PORTIAD

YORNKEY

LESTOCH

WYSTAN

LINAOC

XESTA

VODAEARD

HEIRS
OF
BONE
AND
SEA

HEIRS OF BONE AND SEA

KAY ADAMS

INIMITABLE
BOOKS
UNFORGETTABLE STORIES

Published by Inimitable Books, LLC
www.inimitablebooksllc.com

Library of Congress Cataloguing-in-Publication Data is available.

First edition, 2024
Cover design by Keylin Rivers

ISBN 978-1-958607-09-1 (hardcover)
10 9 8 7 6 5 4 3 2

To those who stare at the stars to feel something.

Some scars are carved into our bones - a part of who we are, shaping what we become.

-Daughter of the Moon Goddess by Sue Lynn Tan

TRIGGER WARNING

This novel includes some sensitive topics that may be upsetting to some readers, and I have done my best to approach them in an appropriate manner. For your comfort, please be aware of the following topics while reading: graphic descriptions of fantasy violence, non-consensual drugging of main characters, depictions of panic attacks, depictions of self-harm, depictions of drowning, suicide ideation, implied torture, menstruation mention, alcohol abuse, and intended filicide (killing one's daughter).

ONE

From the moment I saw the Marama fleet in the sun-speckled distance, I knew something was wrong. And when the black-ened hull of my father's ship sailed into view, I bundled my hair into my arms and ran down from my lighthouse.

Even with a favourable wind and calm waters, the Full Moon and Crossbones were too early. They weren't scheduled to return until to-morrow afternoon, before the Resurrection. Something had brought them home from the mainland too soon.

The first ships were shuddering to a halt against the docks when I arrived, my bare feet sliding over the wet wood. My mother watched as Father's ship slotted into the pier next to us, her face a smooth slate, her dark blue eyes shuttered. Behind her, the diamond spires of our palace glowed red in the sun's last rays, illuminating the coast of our island and the brunt of the damage in the fleet.

"What happened?" I choked, my hair tumbling out of my grasp in my shock. The ocean breeze caught the white strands and whipped them down the shore, a dozen yards of salt-crusted strands that were as sacred to me as my power was to my parents.

In the lengthening stretch of my mother's silence, I looked for our crest—a rising wave adorned with a crown of stars. I could never mask my emotions as well as Mother could. They slipped through the cracks in my walls like pelting rain, filling the corners of my mind, flooding forth in waves that threatened to drown me. Mother's chilly gaze had never been a comfort, so instead, I imagined my lighthouse jutting out over the ocean, red and white painted stone standing tall on the cliffs. The one thing that weathered every storm. Unbreakable.

My fears found the cracks, anyway. My heart knocked against my ribs in rapid bursts the longer my mother stayed silent. I'd never heard of anything happening to Father during his adventures on the mainland. I'd never heard much of anything at all. He kept his escapades secret from me, and I'd learned not to pry. That was to say nothing of what I'd overheard the guards whispering in the quiet corridors at night when they thought everyone else was sleeping.

I didn't like what I had overheard in recent weeks—that my father was losing the war, that it was getting worse, that the chieftess was becoming more worried as the days dragged on. I had meant to ask him about the rumours upon his return. To my knowledge, he wasn't fighting in *any* war—but those thoughts vanished from my mind as his ship rocked up against the dock.

His first mate, Noa, dropped the gangplank with a clunk onto the pier. Wounded crew members stumbled forward, each of them barely managing to bow as they passed my mother. She pressed her lips into a thin line, icy eyes wide and unblinking. Her chest rose and fell with a steady rhythm.

Sometimes I despised her emotionless facade. This was one of those times. To see her react without such passivity might ease the concern clawing up my throat. I could only hope to see a fracture in her facade. She was as silent as a stone statue and just as still, so I scrambled onto my father's ship, shouldering past a surprised crew member. If she wouldn't going to see Father, I would.

Except my father had forbidden me from boarding his ship.

My parents thought it would tempt me to leave our island home, to explore the world. They said my heart sought the horizon, and I would never be happy with our shores as my border. They were wrong. I *was* happy here—happy with my books and my hobbies and my lighthouse. But if the rumours about war were true, then my parents had every right to be concerned. I had to be protected, and that meant I couldn't leave, no matter what my heart wanted.

The ship breathed beneath my feet, the gentle swell of waves lapping the sandy shore, but my stomach dropped at the unfamiliar sensation. I caught the railing to steady myself, breath whooshing out of me at the rise and fall. Mother's piercing gaze drilled into my back.

"Noa!" I called. He stood at the mast, adjusting the damaged main sail, and whirled around at my voice. Confusion drew his eyebrows together, then panic shot them up again. "Where's my father?"

"Princess Kalei," he said in a low voice, crossing the deck. "You shouldn't be here."

"Where is my father?" I repeated, slower, tamping down the fear that would have made my voice break if I spoke any louder. His hesitation was worse than Mother's silence.

But why was he hesitating? Unless…

My back hit the banister as I feared the worst had befallen my father—he was dead. He had to be dead if Noa wasn't answering me. Why else would he stay silent, if not to protect me from the truth?

A small, rational corner of my mind tried to reason with the sharp shards of fear I was swallowing. I shouldn't have been so scared of the possibility. I had the power to bring the dead back to life. No one truly knew what waited on the other side of the Dunes of Forever, but if my father was dead, I could bring him back tomorrow, on the full moon, during the Resurrection. But, the irrational part of my mind shot back with barbed ferocity, *What if they didn't have his body?* I couldn't bring him back if they didn't have his body.

"Minnow," Father's warm voice wove out of the darkness behind Noa.

Relief rushed through me, but when Noa stepped aside, I choked on a gasp at the sight of ruby droplets splattered across his stomach. His linen shirt was torn, hanging by pale threads from one shoulder, revealing a splash work of deep gashes that covered the right side of his ribs. The half-cape that hung over the other shoulder bore the brunt of the burns—char curled up the hem, blackening the once-bright pattern of leaves and feathers. The tatters fluttered in the breeze, small needle pricks dotting the fabric that echoed the cuts on his stomach.

He lumbered forward, clutching his side, face twisted beneath his grimy beard. Blood trailed in his wake, ink-black in the fading sunlight, and seeped between the deck boards beneath his feet.

"You shouldn't be here, Minnow," he grumbled, cupping my cheek in his palm. His skin burned.

I grabbed his hand, pulling it down between us. Nothing of Father reflected in my appearance. My skin was darker than his, even as night enveloped us. He had always been the pale moon to Mother's dark night, yet I shared her ice-chip eyes.

"What happened?" I pressed.

His fingers slipped through mine, slick with blood. Distance gleamed in his brown eyes. I tried to bring him back to the moment, tugging his face to meet my eyes, but he brushed past me with a breathless mumble and stumbled down the gangplank.

"Minnow, meet me in the infirmary," he called over his shoulder, gesturing vaguely for Mother to follow him.

She fell into step beside him as they climbed the stony path through the sandy dunes towards the palace. Her low, urgent voice snaked down the dock towards me, only whispers on a breeze that caressed my skin, dispassionate murmurs without identifiable words.

Noa tilted his good ear to me. "Your father thinks he's invincible."

"He's not." I studied him. The right ear that had been lobbed off in the sword fight that ultimately ended his life, nose caved in from decomposition rot, and eyes milky white after his sojourn to Death's dark shores in another time. "What happened?"

He straightened, watching my father's tattered cape disappear over the dunes. "Perhaps he'll tell you in the infirmary."

I didn't want to wait to be dismissed by my father yet again, not if

Noa had the answers. "Noa…"

"Chief Mikala swore us to secrecy," he said with tight-lipped apathy. "Excuse me, Princess." He dipped his head and returned to the mast.

I frowned. Noa never called my father by name or title to me. He was distancing himself, defaulting to formality to avoid talking about what was happening on the mainland. The rumours I had heard from the guards nagged at the back of my mind as I stumbled down the gangplank. My feet steadied on the dock, but my thoughts continued to lurch as if they were tossing in a storm. Something horrible was happening beyond the borders of my island. My gaze drifted to the dark horizon, barely indistinguishable from the ocean. Stars sparkled overheard and white caps formed on the waves—the only differences I was able to see from where I stood.

Somewhere out there, beyond the haze of the horizon, beyond the line where the sky met the sea, someone had injured my father. I wouldn't allow it, but if I wasn't allowed out there, how could I stop it from happening again? More importantly, what business did my father have fighting in a war I had never heard of? How long had they been keeping it secret from me?

I scrambled up the dunes, the wind behind me buffering against them, and flew past men and women carting corpses to the crypts. My heart pounded against my teeth, a bitter tang at the back of my throat. The dead didn't frighten me nearly as much as Death himself did, but now I began to wonder who all those people were, who all the souls I brought back every month were. People who had homes—families—on the other side of the ocean. Or so I had thought.

The line of carts wound around the side of the palace.

My hair dragged through the sand and across the stone as I bounded over the threshold into the glittering foyer. Moon dust sparkled in the marble beneath my bare feet. Gold veins ran in rivulets through the floor, streaming up the walls to the vaulted ceiling, spilling into the hundred-candle chandelier dangling from a glass dome. The coloured windows flanking the doors stared into the velvet void. Few servants lingered in the corridors, but guards wandered by on their nightly rounds—smartly silent as they passed, merely nodding their heads in my direction.

I hurried to the infirmary wing, my feet a whisper on the cool marble, silencing my approach. Father's voice rumbled through the crack in the door. Mother's soft answer was too low for me to hear. I crept towards the door, back pressed against the wall, tucking my hair behind my ear and leaning forward until their murmurs formed words.

"The Vodaeard princess said she would take me to the other half," Father said, his excited grumble rattling my bones.

I held my breath, trying to recall where I had read that name before. Its mystery eluded me.

"I was so close, Iekika. If I leave now, I can be back in Vodaeard by morning, and the girl can take me to it. I can have the other half of that moonstone in my hand in less than three days. Plenty of time to prepare for the Blood Moon next month."

A shudder crackled down my spine. I had never heard that phrase before, but the way my father said it, almost reverently, made me believe it was important.

"She won't be ready. Why did you call the retreat?" Mother pressed.

I glimpsed her black shawl dusting the floor as she shifted her stance.

Father grunted. A hiss blew between his teeth. "She escaped when I cut out her parents' hearts."

I slapped a hand over my mouth to stifle my gasp. The bloodlust in his voice echoed in my ears. I barely heard him continue over the ringing of violence.

"They bombed my ship. As we retreated, a second bomb exploded at the helm. That's where this came from."

My hand trembled as I dropped it from my mouth. My father was injured. I had to go in there and heal him. But how could I face him, with all my questions, knowing he had killed the monarchs of some kingdom across the ocean? That didn't sound like my father, and the lack of remorse in his voice terrified me. I had never heard him sound so callous before. He was kind and caring. A true chief. He always did what was best for our people.

How was killing foreign monarchs the best thing for our people?

I heard the cot creak under his weight. "Where is Kalei?" he grumbled. "Go find her," he barked to one of the nurses.

Scrambling away from the door, I palmed the fear from my eyes, clenching my teeth to hide the tremor in my bottom lip as a young nurse pushed the door open.

"Oh, Princess," she exclaimed. "Your father is waiting for you." She held the door open for me.

I took a deep breath and let it shudder through me. The slow exhale calmed my racing heart. "I'm here, Father," I said, ignoring the way my mother's calculating gaze tracked my movements across the infirmary.

If I didn't meet her eyes, she wouldn't be able to see the storm behind mine. I was a lighthouse now, strong and defiant. This was the storm I had to weather.

Father's eyes lit up when I stopped in front of him, pride pulling his pained face into a grimace of a smile. A stream of blood dripped off the bed, a pool of rubies in the harsh white light of the infirmary. He reached out to cup my cheek again, fingers still wet. How could this kind face hide a monster? Perhaps I had misheard. I shoved my doubts aside and smiled down at my father.

"Minnow, why do you look so concerned? This was just an accident."

My stomach twisted into a knot. I pulled his hand down again. My father wouldn't hurt anyone for no reason. I had to trust that he knew best.

"Come," he said, tearing the remaining threads of his shirt. The fabric was so stained beyond its original colour.

I grimaced at the crusting blood oozing out of his side and reached blindly for a knife on the tray behind me.

He grabbed my wrist, fingers pinching. "No. No blood."

"Bu—"

"No blood," he said firmly, the force of his tone causing him to cough. He drew his hand back, hacking into the crook of his elbow. Red speckled his lips.

My gaze flicked up to my mother, only to find the ghost of her presence, her absence as startling as her silent departure. Huffing, I knelt on the ground, plucking a strand of hair from the waves cascading down my back. My hair had never seen a trim, but my parents allowed me to use it to heal, only a single strand at a time. I took a moment to crumple it in my palm, rewording the questions on the tip of my tongue.

"You would tell me," I said slowly, eyes locked on the mesh of cuts, "if you were in danger." I meant it as a demand, but it came out closer to a question.

"You needn't concern yourself with that." His eyes bored into the top of my head. "Minnow, you know why you stay on this island?"

"To keep me safe," I murmured. The hair in my palm tickled my skin.

Father tilted my chin up. "Everything I do, I do to protect you. To protect your gift." His fingers drifted to the cord around my neck, down to the silver pendant and obsidian stone resting against my chest. He eyed it hungrily. "Power like yours must be protected. Say it."

"My power must be protected," I whispered. It had always been about keeping this *gift* safe, and not putting myself in danger, lest someone try to take it from me. Or worse, kill me for it. If I was gone, so was my power.

"Do you trust me, Minnow?" His fingers caught my chin again.

I felt every slick drop of blood on my face like a brand, binding me to him, to this island. "Always." My throat burned earnestly, but my face flamed with shame. The word felt like a lie, even though I wanted it to be true.

"Then trust me when I say you don't need to concern yourself over this." His gaze softened, and his hand slid to my cheek again.

I leaned into his warmth, my heart beating in my throat.

"Finish up here," he said finally, dropping his hand.

I leaned forward to press the strand of hair against his wound, murmuring the words to kindle the moon's healing power through me. The obsidian stone pulsed against my chest, warmth spreading down to my fingers, splaying through the cuts and stitching them back together.

"I'm leaving in the morning," he added, almost as an afterthought.

My hand slipped against his side, and erratic light veered from the stone, briefly blinding me. I rose to my feet unsteadily. "You're not staying for the Resurrection?"

Eyes narrowed, he stared at the stone as if he could pick apart its secrets, though not even I understood them. The stone granted me power beyond comprehension, but only I was able to wield it. Its gift remained a mystery. The cord dug into the back of my neck under the weight of his scrutiny. "No," he murmured absently. "I have matters to attend to on the mainland."

"What matters, Father?" I blurted. The stone burned against my dark skin, light flickering in its depths. It had never reacted this way before. I only felt its warmth and saw its light when I used my power, as the moon's gift channeled through the stone. This was strange, and I didn't like the way Father's eyes focused on the necklace and not on *me*. "You've always been there for every one of my Resurrections. Why not this one?"

He rose from the bed, large-chested and broad-shouldered. The skin stretched over his side, still stitching, straining as he moved. "I will not hear any more of this, Kalei." He marched for the door, back through the trail of his own blood speckled across the white floor like red stars in a bleak void.

"Father!" I cried, my voice finally breaking. "Please tell me! What war are you fighting?"

"Enough!" He whirled, the power of his words slamming into me like a gale, forcing me back a step. After a moment, when I was sure I would burst into tears if he didn't say more, his shoulders sagged. "Minnow, I don't know what rumours found their way to you in my absence, but you shouldn't listen to them. Whatever happens on the mainland will never hurt you here."

My parents told me assassins from the mainland had tried to kill me when I was a child, to steal my power for themselves, but no one else could channel the moon's magic. They kept me locked on this island like it was my personal prison, and I learned to love it even though my heart yearned for the horizon. But there had come a time, several years ago, during my first Resurrection, when I had learned that danger lurked much closer to home.

It wasn't some faceless being on the mainland, unable to reach me.

It was Death himself, snapping at my heels every time I dived into the depths to retrieve lost souls. I crossed into his realm—uninvited— too many times. I had always known it was a matter of time before he came knocking.

Renewed fear spiked through me now. I wasn't worried about myself anymore. Father was keeping secrets from me, inciting dangerous affairs on the mainland. If there truly was a war—and I was starting to believe there was—who would keep *him* safe?

He sighed and opened his arms.

I fled into his embrace. The tang of ash and blood clung to him, tickling my nose as he pressed a kiss to the top of my head.

"I'll be back in three days' time, Minnow. Keep a weather eye on the horizon for me."

"I will," I murmured as he strode from the infirmary, swallowing the lie. Three days might be enough for my father, but I needed answers now.

When he was gone, I raced to confront the one person who might have them.

TWO

Cold tears pressed at the corners of my eyes—from the wind, I told myself—as I stared into the red sun until my eyes burned. Everything it touched blazed in orange fire—the whitecaps on the waves, the anger churning in my veins, and the curls of amber hair tumbling into my face. Light sparked on the sea as we cut through the water, but the sky and the world we had left behind were dark.

Death lay behind me. Death lay before me.

There was nothing left for me back there.

My quarry lay ahead, tangled somewhere at the front of the retreating armada. A burnt hull, a charred figurehead, a crisped pennant. My fingers, bloody from obsessively chewing them for hours, dug grooves into the splintered railing.

If only the enemy captain had been standing closer to the explosion.

"My queen." My first mate's voice startled me, sounding much closer than I expected.

A nail cracked as I jerked away from the railing.

He stood straight-backed, his posture rigid from years at court.

A cough built up in my throat, breaking up the dust that had settled there since we set sail hours ago. I hadn't spoken a word in those hours, in part due to my stomach churning in knots like the wind churned the waves. But mostly due to the grief that weighed on my shoulders like the crown I was set to inherit, too soon and too unexpectedly.

"Black seas. Now is not the time for formalities, Talen," I muttered, sticking my finger in my mouth to bite off the piece of chipped nail and spit it over the side of the ship.

As long as I had known him, he had never said a word about the crusty blood on my fingertips or the constant scabs on my bottom lip. Nothing I did could stop the urge to bite my skin—not even when I had tried dipping my fingers in fish oil. He was the only person who seemed to understand what I couldn't even explain to myself.

He waited patiently until I dropped my hand, my fingertip covered in saliva, unsatisfied. "Evhen, you're allowed to mourn."

"Now is *not* the time for that," I grumbled, turning back to the sea. Everything was a hazy, salty, angry blur. Any time something wet landed on my face, I blamed the spray of the ocean because it was easier to blame something I could see than the roiling emotions in my heart. And when I found myself at the prow—leaning into the unknown as if that could bring me closer to the Marama warships we pursued, chest tight and stomach tense—all the words I wanted to scream into the sky died in my throat instead.

I was too young to inherit my father's crown. Tradition declared that monarchs could not take the throne until their eighteenth birthday. It was only age that mattered to my people. I wasn't there yet, but that didn't lessen the burden of knowing I'd be crowned all the same.

Wind whisked my tears away as I agitatedly ran my cracked nail over the pad of my thumb. I tried to focus on what lay ahead, but everything circled back to my dead parents. Even imagining what I would do once we caught up to the warships didn't stop their faces from flashing in my mind.

We had been sailing straight since morning, following the warships at a distance to avoid being spotted, and now that we were so close, I could feel their killer's blood on my fingers.

"We have to catch up to those seas-damned ships."

Talen sighed, shoulders slackening, rough-worked fingers sandpapering across the sparse orange fuzz dusting his jaw. "We're moving as fast as we can," he said. "Besides, we found something below deck you might want to see."

Brow furrowed, I followed him to the hatch in the middle of the ship, the pain in my chest unfurling. It was replaced by an uncomfortable sense of dread. I hated the shadowy places on boats, raised on stories of the ghostly souls of sailors trapped as their vessels sank, of spirits who sailed the seas forever. Ghosts lived in the dark corners of ships and minds alike, and I had enough of them in my life to believe they had followed me here.

My first mate hauled the grate open, and I peered into the musky, fuse-scented gloom. A candle flickered somewhere behind the stairs, the shadows dancing up and down the planks. Heart bursting like a lit explosive, I swallowed and descended into the low-ceilinged space.

The cargo hold was void of actual goods except for a few crates—blankets and ripe fruit—thrown hastily against a wall and three forgotten barrels of explosive powder. We had fled Vodaeard too quickly to pack anything, but I didn't expect to be gone from home long. All I had to do was safely arrive on a stranded island, sneak into the palace, and kill the man who killed my parents.

Easy, if not for the hundreds of warships between my ship and the shore.

From behind the stairs came the distinct sound of someone gulping, followed by a bottle hitting a table. Groaning, I nearly slapped my forehead as I turned to see my younger brother slumped against a post with his eyes shut. A single candle, sitting dangerously close to the edge of the table, illuminated the sheen of sweat on his pale face.

I circled the stairs. Three other bottles cluttered the low table, one of them already empty. I kicked my brother's foot. "Alekey."

He cracked one eye open and sat up, beaming his most infuriating grin. The one that got him out of so much trouble as a child. The one I wanted to cut right off his face with my cutlass.

"Took you long enough," he chirped, his words slurred from the drink. He blinked one eye at a time, staring into the mouth of his bottle. "I think. What time is it?"

"The sun's going down." I wanted to be furious with him, but I couldn't muster the energy. I had no right to be angry at him if he wanted to drink his grief away.

But he wasn't supposed to be here at all.

"Oh, then, yeah," Alekey said, winking up at me. "Took you long enough." He tipped his head back and downed the rest of his drink, wiping the back of his sleeve across his mouth.

I wrapped my arms around myself, turning my face into a frown as fear cut through me like a knife. How was I supposed to focus on killing someone who deserved my wrath when I had to worry about his safety as well? Even if I wasn't really mad, I could at least look like it.

"You know I don't like…" I waved a hand at our surroundings. The light from his meagre candle didn't reach the corners. It played tricks if I stared too long.

"Their ghosts aren't down here," he snapped, suddenly serious, eyes narrowing at me.

My breath stuck behind my teeth. Numbly, I watched him reach for another bottle and fumble with the cap.

"I would have seen them," he growled. Fat tears dripped down his cheeks. "I would have…" His hand slipped, and he threw the bottle down, choking on a sob.

Without a word, I caught the bottle and twisted the lid off. My hands shook as I set it on the table for him.

He hadn't seen them—their faces frozen in fear.

I prayed he never saw their ghosts. I would rather him drink himself into a stupor than live with the images that flashed through my mind. If I couldn't protect him out here, at least I could protect him from that.

"Come up when you're ready," I whispered to the dark. The shadows danced up the walls in answer.

Alekey didn't look up, shoulders shuddering.

Weary down to my bones, I swiped the last bottle and trudged up the stairs, twisting the cap off. Talen raised an eyebrow at me as I tilted the drink to my lips.

"What?" I mumbled around the rim.

"Nothing," he said innocently, jewel glittering in his ear as the last rays of day speared across the sky. Silver specks painted the velvet void behind us.

I lowered the bottle without having drunk a drop, my fingers tight on its neck. "If you have something to say, say it."

"You're not one to drink, Evhen," he said, drawing out each word.

The disapproval lacing his voice grated against my fraying nerves.

"Maybe I should start." I waved my prize in his face, sloshing alcohol over my hand. "And might I ask why you let him get two in before saying anything to me? Seas, he shouldn't even be here!"

"You're deflecting."

I scowled. "Don't presume to know what's going on in here." I tapped my head with the mouth of the bottle and took a genuine swig. It burned on the way down, and I screwed my face into a grimace.

He crossed his arms over his broad chest. "I know you better than you think, *Your Majesty*."

The title scraped against the inside of my skull like a knife's edge. It felt less like an honour and more like a brand.

"Don't call me that," I mumbled, staring at the murky liquid in the bottle. It smelled awful and tasted worse, but maybe Alekey had the right idea. Forgetting was easier with something to aid it.

"Then what do you want me to call you?" There was a challenge in his voice, one I didn't hear too often. My voice of reason rearing his head.

My eyes narrowed. "Captain," I suggested. "Something that doesn't remind me of *them*!" I took another swig. It buzzed in my veins, but stress continued to pound behind my left eye.

"We're all upset, Ev." His voice softened. "You don't see Icana and me ruining ourselves because of it."

My gaze whipped around him to look towards the helm.

The woman in question shook her blunt blonde bob out of her face. "Don't drink and sail," she said sagely.

15

I looked back at Talen, fire in my eyes and fury in my voice. "I didn't see you crying over it, either."

A muscle feathered in his jaw. "You weren't looking."

I stomped to the railing and leaned against it, drawing in a sharp breath of cold air. "What do you think I've been doing all day?"

Talen joined me, only to pluck the bottle from my loose grip and drop it into the wine-dark sea. "Thinking about murder is not grieving."

"It's not murder. It's revenge."

I lifted my gaze from the tumbling waves. In the distance, a white castle rose above the water, flickering between groves of palm trees. And, nearer than I expected, a lighthouse jutted out of the rock, red and white painted stone piercing through the hazy veil of night.

Oh, curse the seas!

My heart slammed into my throat at the sight, and I curled my fingers around the hilt of my cutlass to distract their worrying. The moulded leather grip was a small comfort.

"Douse the lights," I whispered, though I doubted we had been spotted. There was no fire at the top of the lighthouse, and we were still too far away to see the warships, much less the shore.

Talen quickly put out the lanterns along the side of the ship. At the helm, Icana doused her lantern, but there was still a weak, warm red seeping between the boards beneath our feet.

"Key!" I called down into the cargo hold. "Smother that candle."

Below deck, Alekey mumbled exactly where I could smother it. Heat fanned across my face as my first mate chuckle-coughed into his hand.

I stomped a foot on the top step. "Key—black seas, help me—put that light out, or I will put it out with your face."

Grumbling wordlessly but loudly, my brother blew the candle out, and I moved away from the pitch-black cargo hold. Below, I heard him trip over something as he landed with a hollow crash and an exaggerated cry of pain. Moments later, he stumbled up the stairs. A broken bottle hung from his fingers and the remnants of alcohol clung to his tousled black hair. He shook his head like a dog, flinging drops of ale all over me.

I cringed at the smell as droplets stuck to my skin, then grabbed the empty bottle and chucked it overboard.

Alekey watched it drop into the ocean with a splash. "That wasn't very nice," he said, raking a hand through his sopping hair. It stood up on end as he contemplated the excess ale on his fingers.

Movement beyond the lighthouse drew my attention to the rocky outcropping before I could snap at him again. Racing towards the castle on the far side of the island, a girl with the longest hair I've ever seen ghosted through the night, leaving a white haze over the grass in her wake. She was a pale, moon-bright speck against the dark, but she disappeared out of sight as Icana steered us to the other side of the cliff.

Talen dropped the anchor. For many long minutes, we were silent. My heart fluttered in my chest as I stared across a strip of rocks leading to a path through the dunes, mind whirling as violently as the waves over the reef.

"Who in the great seas was that?" Alekey finally broke the silence.

I didn't know, but I intended to find out.

THREE

Noa raised an eyebrow at the plate in my hands, piled with fresh bread slathered in peach jam, crumbly fruit tarts drizzled with custard, and slices of ripe apricot dripping in cacao spread. He might have lost his sense of smell from the Resurrection, but his eyes knew delicious food when they saw it.

It had taken little effort to acquire the plate from the palace cooks—I usually ate breakfast this late at night and spent my waking hours wandering the empty halls while everyone else slept. The moon kept me awake, as the sun kept everyone else awake.

Though, unlike the cooks, Noa always questioned the generous stacks of food. "Are you trying to bribe me, Princess?"

Exaggerating a gasp at his accusation, I drew the offering back, affronted. "I simply thought you'd be hungry after so long at sea."

The growl from his stomach filled the servants' corridor, where I'd found him sneaking out of a maid's cellar room. He crossed his arms over his chest, scarred eyebrow still dancing amid locks of brown hair. "I told you earlier—"

"And you knew he wouldn't tell me anything," I interrupted, lowering the plate between us when it was clear he wasn't going to take it. "I need answers. And you're the only person who will give them to me."

"What makes you say that?" His eyes darted over my head, fixing on something in the corridor behind me. A shadow shivered in his gaze.

"Because I know the way to your heart is through your stomach." I raised the selection of food again and nudged one of the apricot slices towards him.

He caught it before it tumbled off the plate, cacao dripping between his fingers.

"Besides, I can't eat all this by myself."

"Hmph," he grumbled, popping the fruit into his mouth. He brushed past me, snatching the plate out of my hands as he did, and marched silently down the hall.

I stared at the door to the room where he had been messing around with a maid. I didn't even know her name or what she looked like. She was just another face in the palace. It wasn't by choice that I hardly knew anyone—my parents didn't allow the maids or the servants or the guards to talk to me. They weren't allowed to acknowledge me in the halls, aside from a bow of their heads. Perhaps it was for the best. I was a princess, after all. But my heart was lonely, and Noa was the only person who bothered to acknowledge me. I considered him a friend.

And now he was shunning me as well. I hurried after him, eager to escape the chilly cellars. "I only want—"

I nearly slammed into his broad chest when I rounded the corner. He had stopped in the adjacent corridor and whirled around to face me.

"Chief swore us to secrecy," he said again, more forcefully than before. His eyes were dark flashes in the waning torchlight. Fists clenched at his sides.

I held my breath, waiting until he straightened again before releasing it with a whoosh. I opened my mouth, but he set his face into a scowl, shaking his head sharply.

"I won't ask you to tell me what my father is doing on the mainland," I said quickly.

He tried to move down the hall, stuffing a fruit tart into his mouth to avoid my questions, but I ducked past him and blocked his escape.

He mumbled something around the pastry. One foot tapped impatiently, waiting for me to give up.

I hated his secrecy and his loyalty to my parents. I wouldn't have another chance to ask him if he was leaving with my father in the morning. I sighed, feigning defeat. "Just tell me where—"

"Princess," he warned with a low growl, "you know I won't disobey your father."

"Let me talk, Noa," I snapped, the torchlight flickering with my tone. He raised his eyebrow again, bemused. "You don't have to tell me what you know, only where I can find information about the Blood Moon myself." I studied his reaction. He always betrayed so much on his ruined face.

There was the slightest twitch in his eye, a quirk at the corner. So he did know. But he wouldn't tell me.

"No one will know you helped me if you only tell me where to direct my research."

He sighed and scratched his chin. A shadow curved along the wall behind him, and beneath us, the bones of the dead quivered in the crypts. "I don't know," he said hesitantly.

I bit my tongue, relaxing my fingers before the bones in the crypt could rattle the foundation. I couldn't wake the bodies until tomorrow, but with the moon growing to full, the bones were becoming impatient. The dead were waiting to return once more, but I needed to know why I was bringing them back.

There were two phrases my father said that meant nothing to me and everything to him. Now, I could maybe learn more about them.

"Will the library have that kind of information?" I pressed. If the dampness of the cellars and the exhaustion in his eyes were any indications, my time with him was running out. He would soon retire and leave in the morning. I wasn't going to let this opportunity slip through my fingers.

Noa rubbed the side of his absent nose. "I can't guarantee you'll find anything there, and I won't answer any more of your questions."

My breath rattled behind my teeth. His behaviour only made me more curious, but I took his warning in stride, palms tingling with trepidation. Something dangerous was happening on the mainland, but maybe my answers were a lot closer to home.

"Thank you, Noa," I murmured.

He peered at me in the gloom. "Take care how you tread, Princess." His low voice filled the chilly corridor, scraping along the stone with warning. "There are things your father will go to great lengths to keep from you. Whatever you find, I can't promise you will like it."

With that, he disappeared down the hall, taking the chill with him.

I blew out a breath. Shadows writhed between the black stones as if they, too, knew the secrets being kept from me.

The palace was falling asleep when I emerged from the cellars. Dreams crept up behind me, weaving through cracks in the marble stones to fill the bedchambers. A blanket of silence held the palace in its embrace.

This was my favourite time. When the corridors were quiet, and the stones were still. When torchlight flickered along the walls, between pools of ink-black night. When the moon rose in the sky, and its pale light reached me wherever I went, and my power scratched beneath the surface of my skin. This was when the bones in the crypt sang their waking song.

The long-forgotten skeletons themselves had no souls. I could only bring souls back into bodies of flesh when the moon was full—when my power was at its peak. But the bones of the long-dead moved and danced and rattled a wordless melody whenever I called to them, no matter the phase of the moon. The ones I saved from the Dunes of Forever, though—I didn't know their names or their purposes. My parents always curated the souls I retrieved—but why? That question—a single, silencing why—echoed in my mind as I turned a corner and stopped short.

Dressed in a black silk nightgown and standing as still as the statues that lined the hallway, my mother waited. The library was on the other side, and I had to pass her chambers to reach it. She didn't move while I approached, chilling eyes fixed on me in an unblinking stare.

"Good evening, Mother," I said.

As I edged past her in the suddenly too-tight hall, she moved like a viper, latching a hand around my wrist and easing a cry of surprise from me as she dragged me into the antechamber of her rooms. I staggered before getting my feet under me. Dark, thick curtains hung in front of the window to stave off the night air, and a dying fire sat in the hearth. The door to her bedchamber was ajar, a blazing light streaming out of the crack. She pulled me to a stop in the middle of the room and whirled me around to face her. Her shift hardly moved, stiff as her lips. Even the faintest breeze dared not touch her without consent.

"Why were you talking with your father's first mate?" she asked in a low tone, a soft hiss between her teeth. She never raised her voice, never spoke in a tone louder than a whisper, but that made her all the more frightening. Her words tickled my spine.

She also never called Noa my father's advisor—*she* advised him— but it startled me to know she had seen our conversation. Or rather, as I thought back to the twisting shadows in the dark belly of the cellars, she had sent someone to watch my every move. No doubt the spy had already confronted Noa.

I pictured my lighthouse in my mind, its painted stone strong against the sea's battering winds.

"I caught him sleeping with one of the maids."

A pang of guilt soured my tongue. That kind of behaviour wasn't allowed within the palace walls, and surely the girl would suffer the punishment instead of Noa. He would sail away with my father before they even identified the girl, unscathed.

My mother's gaze didn't waver. "And what were you doing in the cellars so late?"

"I often roam the empty halls at night," I said, the truth closer than a lie. "I like the quiet."

Her night-blue eyes glittered like dying stars. She knew I preferred night to day, when I felt closer to the moon as it hung in the velvet-black sky. I felt more alive, more energized by its pull, the way most people felt rejuvenated by the sun's warmth. Even on a cloudy night, I could feel the moon's energy in my veins. And Mother knew I preferred that. So why did she look so suspicious?

"How many of the guards do you pass on your nightly walks?"

My mouth ran dry. I noticed the way she carefully chose her words. Not how many I talk to, but how many I pass by, which was a significantly greater number.

"I don't know an exact number," I said. "I'm usually lost in a book. I'm headed to the library now, if you'd like to help me find a new book to read. I've read so many." As I spoke, I edged around her towards the door, pausing long enough to see her cut a ringed hand through the air.

"It's late," she said, dismissing me.

"Good night, Mother." I dipped my head and slipped into the hallway, letting out a tense breath. It was so hard to keep secrets from her when she saw everything, heard everything. Likely, she knew exactly what I had asked Noa. But she was keeping secrets from me, too.

Soon this web of lies would unravel, and I didn't want to be caught unprepared when it did.

At the end of the Hall of Statues—so named to commemorate all the chiefs of our past in marble and gold—I turned the corner to the library wing. The stone walls here depicted our lineage written in elegant script, the earliest names in an ancient version of our language that few now could read. I ran my hands over the indentations, feeling the history rise and fall beneath my fingertips. My father's name was one of the last. And right under his, mine. Kalei Maristela. The flower of the star of the sea.

The library's massive doors groaned open under my palms. Plush carpets from other lands muffled my footsteps as I entered. The only light came from two guttering torches in the hall. I picked up one of the glass lanterns by the door and coaxed a flame from the torch onto the wick. Open flames weren't allowed inside, lest all our tomes vanish from existence in ash and smoke. Knowledge was precious, as precious as the lives I brought back. The only difference between knowledge and the souls I retrieved from Death's dark shores was that, once lost, it was lost forever.

Worry rumbled through me as I ghosted between the aisles. I thought I was doing the right thing, giving people a second chance at life, an opportunity to start again. But what if I was only helping my father do terrible things on the mainland? He wouldn't give me answers, so I had to find them here amid the weathered books and the ancient parchment. I had to know the truth.

Before I scoured the aisles, though, I drew towards the map in the centre of the library, housed between two thick pieces of glass. The edges were charred from some long-ago fire, the date in the corner unreadable, but the names of kingdoms and faraway lands were still visible in their careful script. Lines crossed the countries and oceans, different colours for different journeys of past explorers. It was the gilded illustrations that had grabbed my attention as a child—the serpents and cauldrons and sirens and horned horses that galloped across the lands—but I started learning the country names as I grew older. Portiad in the north. Yornkey along the coast. Lestoch off the mainland. Linaoc's chain of islands. And there, at the southeast-ern-most point of the mainland, jutting into the sea. *Vodaeard.*

I set the lantern on the glass and leaned closer. Vodaeard was small. Its east, south, and west coasts were surrounded by ocean. On land, mountains bordered it on one side, and there were no geographical markers at its north. It was, in all respects, unremarkable.

What was my father doing there?

My hand dropped to my island nation, directly south of the centre of the mainland. We were a ring of islands around a central lagoon. The largest one was where I called home. I traced a finger over an unidentifiable strip of island—the cliff where my lighthouse stood against the sea. It hadn't shone in years, the mirror at the top broken, but no ships sailed these waters except my father's. We were safe here.

Or so I had thought.

With a sigh, I picked up my lantern and delved into the deepest corners of the library. I had to trust that my father was doing the right thing—that he knew what was best for our nation. Still, I would never forget the chilling tone of his voice as he boasted about killing. Carving out the hearts of monarchs. I had seen enough dead bodies that the scars left by violence didn't bother me, but hearing him describe how he assassinated the Vodaeard monarchy churned my stomach. Bile bit at the back of my throat as I wandered down a dark aisle, but I wasn't here to uncover the truth about what heinous acts he had committed on the mainland. Something else he'd said needled at my mind instead.

I can have the other half of that moonstone in my hand in less than three days. Plenty of time to prepare for the Blood Moon next month.

My mother had said, *She's not ready.* There was only one person in whom she lacked so much confidence—me.

I had never heard of the Blood Moon before, but it was clear they were trying to prepare me for something. And the stone around my neck, a fallen piece of the moon, was only half of a whole. What would restoring it do? That was the knowledge I sought within these pages. Without any friends on this island, I had learned to do things for myself, but in none of the books I'd read had I seen the words "Blood Moon" before.

The lantern light fell on a large leather-bound tome. Faded black script ran along the spine, turned grey with time. I traded its place on the shelf with my lantern to run my fingers over the ridged cover. Black thread embossed on the front created half-moon shapes in each corner.

Curiosity piqued, I angled the books towards the light, catching the glint of silver twined through the black thread. When I opened the cover, the ink on the first page was so faded I could hardly distinguish individual letters, but I immediately recognized the illustrated first initial. Only one other book in the library had a similar style of text, but I had dismissed the stories within as fables—myths.

But there had to be a reason this tome, decorated in a similar style to a book about legends, was gilded in images of the moon. Tucking it under an arm, I snatched up my lantern and hurried to another section of the library, one I frequented more often. The books here contained stories about dragons and sirens, demons and ghosts, witches and pirates. These were the stories I read over and over. These were the stories I knew by heart.

The matching tome, bound in mottled brown leather, was on a lower shelf, tucked between a book about pirates and a book about star-crossed lovers. I pulled it out and set it beside the first on the floor. They were the same size, but at first glance, that was the only similarity. I opened both to the first page.

The illustrated initials were definitely drawn by the same hand.

Heart racing, I gathered both books in my arms and blew out the lantern, plunging the library into total darkness. My eyes adjusted quickly, and I left the library with the hope that its secrets wouldn't remain hidden for long. These books, and whatever stories they told of the moon, could help me understand what my father was looking for on the mainland.

At the bottom of the grand staircase, night twinkling beyond the windows, I slipped through a servant's door. The cramped hallway twisted towards the back of the palace. I knew the path well. The door opened into a cordoned section of the bush gardens, the near-full moon illuminating the entire island. With the ever-present red glow of the volcano's peak above the coconut and banana trees behind me, I hurried towards my lighthouse to examine my treasure.

FOUR

I glared at the gaping hole in the siren's chest. The explosion hadn't done nearly enough damage. A larger blast and better timing might have sunk them on our shores, but the ships and their murderous crews had still been able to flee Vodaeard.

They shouldn't have been allowed to leave at all. They killed my parents, and they would have done worse to me if Talen hadn't been there to drag me out of the throne room to safety.

My fists clenched at my sides, cracked nails biting into my palms. I hadn't felt safe in years. There were no safe places left when war ravaged the continent. And I certainly wasn't safe here, but I needed this. I needed to kill the people who murdered my parents. I needed to kill them all.

Talen hadn't said a word when I told Icana to follow the warships. It was only when we scrambled up the crags that he urged me to think before I acted. To stay close to the boat. In case we needed to make a quick escape.

I hadn't told him I expected to die tonight. He never would have let me go alone if he knew this was a suicide mission. I only wanted revenge on the people who destroyed my life. I didn't care if I died along the way.

The salty ocean wind stung my nose. A gentle swell of waves bobbed the ships next to the dock. I imagined them burning, one by one in the night, but then the image faded like smoke as I turned to face the shining palace behind me. My cutlass bumped against my hip. It would be gratifying to watch the ships burn, but I wouldn't be satisfied until I cut out the hearts of the king and queen and felt their life fade beneath my fingers.

I wanted someone else's blood on my hands for once.

A cobblestoned path cut up the banks towards the castle, empty this late at night. I scoffed as I neared the doors. There were no guards, a false sense of security hanging around the palace like a stain. They had no reason to fear an attack on their own shores.

The door swung open at my touch. Night swept like a wraith into the grand entrance. I slipped in, silently unsheathing my cutlass as I glanced around. Archways spilled into adjacent rooms. A long hallway stretched between a sweeping double staircase. The balcony was gilded in a gold banister. And everywhere—paintings in heavy frames adorned the marble walls. At a closer glance, I recognized some of the artwork. My gaze darted to the statues, the vases, and stolen artefacts on display. Spoils of war.

A sour taste filled my mouth. I left this hall of horrors, ugly reminders of what this nation was doing to the continent, and climbed to the second floor. It felt wrong to run my hand along the banister, the gold cold to the touch, but we relied on wood and stone in Vodaeard. I had never seen so much of the metal in one place before.

No doubt they had mined it from the mainland as well.

Footsteps echoed down the hall to my right, accompanied by two murmuring voices.

Curse the seas!

Heart in my throat and ears pounding with fear, I ducked into an alcove on my left, scrambling up a few steps of the hidden winding staircase until I was out of sight. With my cutlass clutched to my chest, I pressed against the wall. Two guards marched past my hiding spot. One of them yawned loudly.

As their footsteps faded, someone shuffled into the spiralling stairwell above me. My fingers tightened over my cutlass.

I whirled. The tip of my blade came to rest in the hollow of a maid's throat. She was, too, startled to scream, eyes wide, tray trembling in her hands.

She opened her mouth.

I jabbed my blade closer.

She shut her jaw hard, her teeth clicking on impact.

I climbed the two steps between us.

Her shoulders bumped the wall. She didn't take her eyes off me, and for a moment I saw myself reflected in them, a terrified child on the brink of death, begging for my life, pleading with my parents' killer. The image vanished.

I wasn't like that man. I wasn't going to kill an innocent girl.

"The king and queen," I whispered. "Where do they sleep?"

Shaking, she balanced the tray on one arm. "They sleep separately," she said, voice wobbling. "The chief in the west wing, the chieftess in the east, in the Hall of Statues." She pointed in opposite directions as she spoke.

Keeping my sword at her throat, I slowly climbed a few more steps. "Not a word of this to anyone," I hissed.

She fled the stairwell as soon as my sword freed her neck from its point. The spark in her eyes told me I didn't have long before she did, in fact, share this with someone. At the next alcove, I paused in the shadows, heart thumping. Squeezing my eyes shut, I let the image of the chief fill my mind. He deserved to die for what he did to my parents, but I was running out of time. I had to find him before the guards found me.

A reverent, murmuring voice drifted up to me from the hallway I had just abandoned, but it was the single word that stopped me from continuing upwards. Princess.

I twisted around and hurried down the winding stairs. At the bottom, I peered around the corner. My cutlass was heavy in my sweaty grip. On the other side of the double staircase, two guards were rising from low bows in front of the girl with the long hair.

"Your Highness," one of them said as they continued down the hall, and my heart lurched into my throat.

She was a princess.

Which meant she was—No, she couldn't be. The Princess of Death was a monster. This was just a girl.

She smiled uncomfortably at the two guards, two books under her arms, and made her way down the stairs, a trail of white slithering behind her. As I watched, she disappeared into a concealed door at the bottom of the stairs.

So I wasn't the only one sneaking around so late at night.

An idea—half-formed and entirely dangerous—took root as I crept down the stairs before I even realized what I was doing. This girl was the chief's daughter. I didn't have to kill him where he slept—I could kill his daughter and let him know my pain. And no one had seen her disappear into the secret corridor. The palace was asleep. She would be missed long before anyone knew her fate, and that revenge already tasted sweet.

My fingers brushed the concealed door, barely a crack in the wall, only slightly darker than the veins of gold in the marble. The secret passage had to lead somewhere, but I was hesitant to follow her into the dark. I glanced back up the grand staircase, nerves rattling my teeth the longer I stood indecisively. The maid would alert the guards soon. I suddenly didn't want to be here when she did.

I walked out the front door. The princess would return to the light-house soon enough, so I was going to wait for her.

I retraced my steps along the beach towards the dark lighthouse in the distance. There were no trees to hide me from view, only the tall dunes and raggedy palm trees. My heart slammed in my chest when Icana melted out of the shadows next to me without a sound. My cutlass twitched upwards, but I breathed easier when I recognized my weapons master's silent tread.

"Black seas! What are you doing?" I growled, glancing over my shoulder to make sure we weren't being followed. The beach was dark, the night darker still.

"Following you. Talen thought you would get yourself into trouble," she answered.

Shoving my irritation down, I stomped up the banks, the lighthouse looming ahead. "Did you follow me all the way into the castle?"

She nodded. "Not very well guarded, is it?"

I cut a hand through the air. "They think they have all the power. Why would they need to protect what no one else can reach?"

"No one except us," she stated.

"No one except *me*," I corrected, angling towards her as we came to a stop at the base of the lighthouse. Her face was mottled by shadows in the moonlight. "I didn't ask you to come with me."

She blinked her wide blue eyes. "No, Talen did."

I ground my teeth together. She was only doing what she was asked to do. I couldn't help the dreadful feeling that Talen had betrayed me by sending her to watch me. As though he had known all along what I was planning. As though I was a child who needed to be guarded. Someone who couldn't keep herself safe.

I exhaled hard through my nose. Icana was reliable. She didn't deserve my ire in this moment. "I discovered something about the girl."

She raised an eyebrow—or tried to. She had never been good at raising a single brow. Both arched, giving her a look of surprise.

"She's the chief's daughter."

My weapons master blew out a breath. She understood the implication well enough, what I wasn't saying. "What's your plan?"

As I opened my mouth to answer, moonlight landed on a flash of white hair over the rise behind her. I grabbed her wrist, and we ducked beside the lighthouse, pressed up against the weathered stone.

Icana's hand reached for one of the twin blades strapped across her back. I shook my head, holding my breath as the girl's footsteps came closer, shuffling through the grass. The door creaked open, then clicked shut. I winced at the sound. Long seconds passed, my gaze pinned to the sky in anticipation. My heart thudded so loud I thought it would penetrate the stone wall.

After a few minutes, I glanced at Icana. "Climb the tower, kill the princess."

"Good plan," she said, unsheathing her twin blades.

Icana slowly opened the door, so it didn't make any noise. Inside, I craned my neck back. Locks of hair wafted in the air, circulating high above. We climbed the stone steps along the widest edge. Near the top, I shifted my cutlass in front of me and stepped into the circular chamber.

The princess was younger than I expected, only a year or two younger than I was, still round-faced with youth and looking like a child in her rough-spun lilac shift. The hem swayed just above her bare feet. She stood by a large reflective disc in the centre of the room, a thin sabre in hand.

We hadn't been as silent as I thought. A quick glance around the room revealed more weapons—throwing stars, crossbow bolts, gleaming daggers. I eyed the railing behind her. A three hundred-foot fall to the ocean below.

"Who are you and why are you here?" she demanded, her gaze darting from me to Icana.

Something glinted in her bright eyes—bravery or fear—but before I could answer, she yanked on her hair.

Icana leapt out of the way, but a tendril snaked around my ankle and pulled me off my feet. I crashed to the ground, swinging my cutlass towards the hair, but it was already gone, gathered around her bare feet. Curling my lip, I lurched upright and lunged.

The princess skittered over the stone ledge and landed on the other side of the mirror, pulling her hair with her. A strand lashed out, wrapping around my wrist. I stared at it, struck by its gleam, its strength. Of all the weapons in the room, I never guessed her hair would be one of them. But then she pulled, shaking me out of my trance.

I tripped, banging into the stone ledge, hitting my knees against the sharp edge. With a hiss of pain, I glanced up in time to see her jump onto the ledge above me, swinging her blade down.

Sparks flew in my face as one of Icana's sword crashed into hers, and she danced backwards again, hair unwinding from my arm.

"What do you want with me?" she panted. Her voice cracked, fear bleeding through the bravado.

I'd heard that sound before, all too recently. It was the same sound I made when I begged her father to spare my parents. My eyes stung, but I tamped down the memories with bitter rage. Her father had to feel my pain. And there were no guards to come to her rescue.

When I didn't answer—the rage in my eyes sealing her fate—she grabbed her sword with both hands. More sparks flew when our blades clashed. The princess shoved back against me, climbing down from the ledge, panting, eyes bright in the dark.

We stood so close, swords locked together, and I saw my own reflection in her round eyes.

Flecks of white—looking like sea foam—rimmed the outer edges of her ocean blue eyes, her lashes blacker than night. She had a splash of freckles across her nose and a dimple in the corner of her mouth that appeared when she clenched her jaw. Her white hair shone silver in the pale light of the moon. Strands curled around her forehead, flitting in the breeze that howled through the chamber.

My heart pounded against my ribs when the girl pushed me back a step, and my hand slipped on my sword. I slid back across the floor, out of reach from her vicious swing.

The princess threw herself forward. She moved rapidly on her feet, unburdened by the weight of her hair, her jabs swift. I blocked, circling around the chamber as she pursued, but then my back came up against the outside railing, my feet sliding through puddles of water. Wind whipped my russet hair around my face, but I didn't dare look down.

If I tumbled, I'd take the princess with me.

Before I could catch my breath, her sword arced down.

I spun out of the way, and it sparked against the railing, metal screeching against metal. Then she was swinging again. I darted back inside, spinning around to bring my sword up. The bones in my arm rattled when our blades connected. I winced, taking another step back as the girl advanced, swinging madly.

She was messy, but persistent. Her sword crashed into mine again. The heat of the clash burned my face. My arm stung with the force.

Fury sparked in her eyes. Gasping for breath, I tucked into myself and rolled away as the sabre came down once more. It clanged off the floor next to my head, too close for comfort. When I rose to my knees, about to spring up, the princess was already there in front of me.

Her heel cracked under my jaw, splitting my lip.

I fell backwards as blood filled my mouth.

A white ghost loomed over me. I blinked the dazed stars out of my eyes and stared up at the princess.

The deadly point of her blade tilted down towards my chest.

A hollow thud resounded through the lighthouse. Then her sword clattered to the ground. She sank to her knees, Icana's blades at her back and throat.

Chest heaving, I scrambled to my feet and placed the tip of my cutlass under her chin. It caught against a cord. Her eyes widened as I pulled the necklace free.

An obsidian stone hung from the cord, embedded in silver filigree, with smooth planes and jagged edges. My breath hitched as I snapped the string from her neck, earning a yelp from her.

"Please," she said, voice breaking. "I need—"

"What do you know of this?" I snapped. The cold stone bit into my palm as I folded my fingers over it. Her father had killed my parents because of this chunk of rock and now a piece of it sat around her neck like a trophy. If I hadn't been so angry, I might have been sick.

"Nothing!" she exclaimed. "My father was looking for more of it in Vodaeard." She dropped her gaze. "He's going to kill the princess."

"He already tried," I growled, ignoring Icana's warning glance.

The white-haired girl shook her head, wincing as my sword scraped along her jaw. "He's going back. He said he had unfinished business there. Please. I didn't know what he was doing on the mainland."

"*Lies*," Icana hissed, the edge of her blade digging into the princess' neck. Blood rubied up from a thin cut.

Her eyes locked with mine, her conviction wavering.

I narrowed my gaze. "Where did you think all those artefacts came from?"

"Gifts," she replied, incredulous.

"Spoils!" My grip tightened on my cutlass.

Her eyelids fluttered closed in defeat. "I can bring them back," she whispered.

Icana caught my gaze over her head and mouthed a silent curse.

Blood pounded in my ears, echoing with the distant ring of battle, the cries of death from so many hours ago.

The cutlass slipped. She didn't cry out when it carved a line down her throat, but she winced, trembling where she knelt.

I was right.

She *was* the Princess of Death.

A name as familiar to me as it was to almost everyone on the continent, the name of legends and bedtime stories told to scare children into behaving. The girl who brought the dead back to life, who built her father's army to wage war on the mainland. A war for the other piece of moonstone that had sat around her neck. The same rock that had been the cause of my parents' deaths.

The girl had been shrouded in mystery for as long as she had lived. No one even knew what she looked like.

And I was staring at her now like she was a figure of Death incarnate.

"Why should I let you live when your death will end the war?" I said through clenched teeth, fingers tightening on my cutlass.

"Why would I want more people to die in a war I knew nothing about?" she shot back.

Something in her voice rang with just enough sincerity that I believed her—she truly didn't know about the war. It made me question just how much she knew about her role in all of it.

"How could you possibly not know about it?"

"My father never talks about what he does on the mainland," she said, matching my tone. "He forbade his crew and the guards from talking about it as well. I've only just found out when I overheard him boasting about killing the monarchs. I want to help."

I replaced my sword at her throat. A soft whimper escaped her. "I watched your father kill the king and queen. I came to avenge their deaths. How could you possibly help when all you've done is build your father's army for him?"

Her piercing blue eyes widened, sincere terror glistening in their depths as her breaths quickened.

"Let me talk to my father," she gasped. "I can stop the bloodshed."

She truly believed she could reason with a monster. Neither of them deserved to live, but if I survived this night, would my soul be damned to the dark depths from all the bloodshed?

"Why would you want to help us?" I asked.

"Because I'm not the kind of person who sits back while others suffer," she said in a strained voice. Her bright eyes shone with sincerity. She believed she was innocent, but how could she possibly know any better when she hadn't seen the pain the war wrought on the world? She was the person who brought back the people to fill her father's army, the people who invaded my home. Perhaps these monsters deserved more than death for their actions. They deserved to know pain. They deserved to know *my* pain. I could make her understand that, and then I could slit her throat while her father watched and make him see my pain.

I glanced at Icana. She shook her head slowly. This was a risk, letting the princess live, and she had already calculated the odds.

I hadn't.

"Get up," I said, taking a step back.

Reluctantly, my weapons master sheathed her twin blades and let the girl stand.

She dusted off her knees, eyes flitting to the stone in my hand.

"You're coming back to Vodaeard with us."

Her gaze snapped back up to my face. "I thought I was allowed to speak to my father?"

"You will be," I said. Behind her, Icana narrowed her pale blue eyes at me. This wasn't *the* plan, but it was *a* plan. "When he lands in Vodaeard."

Fury shone in the princess' eyes like embers. It vanished when I raised my cutlass again, shuttered behind sapphire glass. Her eyes were like the deepest ocean in colour and mystery. So much raged behind them, but she hid everything with a stone mask.

"And what if the princess decides to kill me before I can speak to my father?" she asked.

I searched her gaze for a moment. She stared back defiantly, but there was no recognition in her face. She didn't know *I* was the princess. But if her fear of dying kept her true to her word, I wasn't going to tell her who I was. Not yet, at least.

"You should worry less about what she decides and worry more about what I have yet to decide," I said carefully.

Icana scoffed, but the princess paled. She believed her fate was in my hands—and it was, as long as she didn't know I was the princess she was trying to save.

"Can I bring those with me?" She pointed at something against the stone ledge, two leather-bound books that had been knocked aside in our scuffle. "They're only fairytales," she added.

I gestured for Icana to retrieve them. She scowled at me as she did and shoved them at the princess.

The girl clutched them close to her chest. Sorrow fractured in her gaze when she cast a final glance around the lighthouse.

"We don't have time for this," I muttered, motioning with my cutlass. "Let's go."

Icana took the lead, and I prodded the princess in the back.

I carefully stepped around her trailing hair, marvelling at the way it shone in the moonlight that speared through the slanted windows—glistening silver and translucent opal and sparkling pearl.

As we stepped into the rain, an alarm rang out across the island.

FIVE

Alarm bells trilled through the night, clanging deep in my bones and rattling my teeth more than the fear that was squeezing icy fingers around my heart. My bare feet slid over the soaking scraggly grass as I twisted around, searching the distance for my father. He would come. I could end this here.

The girl followed my gaze, honey-coloured eyes as cold as the distant stars, and then pointed in the opposite direction with the glittering tip of her cutlass. Drizzling rain plastered red curls against her cheeks, and it might have been the shine of the rain in the moonlit night, but there was something akin to remorse in her eyes when she caught my gaze, in the way she grimaced at me.

I shook myself and turned around.

The only thing this girl was capable of was anger. Her warning speared through my mind. The Vodaeard princess might spare my life, but this girl might kill me before then.

I followed the blonde down the sloping cliff to the crags. Rain soaked the hem of my dress. As we neared the shore, grass gave way to gravel, slick mud sticking between my toes. A small boat bumped against the rocky shards, unlit lanterns hanging from the railings. *Grey Bard* was written in slanted red paint along the hull.

"You came in that?" I said as the blonde girl jumped aboard.

They were braver than I thought, to risk the reef in so small a vessel.

One of the men on deck loomed over the side, frowning down at me. His orange hair was pulled back into a low knot, which revealed a jewel in one ear and a sparse beard over his jaw. Hooded eyes looked at the red-haired girl behind me. A silent conversation passed between them before he reached down to help me aboard.

Clutching my books like an anchor, I wobbled unsteadily on the deck as she scrambled over the railing behind me.

"What is she doing here?" he asked, talking around me as though I were a ghost, unseen, unwanted, unwelcome.

"Captain," the blonde girl called from the helm. "A heading?"

"*Captain?*" I echoed in surprise, making my presence clear by turning to face the red-headed girl.

She shoved her cutlass into its sheath and fixed her unruly curls into a bun at the nape of her neck, staring at me with harsh scrutiny. "Vodaeard," she answered, dismissing my question with a glare. "Get me there first, Icana." She marched across the deck to a door beneath the helm, metalwork laced through the glass panes.

"They'll outdistance you," I said, hurrying to match her pace. Another boy sat on the stairs, younger than the others, with a mop of dark hair across his angular face. His watchful eyes stared at me intensely. When I caught his gaze, he winked, and heat flushed up my neck.

"Talen, take her below deck," the captain ordered as the boat rocked away from the shallows.

I stumbled as the small vessel lurched over the waves, frazzled by her ferocity, the boy's burning stare, and the jostling of the ship.

The burly man caught my elbow, pulling me towards the centre of the ship.

"Captain!" I yelled, my voice pitching to a high shrill in panic. "You said I could talk to my father!"

She narrowed her golden gaze at me across the deck. "I said you're coming to Vodaeard with us. You're not a guest, Princess. You're a prisoner."

"I came willingly!" I cried. The man's grip tightened on my elbow, sharp enough that my veins tingled. My fingers dented the leather spines of my books. "I came here to help you save the princess, not be your bargaining tool."

She waved a hand dismissively. "You can do both."

The man dragged me to a hatch and hauled it open. I wasn't afraid of any shadowy dwelling, but it was the uncertainty that came with facing an unknown future that made me dig in my heels. "And what will you do when his ships overcome yours? You'll sink."

Her glare burned through me, hostility warped in the shroud of fallen night. "Then you'll drown with me."

Her words shoved me over the edge and the man pulled me down into the dark depths of the ship's belly.

Clutching my books, the only bit of home I had, I glanced around the cramped cargo hold as he lit a candle. The wavering flame didn't even touch the corners. It revealed a low table, a chair, and a few crates. At the top of the stairs, stars speckled the void, but I didn't feel the moon down here. There were no bones, no crypts, no lost souls waiting for me.

The boat slammed into the reef. It thrashed through the waves, and I tripped over my hair, yelping as I landed in something sticky.

The man looked down at me, eyebrows arched. "Nice hair," he muttered, stepping over me.

I peeled my arm off the floor. Face twisted in disgust, I worked on pulling strands of hair from a foul-smelling puddle when the hatch clanged shut above me, sealing me in with shadows and doubts.

"All right," I whispered to the shadows, dragging myself off the floor. "You don't scare me."

The candle flickered warmly as I set my books on the table. Around me, the ship groaned and creaked, the sounds popping through the dark like something sinister. My heart jumped at every small noise and my stomach lurched with every big tilt of the ship. I wasn't used to the rolling sensation, the rises and falls that had my stomach flopping every few seconds. Bile stung the back of my throat, and I leaned back against the post, closing my eyes. A second later, the boat dropped with the waves, and I lurched forward.

Shutting my eyes was a bad idea.

The grate above me opened again sometime later. I breathed in the stench of ale and explosive powder—why was there explosive powder down here?—trying to focus my thoughts elsewhere than the bile filling my mouth.

"Here," someone said. The dark-haired boy held out a green-tinted bottle. Liquid sloshed within. "That will help with the…everything."

I unscrewed the top. The awful scent of alcohol hit my nose, but I tossed back a gulp, choking as it burned. "That's disgusting," I spluttered.

"Yeah," he agreed, folding his gangly frame onto the floor on the other side of the table. He uncorked his own bottle, raised it in the air between us, and took a swig. In the weak glow of the candle, his face was pale. Hollow cheeks sunken with deep shadows. His eyes glittered at me over the flame, cast in gold. "What's your name?"

Leaning back against the post, I frowned over the rim of my bottle. "I'd rather not tell."

He clicked his tongue against his teeth. "We have one for you," he said. "The Princess of Death. A fitting moniker, I think."

My heart fluttered in my throat. I set my bottle down, staring at the edges of the books in front of me. The thread shone in the candle-light. "And what do they tell you of me?"

At home, the guards whispered. They spoke the title with reverence, fear, awe. Like I was somebody to be worshipped. A hallowed thing, like the moon itself.

This boy spoke as though the title left a sour taste in his mouth. He tapped a finger against his teeth. "I don't really care what everyone else says. I care about what *you* say."

I tilted my head, studying him. He was drunk and the smell of alcohol hung around him like a haze. Dark hair stuck to his forehead from the rain. But he wore fine clothes, costly materials that signified wealth. His teeth were perfectly straight, perfectly white—not brown stubs like the pirates in my stories. He wasn't like the others.

"I *say* I've been kidnapped by pirates who lack a moral code." I narrowed my eyes. "I say I've left my island for the first time in my life and held against my will the day before a Resurrection. I say I've been treated unfairly my whole life. I say I've been *lied* to, held to an impossible standard, and used for my power."

His lips quirked. "I thought you said you came willingly."

"You heard the captain," I said. "I'm a prisoner."

"A willing prisoner," he mused, chuckling.

I frowned and narrowed my eyes. "I came with a warning for the Vodaeardean princess, and your captain turned me into a prisoner."

"She's using you for leverage," he shot back, quick as a whip.

"With my life!" I exclaimed. "That doesn't exactly incite confidence in your captain's leadership skills."

He sat back, kicking his feet up on the table and crossing his ankles. His eyes sparkled in the warm light. "Fear keeps people in line. Surely you should know that."

I ground my teeth. "I'm not afraid of her."

"Then what are you afraid of?"

His words knifed through me, cutting open the parts of myself that I tried to hide from the world. The parts that bled every month to please my parents. The parts that ignored any deep yearning for the world beyond my shores.

I scowled, which he seemed to interpret as a hard-won victory, a grin slashing across his mouth. He was sharp in the mind, quick with a retort, his eyes seeing much more than what lay on the surface. And he hid it all beneath a drunken stupor.

He was smart, and smart was dangerous.

"Who are you?" I said. Someone with his intelligence would have had an extensive education. He was wealthy, attractive—if I was being honest—and that made him a mystery.

"You didn't answer my question, Princess."

And I wasn't going to. I had made it clear I didn't trust them, especially with something as fragile as my fears. I would hide them away behind the stone walls of my lighthouse, would learn to carve my face out of marble. I would do whatever I needed to survive this. Because if they were going to gamble with my life, I would make them regret ever crossing the Princess of Death.

The grate above us ground open. With a sigh, the boy rose from the floor.

"My name's Alekey," he said as the captain came into view around the stairs. He winked again, clapped the redhead on the shoulder, and staggered up the steps.

She rolled her shoulder, frowning as Alekey stumbled over the top and fumbled with the hatch. Her pretty face, ringed by curls burnished gold in the candlelight, twisted into a scowl when he crashed onto the deck above us and yelped in pain. She didn't look at me until the sound of his stomping faded. When she did, anger shone as bright as any volcano burst in her eyes. They seemed to change colour in the candle-light—shifting from onyx to topaz and finally settling on citrine.

It took only a glance to realize she believed his charade. The drunken boy who saw too much, who knew too much—overlooked and underestimated. She was the fool in his play, and she had no idea she was acting the part perfectly. She was already a puppet on someone else's string. What was one more thread to tug?

"The captain graces me with her presence," I simpered, affecting a short bow where I sat. "I am honoured."

She bristled. "You're mouthy. I don't like you."

"The feeling is mutual."

Eyes narrowed to slits, she crouched on the other side of the table, black leather pants stretching over her thighs. The cuffs of her billowy crimson shirt were pushed up to her elbows, and the ties are the collar were undone. I glimpsed pale skin and curves, and then my eyes snagged on the cord around her neck. The obsidian stone rested like a black stain against the hollow of her throat.

She noticed where my gaze landed, on *my* stone around *her* neck, and didn't move to hide it from view. "What did he talk to you about?" she asked, resting her arms on her knees.

Like pulling a shard of seashell from my foot, I jerked my eyes to her face.

"He was drunk," I said. "I could barely follow the conversation."

She frowned deeper, dissatisfied with my answer. Perhaps she had hoped I would divulge something if I thought he was too drunk to retain anything.

"I don't appreciate what you are doing, Captain," I added. "I offered to help, and this is how you treat me? Stuck in some foul-smelling prison cell with a single candle and no food?"

Her brows crinkled in the centre of her forehead. With an air of annoyance, she flung a hand towards the crates against the wall. "There's fruit if you're so hungry."

"Is this how diplomacy works on the mainland?" I tucked my legs beneath me, curling a long strand of hair around my hand.

Her gaze darted to my hand, and she dropped hers to the hilt of her cutlass. "Don't try that again," she warned.

"You might call me a prisoner," I said, twining the strand through my fingers, the moonlight glow tumbling over itself, "but my offer still stands as a willing compromise."

I watched her eyes follow the tangled loop. My hair was a weapon. She knew that, and she was cautious of it. As my words sank in, her gaze wavered, and she looked up at me.

"What offer?"

"I can bring them back," I said. "The king and queen. No one has to die. No more blood has to be shed."

She sat on the floor, legs crossed. The stone hung heavy around her neck. "Do you know why they died?"

I dropped my gaze quickly. Before my stone walls fractured. I didn't know the why, but I knew the how, and it horrified me still to think my father had done it.

"They weren't willing to give up a secret," she said, her voice trembling with rage. "Your father cut out their tongues when they refused to talk and then carved open their chests and reached in and—"

"Stop," I whispered, the pain in me as fresh as the cuts she was describing.

"And pulled out their hearts—"

"Stop!"

"And painted the throne room with their blood, so don't tell me no more blood needs to be shed!" She glowered at me through the tears swimming in her eyes.

I shook, not wanting to believe my father was capable of something like that. His arms were strong, but were they strong enough to snuff a life without hesitation? I had forced myself to believe I'd misheard him in the infirmary because I had been too scared to believe it then. It didn't seem within his ability to do something so vile and yet show no remorse. I had fallen into his arms, scared for him, for his safety, and yet he had been lying to me.

It was still hard to believe.

She clambered to her feet, lip pulling back over white teeth as she snarled, "Enjoy the night, Princess. It might be your last." She blew out the candle and stomped up the stairs, away from the inky darkness of the cargo hold.

I listened, heart in my throat, as she slammed a bolt over the hatch and locked me in with the shadows.

SIX

The cargo hold swallowed the night behind me in shadows. My heart hammered against my ribs so hard it bruised. Eyes squeezed shut, I listened to the rush of the ocean around us. Sails snapped overhead, waves slapped the hull, and a gull screeched in the distance. I breathed deeply through my nose. Fresh ocean air hit my face, salt stinging my lips and rain pelting my face. The obsidian stone burned against my chest in the light of the near-full moon as I leaned against the railing, ignoring the stares of the rest of my tired crew. Alekey's eyes burned the hottest on my back.

The princess was manipulating me. Every moment from the lighthouse to now had been a clever manipulation, designed to make me believe she had no role in any of this. She didn't want to help me or my kingdom—she only wanted to keep her life. She would say and do anything to survive this war.

"Ev?" Talen's voice cut through the thoughts swirling in my head.

"She can't know who I am." My voice was a whisper through gasps of panicked breaths. This entire plan hinged on her believing she could stop the bloodshed. As soon as she found out I was the princess, her cooperation would end. It needed to last as long as possible in order to reach Vodaeard alive. "I need her to think we're taking her to Vodaeard to meet with the princess. Her father needs to know my pain."

Sighing, Talen scraped a hand over his jaw. He leaned against the railing next to me. "What did she say?"

I made a face, clutching the stone between my fingers. My voice was low enough that only Talen heard me when I spoke. "She said she'd bring them back."

As much as I wanted to see my parents again, hold them and say goodbye, I couldn't. Mortality was inevitable. Everyone died. Even if she did bring them back, they wouldn't be healthy and well. They'd be deformed from the blows that killed them. Heads caved in. Chests carved open. Dead, dead, dead. Their souls were gone, adrift in the Endless Seas, a place of peace our people went to after death. I couldn't bear the thought of seeing them like *that*, even for a few extra minutes.

I shook my head fiercely. The wind snatched my hair away from my face as I did. "She's only trying to save her own skin."

In this world, it wasn't our job to manipulate mortality. The Endless Seas were unforgiving and judgemental—I had already been willing to risk everything to shed more blood, not knowing if there would be a place for me there if I had killed the chief. There were implications of messing with fate, and the Princess of Death made a mockery of that. She had to have known what she was doing. It went against nature.

It frustrated me, how quick I was to believe her in the lighthouse. There was something so captivating and poisonous about her. She had wedged herself beneath my skin and in my lungs. Every breath felt tainted—acidic—with her so close. And the storm in those eyes. Swirling blue and white like ocean waves. It was those bright eyes that remained splashed across my mind, rather than her silvery-white hair or even the freckles dotting her tiny nose like a constellation.

The railing warped beneath my fingers. The high of battle clanged around me. I needed to focus on what lay ahead. The blood running hot in my veins demanded revenge, and I would have it when her father landed on my shores again.

She would never be able to convince such a monster to be anything other than a monster.

And so, the monster had to die.

But first, I had to know why her father was looking for more of this rock. I twisted the stone in the moonlight, watching the pale glow reflect off the smooth planes and fracture in the jagged edges.

"Pretty," Talen muttered next to me.

I shook my fist as if the answers would fall out of the stone. "They died for this."

Talen raked a nervous hand through his hair. He understood well enough what I wasn't saying. If the rock gave the princess her twisted power, what could more of it do? My parents had died to keep the moonstone's secret. And I had almost given him exactly what he wanted.

I drew my arm back.

Talen snatched my wrist, yanking me away from the railing. "Is that such a good idea?" he said in a low voice.

"This is the reason they're dead!" Salt filled my mouth as tears threatened to fall again. Below deck, the princess had goaded me into reliving those recent memories. If this chunk of moonstone was why I would never see their faces again, I wanted it to sink into the black seas, lost forever. Drowned with the ghosts that haunted me.

"Sinking it won't give you the answers you want."

"It means *something* to her." I stared at it, a black stain on my palm. "All that horrendous power wrapped up in this hideous thing."

"How do you know it's not her?"

"Because she looked terrified when I took it from her." It was as cold and distant as the stars fading out of the night sky. I closed my hand over it, snuffing its unfathomable pull. If I stared too long, I'd tumble overboard and sink beneath the waves. "It's connected to her power. It should be destroyed."

"And if there is more of it? Destroying this one piece won't stop them."

My eyes fluttered closed.

As always, he was right. There was a reason Talen had been my father's advisor and trusted friend.

Sighing heavily, I slipped the cord over my head. Exhaustion was creeping up on me like a wave. We had all been awake for too long, but I was too scared to close my eyes. Only darkness awaited in my dreams. "Where are we headed?"

"Lafori," Icana confirmed from the helm. "There's a port there. It should be beyond the blockade's reach."

The reminder that the princess had been right grated against my nerves. It should have taken us less than a day to sail back to Vodaeard. We hadn't been past the reef for long before Icana noticed the warships in the distance, mere specks on a black horizon. Her keen eyes were better attuned to the night, picking out the bobbing lanterns from the fixed stars. We'd adjusted course quickly, another hasty plan put into action—dock in the west, wait a few days to make sure we weren't followed, and then slowly sail along the south coast back towards Vodaeard. From Xesta, on the other side of the mountains, we would walk. It would take significantly longer, weeks at most, but they wouldn't expect us to cross on foot.

I wanted my home at my back and my enemy in front of me when I had my revenge.

"Doesn't that bring us dangerously close to the siren lagoon?" Key piped up from the other side of the deck. He'd been drinking constantly since we set sail—I was surprised he was paying enough attention to know where we were headed.

I squinted at him through the gloom. Night blanketed around the small carrack. He was little more than a shadow on the deck. Another ghost. The bottle in his hand glinted in the moonlight as he raised it to his lips.

"He's right," Talen said, peering sideways at me, his mouth turned down at the sides. "Those are bad seas."

"Sirens aren't bad seas," I muttered, dismissing their misgivings with a wave of my hand. "They won't bother us." I tilted my neck back to give him my best impression of a reassuring grin. He only frowned harder. I blew out a breath, his lack of trust cutting deep. "I'm not going to meddle in *more* magic. We just need to get around the blockade."

"And I just want you to be careful," he murmured. His frown smoothed, but worry glinted in his eyes. It drew creases in his forehead.

I wanted to rub those lines away, but I didn't know how.

"Ev, you're exhausted. This is taking too much—"

Frustrated, I twisted away from him, marching towards the quarterdeck. "I'll sleep when I've had my revenge."

"I don't just mean sleep," he argued, chasing my heels. "You haven't let yourself mourn. Even Key mourned."

I scoffed. What Alekey was doing wasn't mourning. I wasn't even sure it could be considered functioning.

Movement in the shadows beyond the glass doors startled me, but it was only Talen's reflection coming up behind me. "I don't have time to think about that right now," I told him.

He seized my arm before I opened the door. "When will you let yourself think about it?"

My throat tightened around all the words I wanted to say. "Later," I said instead, swallowing every other truth and lie. "When I've had my revenge."

Nothing else mattered until the blood of my enemies dripped from my cutlass. Until their blood replaced the blood of my parents in the throne room. Until I was crowned queen, a year too soon.

I was owed as much.

Reluctantly, Talen let me go. He could only say so much—reason with me so much—and he knew this course was mine to tread as long as I needed to tread it. And I knew he would be there with me every uncertain step of the way.

Taking a deep breath, I opened the door to the small, cramped captain's quarters for the first time since we started our journey from Vodaeard. The ghosts that lingered there were too much for me to handle then, but I had nowhere else to go now, and I needed to be alone.

The room was barely large enough to fit a small cot, a small table, and a small closet. Candles and papers crowded the table. More were tacked to the wall. I rifled through the sheets on the desk. Most of them had been surprise gifts for my parents when they went on their excursions out to sea. They were never gone long, but Alekey and I used to write letters, wrap them in twine and messy wax seals, and hide them all over the ship to find as they sailed. The notes never said much, only silly childish things, but our parents had kept every single one. The ink was so faded with time I could hardly read the scratchy, scribbling script.

A lump formed in my throat as I absently bit a nail. I wasn't the same person who had written those letters so long ago. I wasn't the same person I had been only days ago. So much had been lost in such a short amount of time.

Talen was right. I hadn't let myself grieve. But it felt easier to hold onto my anger instead of my agony. If there was one thing I was good at, it was being angry. I certainly wasn't good at saying goodbye. These notes were proof of that. Every time my parents set sail, even for a day, I was with them. I never had to say goodbye. They always came back.

A tear spiked down my cheek. I clamped a hand over my mouth to stifle my sob, but it burst out of me like a lit fuse. Emotions I had dammed crashed over me all at once, drowning me in sorrow, grief, agony. Gasping through the tears, I blindly reached for the cot and lowered myself onto the scratchy sheet, grabbing at the threads to keep them from unravelling all around me.

It still *smelled* like them.

An explosion blasted into the side of the ship, knocking me out of the cot with such force that I cracked my nose on the floor. As blood burst in my mouth, the metallic tang coating my throat, another explosion rolled the ship sideways. The closet crashed across the door, the only thing not bolted down. Maps and letters covered the floor. Blood from my nose dripped across a map beneath me like a series of *X*'s.

My first thought was, *pirates*. But then I remembered we weren't flying any colours, which made us pirates as well, and no pirate crew would attack such a small vessel. We weren't large enough to be carrying any precious cargo. The effort wasn't worth it for the few bottles of rum below deck.

Unless it wasn't bottles of rum, they were after.

Black seas! The Marama navy must have spotted us.

I staggered to my feet, listing sideways as I scrambled over the wardrobe. The doors ground open, hinges busted, to Talen and Icana peering over the side. Key stood by the centre mast, rope in hand.

"The warships?" I called before taking stock of our surroundings. A clear sky greeted me, the sun blinding on the crashing waves all around. Something roiled in the ocean beneath us.

"Worse," Icana gritted.

What was worse than the warships?

I got my answer a second later when a fish's tail jumped out of the water. Multicoloured scales flashed wickedly in the sunlight. Its screech pierced the air before it dived again. I clamped my hands over my ears, screaming as the sound clawed at my skull.

Sirens. We were in bad seas, indeed.

One of them leapt out of the foaming sea in front of Icana, A webbed hand curled around the banister. She danced back, swinging both swords at the creature. With a hiss, it launched backwards through the air. Its tail sliced into Icana's cheek with enough force to draw blood.

"No!" I cried. The boat skidded sideways over the waves, and I lost my footing, crashing into the staircase. "Don't hurt them," I warned. A sliver of wood stuck out of my elbow.

"They attacked us!" my weapons master shouted over the sound of churning waves and whipping tails. "Unprovoked!" she hollered at the sea, waving her swords threateningly. I wouldn't cross Icana with a butter knife, but sirens were not of this world. They were bound by different laws, different nature.

And they were angry.

Another screech rent the air, knocking all of us off our feet. Bent against the horrific sound, I looked up in time to see two sirens clambering over the edge of the boat. Their skin glimmered as they shed their scales. Flesh rippled like water over the legs that replaced their fins as they strode across the deck towards me.

"Don't touch her!" Talen shouted. He snatched one of Icana's blades from her and ran across the deck.

One of the sirens turned to him, ducked beneath his lunge with lethal grace, and slammed a hand into his chest to shove him backwards.

His forward momentum stopped with a resounding crack. He flew through the air, crashing into the mast and landing in a heap beside Alekey. The mast bowed under the impact. Talen didn't move.

Gasping, tears stinging my eyes and blurring my vision, I looked up at the approaching sirens. One of them reached for me, fingers like claws. I smacked its hand away, scrambling backwards as I fumbled for my cutlass. My back slammed into the staircase. Fingers closed around my throat and lifted me off my feet. I scratched at the siren's arm—flakes of flesh fell away to reveal scales hidden underneath—as the other one reached for the cord around my neck.

"Let go of her," a cold voice snaked across the deck.

The princess stood at the top of the hatch. Alekey held it open for her as spindly strands of her hair snapped like a pennant in the wicked wind that stormed around the boat.

The two sirens whipped their heads around. With a hiss and strength unworldly, the one holding me threw me aside. Something inside cracked when I slammed into the raised edge of the cargo hold hole, and I choked back a cry of pain, spitting blood onto the wooden boards of the deck.

The princess' bare feet shifted into view in front of me. Squinting in the sun, I gazed up. White hair shone like a halo around her head. As my vision darkened and my head dropped to the deck, I distantly realized she looked exactly like a vengeful spirit from books about the Endless Seas. Like a ghost to haunt my nightmares.

Something bit into the back of my neck. I blinked up at the princess. Nausea filled my mouth. The moonstone glowed in her hand as she dragged the sharp edge across her wrist. Blood spilled over, and the *air* changed as she raised her arms to the sea. Sweat beaded on my forehead, my tongue heavy in my mouth. The wind ceased, pressing in against the ship on all sides. The two sirens shifted anxiously as white light shot down the length of the princess' hair.

Beneath the ship, the ocean bubbled. Steam rose off the surface and fell back in a blanket of fog over the boat. I pushed myself to my knees. Her hair continued to glow as she strained, face twisted in pain, fingers curling into claws as *something* moved in the waters.

The sirens hissed, edging towards the railing. As they approached the side, several bony hands clamped over the wood. Icana cursed loudly when a face loomed near her, scales and flesh and hair flaking off from salt-encrusted bones. The bloated body pulled itself over the edge. My weapons master skittered away from the decayed siren corpse. The tail didn't transform into legs. Parts of it split open by gaping wounds to reveal hundreds of tiny fish bones lining its length. Behind me, Alekey vomited at the stench that filled the stifling air.

"Moon-blessed!" the two living creatures hissed, tongues darting between their teeth. They threw themselves over the side of the boat, tails glittering briefly before they disappeared beneath the surface. The others thrashing through the water followed, and the crashing waves stilled at once.

Swaying on her feet, the princess dropped her arms. A haze surrounded her as the glow in her hair faded. The bony hands unlatched from the railing and splashed into the ocean, and the corpse on the deck fell to the boards, once more a dead thing.

Icana prodded it with her sword, just to make sure.

Pain jolted up my arm as I pushed myself to my feet and limped to the side of the boat. Nothing moved beneath the glassy surface, a still world hiding in the depths.

The princess and her infernal white hair ghosted in view next to me, breathing heavily. A nervous giggle squeaked out of her.

I twisted to face her. "Why did they call you that?"

"What?" she panted. Red spread across the tops of her cheeks, eyes brighter than sapphire gems.

"*Moon-blessed*. What does that mean?"

She turned and regarded me, head cocked to the side. Joy danced across her face as she came to some realization I didn't understand yet. "You don't know anything about me at all, do you?"

I slammed my arm across her throat, pushing her against the railing so hard the wood—or her spine—cracked.

Her chest rose and fell unevenly, but there was no spark of fear in her gaze.

Why wasn't she scared?

"Captain," Icana warned. Feet shuffled over the deck towards me.

The princess didn't move, staring at me with her mouth slightly open.

"C-captain," Talen's voice croaked behind me.

Relief shattered the icy rage in my veins. I jerked away from the princess, looking across the deck at him. Blood speckled his face, but he was on his feet. *Alive.*

"Talen, are you—"

He cut a hand through the air, and I flinched at the pain in his eyes. Guilt soured my stomach. I should have made sure he was alright first. He didn't seem to want my worry as he limped towards the crew quarters on the other side of the ship.

My cutlass came to rest over the princess's heart. "This is *your* fault!" I could have lost Talen. I could have lost them all. I was gambling with too many lives, all for the piece of rock clutched in her palm.

"I saved your life!" she cried. Fear finally shone through the sheen in her gaze, battering against the walls she had so carefully built. "A little respect would be nice."

A manic laugh burst out of me. "Respect is a mutual transaction, Princess! Show me some, and I'll consider showing you some in return. Get below deck before I feed you to the sirens."

Anger flashed in her eyes. Huffing, she stalked away. I stepped out of the way of a snapping tendril of hair, and she disappeared into the cargo hold, another ghost to add to my collection.

"That contradicts itself," Key murmured, perching on the edge of the hole, searching the dark beneath as if he had lost something.

"What?" I snapped at him.

He looked up, eyes boring into me with a kind of wisdom I hadn't expected from him. Maybe he was paying more attention than I thought. "You want her to show you some respect, but you refuse to give her any first. Like you said, 'it's a mutual transaction.'" He got up, dusted off his pants, and walked away without another word.

I pinched the bridge of my nose. "Icana—"

"I'm not picking sides, Captain," she called from the helm. She had tucked her short blonde hair beneath a wide-brimmed hat and squinted towards the horizon, guiding us towards clear skies and good seas.

Chastened, I say, "I was only going to ask how much farther to Lafori." The words are quiet, all the fight gone for now.

SEVEN

undled in the corner of the cargo, I tried to sleep. But I shuddered every time I closed my eyes, visions of the dead sirens rising out of the water haunting the shadows around me. The stench of ocean gore permeated the air, long after they had disappeared again into the depths. Flashes of flesh and scales peeling off—like they were in a constant state of transformation, between something not entirely siren and something not entirely human—tormented my mind.

I had never seen so much decay and rot before. The bodies of the people I brought back were well-preserved in the icy crypts. These bodies had been bloated beyond recognition, eaten away by whatever lurked in the murky depths of the ocean, slithering like they were still alive. The bones had moved at my call, and the sirens who still lived, who witnessed their kin revived, had recognized something in me.

It was the only thing I could think to do to save the captain.

Moon-blessed, they called me. It wasn't like what the guards whispered in the dead of night, quiet and reverent. It was as much a mystery as the dark side of the moon. But the sirens seemed to understand. They knew why the moon had given me this power.

And it seemed to frighten them.

I yearned to hold onto that feeling all the time. The feeling of staring down the most terrifying creatures in the world and having them look at me in fright—of commanding death in front of these creatures who transcended this realm entirely.

The moonstone pulsed in my palm. I unfurled my fingers to stare at it. The moon's power glinted along the jagged edges, caught in the mesmerizing current of the depths. I sat up, crossing my legs. For years, this stone had guided me to Death's dark shores, and for years, this stone had pulled me back. I had put my trust in it, in the moon's ability to bring me safely home.

But I always thought I had to see the bodies to resurrect them and the bones to move them. What I had done with the sirens was something else, something that left me feeling off-balance. I hadn't needed to see their bodies or their bones to bring them to the surface. I'd simply *felt* them.

So if I delved into the depths now, without any bodies around, would I see any lost souls?

The drying blood on my wrist was clotted brown over the ripped flesh. It didn't match the dozens of neat, half-moon scars that covered my wrists. Those had been done by a steady hand, a sharp knife. Blood was the only way to open the doors to Death's dark shore.

I ripped at the wet scab and closed my eyes.

Colours blended into a tunnel, grey and blue, and green and black, swirling around and around like water tumbling over itself as I plodded towards a piercing light at the end. Blood sprinkled the tunnel behind me, a ruby trail to guide me home. This was the usual path I walked during a Resurrection. Death's door waited at the end of the tunnel, beyond the hook, the net, the sail, the ship—the normal tools I used to bring souls back from the depths. And beyond that, I knew what I would see—the black beach. The slate sky. The Dunes of Forever.

I didn't make it nearly that far.

"What are you doing?"

The screeching voice dug like a fishhook into my abdomen and yanked me out of the tunnel. My eyes flew open to see the captain looming over me, the tip of her cutlass kissing my throat. My heart hammered in my chest like I had been torn out of a nightmare, a frenzied pulse in my veins.

The stone continued to glow in my palm, a steady flash of light. She snatched it from my icy fingers, and it winked into darkness, the swirling light fading into its deep void.

"What were you doing?" she asked again, voice low. Beneath the threatening tone, though, there was a hint of something equally dangerous—panic.

My brow crinkled. Before I could answer, the flat of her hand connected with my jaw with a loud smack. I gasped, my skin sizzling.

"Black seas," she muttered, pacing away from me. Her sword snicked into its sheath, and she raked a hand through her hair, tangling knots in her fingers. She rounded the low table, and I wondered if she was putting it between us for her benefit—or mine. Deep shadows flared in her tawny gaze when she exclaimed, "You're intolerable!"

"And you're insufferable," I shot back, bounding to my feet. Her hand darted to her sword again. I rolled my eyes.

"That's the same thing," she said, slowly relaxing her shoulders. The obsidian dangled from her fingers, no reverence for something with so much power. No reverence for it, no reverence for me, no reverence for the moon. She didn't deserve to be holding something so sacred.

"No," I said, tearing my gaze from the stone to her face. "Because you will tolerate me, but I will not suffer you."

Something ugly flickered behind her beautiful eyes. I knew if I stared too long, I would be the first to crack. My lighthouse walls could only weather so much hatred, and I was exhausted. Her moods were too volatile, the arguments constant—the fear that had taken hold of me since she entered my lighthouse was ever-present. It seemed so long ago already. I was tired of withstanding everything she hurled at me.

Her gaze was the first to drop, narrowed to slits when they landed on my books. She sank to the ground, legs crossed, and motioned for me to take a seat.

Still wary of her, I slowly folded my legs beneath me and let out a shaky breath.

"Tell me what happened up there," she demanded. Methodically, as if it were a ritual, she wrapped the frayed cord of my necklace around her wrist and cinched it with her teeth.

"There's nothing to tell," I said. "You were in danger. I saved your life."

Her eyes bored into mine again, fiery and icy at the same time, picking me apart. Chaotic thoughts clashed in the honey depths of her gaze, but I was the first to look away this time. I stared at my hands in my lap, the half-moon scars, the flaking blood.

"I do not know how my power works," I admitted. My fingers felt hollow, numb. They always did after I dived into the depths, as though I left pieces of myself behind every time. As though the moon's energy had all but left me empty. "My parents told me I was born with it, but I have never been able to use it without that stone. When I grabbed it from you, I...*felt* the sirens deep in the ocean. I didn't think. I just raised them to scare the others away. I didn't know I could do that without seeing their bodies."

"What do you mean?" she pressed.

I lifted my head. Her gaze had gone distant, but she was attentive, piecing the information together. I didn't know what picture of me she was forming in her mind. If it looked anything like the terrifying Princess of Death that they called me on the mainland.

"Every month on the full moon, I can bring the dead back to life." The captain scoffed, earning a glare of daggers from me. "Life is precious, Captain. I know that better than anyone. Why are you so quick to dismiss what I do as vile?"

Her eyebrows narrowed. "What you do is an affront to nature. Death comes for us all, as it should, in its own time. Who are you to say it doesn't?"

"You heard the siren. I'm moon-blessed," I reminded her. "My power is a gift, and I treasure that. As I was saying, my parents bring me the bodies of people they want raised, and I search for their souls in the…afterlife, I suppose you call it. I have to see their bodies to find their souls. I didn't bring the sirens back to life, but I moved them without seeing them."

A frown creased her forehead, lips puckered as she pondered. "Every month?" she repeated. Some pieces were falling into place, but I couldn't see the picture she was painting.

I nodded. "It's the full moon today."

"It's day. There's no moon out," she said, brow furrowed.

I refrained from scoffing at her ignorance. "That doesn't matter. The energy is still there, regardless."

She ran her tongue over her teeth and chewed the inside of her cheek. A cracked nail picked at flakes of dead skin on her lip. As I watched, waiting for her to talk, she ripped a piece of skin too far. A drop of blood beaded on her lip. Without even wincing, she clamped her teeth over her lip and shifted her gaze to me, bright in the amber candlelight.

"Captain," I continued with a weary sigh, "I want to be able to help you, but—"

"And what of the sirens?" she interrupted. She pressed a finger to the droplet of blood and smeared it across her thumb. It wasn't the only bit of blood I had noticed since coming aboard. Scabs surrounded most of her nails, the skin discoloured where it had healed over and over.

I hesitated. "*What* of the sirens?"

"They recognized something in you," she said. A shiver shuddered up my spine at the reminder. "I know sirens are bad seas, but do they have the same kind of power as you?"

A healthy dose of fear laced her words, but her eyes glinted with curiosity, as though she had stumbled upon something extraordinary.

"Why were we so close to the siren lagoon, anyway?" I asked. The gilded map in the library flashed in my mind. The lagoon was a crescent-shaped island off the west coast of the mainland. All the stories

I had read told of a perpetual storm that sunk ships that sailed too close. But there was no reason for us to be in the western waters.

"Your father's blockade."

The excitement I expected to feel wasn't there. Instead, a chill prickled my body. We were so far from my father, from my home, from everything I had ever known, yet somehow sailing around blockades and surviving siren attacks felt a lot like diving into the depths. The pain, the uncertainty, and the cold that followed.

"If he has already formed a blockade, we may never get through," I said, keenly aware of the defeat tinging my voice and unable to stop it from spilling over.

"You don't need to concern yourself over it," she muttered.

My breath lodged in my throat. Those were the same words my father told me in the infirmary. The same dismissive words that had led me to this exact moment. If he hadn't been so quick to ignore me, I would have still been safe in my lighthouse.

I wasn't going to let her ignore me now.

"You have no right to tell me what I need and needn't concern myself with," I said quickly. "Especially when I risked everything to help you save your princess. You are bargaining with my life, Captain. I am already involved. The least you can do is tell me your plan for getting around my father's armada."

Her head twitched, eyes narrowed to study me as her nostrils flared. It was hard to read her in the low light when she wasn't actively loathing me with every vein, every muscle. Perhaps no one had ever dared to speak out against her before. Perhaps she was imagining all the ways she could cut me open with her sword.

"You clearly know your geography," she said, leaning back against the post. "You tell me." She threaded the loose ties of her shirt between her fingers. The same thing I had done with my hair the last time she came down to talk.

So, she was paying attention, after all.

I reached for one of the books between us.

"I'm not interested in whatever strategic advantages you *think* you have. My father will sink this small boat." I thumbed to the first page, the letters traced in gold. When she didn't move, I briefly glanced up at her. "Why are you here?"

She jumped to her feet, open hatred plain on her pale face. "I want to know what makes you so seas-damned special," she hissed.

"Are you jealous?"

She seethed, nostrils flared. "I don't think power like yours should belong to any one person. So, no, I'm not jealous." She leaned across the table, shirt billowing open. I held my breath, staring up at her while my heart hammered in my chest. "I almost tossed this into the ocean," she said, raising her wrist between us. The obsidian swayed. "All that power…it's caused so much pain and suffering. And maybe the sirens had the right idea of trying to take it. Maybe they recognized how dangerous this is."

"And maybe they want to use it for themselves," I said. My tongue trembled over the words at the thought of losing the stone to the depths. I was nothing without the stone. I was nothing without my power. And even though I couldn't let her see how frightened I was, it was hard to keep my walls from crumbling around me.

"You don't believe that," she said. She was right. The sirens didn't need my power. They had their own, different and frightening.

My gaze dropped to my books, curiosities bound in neat pages and illustrated script. Maybe they weren't stories after all. Maybe fiction was closer to fact. There had to be a reason this book was embossed with symbols of the moon.

"If you cross me again, I will throw it overboard," the captain threatened, circling towards the stairs. She peered at me between the slates, studying me, ripping me apart. I tried not to squirm under her scrutiny, the heat of her gaze flushing my cheeks. "Why you?" she murmured to herself.

"I've been asking myself that same question for years," I told her. The pages crinkled as I searched for the right story. "Is that all, Captain?"

"For now." She stomped up the stairs, and this time, the hatch didn't slam shut.

I exhaled shakily. Ever since my father's ship had returned, I had felt as though I'd been observing a dangerous play from behind the curtains. Unable to speak out, unable to stop the events from progressing as they were. I was observing my own life from the outside, every moment worse than the last. Pieces moved around me on a grand scale, and I was the only one who couldn't see the final image.

I thought my role in life was simple. I was the Princess of Death, who granted life under every full moon.

But it didn't feel that simple anymore. I wasn't sure where I fit. On a boat sailing to save some foreign princess that my father wanted to kill? In my palatial home waiting for the next full moon without anyone to talk to? My whole life, I had longed for the horizon, the open ocean, freedom from the expectations that chased me into the depths and back again.

I was finally sailing towards that horizon, and I still felt trapped. Everything was moving around me, and I couldn't keep my head above the water.

I was drowning.

The fairytales in my books swam before my eyes, the words lost in the thoughts tumbling through my mind like a thunderstorm. I wanted to be home. I wanted to be safe. But I had been courting Death for too long to be safe anywhere. He always sent his messenger when I lingered in the depths too long. Now his messenger was chasing me across the world.

Silver glinted on the page in front of me, and I pulled my attention out of my thoughts towards the book. My breath hitched at the etchings of fractured crescents on the parchment. I drew the book closer, squinting at the faded letters.

It started as all fairytales did.

In another time, in another place...

But the rest of the opening paragraph made it clear this was one I had never read before.

> When the world was young, and water covered its sur-face, a piece of the moon fell from the sky. It stole light from the stars and sun and landed in the ocean with a mighty splash. When it landed, it broke apart, pieces scattered across the world. The largest piece created an island, but the smaller pieces were lost.

That explained why the book was covered in moons.

> The chief at that time followed the path of light through the sky and water and named the island Marama. He searched the world for the other pieces of the moon, for he believed he was owed them for naming the island after the moon goddess. He gathered as many pieces as he could find, but he could not find them all. Years passed, and the chief feared he would never claim all the pieces. One night, as the elderly chief lay sick in bed, light danced across the sky. He chased the light, through water and sky, to a girl on a crescent island with a marvellous power.

But the story wasn't over yet.

> She communed with the dead and harnessed the power of life through a black stone that sat in a silver clasp around her neck. The chief wondered at her power and craved it for himself. He slaughtered the girl, who was secretly an old woman who had been the first to touch the fallen moonstone long before the chief landed on his island. The power of the moon kept her young with

a special song. Upon her death, the moon turned red as blood that hour, and by killing her, the chief was granted the power he always sought. *Immortality.*

"What are those?"

I jumped at the voice, slamming the book shut. The words painted a bloody picture in my mind, and my heart beat like the fast wings of the hummingbirds on our island.

A bottle clinked onto the table across from me, and Alekey peered down, raising an eyebrow. "Are you okay?" he asked.

"Fine." I swallowed, mouth dry. Panic pounded behind my eyes. "Just...lost in a book, I guess." If this story was true—if this legend of the moon and death and immortality was real—then my father was planning something much more horrific than I ever could have imagined. And if this had anything to do with the Blood Moon I'd heard him mention, then I only had a month before he planned to sacrifice me to gain this fabled power.

"A good one, I hope," he said, dropping to the floor. He reached for the second book, cracking it open and squinting at the letters.

"Fairytales," I answered, voice shuddering. Why couldn't I tell him what I had read? The horrific image it painted stained my mind. I longer for nothing more than to scrub it from memory. My father would never plan to do something like that to me, his *Minnow.*

Alekey hummed as he paged through the various stories. An image of three girls with fishtails flashed between the pages. He flipped back. The mermaids sat on a rock, watching a boy fly in the air around them. He ran a finger over the colourful tails. "Hey, those look like—"

"Sirens," I said, grateful for the distraction. Panic blurred my vision as I tapped the scales lining the edge of the page. "Mermaids in this version."

"What's the difference?" A lock of hair flopped into his face as he studied the image. It was hard to tell what information he was tucking away in his mind, or why.

"In the stories, mermaids are all girls. Sirens are something else entirely." When sirens shed their scales and grew legs, there were no distinguishing features. Not entirely human, not entirely siren. "I think these aren't only *stories*," I added, watching him carefully.

He shoved a hand through his hair as he looked up at me. The slanting sun above us and the twisting shadows around us carved his face in marble, gold chips for eyes, sharp relief under his cheekbones. He didn't look like a child in this light. "What do you mean?"

I blinked, my eyes darting up from his jaw. "I…" I swallowed, feeling a blush crawl up my neck, momentarily forgetting my own horror. "I think there is some truth in the legends."

His grin did something inexplicable to my stomach. "And what do the stories say of you?"

I pulled the book back and shut it, sealing all its stories inside. Some truths were too dangerous. And some truths I was too scared to bring to light yet. "Why did the captain send you down here again? She believes you're drunk."

A laugh burst out of him. He took a swig from his bottle, coughing. "I *am* drunk," he said. "And she didn't send me. I came to ask if you're hungry. We're nearing Lafori, and I don't want to be stuck on board if you're not coming with us."

I tried to picture it on the map in my mind, but I couldn't place it on the mainland. The promise of leaving this boat was enough to lift my spirits, though. I wanted solid ground beneath my feet again and as much distance as possible between me and this book. "The captain is allowing me to go ashore?"

He shrugged. "She'd rather you come than have her bring you food later. She is 'not a seas-damned servant.' Her words, not mine."

"All right," I said, rising from the floor. I dusted off the hem of my lilac nightgown. The book with its glowing moons stared up at me from the table. A shudder ran down my spine.

"Great," he said, eyes shining. "Now…we should probably tell the captain you're coming." He bounded towards the stairs, winking at me.

"You didn't ask her first?"

"Sometimes it's easier to ask for forgiveness than permission." He clambered up the stairs, abandoning his bottle of rum on the table behind us.

I followed him into the streaming sunlight and right into the captain's icy glare.

EIGHT

The sun was sinking below the horizon, aquamarine darkening to sapphire as night fell in thin swaths across the sky, but the thrill hadn't left my veins. It had only been a few hours since the siren attack. And then the princess stepped out of the cargo hold with her hair hazing behind her and Key announced she was coming ashore with us. The thrill quickly fizzled past annoyance and settled on rage.

I pinched my eyes shut, took a deep breath, and whirled on him as he strolled past me and leaned against the railing.

Icana guided us next to an empty dock in the small port town where houses dotted the road, lifted on stilts and shielded with tarps. The chances of anyone recognizing us here were slim, but there was no reason to bring the princess ashore.

"Alekey," I ground out between my teeth. He tilted his head back to grin at me. "My cabin. Now." I snapped my fingers. As he crossed the deck, I glanced at Talen. "Watch her."

My father's advisor folded his arms over his chest in his best approximation of an intimidating stance.

The princess ignored him to lean over the railing, straining to be free, the wind whipping through her hair.

I followed Alekey to my quarters and slammed the door shut behind me. His eyes, always a shade darker than mine, roved around the room, landing on the letters and maps scattered over the desk. Something broke behind his eyes. A sad smile touched his lips. "They kept them."

It was like a punch to my stomach. I bit my lip as he rifled through the letters, the pain chasing my tears away. Talen was right. I hadn't let myself mourn. But neither had Key. I had been living with their ghosts while he had chased them away with the drink. I didn't think there was enough rum in the world to erase those memories from my mind.

"Key," I murmured.

He chuckled at one of the letters.

"I can't have her come ashore."

"Why not?" He didn't look up, but his jaw tightened. He was listening, but how could I make him understand that I had to protect him? He was still my little brother, and this world was too big for him. Too big for us.

"She's dangerous," I said.

He turned to me, hand resting on one of the letters. "She's scared."

I scoffed. "What would you know?" Biting words were easier. Anger was easier. And if my brother hated me at the end of it, at least he would still be alive.

He frowned, brows pinching together. It struck me how much he looked like our mother. He had the same dark hair and soft jawline. I had our father's unruly sunset curls and sharp cheeks and love of the sea. He had taught me to sail before I could talk, but Alekey always preferred the beach.

He shouldn't have been here. Our parents shouldn't have died. So many *shouldn't haves*, and yet...

"Unlike you," he said, and I flinched at the knife's edge in his tone despite how much I deserved it, "I've spent my time trying to be nice to her. I think she really wants to help. You do realize she's trying to make sure *you* don't die, right? You're just being a bitch to her because you can."

The word felt less like a stab and more like a slap coming from him. He knew better insults. He was also drunk, so I let it slide.

"She's the reason our parents are dead," I snapped. "Whether she knows it or not. Have you forgotten that in your drunken stupor?"

"Black seas," he muttered, rolling his eyes. "Do you ever hear yourself, Ev? All you can think about is your revenge. They were my parents, too, and I don't want to kill her because of it. Maybe, just *maybe*, she's different. Maybe she can stop it all."

I narrowed my eyes. The princess didn't want to die. That was the only reason she gave for her motivations. But Alekey seemed to believe her, seemed to believe she was innocent. Either she was a better actor than I expected, or my brother wasn't as incompetent as I thought.

Or he was just too enamoured by her stunning eyes to think clearly. That would make two of us.

"Besides," he added with a smirk, "if you don't let her come, you'd have to bring her back some food later."

My teeth screeched together. "I'm not a seas-damned servant."

His eyes sparkled in the dying sunlight that cut through the porthole. "I knew you would say that!" He loped past me, shouldering the door open. "I'll keep an eye on her if you want."

The princess watched us from the gangplank, not bothering to hide her interest in our conversation.

"You'll keep your eyes to yourself," I snapped at him, warmth burning my cheeks that had nothing to do with the setting sun behind us.

Alekey laughed, bounding away to join the princess at the side of the ship and offer his arm.

A strange sensation settled in my belly when she let him lead her down to the dock, but then she glanced back at me, eyes as wide as the sea, and my mind went blank.

"Captain," Talen coughed. I looked at him wildly, snapping my mouth shut.

"What?"

He lowered his voice. "Careful who you let know your heart, Ev."

Traitorous heart fluttering, my stomach flopped uncomfortably. "I'm not jealous of Alekey."

A grin flickered across his mouth. "I didn't say you were."

"But you are," Icana called from the helm, slinging a bag over her shoulder. Her twin blades rested nicely against her back. She fixed a final piece of rigging and crossed to the gangplank. "Don't stray from your course, Captain."

Her boots thudded as she hit the dock. Talen glanced back at me and gestured grandly towards the railing. I huffed, pushing myself ahead of him. They would both keep me in line if I strayed too far.

But who would keep Alekey in line?

My legs adjusted to land quickly. The princess wobbled, even at a distance, as they climbed onto the street. Her bare feet curled into the pavement like it was grass. I watched as she tilted her face to the sky, drinking in a deep breath. The full moon broke the horizon behind us. Her hair soaked up its light like a pale river.

It was stunning.

Pushing that thought deep down, where it would never see the light again, I stepped around her trailing hair, nudging it aside with my foot. "Do something with that," I muttered.

She pulled long strands away from my boots and scrunched up her nose at me. "I need something to braid it with," she said.

I was already walking away, marching towards the tavern at the end of the road. Noise spilled from the open door.

"That would be a *you* problem, Princess," Talen told her as he followed me. He jutted his chin towards a sign next to the door, giving me a warning glance. NO WEAPONS ALLOWED.

My hand drifted to my cutlass as I tilted my head back to read the sign above the door.

The princess shuffled onto the porch behind me. "The Fetching Fledgling," she said. "Sounds…snuggly."

I glanced back at her and caught Alekey staring at the building next to the tavern and its bright red sign over a bright red door.

"The Loose Goose broth—"

I choked in disgust and grabbed him, shoving him into the tavern ahead of me.

Talen doubled over laughing, clutching at his side. I smacked his arm.

The princess shifted past me, a furious blush on her cheeks. Her hair continued to trail behind her, swept into the tavern with the ocean breeze that seemed to follow her everywhere.

Someone whistled from the second storey of the house.

Talen waggled his fingers. Icana craned her neck back to make eye contact with the woman hanging out the window.

She made a show of yanking her blades from their sheaths, twirling them around her fingers, and then slamming them into the basket of weapons beside the tavern door before she entered.

With a sigh, trying to scrub the embarrassment from my mind, I pulled my cutlass free.

"Are you sure?" Talen asked, his voice made husky from his laughing fit. He eyed the tavern over my shoulder, the rolling chatter and clinking plates and the permeating smell of ale.

"No," I said. There were already a dozen swords and daggers in the basket, but that meant no one inside was armed. I carefully placed my cutlass next to Icana's blades. "But I'm hungry."

He took an extra long time digging daggers out of various hiding places on his body and depositing them in the basket. And when the basket became overcrowded, he set them in neat rows on the porch. I left him to disarm himself and stepped into the dimly lit room, following the curving river of white hair to the princess in a dark corner. She bounced on the edge of the bench next to Alekey. Two tin cups of ale had already found their way to the table. Icana sat across from them, tucked into the corner with her back against the wall, watching the crowd.

"That is a lot of hair," someone mumbled at the table next to us.

I glanced over and deemed them unthreatening. "She's growing it out," I said as I swung my leg over the bench beside the princess.

Her leg bounced up and down, fingers clutched in her lap. "I've never been to a tavern before," she exclaimed, eyes wide.

I clamped a hand over her knee, stilling the incessant twitching. "Don't get used to it." After a lingering moment too long, I snatched my hand back as if her skin burned and waved to the barmaid across the room.

"What'll it be, cutie?" she asked, winking. I blinked, glancing sideways at Alekey, but it seemed her eyes were locked on me.

Icana leaned forward, crooking her finger at the barmaid. She whispered something in the girl's ear that made her blush scarlet. "I'll bring that right away," she said, shyly tucking a strand of hair behind her ear. She scurried to the bar, and every few moments, glanced over her shoulder. Icana watched her, a sultry tilt to her chin, her burning gaze warming the entire room.

"Get a room," Alekey moaned, ducking his head into his cup so he didn't have to see my weapons master undressing the girl with only her eyes.

"I plan on it," Icana told him.

The princess ignored them, but it was hard to ignore the pink tinge on her cheeks. Her leg was bouncing again, even harder to ignore. I shifted away from her as Talen slid into the opposite bench, a high colour in his cheeks beneath his beard.

"What did I miss?" he asked, breathless.

"Not much, apparently." If I had known coming ashore was going to lead to so much unabashed flirting, I would have avoided port altogether. But we had been sailing for too long to avoid coming ashore to eat. My crew was hungry.

And the princess was restless. I felt her fidgeting, even at a distance. She continued to bounce her leg.

I slapped my hand on the whorled wood in front of her. She jumped. "*Stop*. Bouncing."

"Captain," Talen said, sarcasm dripping from his voice. "Do you need to take some air?"

The princess' leg slowed when she saw the murderous glare I shot at him. "Sorry," she said quietly.

"Don't apologize to her," Alekey said on the other side of the princess. "It'll make her think she's allowed to be a bitch."

Rage boiled my blood. My hand dropped to my empty scabbard, and finding it thusly empty, I shoved myself from the table as the barmaid returned with a tray of food. She sidled between Talen and Icana. I stalked towards the bar before I could watch them flirt, dropping into a vacant seat.

"Rough day?" the man behind the counter asked. He slid a glass of tawny liquid towards me.

I scoffed and took a gulp. It burned my throat and cleared my head. "Rough life," I muttered in response. I tossed back the rest of the drink. "My parents are dead, I'm running around with the daughter of the man who killed them, I can't get home because that same man wants me dead, and my crew doesn't seem to respect me anymore. We were attacked by sirens today, and I haven't slept in…I don't know how long, and I just want to go home, but I can't because—"

"The man who killed your parents wants you dead," he said, nodding. "I follow ya."

I shoved a hand into my hair. Across the room, the barmaid's screeching giggle pierced through the noise. I grimaced as the barman glanced over. He cocked an eyebrow.

"That your crew?"

"That's my crew," I mumbled. The words didn't sound right or taste right. I squinted into my empty glass.

"So, who does that make you?"

"Princess Evhen Lockes of Vodaeard," I answered, brows pinching together as the truth tumbled out, unbidden. He swam in my vision. "Who are you?"

"The guy her father paid off to drug you."

The words landed a moment too late.

"Shit, seas, fu—" I stumbled off the stool and into the broad chest of someone who smelled like death.

The stranger clamped a hand over my mouth. Rot smeared across my tongue. My arms refused to move, too heavy at my sides, tingling numbly. My head felt leaden as I looked up at him.

He spun me around, something sharp stabbing into my side. The room spun around us with blurred lights and muted voices and sticky air.

Warmth clung to my skin as he shoved me towards a door on the other side of the bar. I tried to look over my shoulder, to search for my crew, but even my head refused to move on my command. My eyes rolled back, the drug slugging through my veins.

"Let go of her."

The princess' cold voice was like an anchor, yanking me out of murky grogginess into the hazy tavern. We turned, the length of the bar between us. A knife nicked my throat. One hand twitched up to scratch at the man's arm.

The scene before me confused me. The tables were empty, the other patrons circling my crew, swords flashing in the firelight.

Someone was sprawled on the floor at Icana's feet. My weapons master held a crossbow, glaring down the length of the bolt, and the barmaid she had been flirting with cowered in the corner.

Alekey was drooped over the table. A pang of fear spiked through me, muddled by the drug, but I tore my eyes away from him to the princess. She stood at the head of the table, bare feet planted in a disgusting puddle of ale, hair wrapped around her wrist like a whip.

"I said *let*. Her. *Go*," she repeated.

I followed her voice through the haze, but when I tried to fight my way out of the man's grip, nothing moved. His knife dug in a little deeper.

"Tell her to lower her weapon," the man growled in my ear, peeling his hand away from my mouth. I gulped down air, my tongue feeling like cotton. I tasted blood, and I didn't know if it was my own or not.

When I didn't say anything, the man spoke to Icana. "Lower your weapon. We just want her." His blade jabbed harder into my side, causing a trickle of blood to caress my leg.

The princess didn't know who they were. She didn't know who I was. She didn't know her father had paid these men to kill me, and yet she stood like she was ready to fight for me. Her eyes darted to the side.

My lips stuck together as I opened my mouth, everything moving too slowly. "Ica—" I mumbled, swaying in the man's grip. He shifted his arm across my chest, and the princess moved.

She snatched the crossbow out of Icana's hands.

She aimed.

And then she shot me.

NINE

In the span of a breath, time slowed.

The bolt flew across the room, pierced through the captain's shoulder, and buried itself in the man's chest before I inhaled. He was someone I had brought back once—that much was clear by the rot peeling off his skin—but I didn't know him. I didn't know anyone in this tavern. And I didn't have time to think about it because when the man howled in pain, movement flurried around me.

The other two, still-alert crew members leapt forward, diving under swinging swords, grabbing plates, cups, and cutlery to use as weapons. Talen darted to his captain, slipping an arm around her as she pitched forward, blood pouring down her arm.

She caught my gaze through the fray, a stunned expression on her face. As Talen dragged her towards the door, she dipped her head at me—perhaps the only amount of gratitude I was going to get for saving her life. A second time.

Or maybe they had poisoned her with whatever afflicted Alekey and she wasn't thinking clearly.

That was probably it.

Icana tore the crossbow out of my hands and smashed it into someone's face. I ducked around the table as they crashed to the floor. Alekey moaned when I prodded his shoulder. Worry twisted my stomach for the soft-hearted boy. How did he get wrapped up in all of this?

Glass shattered into the wall above my head, startling me out of my thoughts. I twisted around, eyes narrowed as I scanned the room for a sword or a shield. A flash of steel glinted on the floor between two unconscious bodies. I pulled the short dagger towards myself with a strand of hair.

Before I could use it, Alekey's hand clamped around my wrist and he tugged me away from the table. We jumped over more bodies, more *dead* bodies, and burst onto the porch. The captain and Talen were already at the dock. Blood splattered the road behind them.

Icana hurried us towards the boat. Alekey collapsed the moment his feet hit the deck. I pulled my hair over the railing, running my fingers through its length, stunned at the shocks jolting up my arm as my power clamoured in my veins around so much death. The blonde bounded to the helm, loosening the sail as she went, and spun the wheel around. We jostled away from the dock as the tavern patrons spilled out onto the street behind us.

Before the boat had scraped past the edge of the dock, Talen marched over to me, seized my shoulder with one hand, and slammed his other fist into my jaw.

I collapsed onto the blood-soaked boards with a crunch of bone and a yelp of pain, tears springing to my eyes. Vision blurry, I placed a hand against my mouth, wincing at the pain blossoming across my jaw. I couldn't tell if it was broken or not, even as a bitter tang stung the back of my throat and blood dripped from my lips.

Talen's dark form loomed over me, shadowed in the light of the full moon.

"Stop," the captain ordered, shifting in front of me.

"She tried to kill you," Talen growled, hands clenched into fists.

"She saved me!" The captain smacked his arm. Her face scrunched at the sharp movement.

I stared, unable to talk or move. My vision swam red, then black.

The captain's voice, like an ocean breeze cresting through palm leaves, kept me anchored. "If she wanted me dead, I would be."

His glare cut through me. "Were you trying to kill my captain?"

I shook my head, eyes watering as pain spread over my nose. A low moan tickled my throat. The boat tilted around me, as though something was stuck against the inside of my head, throwing me off balance and making the world spin in a riot of colour and pain. My stomach roiled, hot and cold and decidedly ill, as a string of blood hung from my bottom lip.

I was going to be sick.

"Take her to my quarters," the captain said. "And try not to kill her." She massaged her arm and tilted her head back towards the cloudy sky, pain rippling across her features. "Fuck!"

Talen reached down, but I swatted him away, staggering to my feet. The boat shifted under me, and I listed sideways, catching myself against the railing. Bile stung the back of my throat, burning my eyes, but there wasn't anything inside for me to empty. Blood and saliva streamed down my chin. I whimpered through the pain.

"Are you done?" Talen grumbled. He stood next to me, arms folded across his chest, blotting out the stars with his glare.

I glared back, the best I could do with a swollen jaw. My left eye was beginning to puff up. If it wasn't for the pain spreading under my skin, I wouldn't have minded not seeing the crew or the ocean for the rest of the night. I pushed myself away from the railing and strode through the gilded doors into the captain's quarters, slamming them shut behind me. The panes shuddered with the force, but the world finally stilled around me.

I lowered myself onto the low bed, dropping my head towards my knees. The scent of sea salt and dust wafted into the air as the mattress sank beneath me. Curiously, it reminded me of the captain. My fingers brushed the undisturbed sheets next to me. When was the last time she slept here?

After some time, the door creaked open.

I raised my head, squinting through one swollen eye, to see the captain enter, medical supplies in hand. Blood stained her shirt. Her right arm hung uselessly at her side, scarlet dripping from her fingers in slow drops. She winced as she shut the door behind her.

"I'll thank you to never shoot me again," she said. She pulled the chair out from under the desk with her foot and dropped into it with all the grace of a drugged pirate.

I nodded, squeezing my eyes shut. The pain was beginning to radiate across my forehead in sharp spikes.

"Look at me," she instructed. I lifted my head, flinching when her hand moved. With a huff, she took my chin such softness in her fingers that I wondered if they belonged to the right person. "Black seas, you look worse than how I feel."

I didn't mean to laugh, but it ground out through the bruised bones in my jaw, scraping over my teeth. A tear slipped down my cheek at the ripple of pain it caused in my throat.

She grinned, a malicious slash across her mouth. "Is it awful of me to think you deserve this?"

I tried to protest, but she locked my jaw in her grip and shook her head at me.

"Nope. For once you can't talk. I'm going to enjoy it while it lasts."

I settled on glaring at her through one eye, but I assumed some of the effect was lost amid the swelling.

"Now, I don't know much about medicine," she continued, pulling her fingers from my chin to pry open a bottle of ointment with one hand. "But this was all I could find below deck."

She spilled the liquid on one of the rags, using her teeth to cap the bottle again, and shifted closer. I held my breath as she pressed the rag to my jaw. Her touch was so gentle I barely felt the callouses on her fingers that rubbed against my broken skin as she dabbed the blood away.

"I'm not going to apologize for Talen," she said quietly, focused too keenly on my mouth, which had gone dry the moment she touched it. "You *did* shoot me. But I know you didn't intend to kill me. Those men did, though. Your father paid them to drug me."

My heart dropped through the mattress. I tried to pull back, to say something, but her fingers tightened and she shushed me.

"The plan was to restock in Lafori," she continued. Why was she telling me this? "We were going to sail across the southern coast, dock every few days to restock, and ditch the boat in Xesta to cross the mountains on foot. I had hoped we'd be able to get past the blockade that way, but it seems he already knows where we are." Her gaze flicked up, just for a moment.

I found myself lost in her honey eyes. My mouth felt so tender and raw and open in her hands. She averted her gaze again, and I struggled to take a proper breath.

"I don't want you coming ashore with us again," she said. A muscle feathered in her jaw. My heart was well past the mattress now. I felt it sinking further into the ocean depths. "I let my guard down today, and if anything had happened to my crew…I'm not risking any more lives just so you can have a taste of fresh air. You'll stay on board with Alekey, read your seas-damned fairytales, and when we get to Vodaeard, you'll tell your father to end this war. I won't let anyone else die over this stupid piece of rock."

Slowly, the pain began to ease beneath her fingers, but everything else tingled numbly. My chest tightened as if she had secured a noose around my throat by condemning me to the ship. I knew she viewed me as a prisoner, but I hadn't expected to feel so much guilt over what had happened in the tavern. As though it was my fault she had nearly died.

She blamed me for it.

What was the point in telling her that I was going to die one way or other over this stupid piece of rock? I reached up and tugged her hand away from my face.

She yanked back, as if I had stung her, and then threw the rag down. Her lip curled as she snapped, "Heal it yourself, then."

82

I couldn't heal myself, but she didn't know that. I shifted away from her, the moment suffocating under tense silence. She wanted me to be silent, so I was going to be silent, reminding myself that I was trying to do the right thing. Even if the people I was stuck with were unwavering in their prejudices.

She shoved the chair back, kicking it out of her way. It crashed into the desk and toppled over.

I glowered up at her, her insatiable rage tearing through me. She was only a puppet, pulled this way and that by some unseen force. Someone would have to cut the strings eventually. And I wasn't sure I wanted to be the one to do it.

I wasn't sure I wanted anything to do with her after this.

Even if her fingers had been the softest thing to caress my skin. Even if she smelled of the ocean and sun and all my favourite things.

She snatched up a roll of gauze that had fallen from her lap and unravelled a strip, tearing it with her teeth. Edging past the fallen wardrobe, she wound the gauze around her shoulder, over and over, and cinched it with her teeth as she yanked the door open. Mumbled curses filled the night and the door swung shut on her wretchedness.

I fell back onto the bed, flinging an arm over my eyes. The movement jostled my jaw, earning a groan, but the pain passed quickly. Everything felt heavy, confusing, uncertain.

My father had paid those men—men I had brought back to life—to hurt the captain. That meant he was looking for me, but I didn't feel better with that knowledge. He wanted to kill the Vodaeard princess, and I had the sickening suspicion he would have allowed those men to kill my captor, too. How could any of this be the moon's plan for me?

I finally let the exhaustion I'd felt for two days drag me down into a dreamless slumber.

I slept through the night for the first time in years. Night was my domain, when the moon's silver disc guided my steps and stars speckled the deep velvet dome. Most people woke with the sun, its warmth stirring their bones to move. I woke with the moon, its reflected light filling my veins with energy.

When I finally woke, tucked beneath the sheets, the sky beyond the porthole was painted with even strokes of lilac, peach, russet, ruby. Thin lines of yellow rimmed pewter storm clouds in the distance. Lightning jolted through the sky as I sat up, wondering who had tucked me in.

A soft rap sounded on the door. I recognized Alekey's dark hair through the warped glass and tried to open my mouth to call out to him. Pain crackled through my bones.

The door creaked open, and he poked his head in.

"Oh, you're awake!" A grin split his face. He shouldered the door open, balancing a tray in one hand and carrying a bottle of medicine in the other. My stomach growled when the scent of fresh bread and chocolate hit my tender nose.

"We've been docked for a few hours," he explained, setting the tray next to me on the bed. Slices of orange and banana tumbled in a tin bowl next to a plate of chocolate-coated pastries. "The captain and Talen went ashore to find some food. She thought you might be hungry."

Warm tears pricked my eyes. I told myself it was due to the pain of trying to open my mouth, but deep down, I was touched by the captain's consideration.

I picked up a slice of banana and stared at it.

"Here." Alekey offered the bottle of medicine along with a rag he had tucked under his arm. "I think this is supposed to make it less painful."

There wasn't enough medicine in the world to ease this pain, but at least no one was actively trying to kill me at this moment. And Alekey was the only one who had been nice to me so far. That made this situation slightly more endurable.

I flicked my gaze up to his face, gesturing as best I could with the parts of my face that could still move.

He chuckled, low and deep and rich as honey. "Fine," he said. He shifted the tray to the chair and angled towards me.

Our knees knocked together as he doused the rag with the sweet-smelling medicine.

"You know," he murmured while he dabbed my jaw, breath fanning my face, "we weren't having nearly as much fun before you came aboard. Now we have people trying to kill us! It's all rather exciting, I think."

He looked up at me and leaned back to laugh so he wouldn't jostle my jaw. I stared at him, eyes wide.

"It's a joke, Princess," he said. His eyes continued to sparkle with mirth, but his jaw clenched, a muscle jumping in his cheek. "None of this is fun, actually. These past few days have been the worst of my life. I think I'm becoming immune to rum." A knot appeared between his eyebrows. "What does your father want with...the princess, anyway?"

I couldn't answer, and his next words were sharp, knife-laced in the cramped quarters. His sudden anger wasn't directed at me, though. It went to someone much closer and yet so far away. "I lied before. The captain didn't care if you ate or not. I'm pretty sure she hopes the princess will kill you when we get to Vodaeard. It's only fair for what your father did to her parents." He shrugged at my horrified expression. "Her words."

I yanked his hands away from my mouth, flinching as if he had been the one to strike me. His fingers folded over mine, and when he caught my gaze, his eyes softened, a deep gold like the sun-kissed ocean.

"We're in dangerous seas, Princess." His low voice rumbled through my bones. Warning laced his words and sharpened his gaze. "I'm only telling you to be careful around her. She's not who she says she is."

My jaw cracked open, bone scraping along bone, a cut on my lip splitting. "And who is she?" I croaked. The words shattered against my teeth.

"Dangerous," he said. "She only cares about getting revenge on your father, and nothing will change her mind." He wrapped a finger through my hair. "Don't get close to her."

"I'm not—"

"Trust me," he said with a crooked smile. My stomach fluttered at the way he dipped his chin to look up at me through long, black lashes. "She only wants to use you. I want to make sure you don't die at the end of this."

"Me, too," I whispered, pinching my eyes shut. I thought my path had been clear, but the tunnel was getting murkier with every passing moment. It was like diving into the depths and not knowing if I would survive this time. All I wanted was to talk to my father and hear his truth. He was going to hurt the Vodaeardean princess if I couldn't convince him otherwise, but if the story was true, I wouldn't live long enough to bear the guilt of her blood on my hands.

The captain didn't want me to live at all. In her eyes, I was responsible for so many deaths already. To her, it didn't matter that I had brought back so many lives. That I could bring back more if she let me help her save the princess. I didn't want the blood of innocents on my hands, but I also wanted to survive to see this war end. That would be impossible if my father found the other piece of the moonstone.

The thought that Death waited for me at the end of this journey frightened me more than the captain's vengeful glares.

"Can I tell you a secret?" Alekey asked. His thumb brushed the non-injured side of my cheek. I opened my eyes to his golden gaze, shadows painted in the sharp lines of his face from the setting sun. "Promise me you won't get scared."

I nodded, shivering. He didn't want me to die. He didn't want the captain or the princess to kill me. That much was clear. And I realized with a start that I had already decided to put my trust in this gentle, dark-haired boy who drank too much and saw too much.

He dropped his hand from my face, leaving a warm blush beneath the bruises, and clutched my fingers tightly. A tremor racked through his hands. He didn't raise his head when he spoke, so he didn't see the panic in my eyes when he said, "I'm the prince of Vodaeard."

TEN

As the night carried with it a vicious storm kicked in from the ocean, one day at port in Costun turned into two. The last strokes of a fiery sunset brushed along the edges of heavy pewter clouds. Rain slanted across the ocean, churning the waves against the dock, and slammed like a sheet of glass against the tiny hovel Talen and I were holed up in. Through the slated window, I watched the Grey Bard rise on a crest and drop in the swell.

I winced when the princess staggered onto the deck. All I could see through the streaking rain was her hair, white as a river of light, dragging through the haze. A figure stumbled behind her, shadowed in the gloom. A fork of lightning illuminated both the princess and Alekey.

"Should we have told them a storm was coming?" I muttered, sipping the scalding tea in my hands. It chased away the chill of the storm but did little to ease the discomfort in my belly. Storms at sea could quickly turn violent, and my little boat wasn't equipped to weather such a beating.

From his spot on the second bed, Talen shrugged, licking his fingers. "I think they'll figure it out."

I twisted away from the window and crawled onto my bed, reaching for a slab of meat on the tray in front of him. The seasoned juices ran down my chin. "Can I ask you something?"

"Hm?" He locked his fingers behind his head, closing his eyes.

I balanced the cup of tea on my knee. "Why did you hit her?"

Talen was my voice of reason, my father's advisor. He wasn't prone to violence—he often discouraged *me* from reacting as such.

I had a temper.

He had a calm head. And even though it had thrilled me to see him snap and lose control, it had bothered me more.

His brows came together, not in confusion but frustration. "She tried to kill you."

"No, she didn't," I said. My fingers clenched around the fragile teacup. I didn't know why I was still defending her or why seeing her injured bothered me so much. Maybe it was because I hadn't been the one to break her jaw. "Neither you nor Icana would have taken that shot. She saved my life because you both were too scared to see me get hurt."

He sat up, swinging his legs over the edge of his bed to face me. Red burned his face. "You could have died!"

"Icana is an excellent shot!" I pried my fingers from the teacup before it shattered and set it on the small table between the beds. A candle flickered warmly, but his face was too far in the shadows for it to cast any light on him. "She could have done the exact same thing. Would you have punched *her* if she had?"

His fists balled into the sheets. "Why are you defending her? You're the one who wants her dead."

"I'm not defending her." I was. "I just want to make sure you know what you're doing when you lay hands on her. We've kidnapped the chief's daughter. He won't listen to a word we say if she's hurt."

His eyes narrowed, searching my face. I felt him picking me apart, piece by piece, looking for something that made sense within the chaotic swirl of my thoughts. My mind hadn't stopped moving since we left Vodaeard, and it wasn't bound to anytime soon. I was playing a dangerous game with so many lives hanging in the balance, and I didn't know what waited for us at the end.

"I thought your plan was to kill her in front of her father when we reached Vodaeard," he said. "What changed?"

"Nothing," I said, frustration grinding through my voice. "I didn't have a plan for when we reached Vodaeard. I barely had a plan for getting off her island. I—" I closed my eyes, stemming the tears. "I expected to die there."

"What?" he blurted, and I felt the air change as he lurched forward, the confession knocking him off balance.

"I didn't want to tell you because I knew you never would have let me go alone—"

"Of course, I wouldn't!" He jumped to his feet, shifted to my bed, and grabbed my hands. I hadn't realized they were shaking. "Ev, what is going on? Why didn't you tell me that was a suicide mission?"

I scoffed at the ridiculous question, but it turned into a choking sob. "I didn't want to live in this seas-damned world without them. I wanted to avenge their deaths, and I didn't care if I died doing it. Alekey was never supposed to be on the boat. It would have been easier if he hadn't been there."

"Getting yourself killed would have been easier if your brother had stayed back home?"

"Yes!" I tore my hands from his grip. "He didn't need to see me die as well."

"You would have just left him all alone? Black seas, Evhen!" The bed bounced as he stood. He paced to the edge and whirled around to face me. "Pardon my language, *Your Majesty*, but that is the most fucking selfish thing I've ever heard you say."

"He wouldn't have been alone!" My voice rose to a tremor. "He would have had you and Icana and everyone else! No one wants me to be queen! They won't follow me, they won't crown me."

"That's no reason to get yourself killed!"

His words slammed into me with such force that I couldn't stop myself from gasping as a sob rattled in my chest.

"Why her? Why me?" I choked, tears streaming down my face.

Every part of me ached, but it was the images swirling in my mind that wouldn't let me have peace. My parents, over and over again, their heads bashed in, throats cut, eyes gouged—every terrible thing the Chief of Marama could think of, he did to my parents that day.

And I had screamed and screamed and screamed the entire time, while my parents begged with their last breaths until their tongues were cut out and they choked on their own blood. Talen had whisked me away from the throne room, and I had continued to scream and scream and scream until I was numb and cold and empty.

I hadn't since. It had only been a few days, but I had been too scared to shut my eyes willingly, afraid of what I might see crawling out of the shadows of my own mind. But now they were there, flashes like lightning against the inside of my eyes, bursting like lit fuses through my mind, pounding against my head as if they were ghosts demanding to be let in, to haunt my waking thoughts as well as my nightmares. All that bloodshed, all those ghosts—I thought it would end if I took the princess' life that day in the lighthouse. But it never would. No amount of revenge could stop what had already begun.

And the tears continued to fall.

"Shit," Talen muttered. The bed sagged next to me, and his strong arms pulled me against his chest. His fingers tangled in my knotted hair. "I didn't know you were hurting this much."

I hadn't wanted him to know. I hadn't wanted anyone to know. Grief was something I had to bear alone. It had broken me apart in more ways than I could count, scattered pieces of me across the ocean. It would take more lifetimes than I was afforded to find them all and rearrange them into some semblance of the person I had been only days ago.

His arms formed a strong wall around me to keep the rest of the world at bay for a few minutes, but I knew it would have to crumble soon. I had chosen this path. My grief had chosen this path. I had to face it, even if I didn't understand the consequences of my actions. Even if I didn't have a plan beyond tonight.

"You have people who would follow you anywhere, Ev," he murmured against my hair. "Me, Icana, even Alekey. What are you trying to prove by dying?"

I pulled back, roughly palming the tears from my cheeks. "That

I'm worthy to lead them." It was a pathetic excuse for what I had done, but it was the only one I had. "If I could end this war, they would have to follow me. They would have to crown me."

"Is it so bad to wait another year?" He dropped his hands to his lap, searching my face. Looking for answers.

I didn't have the ones he was looking for.

"I was never supposed to be queen so soon." I picked at the loose skin around my fingers. "They were never supposed to die. But I don't want to wait another year if I can end this war today."

"How?" he pressed. He seized my fingers again, stilling them. He didn't say anything about the blood welling up along my nails. "How does this end with you stopping a war?"

I wiggled my hand free and shoved my fingers through my hair. "I don't know. I don't know how any of this ends. What if the only way it can end is with her death?"

The door to our room swung open, and Talen and I jumped, breaking apart to see the princess hovering in the entrance. Water cascaded down her hair. She looked even younger, soaked through, her lilac nightgown clinging to her legs. Heat fanned across my face.

"Alekey was right," she whispered, voice cracking around broken lips. Her eyes caught mine, wavering in the flickering light.

It took a second for the words to register. "What?" What had my brother done now?

"You do want me dead." She shoved past Alekey, who crowded the hallway behind her, and stormed away. Her hair squelched in the carpet behind her.

"Wait!" I jumped to my feet, shaking my head as Key meandered into the room. "What did you say to her?" I yanked a cloak from the hook on the wall and ran after the princess. Icana, a miserable sour turn to her lips, stepped out of my way. "Wait!" I called after the princess, slinging the cloak over my shoulders.

Her hair left a trail that streamed down the hallway. It smacked onto the pavement outside, flowing behind her like it was caught in a perpetual river. Water splashed up her bare legs, soaking the bottom of her dress, but she didn't seem to care.

"Stop!" I snatched her wrist, pulling her to a slippery stop in the street. She glared at my fingers like they were bars on a cage, and I yanked my hand back as if her eyes burned. My chest heaved as I met the full force of her glare. "What did he tell you?"

Lightning crackled overhead, reflected in her ocean-blue eyes. "Enough," she spat, wincing at the force. Dark bruises covered the left side of her face. Her cheeks had sunken into hollows since the last time I truly looked at her. But she was speaking again, and every word was another knife in my ribs. "And I heard enough. You want me dead." She spoke without moving her mouth much, pain glittering in her eyes. "And so, apparently, does my father."

"Well, that makes my decision a bit easier," I mumbled, too shocked by her declaration to say anything else I wanted to say.

Her hand lashed out, smacking across my cheek with the sound of thunder. I blinked in surprise, too stunned to respond in kind. Rain pelted against my stinging flesh.

"I am the Princess of Death," she enunciated through clenched teeth. Blood stained her perfect and cruel smile. "I am not your prisoner or your bargaining tool or your plaything. You would do well to fear me as the sirens did."

A chill snaked down my spine. Her words split my veins open, filling me with ice and fire. I stared, breathless, terrified, and then a familiar emotion curled around my heart. Rage melted my features into stone. A slow smile curled my lip.

She took a single step back.

If anyone was going to kill her, it would be me.

"I told you not to cross me, Princess."

I unwound the rock from my wrist and spun towards the dock. Thunder drowned out her cry as she grabbed at my wounded arm. Through the pain bursting along my shoulder, I ground my teeth together and smashed my fist into the side of her head.

She collapsed onto the dock with a wail. The sound of crashing waves stole her pleas to the depths.

At the edge of the dock, I looked back at her, dangling the necklace over the waters. "Why did they die?" I screamed at her.

Thunder answered with a quaking rumble.

She whimpered and raised her head, peering at me through strands of clumpy hair, blood and water stringing down her chin.

My hand tightened on the cord as the wind threatened to whip it from my grip. I wanted to sink it, but I wanted to see her suffer first. "Tell me why your father cut out their hearts!"

Lightning exploded into the ocean next to us, easing a cry of alarm from her.

She ducked her head and cowered against the raging storm.

My raging storm.

"I can't," she said, voice straining, a cry of pain crackling through the thunder. She pushed herself to her feet, swaying as the dock shook with the waves. Her eyes glared red, rimmed in agony, skin torn and jagged around her lips. "I don't know why."

"Seashit!"

She took a staggering step towards me and stopped, gasping between laboured breaths. Rain streaked her face, her freckles dark in the flashes of lightning that surrounded us. Sobs choked her voice, and blood spattered her lip. "I will do anything I can to help you if it means my father doesn't get what he's after, but please do not throw it away."

Then she did something that stunned me even more than a slap.

She knelt on the dock at my feet and bowed her head to touch the wood.

ELEVEN

When I finally raised my head, heart beating a rapid rhythm in my chest, the captain was gone. A pained gasp shuddered out of me. I pitched forward, hands skittering across wet splinters. It had been foolish to think subservience would placate her, but I hadn't known what else to do short of shoving her into the raging ocean. She would have dragged me with her, and I had survived the depths too long to be drowned at sea now.

And she still had that damned-to-the-depths necklace that was the cause of all my pain and fear.

I tilted my head back towards the silver sky—the heavy clouds, the churning winds, the pelting rain—and screamed. Blood trickled down my throat. Pain screeched along my jaw. And when there were no more screams left in me, I let my tears spill over and wash away in the rain.

Somehow, the storm around me was quieter than the one inside me.

My whole life, I had known two things. I could bring the dead back from Death's dark shores. And I needed the stone to do it.

But the story of the first chief proved that I didn't *only* bring the dead back to life. If the moonstone pieces were reunited and my father slaughtered me, he would gain immortality. He would never need me to resurrect him if he was immortal.

They wouldn't need me at all.

Another thought twisted through my tumultuous mind. If the legend was true, and my parents killed me beneath the Blood Moon, how was I to grant them both immortality? Wouldn't it require much more power than anything I had ever used?

The scars on my wrists twinged as stabbing rain chilled me to the bone. They had never healed properly. Dozens of small crescents circled my wrists like pieces of jewellery. Like brands.

The thought startled me so much, I gasped, shoving my hands between my legs. Rain poured down my back, and my veins were ice in the chilling torrent. I had never thoughts of the scars as anything other than something to be proud of. They displayed to everyone who met me how strong I was. Bleeding every month to bring life back into the world. It was a testament to my power, my gift. I was the only person in the world who could bring lost souls back from the dead. The scars were proof. But they felt different now that I knew the truth about my power. Like I had been branded as a tool for someone else's greater purpose.

The realization shot through me in the same moment lightning struck the boat next to me. My parents hadn't been preparing me to enter the depths without the stone. They had been preparing me to be a goat for the slaughter.

Heat washed over me, and I looked up to see our ship in flames. Tongues of fire licked the sky, the roar washed out beneath the crash of thunder. The wood moaned and shuddered, then *cracked*. I scrambled to my feet, embers landing hot on my clothes, sizzling in the rain.

A shout tunnelled down the dock. I winced at the captain's shrill voice, afraid I had somehow angered her more than humanly possible, but when I turned to her, the panic on her face broke something inside of me. All the words I had longed to say since we set sail—why should I fear her anger anymore when I was destined to die anyway—soured on my tongue.

"Cap—"

She shoved past me with enough force to knock me over, the wet boards sliding under me until I teetered against the edge. I caught myself with splinters in my hands. Shaking the hair out of my face, I looked up to berate her, only to see her already on board the burning boat.

A curse died on my lips the moment she dove into the flames. A moment passed, then two, and when she didn't reemerge, I followed her.

Lightning had split the main mast in two, the massive beam laying in pieces across the deck. Fire curled up the unfurled sail. Glass shattered, wood cracked, and the captain screamed from somewhere within the smokey cloud. My bare feet slid over the deck as I hurried towards her quarters.

The painted glass panes in the door had burst inwards. Shards littered the cabin, pieces glittering like red stars across the floor. The captain was grabbing loose parchment when the upper deck above us groaned. A crack formed in the low ceiling.

"What are you doing here?" she shouted at me. The boat shuddered beneath us, rolling on wild waves, and she stumbled against the desk. Papers fell from her arms in a flurry. "Shit!"

"Saving your life—again!"

"I didn't ask you to!"

"You want to die in an inferno?"

A wave tossed the boat against the dock, and she pitched forward, grabbing the desk for support. My shoulder slammed into the door frame. The ceiling bowed inwards.

"We have to go," I told her, reaching for her arm.

Why did I insist on saving her for a third time? Half of my problems would disappear with her, but the tears on her face rattled me to the bone. This girl who didn't cry and didn't feel, who only raged and hated the world into which she had been born. Who wanted nothing more than to see me die for something I hadn't done. Who hurt deeper than anyone realized.

How had her stinging words cut me open so wide that *she* had settled in the hollows?

Her fingers scrabbled for the papers. The parchment crinkled in her trembling grip. She palmed tears from her face, and I realized I meant what I said to her on the dock.

"How can I help?" I whispered.

She stared at me, mouth agape until a chunk of the upper deck crashed through the air between air. Smoke billowed into the cramped room, choking my lungs. I staggered out the door as more pieces tumbled through the hole. The captain jumped back from the falling boards, arm over her mouth, the smoke quickly obscuring the panic on her face.

"Evhen!"

I whirled around at the first mate's voice, startled to realize it was the first time I had heard someone say her name. He barely acknowledged me as I pointed into the cabin, and he shouldered his way through the collapsing door frame. The deck buckled inwards, fanning the flames towards me, and I scurried away from the captain's quarters as boards crumbled above and below. My foot dropped through a hole in the warped, wet boards beneath me.

"Get out of there!" someone shouted from the dock. Through curtains of smoke, I glimpsed Alekey's dark hair, pale arms waving at me.

"She's still in there!" I shouted back, coughing as smoke coated my throat. Pain screamed along my jaw, and I bit my tongue to keep from crying out loud. Tears stung my eyes. I yelped as more pieces of the deck collapsed around me. The shadowy innards of the ship gaped into the night.

"You can't save her!"

I twisted around to see Alekey gripping the railing, staggering towards me.

"I can try!" I called back.

If I couldn't save at least one more person from this war, then what was the point? And the captain seemed like the kind of person who desperately needed saving.

From herself.

Movement broke through the haze of smoke as part of the staircase tumbled across the door. Talen stumbled back, the captain in his arms, choking as the air around us shifted.

The explosive powder!

Screaming at Alekey to get off the ship, I swung a thick strand of hair at the collapsed railing and yanked it away from the door, gritting my teeth against the pain bursting across my scalp.

Talen staggered out of the ruined cabin, the captain unconscious in his arms, a gash in her forehead bleeding into her eyes. Without thinking, I caught her wrist, felt my fingers touch the cool stone dangling from the cord she had wrapped there, and plucked a strand of hair from my head to press against her wound.

Talen didn't notice the skin stitch together as he carried her to the dock, too focused on getting her to safety before the ship sank. I hurried behind them, heart pounding as the rain continued to fall.

The *Grey Bard* exploded that night. And the captain hadn't spoken to me since.

We'd been walking for three days already, a shroud of tension suffocating any attempt at conversation, through quiet towns and down empty roads and over rolling plains. We kept the ocean to our right, following a hidden map in the captain's mind, to places whose names I had only ever read in our library and whose names I had never read anywhere. Avoiding larger towns, we diverted our path north or south as the captain saw fit to keep us hidden from busy roads and prying eyes.

We slept amid the trees, in abandoned clearings, and washed in stale water that wasn't suitable to drink. The weather remained in our favour as we crossed from dense woods into flat farmlands, bleached yellow from the unrelenting sun, the haze in the distance playing tricks on my mind. Clear azure skies offered no shade. Sweat poured down my back, my hair dragging through massive stalks of corn, as noon approached on the third day.

Alekey was the only one who deigned to talk to me, walking beside me with a good-natured smile. His dark hair was plastered to his forehead with sweat, but it seemed nothing could dim that dazzling grin. He told me when we passed from Azria to Oximeen though there were no borders or signs to denote the departure from one country and the arrival into another. It wasn't until I asked him how much farther to Vodaeard that his grin faltered and he fell into a miserable silence that lasted well into the evening.

That was when I felt a stab of pain in my lower abdomen and froze in the middle of the path we forged between rows of wild wheat. Mottled sunlight streamed through the bubbly clouds on the horizon, painting the sky pale yellow as night chased day. At that moment, I longed for darkness to obscure my face as I weakly called, "Captain."

She whirled around, eyes blazing hot, a lashing on the tip of her tongue before she saw my face.

I bent over as pain radiated outwards.

"Shit," she muttered, shoving a hand through her hair. It caught the last rays of sunlight, creating a fiery halo around her face, my favourite golden-red colour of sunset-kissed seas. A weary laugh welled up inside of me at the comparison, but it came out as a groan over my sore lips.

Icana—quiet, reserved, guarded Icana—pushed Alekey aside and guided me to the ground, rubbing my back as I put my head between my knees.

A low moan escaped my lips. I was in too much pain to be surprised by her gentleness, or else I would have kept her and her twin blades as far from me as possible. As it was, I'd rather her cut me open and tear out the thing that caused me so much pain every month.

"What's wrong?" Alekey asked.

His concern warmed my heart, so I tried to ease his worry—I raised my head, tilting my chin towards the sky and breathing evenly through my nose. "I am plagued by the moon," I declared, wincing at another stab of pain.

He blinked. "What?"

A broken laugh scraped along my jaw at his ignorance. I ducked my head again, breaths shuddering in and out as Icana continued to rub circles on my lower back. Somehow her deadly hands eased the pain.

"Her cycle," the captain snapped at Alekey. He sputtered—was he embarrassed or ashamed?—as the captain crouched in front of me. She rested a hand on my knee, her skin warm through the fabric of my dress, and I was once again taken aback by her gentle touch.

I raised my head to meet her gaze—how could she possibly be so gentle in my most vulnerable moment?—lost in her honey eyes as our shadows lengthened and tangled on the path.

Her brows knotted together in the middle.

My stomach flopped the same way it did when Alekey smiled at me. "Thank you for saving my life."

There it was—that first moment of trust. A glimpse through that beautiful window, to a place within her where memories fractured and love scarce saw the light. She had buried those parts of herself so deep so as to never be hurt by them again. And she was trusting me, just for the moment, to understand that.

Respect is a mutual transaction, she had once told me. So was trust—and in this moment, she was giving me the chance to trust that she wasn't going to hurt me. She was letting herself be vulnerable to me, opening that well deep inside of her for a brief glimpse.

Alekey's warning rang in my mind, but I had little choice. He had told me the truth whereas she had let me see herself bared to the world. I had to trust that meant something. And if it didn't last until morning, at least I had this moment.

A pang of guilt twinged through the pain in my belly. The captain didn't know I had healed the wound on her forehead, and Talen hadn't mentioned it either. It wouldn't be fair to withhold it from her any longer, not if we were allowing ourselves to be truthful with each other.

"Captain, I—" A fresh bout of pain washed over me, and I twisted to the side, spitting something unmentionable on the ground. "Ow," I moaned, fresh tears springing to my eyes through the renewed sting in my jaw.

"You're not so frightening," she said, her tone light but the words mocking. I looked up at her through narrowed eyes, some of the effect lost between the pain and shadows when I dropped my head to my knees again.

"Leave her alone," Icana murmured, her voice a soft drone. It was the kind of voice I expected from a caring mother. Not someone who could cut me in half with her small finger. Still, I was grateful for the comfort of her hands on my back.

The captain rose to her feet, shifting, the moment stifled in the anxiety biting at the air around us. "We need to keep moving," she said in a low voice. "Can you walk?"

I nodded, slipping a sweaty hand into Icana's. Blood trickled down my leg as I stood. The captain ushered Talen and Alekey away through the wheat stalks while the blonde helped me clean up as much as possible before we rejoined them on the path they had trampled in the field. Ahead, chimney smoke billowed into the darkening sky, dozens of plumes.

I breathed a sigh of relief as the wild fields smoothed to tended crops and the first houses came into view. Stars appeared in droves overhead, no clouds or trees to obscure them anymore.

"Why are you helping me?" I asked Icana as we approached the sleepy village. We rounded a small house to a small road and followed the captain's ambling gait to the only inn along the dusty street.

The woman glanced down at me, a stern set to her sharp jaw, and I noticed for the first time how pale her eyes were. They were the palest blue I had ever seen, like the sky at high noon, nearly white around a black centre. She offered me a small smile, the first time I had seen anything other than a scowl touch her lips.

"I know how bad it can get. The captain," she added in a hushed voice, eyes darting up the street, "has never bled, so she doesn't truly understand the pain. But I do, and so I must help."

Up the road, the captain glanced back as if she had heard Icana's admission. She grimaced at me as she disappeared inside the inn with Talen to inquire about rooms. She might not know the pain, but she could empathize. At least she hadn't said I deserved it.

"Well, thank—" Sickness swallowed my words. My stomach lurched, and I barely reached a flowerpot outside the inn in time before I vomited into it.

TWELVE

Dawn cracked between the bleached-white shafts of wheat in the fields behind the inn, the sun casting a dusty sheen over the rippling crop sea. Pale yellow fingers peeked between the slates in the window. Dust motes swirled in the air, caught in slanted beams of light. And I burrowed deeper beneath the covers, content to stay in this peaceful moment forever.

It was the first time in three days I had something other than lumpy moss and twisted roots digging into my back. And even though the mattress sagged, the frame creaked, and the blankets smelled moldy, I was grateful for the lock on the door and the shutters on the window. I trusted Talen to take care of Alekey and Icana to take care of the princess, and I had finally gotten a proper night's sleep. The first in days. Exhaustion had worn me down to frayed nerves. If the princess hadn't looked so utterly pathetic last night, I might have ripped out her throat when she had spoken.

As it was, she lived, sleeping as peacefully as possible in the adjacent room. Icana had willingly offered to look after the princess—she was doing her damnedest to help the girl through her pain—and as far as I was aware, she hadn't killed her while they slept.

What a tragedy that would have been.

Snickering to myself, I sank deeper into the sagging mattress, arms spread wide to welcome the morn. Light filled the room through the cracks in the window, chasing away the shadows of night that lingered in the corners. This was undoubtedly the worst bed I had ever slept in, but anything was better than the wilderness.

The only time I had ever tolerated sleeping outside was when we visited our grandparents' house in the country and watched the stars from their lawn. Vodaeard was built in levels on a rock quarry cut out of the ocean. There were no green fields to lie on under the sky, and the estate my mother grew up on smelled of honeysuckle and lemon. That alone made the long summer nights beneath the stars tolerable.

An ache that had nothing to do with missing my bed and everything to do with missing my parents pulsed in my chest. I sat up, a weighty grief pushing down on me. I hadn't dreamt about their faces, but the images flashed before me anew, painted across my mind in stark relief against the even strokes of sunlight.

The last three days had been the worst by far, and the devastation of losing everything when the *Grey Bard* exploded was building in my chest again, along with the guilt of knowing it had been partially my fault. Icana had built the explosives we planted on the chief's ship before our escape, but then we foolishly left the powder in the cargo hold. If I hadn't been so focused on getting my revenge, I would never have risked travelling with such dangerous goods.

I swung my legs over the side of the bed and rubbed my forehead, easing the ache now spreading behind my eyes. A tear welled, threatening to unravel me completely. Again. I palmed it away. I had shed enough tears of frustration and anger.

The boards were rough beneath my feet as I crossed to the window and threw open the shutters, gulping down a breath of fresh air to clear my head. Autumn was on the cusp behind summer, the air heavy and fragrant, the crop tall and ripe. Harvest had already reached the mainland, and I hadn't even noticed.

A clear blue sky stretched overhead, unbroken as far as the eye could see. Wheat shafts swayed in the breeze. Humid air, so hot so early, kissed my skin, easing a trickle of sweat to my brow. It felt exactly like the summers we spent in the country as children.

I pinched my eyes shut. Those days seemed like they had existed forever ago. Alekey and I weren't children anymore. We would never be able to recall those days again. When our parents were alive and happy. But the war had ruined that. Had ruined us. I wanted to make it right, for me, for Alekey, for the children who had been born into this ravaged world. But doubts nagged at the back of my mind. I had hesitated once. Would I hesitate again when the time came to kill someone? All that foolish courage and false bravery had vanished the moment we left the lighthouse.

I had meant to die on that island.

And what would the princess do when she found out *I* was the girl she was trying to save? What would happen to that fragile trust we had forged last night?

There was only one way to find out—but that was still weeks and half a continent away. I needed her by my side when we crossed into Vodaeard. Which meant I needed her to believe I was taking her to the princess.

A knock rapped at my door. I pulled my shirt over my head and cracked the door open, peering into the empty hallway.

Across the hall, Talen stuck his head out of his room. His orange hair stuck up at the back, and red lines creased his cheek. He dragged a hand down his face. "Mmf," he mumbled.

"Did you knock?" I asked.

He shook his head, scrubbing the sleep away with both hands, eyes suddenly alert. "Did you?"

"No." Unease settled in my stomach. I glanced into the shadowy room behind him. Alekey was a lanky bump beneath the blankets on the other bed. My gaze slid to the door next to mine. If something had happened to the princess…

"Do you want to knock?" I asked Talen.

He coughed. "No. I rather like my head on my shoulders."

Icana's morning wrath was infamous in the palace. No one would dare wake her out of her slumber at risk of losing a finger. Or worse.

Masking a panicked laugh with a weary one, I quickly rapped on Icana's door.

The door flew inwards a few moments later, and I jumped back. Relief at seeing her alive quickly morphed into the astute fear that she could mangle me and make it look like an accident, simply for knocking too early.

She glowered at me from the other side of the door, eyes blazing with the fire of a thousand suns. The heat of her glare was as hot as the furnace I assumed she wanted to throw me into. "*What?*"

Black seas, I was her *queen*. What did I have to fear from her, even if her sharp tongue could cut me open as well as any blade?

Apparently, everything.

Beyond her, the princess' eyes fluttered open. "Captain!" she exclaimed, clutching the sheets to her bare chest.

Oh, seas, I would rather be victim to Icana's little finger than be witness to what lay beneath those covers.

"Is something wrong?" the princess pressed, sitting up.

"No, I—" I glanced from her to Icana and quickly back. No, she was definitely the less torturous of the two options. "Nothing. I'm sorry if I woke you."

Icana's fingernails dented the door. I flinched at the sharp sound then asked the princess, "How are you feeling?"

"Truthfully?" she murmured. That single word did something inexplicable to my heart, my resolve. She wanted this to work. I needed this to work. "Hungry."

"I can have some food sent up," I said in a whisper of a breath.

"And coffee?" she called as Icana slammed the door shut, the force of it rattling the window at the end of the hall.

Blowing out a shuddering breath, I glanced up to where Talen hovered in the doorway to his room. "Next time, *you* knock."

"She didn't kill you," he offered, unhelpfully. "Progress."

My fingers drifted to my throat as if the ghost of the knife in her glare lingered there. "If I die in my sleep, my ghost is going to haunt you."

"I don't believe in ghosts." He turned, nudging the door with his foot. "I'm going back to sleep."

As I loosened the tension from my arms, the fear of Icana's wrath seeped from my skin, dropping between the boards, through the foundation, and into the earth where it would remain. And after I had stuffed my legs into my pants and my coins into my pouch, I ambled into the common area of the inn. The owner was kind enough to send up a plate of food and pot of coffee, and as I walked out into the skin-sticking morning air, I briefly wondered why I was being so accommodating. At least I wasn't the one serving it to her on a silver platter.

The town was so dismally small I made a complete circuit before the last stars winked out of the azure. Aside from the inn, there were twelve other white-painted farmhouses and one grey-stone house of worship. Each house sat at a distance from the road, the crisp lawns rolling towards bright gardens lined with fruit trees. The tavern was on the lower level of someone else's house, and each homestead doubled as a market for ripe fruit, fresh bread, and sweet corn. Anything they grew themselves, they sold themselves.

The options for clothes were a little less than optimal.

A few extra coins bought delivery to the inn—the people in this town were more than happy to oblige—alongside a meagre selection of shirts and dresses for my crew and the princess. The town woke around me as I strolled. Young children ran into the street to play and older children hurried into the fields to start their chores. The tavern beckoned, a deep pull in my bones and a welcome reprieve from the stiflingly hot morning. It was empty so early, but the owners were quick to offer me a seat and food and their strongest tea. A steaming plate of mouthwatering breakfast meat, delectable fruit, and crisply toasted biscuits arrived in front of me a few minutes later.

The door behind me cracked open. Hot air brushed along my spine as Talen slid onto the bench opposite and plucked a sausage from my plate. His throat bobbed as he swallowed.

"I was going to eat that," I told him.

Alekey's lanky form was a freshly coifed shadow as he dropped onto the bench next to me. His fingers retreating out of reach of my fork.

"Seriously? Can't a girl eat her breakfast in peace?"

"Not a chance," he said around warm bread. He licked his fingers loudly. "Damn, that's good."

"I wouldn't know."

With a mirthful twinkle in his eye, Talen reached for another piece of meat. I wrapped my arms around my plate like a protective barrier, baring my teeth at him.

He tossed his hands up in defeat and called for one of his own.

"I thought," I said pointedly, peering up at him as I bowed over my food to keep my brother's fingers from finding another baked treasure, "you were going to sleep in."

Talen waved a hand through the air. He had tamed his hair, as much as his curls could be tamed, but he was in desperate need of a shave. "I was already awake. Thought you might be lonely."

"Or wanted to be alone," I muttered.

"No one *wants* to be alone," my brother murmured. When I glanced at him, an anguished gleam in his eyes, he was unwaveringly focused on the table. His finger traced the whorls in the wood.

I caught Talen's keen gaze across the table. Shame crept up my neck. How could I have ever thought of leaving Alekey alone in this world was the best course of action? It had been selfish. *I* had been selfish.

But I still had to protect him. If not as his sister, then as his queen. And queens had to make the difficult decisions—every decision I had made so far was with the hope that I could give him a better world to grow old in. And even if I survived, eventually he would have to learn to grow old in a world without me.

I pushed the fruit around on my plate. "How's the princess?"

Alekey's head shot up. "Why?" He twisted to face me, his most infuriating grin on his face. All that melancholy—gone in an instant. "Why do you care?"

"I care," I said through my teeth, "because I want to get home. We've been gone too long already."

"You mean *you've* been gone too long," Alekey argued. "I'm just the prince. You're the one who's supposed to be there...ruling." He cut a hand through the air, face scrunched up ponderously. This was the first time since we had left that he was sober. It didn't suit him well.

I stabbed a slice of pear. Annoyance tasted bitter. I had been annoyed at our traditions for so long that the feel of it at the back of my throat was so common to me. "They won't let me rule," I grumbled. "No one wants an underage queen."

"They don't really have a choice," Talen said. "You have to make them see that."

"They don't want *me*," I said, setting my fork down to stare across the table at him. His eyes searched mine, and I tried to make him understand without saying it out loud. No one in our country believed I was the optimal choice to rule. I was brash, abrasive, quick to temper, and I adamantly refused to listen to counsel. I always imagined I had years to change all that before anyone expected me to make any decisions. My parents were still supposed to be alive.

Finally, Talen sighed, scratching the fuzz over his jaw. "Either way," he said, "we have to get home before we worry about your crown. How long do you think the princess will be...ah...incapacitated?"

A withering glance found its mark in the centre of his forehead. It wasn't like Talen to get squeamish or uncomfortable at the mention of someone's cycle. Alekey, most certainly—he had his head buried in his hands again. "I want to leave by morning. But I won't make her walk if she's in pain."

"It can't be *that* bad," my brother mumbled into his palms.

I smacked his shoulder. "You don't get to say whether it's bad or not. Even I don't get to say whether it's bad or not." He knew I didn't suffer from it, but he also knew how it had affected our mother. "We're only a week or two from the mountains," I added. "A few extra days won't hurt."

Talen's eyes pierced into me—not for the first time since the princess joined our crew. "Are you defending her again?"

My glare stabbed him with as much force. "I'm just saying…I don't mind a slower pace. I'm not exactly looking forward to facing the man who killed our parents."

"You'll kill him, won't you?" Alekey raised his head. The anguish in his eyes stirred something in my heart. I had to do this. For him. For my people.

"I hope so," I said with a heavy sigh. It was up to me to make the hard choices. Sparing that man's daughter was a difficult option to pick, but killing him was an easy and obvious decision to make. I just couldn't afford to hesitate again.

I continued to push fruit around my plate, the sweet juices souring on my tongue, while Alekey dived hungrily into his plate. Talen's fork scraped thoughtfully across his plate for a few minutes.

Something that had been bothering me since we left Costun nudged to the front of my mind. "Does anyone else feel like we're being watched?"

Alekey made a show of looking around. "We're the only ones in here," he said, ever observant.

I huffed through my nose. "Since we landed. I haven't been able to shake the feeling since…you know."

"We were drugged," my brother said, face twisting. We shuddered at the same time, the memory cloying, crawling.

"Icana hasn't said anything," Talen said. And we all knew the weapons master would have noticed. She was a fox—keen eyes, sharp ears, and an even quicker bite.

We ducked into our plates again as another patron entered. Heavy footfalls crossed to the counter.

"What about those knocks earlier?" Alekey whispered. I glanced sidelong at him. I thought he had been asleep during that.

"Probably some local children playing," Talen said dismissively, but I caught his gaze again. Worry shimmered behind his eyes. The muscles in his jaw ground over each other.

I murmured an agreement I didn't believe, my spine tingling. Why now? If we were being followed, why hadn't we been ambushed on the road? Had we dropped our guard so much now that we were be-hind solid walls again? I didn't have the answers. Neither did Talen. But neither of us believed we were safe.

As day listed towards night, and bugs chittered in the fields and smoke poured from the chimneys, we returned to the inn. Hot air followed us through the cramped corridor. The door to Icana's room was open as we passed, and I glanced in.

The princess was sitting up in her bed, a fresh colour in her cheeks, playing a child's card game with my weapons master, who appeared to be losing—and not enjoying it. It took a moment of staring before I real-ized the princess' tangled hair was braided in a tightly coiled knot.

She glanced up, her deep ocean gaze finding me over the top of Icana's head. "Captain," she said with a dimpling grin, her voice as warm as the last rays of sunshine filtering through the windowpanes, casting rainbows of light across the floor.

Blinking, I forced myself to remember why we were here, annoyed with the distracting thoughts clouding my mind. I couldn't even go a full day without thinking about her hair or her eyes. "Did Icana do that?" I asked, gesturing to the braid.

"I have many talents," the woman murmured without looking up.

"Card games, not among them," the princess teased.

My mouth fell open when Icana didn't immediately decapitate her. Instead, she calmly set a card down on the pile.

The princess snatched it up and threw her cards down with a vic-torious whoop.

A smile spread across my face like a small itch. Horrified, I quickly masked it. "Think you'll be good to leave in the morning?"

Her nose scrunched as she pursed her lips. She nodded. "Probably. Thank you," she added as I turned to leave. "For letting me rest."

Seas, I was being too accommodating.

Mumbling something incoherent, I retreated to my room—and stopped short. Tucked between the door and frame, mostly out of sight, a glass bottle sat on the floor, filled halfway with water. A rolled piece of parchment floated within. Brows knotted, glancing around to see if anyone else noticed, I picked it up and brought it into my room. My heart spiked at the sheer strangeness of it. Who was leaving message bottles in front of random doors?

Or maybe, remembering the knocks from earlier, not so random after all.

A ceramic bowl for washing sat on the vanity in front of the mirror. I glanced up—a confused, tired Evhen peered back at me from the looking glass.

Bits of myself reflected bits of my parents. My father's hard jaw, his unruly hair, my mother's eyes. It wasn't the time to mourn them, so I let out a shuddering breath and popped the cork off the bottle. I dumped the contents into the washing bowl, my hand underneath the spout to catch the note.

And then I screamed.

The door crashed against the wall, shaking on the hinges, as Talen pounded into my room a moment later. The glass slipped from my fingers and shattered on the floor as the liquid burned my hand. Red welts bubbled over my skin. Tears streaked down my cheeks. I swore, trembling, as Talen grabbed the pitcher of water next to my bed and threw the contents over my hand. A fresh curse burst out at the sizzling sensation. I doubled over the vanity as Icana darted into my room.

She checked the wardrobe, the underside of the bed, and behind the curtains.

"Seas, fuck," I gritted. Pain roared in my ears as loud as a maelstrom, burning beneath my skin. My hand trembled uncontrollably, red and sore and bleeding. "What in the black seas was that?"

"Poison," Talen said, jaw clenched so tight his teeth scraped together. He grabbed a towel from behind the door and, grimacing apologetically at me, wrapped my hand in it. I swore, sucking in a sharp breath. The room spun through the jabs of pain while tendrils of light exploded across my vision.

"Who puts poison in a bottle with a note?" I ground out through clenched teeth. The searing agony subsided a fraction as he patted my hand dry. With my other hand, I plucked up the folded parchment from the washing bowl, hissing as the lingering poison stung the pads of my fingers.

Silent as a wraith, Icana appeared at my side a moment later, tugging on leather gloves with her teeth. Of course, she never went anywhere without her gloves. The wax seal cracked, spraying poisonous bits into the air. I cringed back as she pried the paper open, spreading it over the vanity. Smudged ink ran in rivulets over the paper, but the letters were clear enough.

WE KNOW WHO YOU ARE, YOUR MAJESTY. MEET US AT THE EDGE OF TOWN. MIDNIGHT. ALONE.

A lump stuck in my throat. There was no one else it could be addressing. The princess was only that—a princess. And Alekey was just a prince. I was the queen. Underaged, come-into-my-power-too-soon queen.

Talen gently rubbed my hand, searing my raw skin, as he read the note. "You can't go," he said. "It's a trap."

"Of course it's a—fu—" I hissed in pain as he unwrapped my hand, cold air hitting my skin again. "They made no demands. They just said to meet them. I'd be a coward not to go." Anger was a fire licking at my heels, spurring me into rash action. Like every other moment thus far, I was making half-planned decisions only to deal with the consequences later.

And like every other moment thus far, Talen was there to be my voice of reason. He argued, "You'd be dead."

But I didn't want reason. I wanted revenge.

Eyes blazing in a way that scared most people, I shouldered past him, snatching up my cutlass from the corner.

The princess floated into view in the hall, eyes wide, robe cinched around her waist. "What's going on?" she asked, voice tinged with more worry than anyone else on my crew. Her eyes darted to my hand as I unsheathed my cutlass. "What happened?"

113

This truly was her fault, and she had no idea she was to blame.

My heart was still racing, the high of the attack coursing in my veins. Her worry, her gentle tone, her bright eyes weren't enough to calm me.

"Move," I barked. I didn't wait for her to oblige before I shoved my way into the corridor. The walls seemed to press close, shutting me out from the rest of the world, tinged red like the welts on my hand.

"Ev—Captain!" Talen shouted behind me, remembering almost too late that I didn't want the princess to know who I was. "This is foolish."

"Don't try to stop me," I growled, striding towards the stairs. "I'm going to have my revenge one way or another."

"I won't let you go." His hand seized my wrist, holding tight, pulling me around to face him.

The words building up in my chest stung worse than anything I had ever said to him before. I regretted them before they even left my lips. "Let me go. That's a fucking order."

He pulled back as if I had struck him with something much worse. I was his queen, whether I had been crowned or not. Whether anyone else believed it or not. He knew he had to obey me.

But the look of betrayal in his eyes made it hurt all the more. I shoved that image away, thinking instead of my cutlass running with blood, and I whirled around, stalking out of the inn and into the night.

Night hadn't fully fallen by the time I reached the edge of town. The sky in the distance was painted pink in one direction and sapphire in the other, the colours bleeding together high above. Nothing moved in the streets, and only candles flickered in the windows of every house I passed. Smoke billowed into the sky from the few chimneys. Somewhere, a sheep bleated.

The note had said midnight, but I had never been one to listen to directions. Which was why I was here early, waiting.

The spreading night at least brought a touch of cool air, which stung the hideous welts on my hand. I tightened my grip on my cutlass. Thankfully I hadn't lost the use of my right hand, though my arm still stung something fierce. Despite Icana's training, I wasn't a very good swordsman with my left hand.

I waited at the edge of the town. The road stretched far ahead, disappearing through winding hills and shadowy fields—everything ahead cast in a gloom of deep blue, but nothing moved in the dark. Nothing lurched at me from the quiet. Night bugs twittered in the fields, screeching their nightly melody along the side of the dusty street. Anger buzzed in my veins still. Trepidation gnawed at my stomach. What did I think was going to happen out here? I shifted from foot to foot in anticipation. Was I going to cut open some fools who dared crossed me?

Or was I the fool who was going to get cut open?

Movement rustled in a copse of trees next to the road. I eyed the shadows warily. Knee-length yellow grass parted before me as I pushed towards the trees. My heart hammered in my chest, drowning out all other sounds. Even the bugs seemed to grow silent. A collective breath held against the night.

A chill snaked down my spine, nearly shattering my resolve. This was utterly foolish. Talen had been right. As always.

I was about to turn back when someone lumbered behind me. Too slow—always too slow—I whirled around. A hand clamped around my neck before I could raise my sword between us. Slimy fingers squeezed my throat. Panic burst in my chest, lungs screaming for air, and I dropped my sword to scratch at the man's hands. Skin flaked off beneath my nails. He smelled like rot. Like death.

All that foolish courage and false bravery—gone.

He released my throat with a jerk, my skin tearing beneath his nails, and grabbed my shoulder to knock out the backs of my knees and drive me to the ground. My limbs cracked at the impact and pain crackled in my jaw. I squirmed, trying to get up, but his grip pinched a tender spot in my neck that made me see bursts of light when I moved.

Two others slipped out of the trees ahead of me, like oily snakes in a nest. I recognized one of them from the attack in the tavern and lifted my chin to scowl at him. The other barely acknowledged me—part of his right ear was missing and his nose was caved in—as he polished a curved blade that gleamed silver in the half-moon rising over the parched fields.

"What a curious turn of events," said the man from the tavern. His earlobes were missing, and the stench of decay hung around the three men, cloying at my throat. I gagged. "You came alone."

"You told me to," I spat, unable to keep my mouth shut around people who would sooner cut out my tongue.

"And you're not the type of person to listen to orders," he said. "Otherwise, you would have stayed in Vodaeard where you belong."

I spat at his feet. He chuckled. The sound grated down my spine, a furious *tap tap tap* against my bones.

"Sorry to disappoint," I told him.

With an air of drama, he draped a hand over his chest. Seas, he was worse than the man who killed my parents. At least the chief hadn't wasted time with mockery. "It's not me you're disappointing," he simmered. "It's everyone else, dear. The people you want to protect. Especially that younger brother."

My blood ran cold, draining out of my face and into the field beneath my knees. Talen and Icana would never rise to such easy bait, but I couldn't let anything happen to Alekey. "What do you want?"

"Not what we want," he said, infuriatingly cryptic. Was this how they interrogated people in Marama? I doubted the chief had any use for prisoners. "It's what you want."

Refraining from rolling my eyes, I gritted my teeth instead. "And what's that?"

"You want to give us the princess."

I barked out a laugh that earned a sharp pinch in my neck and a wince. "Guess again."

"No one else has to come to any harm. Especially not—what's his name—Key?" An awful grin spread across his face. My fingers twitched for my cutlass to cut it off. "Key Lockes. It's cute."

My mouth opened before I could stop myself from snapping, "Keep him out of this." They were only baiting me, I knew that, but desperation made me say foolish things. Alekey didn't deserve to be hurt because of me.

"Then return the princess. And surrender yourself to the chief."

My chest heaved as if a door had slammed shut on my options. My future. Surrender was death. For both of us. I hadn't forgotten what the princess had told me that day on the dock before she bowed and offered herself to me entirely.

Her father wanted her dead. I had meant to ask her about it before the *Grey Bard* sank, but I would never get that chance if I surrendered now.

But I couldn't damn the princess to her fate either. Not when we were so close to lasting trust between us.

I shook my head. "No deal. She'll get to see her father in Vodaeard. I promised her that much. But not sooner." I was a queen of my word. The princess would have her chance to talk to her father, on my terms.

The man narrowed his eyes and lowered his voice. "You're playing a dangerous game here, Your Majesty."

My breath clipped my teeth at the title. "Not a game." My lips quirked as I remembered what the princess said. *My life is not a bargaining tool.* "A gamble."

He ran a hand over his jaw. "A foolish risk, to be sure. The chief has an army. What do you have?" His eyes lifted from me to the road behind us. "Two fools who don't listen to orders." He raised his voice to be heard by the two fools who had followed me, and panic burst in me anew.

From somewhere behind me, swords rang out in the air.

I twisted my head to see Icana and Talen, shadows against the late sunset, at the edge of the field. A quick glance revealed they were alone. Which meant they left Alekey alone. And they left the *princess* alone.

I wanted to scream at them for abandoning my brother, but fear wrapped frozen fingers around my throat and anger scraped my tongue like shards of ice. My mind whirled through the panic raking claws in my skull.

The man holding me down was briefly distracted by my crew mates. It didn't last long, but it was still long enough.

I jerked my elbow back into his groin. His fingers released my neck as he doubled over with a grunt of pain. I reached back, curled my fingers in his shirt, and flipped him over my head.

He smacked into the ground, his fingers grabbing for anything—hair, skin, clothes, anything.

I threw myself to the side as Icana darted into the field, silent and deadly as a wraith. The raw skin on my hand screamed when I brushed the ground, searching for my sword. My knuckles hit the hilt, and then I was on my feet, running before I even registered the fight breaking out behind me.

Talen was a blur as we passed each other—him in a frantic hurry into the fray, me in a frantic hurry towards the inn. If anything happened to Alekey...I couldn't let anything happen to—Oh seas, what if...

I burst through the door to the surprise of the owner and raced up the stairs, my heart pounding in my ears, drumming a beat to my brother's name. The hallway blurred in front of me, tilting to the side, empty.

I couldn't let anything happen to Alekey.

The princess leapt out of her room into the hall, braid swaying mere fingers off the floor behind her, brandishing a small knife. A memory flashed, so far from this night, of the first time I had seen her in the lighthouse. It faded just as quickly. I didn't have time to think about why Icana had given her a dagger.

I couldn't let anything happen to Alekey.

The Maraman royal stumbled into the door as I pushed past her. The door to Alekey's room was still open. I froze, lungs burning.

My brother sat on his bed, a quizzical quirk on one eyebrow. "Ev—"

Relief crashed over me like a cold wave, and Alekey grunted when I locked my arms around his neck, holding on as though he was the only thing that mattered in this life.

THIRTEEN

Dawn broke over the cornfields in fractured bursts of light behind spindly clouds. I lay in bed as watery light seeped through the cracks in the windowpanes, chasing away the shadows but leaving the fears. The problem was, I didn't know if the fears were mine or the captain's. She was staunch, fearless, everything I should have been considering how many times I stared Death in the face and said, *Not today*.

But she had been in such a frantic state when she burst into the hallway last night. Sickness had coiled within me, seeing her like that, but it could have been the pain jabbing at my lower abdomen. And I hadn't lingered when she threw her arms around Alekey.

Despite everything the young prince had said about the captain, a strange emotion had settled into my heart, heavy and decidedly bitter. It kept me up all night, tossing and turning in discomfort, wondering at its foreignness. Dawn found me awake before anyone else, eyes open wide to the world and a cataclysmic storm swirling within. In the long minutes of silence, I took the image of my lighthouse, built it up stone by stone around my heart, and sealed myself from the chaos.

But the emotion continued to nag at me, finding cracks in the foundation, even when Icana woke up as a defiant stream of sunlight beamed on her face. She rolled out of bed, quite literally, and announced she was going downstairs for some food.

The captain knocked on the open door a few moments later.

"We're leaving soon," she said, and then seemed to remember the cup of steaming coffee in her hand. She blinked, a strange colour creeping over the collar of her shirt. "I…for you."

The foreign feeling returned tenfold as I crawled out of bed and took the cup from her before she decided I was ungrateful and snatched away the only thing that gave me comfort. Why was she offering it like a peace treaty? She avoided my gaze, and something in her pinched expression told me it was better not to ask about the angry sores on her hand.

As soon as the aroma hit my nose, though, all cloudy thoughts gave way to the singular joy I found in a good cup of coffee. I could even forgive her for—well—everything.

"I honestly don't know what you like about that stuff," she muttered, turning up her nose as I burnt the tip of my tongue in my eagerness.

"Consider some coconut," I mumbled, eyes fluttering closed. The scent itself transported me back to my lighthouse.

"A what?" she blurted.

I cracked open an eye to peer at her through the wafting steam. It made her blurry, hazy like an afterimage from a burst of lightning. Instead of educating her on traditional island delicacies, I took another sip, retreating to the window sill.

"Be ready to leave in ten minutes," she told me.

I caught her reflection in the glass. The words building in my chest soured around the coffee in my stomach when I remembered my situation, morning beverages aside. "I don't have anything of value here, Captain. I'm ready to leave now."

Her expression clouded, and she left without another word.

Leaning against the cool pane, I watched the small crew move from room to room, always underfoot of one another but never tripping over each other. They moved like a nebulous unit, a swirling storm with the captain at its centre. The strange emotion returned when she stopped in front of my door ten minutes later and announced they were ready to leave, arm linked through Alekey's. His hair flopped into his eyes while she had pinned hers back in a loose bun.

The feeling festered, unrecognizable until we were out of the inn and walking down the road. Until we neared a small house of worship, its doors flung open wide. Until I heard the singing voices from within, accompanied by the hollow sound of an organ.

Jealousy. I was *jealous*.

Putting a name to the foreign emotion startled me. It sat uncomfortably in my belly, roiling and coiling, but it didn't make sense. What could I have possibly been jealous of?

My feet carried me towards the doors of the worship house. Fragile rays of sunlight beamed down the centre aisle, pouring rainbows through the coloured windows above the doors. Beautiful notes drifted up to the rafters, carried by sweet music and bitter incense. Rows on rows of people crowded the small space, facing an altar at the far end. The figure on the altar was faceless, featureless from where I stood on the steps, but it glinted gold and white as the sun caught it over the wheat fields.

"Princess?" Alekey said behind me.

I jumped, his voice breaking through the calm silence, and turned. The others had moved on, past the low town wall.

His dark hair drooped into his eyes, less gold and more yellow in the straining broken light, that easy grin on his face. A high colour kissed his cheeks. As the sun rose higher behind us, finally peaking above the ropy strokes of clouds, realization struck me with the intensity of all the sun's blazing warmth.

I was jealous of Alekey.

Why was I jealous of him?

"Key!" the captain called from up the street, and I knew.

"The captain beckons," he said with a wink. "Come on."

I glanced inside the chapel once more, thoughts crashing into each other like waves on a rocky shore. A pang of longing shot through my chest. The melody of the parishioners' mingled singing voices needled my mind. How could I possibly be jealous of a dark-haired, soft-spoken boy who saw too much when there was war—one caused by my own father—ravaging this world? Shame stabbed through my ribs as I watched the worshippers sing. These people were at peace. There was no war here. No danger. They were safe, having found comfort in their faith.

It was so at odds with how I felt, so far from my island, the moon so out of reach—my connection to it still on a cord around the captain's wrist. Like a treasure she had claimed and mocked me with.

I had nothing to be jealous of. But the feeling lingered on my heart, and my mind clouded as I followed the prince back to the group. Behind us, lost in a cloud of dust, the singing faded.

The stone swayed below the captain's ruined hand, swallowing the bright light, a stain against the world as ugly as the welts covering her skin. She had wrapped her hand in a bandage, hidden it away, but she hadn't spoken about what had caused it.

It pained me to think the fragile trust we had formed in the field had fractured.

Truth burned the tip of my tongue like coffee, but decidedly less tasty. I could heal her hand if she let me. I could heal her shoulder—if she trusted me.

But something had severed that bond in the hours since she injured her hand, and she refused to let me even acknowledge it.

As we walked between the rolling hills, their boots crunching on the gravel, my bare feet burning in the dirt, the answer glared at me from the cord around her wrist, swaying back and forth with every step forward. My stone. My power. My parents. Everything, all paths, came back to my horrible power and my horrible parents. They had caused her more pain than I was realizing.

I had nothing to be jealous of when my world and my life hung in the balance from her wrist like the scales of justice.

The words she spat at me on the dock scraped the inside of my skull like hot coals. *Well, that makes my decision easier.* If she could resist killing me, it was because someone else was going to.

And that someone else was my own father.

My fears were my weaknesses. They always had been. I had never been able to mask my insecurities, and anyone with sharp enough eyes had seen right through me. Walls and stones and lighthouses did little when my mother's cutting gaze always tore them down. I had to be strong, not like my lighthouse, but like the ocean. The vast depths. The undying shores. I was the Princess of Death, and I could be strong.

I could survive.

The lighthouse walls strengthened around my heart—another layer added slowly—brick by brick, stone by stone, reinforcing my protection against the storm. I had to seal myself away from the rest of the world, from the captain, just as she hid her pain from the world. I had to lock away the parts of me that wanted to believe I was doing the right thing. Because no matter how hard I believed it, I was still in danger. Nothing could change my fate now. It was a constant, uncertain nagging in the back of my mind. I had thought I would live to see my family, my home, and my lighthouse again. But if the story was true, Death waited for me at the end of this journey one way or another.

I was the girl who could talk to the dead, and that was where it had all gone wrong.

Two days crawled by, each day longer than the last, growing hotter and hotter as we passed through one-road towns and sparse farmlands. Sweat trickled down my back, settling into the hollows of my hips. Though my heavy braid swayed several fingers off the ground, it felt as though it had been dragging through dirt. It lost its sheen as the days wore on.

On the third day of walking, night was still hours away when we reached a small city growing out of the fields. Paved streets twisted through white stone buildings, and brightly coloured banners streamed between the buildings, providing pools of shade every few steps. The sounds of laughter and chatter filled the air, which tasted of meat and bread. People bustled up and down the winding streets, talking excitedly with one another and calling out to friends. It was the liveliest place we had come to thus far, and a stab of longing clenched around my heart.

While I rarely participated in anything other than Resurrection Days, I missed the festivities and celebrations on my island. I missed the village. I missed the night guards, who often spoke too freely when I roamed the halls in crypt-like silence.

The captain moved next to me as we followed the twisting labyrinth, between tangles of bushes and tightly packed buildings. She had unpinned her hair, letting it fly in loose tendrils around her face, the sunset glow permanently caught in her strands. Bits stuck to her eyelashes, and when she raised her injured hand to brush them away, my eyes snagged on the swaying stone. It was so close and yet so far.

She saw my staring and lifted the stone between us.

"I want to ask you about this," she said, her voice low enough for only us.

The chiselled edges mesmerized me, sharp and jagged and all the things I never could be. My mouth was dry when I finally tore my eyes away from its tantalizing pull to her face. "What do you want to know?"

This was the conversation I didn't want to have. It was the one I *had* to have. One that would cut me open, bleed me out, and reveal everything I wanted to hide from the world. My vulnerabilities, my insecurities, my weaknesses. All wrapped up in that precious stone. It captured the sun as we stepped from one pool of shade to the next. The light bounced around the broken edges in time with the beat of my heart, always in harmony.

"That day on the dock," she said, running her fingers over the smooth planes, sunlight sparking against her fingertips like fire. "What did you mean your father wants to kill you?"

I bit my tongue as the truth rushed up. Would she even believe me if I told her? Instead, I let my next words lash out like a snake's tongue. "Don't think I've forgotten what you told me then."

Surprise blinked across her face, rapidly replaced by the same cold anger that held frozen me to the bones on the dock that day.

I hated feeling so powerless, made so insignificant under her glare.

Instead of threatening me the way she had done then, she threw my words back at me, sharp as knives. "Don't think I've forgotten what *you* told *me*. You said you would do anything to help me. Are your promises worth naught when you believe me weakened?"

Frustration and weariness collided in my chest, pulling at my bones, and filling the hollows and holes. In my mind, I didn't deserve to be treated like this—like the villain in her story. But every time we opened our mouths around each other, we started yelling.

She had taken my life from me when I had been a willing prisoner, as Alekey called me. She had taken my stone, my power, my choice, and she still frightened me with just her eyes. I had been stripped bare, and she still found ways to tear me down. Each word was another cut, another scar. I was tired of it.

"Captain," I said, all my frustration and exhaustion grinding through that single word until my voice flattened, "I don't believe you've been weakened. But we are not anywhere nearer to finding a compromise that doesn't end in our deaths. I want to help you—"

"Then answer me," she snapped, nostrils flaring.

My feet skidded to a halt at the corner of an intersection. "*But* you cannot keep demanding things of me without giving me anything in return," I continued.

She turned to me, her face falling into shadow. Darkness hung around her like a cloak. Her walls were built so high no one could breach them.

She had torn mine down to rubble. Maybe she just needed someone to do the same, and suddenly I wanted to be that person. Someone had to take the first step towards trust. "My name is Kalei."

She seemed startled. As if I had confessed something more important than my name. As if I had crossed a boundary that wasn't meant to be crossed and she didn't know what to do with the information.

I held my breath, waiting, watching. There was no easy way to build trust with her, only my way, and the choice was hers to take what I offered.

"Evhen," she said quickly. A thrill coursed through me at hearing it come from her mouth for the first time. A name so unlike anything I had ever heard before. A soft name for someone so hard.

I smiled. One more step. This was what she wanted to know.

"The stone can grant him immortality."

"What?" she blurted, reeling back.

This was what she wanted to know, so why was she making it sound like I had been lying to her? Why did she sound so betrayed, affronted?

My breath blew past my lips in a curtain of annoyance, and started again. "In the legend—"

"Legend?" Her voice slammed into my ears and broke against the wall behind me. It scraped along the ground, curling up the street until her whole crew turned at the sound. "You mean to tell me that you don't actually know anything about this stone or why your father is waging a war for more of this shit?"

"I am *trying* to tell you," I said, attempting—and failing—to mask my growing annoyance. "In the legend—"

"This isn't a story, Princess!" It irked me more than it should have that she used my title mockingly when I had given her my name only moments ago. "This is reality. You can't believe everything you read in those seas-damned fairytales of yours."

I bit my tongue against the barrage of words that stemmed from a well of anger. Anger sunk ships and burned hands. Anger was the darkness that surrounded us like a pall and clouded our minds. It fuelled the fire in our hearts against each other. Taking a step towards trust was the wrong way to approach a tentative alliance. Any potential for something more required putting aside anger, but she had built her walls out of fire—not stone. I wouldn't yell to force her to listen to me anymore.

"From what I've read," I continued, ignoring her scoff, "if the pieces are reunited, my parents will have everything they need—"

"I'm not listening to this," she said, turning away as Alekey approached us. "I am not risking *everything* for a stupid story."

"There's some truth in legends," the prince said, his voice soft, brows knotted in the middle of his forehead. I recalled telling him about the sirens of stories, the mermaids of myth, and I knew he had been paying attention all this time.

"What would you know?" Evhen snapped at him. A banner shifted overhead. It swayed in the gentle breeze that twisted through the streets. Sunlight glinted in the open hostility in her topaz eyes. "You're always drunk. What would you know of legends and myths?"

A thread in my chest twisted, a deep pang for the hurt expression on his face. He didn't deserve to be treated this way anymore than I did.

"Captain," I said, voice hard, the word sneering. "Alekey has been nothing but kind to me, and you have been nothing but awful. He is right about the legends and he was right about you."

That cruel, slow grin spread across her face.

Even Alekey seemed perturbed by it, looking away from her wrath.

"And what else did he say?" Her voice coiled around me like a slithering, living thing, ready to strike. To bleed. To kill.

But I knew something she didn't, something that had terrified me from the moment I discovered it, but it was the one thing that could stop this superiority farce.

I rolled my shoulders back and straightened to my full height—still several fingers shorter than she was, but it was enough of a posture to earn a curious quirk of her chin. "He told me he is the prince, so there is one thing stopping you from killing me, and that is permission from a member of the royal family. From him."

For a fleeting moment, almost too quick for me to notice, terror flashed in her eyes as she glanced at Alekey. Then that cool gaze landed on me again. "That is still a decision for the princess to make, not him."

She began to walk away, and the noose tightened. Red and gold and black seeped into my vision like ink stains in water. "Why do you say things as if with her voice?" I called. She froze. Turned. "I offered to bring them back. Why do you act like the princess won't want that?"

"Wait, what?" Alekey blurted, standing between me and Evhen. "You knew about this?" he said to the captain, his tone accusatory.

Her eyes widened and locked on me. For the first time, I saw fear in her gaze.

Why did the captain look so frightened by his tone of voice? That's what all this hinged on—she couldn't kill me until I talked to the princess, because I would offer to bring her parents back from the depths.

Alekey spun around to face me. "Can you really do it?" Hope laced every word.

"Yes," I whispered, too startled to say anything else.

He glanced over his shoulder, a different kind of hurt curling his shoulders. "Why didn't you tell me?"

Why did he make it sound like she had done something awful by not telling him?

"Key…"

He whirled, anger sparking like hot coals in his eyes. "Why didn't you tell me she offered to bring our parents back?"

Our.

Oh.

How hadn't I seen it before? The truth was glaring me in the face, in the form of golden eyes, honey and yellow, the sea kissed by sunset. They were the same colour, though Alekey's a shade darker. Still the same, nonetheless.

A breath shuddered in. My shoulder knocked into the wall as the skies tumbled around me, rapidly descending to darkness.

They were the *same*.

All this time, I thought she had been taking me to plead in front of the princess in Vodaeard. She had led me to believe the princess would decide my fate. I had been courting Death for so long, I hadn't realized he could come to me in the form of a red-headed, honey-eyed, sea-hardened Vodaeardean princess.

A warning sirened in my head. Well, that makes my decision a bit easier. Not Captain Evhen, but Princess Evhen had said those chilling words to me that day on the dock. Because Princess Evhen wanted me dead. Because Princess Evhen was going to kill me in front of my father.

As my father killed her parents in front of her.

Your death will end the war.

That moment from the lighthouse, so long ago already, flashed in sharp clarity through my mind. The memory left a bitter taste in my mouth. She had been right. Of course, she had been right. My death would end the war, and that is what she had meant to do all along.

She was never going to let me bring her parents back.

She had never even considered it.

Because Evhen, the princess of Vodaeard, wanted revenge.

My knees hit the street, scraping the stone. They were still arguing, loudly, their voices clawing against the inside of my skull, cutting through bone and marrow and thought.

Alekey turned back. "Kal—"

When I pitched forward in a faint, he was too slow to catch me.

FOURTEEN

Alekey slammed into my shoulder, too hard to be accidental, as he passed me on the road. A low groan built in my throat at the blood seeping through the ratty bandages. The wound hadn't healed properly in the days since the princess shot me in the tavern, but it seemed more agitated in the days since she had fainted. It burned beneath the bindings. I rubbed my arm, barely noticing how my fingertips warmed at the touch.

He had become increasingly distant, ever since we landed, but now guilt gnawed at me for not telling him about the princess' offer sooner. It wouldn't have made a difference—it was my decision to accept or reject her—but I was still to blame for his shift in attitude.

An uncomfortable sense of responsibility rolled uncomfortably through my stomach. Alekey's anger at me and the princess' distressing silence—the truth had come out before I could stop it, and an irreparable rift had come between all of us. I felt as though I was watching everything unfold from outside of myself. Like I was trapped on some abandoned shore with a world of raging ocean between me and the people I loved most.

As if I had somehow caused all this grief and I could only watch as everyone else suffered.

"What's he so pissed about?" I grumbled to Talen, even though I knew perfectly well what it was. It was easier to twist this emotion into anger because anger was all I knew. I had forgotten what anything else felt like the moment I watched my parents die.

A part of me believed I would never know joy again. I wasn't sure it existed in this world, especially not for people like me. We didn't deserve to know joy. At least, not until someone else's blood stained our memories.

"Ask him, not me," Talen grunted.

Frozen in place by his snappish tone, I pinched my eyes shut. Even my voice of reason was angry at me, and he had every right to be. We had all left pieces of ourselves scattered across this seas-damned continent, that we were never supposed to be crossing on foot, too broken by recent events to ever be whole again. What kind of people would we be when we emerged on the other end of this quest? Not the same as we were when we started. And I deserved every single one of their verbal lashes for it.

I never should have left Vodaeard. Never should have let revenge consume me. The only thing a responsible queen would have done was wait. Wait to rule. Wait to die.

The princess had seemingly come to her own conclusions about what waited for us at the end of our journey, and it was *her* silence that bothered me more than Alekey's anger. She was quiet, remorseful, hunched into herself as if by dragging her feet, she could prolong our arrival at Vodaeard. She was terrified by whatever waited for her. I knew why her father wanted to kill me, but I still didn't understand why she thought he wanted to kill her.

I racked my brain for the memory, trying to sort through all the things I *wished* I had said and all the things I had *actually* said. She had been talking nonsense before she fainted. Something about legends and myths. I watched her from afar, chin tipped towards her chest, bare feet shuffling over the ground without a care for how hot the ground was or how dusty the roads were.

What had she been trying to tell me?

Why hadn't I tried to listen?

"Xesta's ahead," Icana announced, breaking the stale silence around us so suddenly that the princess flinched.

Ahead, the sun's haze played tricks on the road as I peered into the distance, pulling sticky strands of hair away from my neck. I hadn't realized how close we already were.

It was the largest kingdom in the south, a massive trade route between the east and the west, and more and more people were filling the streets leading to King Ovono's domain. We had probably already crossed the border, and I hadn't even noticed.

I rubbed the ache growing behind my eye. We would be recognized immediately. Not that it would have changed anything. We would have come to Xesta one way or another—on foot or by boat—but we had also been attacked in towns too small to be governed by any law. If we were identified in those small communities, there was no way we could slip through unnoticed here.

And there was no telling what the princess might do now that she had lost all tentatively-placed trust in me.

I didn't know how to build that again when she expected me to believe her fairytales.

Icana and Talen looked at me as if I held all the answers. Why did I have to be the one who knew what we were doing? Why did I have to be the one who had all the plans? All my plans had crumpled to dust before we even left Vodaeard, hastily thrown together as Talen whisked me away from where my parents' bodies cooled in the throne room. Why did I have to be the one who held the fate of my entire nation in the palms of my useless hands? They weren't big enough for so much responsibility.

My voice of reason and my master of weapons expected me to say something. I couldn't recall a time when so many pairs of eyes needled into me with so much intensity all at once. I could barely recall anything that happened in my life before my parents died. It was too painful to think about any memories that included them. But I had never been one to squirm beneath scrutiny. Even if I didn't always know what I was doing, I acted as though I did.

But now I couldn't muster up the act with all of them staring at me.

My mind blanked. No memories, no plans, no acts, nothing. We were passing through yet another small town before the capital city, cramped stone buildings packed tightly together in the middle of a low stone wall enclosure. And I did the only thing I could think to do.

I ran.

Gravel kicked up under my feet, biting my ankles as I tore through the narrow streets. Piercing bits of rock scraped my arms from the rough-stone structures all around me. An alley squeezed me out into a quiet garden nestled between buildings on all sides, weeds over-grown in the cracked dirt. Colours burst from bending bushes and burdened branches. An overly sweet smell cloyed the air, a mix of ripe and rotting fruit, and I caught myself against a rusting gazebo, heaving dryly. Chest tight, I sank to the ground amid towering bram-bles, head between my knees as I sucked in shuddering breath after shuddering breath.

Heat fanned across my face when I heard movement over the stones lining the path behind me. I palmed panicked tears from my cheeks, and my head fell back against the twisting metal fixture as the princess stepped into view.

She lifted the hem of her dress so it wouldn't get caught in the crawling vines.

My chest rose and fell in rapid bursts, pain spiking behind my eyes, sweat pooling in my palms. "You are the *last* person I want to talk to right now," I said between gasps, squeezing my eyes shut when she sat next to me, her shoulder brushing mine—warm skin burning mine.

She didn't say anything for a long time, her foot rocking back and forth in gentle waves

The sensation of the movement against my leg reminded me of the swell of waves beneath my ship, the up and down, the rise and fall. I pictured my cabin on the *Grey Bard*, the warbled knots in the wardrobe, the scratchy bedsheets that smelled of dust and death, the letters from me and Alekey to our parents. Slowly, my breaths evened and my racing heart tamed to a steady tempo.

A bird chirped in one of the trees crowding the space. The ground smelled of fresh water, bright and clear and earthy—tangy against my tongue, and sharp like bristling thorns. Sunlight kissed my skin, and then I became keenly aware of her body next to mine, the hesitant brush of skin against skin. Her hair, tickling my arms, smelled of moonlight, a silvery scent I couldn't explain with words in the same way one couldn't describe the scent of sunlight.

I opened my eyes and found her azure gaze locked on my face.

"Why did they send you?" I asked, brows pulling together as I studied her face. Freckles dotted her nose and her mouth quirked up in the middle. When her lips pulled into a smile, I realized with a start that I'd missed something I had never seen before.

Her eyes were still clouded, though. "They didn't send me," she said. "I offered to come."

"Why?" My voice strained around the word. Why would anyone want to be witness to the mess that was my life? Why would anyone offer to even talk to me when I had been an ass to everyone for days? Fatigue had made me insufferable.

The words she had spoken to me that day so long in the cargo hold echoed in my mind. *You will tolerate me, but I will not suffer you.* I hadn't realized how vile I had been from the start, so focused on my lust for revenge that everything else had been pale specks compared to that one burning thought that spurred me on—even my own cruelty.

She shrugged her frail shoulders. "I meant what I said." Before she elaborated, my mind sped through all the things she had ever said—the bad, the good, the threats, the promises. "I will do anything to help you. Of course, I hadn't known you were the princess then, so I was speaking to Captain Evhen, but when I make a promise, I keep it."

My head dropped into my hands. "Does that promise also apply to Queen Evhen?" It was the first time I had said the title out loud, and I didn't hate how it sounded. A little awkward, all things considered, but it was my title and I was going to wear it with honour.

When she didn't reply immediately, I raised my head.

She was staring at the flowers around us, the bright flashes of colour that hadn't wilted yet, red and pink and yellow petals hiding beneath the leaves. Her fingers brushed the colours like paint. "When I realized you were the princess," she said, her voice so low I had to lean closer, "I thought you were going to kill me right there in the street. And then I thought you were going to kill me when we reached Vodaeard. Because my death would end the war. Because my father killed your parents and you wanted revenge on him for it. And I was scared. I thought...I thought bringing them back was what the princess would want...what you would want. But it was what *I* wanted because it meant I would live. All you wanted was revenge."

She wasn't wrong, but before I could say anything, she lifted her eyes to mine again, and there was no fear in them. Understanding sparkled in their depths.

"Then I thought—why haven't you killed me yet?"

I closed my mouth. It was the one question I couldn't answer. Why had I spared her life time and time again? Why had I defended her when I should have killed her?

"That question has been burning through my mind for two days," she continued. She tugged a bloom with purple petals from its stem and placed it in my palm. "But I have another question for you. Why did you run?"

The spiralling shape of the flower spun in front of my eyes, larger petals curling towards smaller ones in the centre, surrounding a clump of pale yellow pollen. A tiny black beetle darted between petals.

"Where I'm from," I whispered, unable to bring myself to look at her and let her see all my insecurities laid bare, "children come of age at eighteen. Tradition declares that I cannot be crowned for another year. It's an archaic law from when Vodaeard was much larger, but the people haven't forgotten. No one will accept me as their ruler, but everyone expects me to have all the answers already. When I left, I never thought I would see my home again. I thought I was going to kill your parents where they slept and then die by their guards."

The princess didn't respond to the revelation of my intended death.

"Then I thought you were going to kill me in your lighthouse. Then I thought the sirens were going to kill me. Then the fight at the tavern. Then the poison." My voice had lost all traces of emotion, as though I had raged the feelings away only to be left with cold apathy. "Somewhere along the way, I realized I don't want to die, but I can't seem to figure out how to make a plan that doesn't end in my death. And Alekey is pissed at me for seas-know-what, and Talen and Icana keep looking at me like they expect me to make all the decisions, even though every single one so far has ended badly, and I can't do anything right, so why should everyone even want me as a queen, and—"

Her hand folded over mine, cutting me off so abruptly I bit my tongue.

I yanked my hand out from under hers, the crumpled flower falling like ash from my palm, and scratched at the offending tears that streamed down my cheeks, as if I could hurt them for betraying me. Sorrow was the one emotion I refused to let anyone see. It was the most useless—and most terrifying—emotion. Crying wouldn't bring life back into my parents' bodies, but it could bring danger to my doorstep. And I was allowing that danger to walk beside me, to see my insecurities, my vulnerabilities.

I jumped to my feet, brushing off dirt and twigs, and narrowed my eyes down at her. "Now what?" I snapped. I had trusted her with the deepest parts of myself. Only a fool would think she wouldn't use that against me.

Sighing, she pushed herself up, running a hand over the rough-spun fabric of her dress. The dress I had bought her. Deepest blue, like her eyes. Hemmed in white. Like her hair.

Black seas, I had been a fool.

"Why do you do that?" she asked, tilting her face up to peer at me.

"Do what?" I had been a fool to show her weakness, to show any of them weakness. Talen and Icana might never mention it again, but no one would let me lead them when they discovered how I had reacted to a simple decision like *To Go or Not Go to Xesta*—that I had run again.

Her nose scrunched. Sunlight danced across her freckles like sparks on ocean waves. "Pretend like it is everyone else's fault when they see you act human."

"Do you think I didn't cry when your father cut out their hearts?" The raging, horrific screams echoed in my mind, as fresh as if they had happened yesterday. Blood splattered my vision. "Crying didn't stop him from killing them. Crying didn't stop him from turning on me. My tears didn't earn me any sympathy from him. So, yes, it *is* everyone else's fault because this world doesn't take pity on crying children—it tramples them."

I spun away before her face could crumple under the realization that horrors followed me everywhere. It wasn't my responsibility to ease her into this world. It wasn't my responsibility to be gentle for the sake of her fragile reality. This was my reality, and she would have to learn the horrors firsthand. Just as I had to. And there was only one way for someone like me to face it—with an army and a lot of courage.

I stomped over vines and crushed flowers beneath my boots. This defiant space of tousled green amid the tough stone and parched dust disappeared behind me like a bad dream as I found my way back through the packed alleys.

Talen, Icana, and Alekey had moved off the road, laying in the crisp wildflower field to the side.

My weapons master raised her arm to shield her eyes from the unrelenting sun as I approached. "Verdict?" she asked.

They wanted me to make a decision. So I would.

"I need an army."

Massive gates set in an enormous stone wall greeted us at the entrance to Xesta. Even from a distance, all I could see above the walls were the very tops of the tallest spires spearing the sky.

Two winding lines stretched half a league over the paved road leading to the gates, one occupied by laden wagons and travelling wares, the other comprised of families and groups of people clamouring for a glimpse of the castle. We joined the second line, passing through with little commentary in a matter of minutes, while the other line hardly moved as guards scoured each and every wagon, cart, and barge.

The kingdom was a bustling network of merchants—peddlers, callers, fishers, and butchers lined the main thoroughfare to hawk their goods. A green space curated with local and foreign plant life filled a wide circle directly in front of the gates, cordoned off by thick rope, forcing everyone to go left or right to meet up again on the other side.

A gasp whooshed out of the princess' mouth at the sight waiting for us at the end of the road—Xesta's crown jewel, King Ovono's castle, a series of spindly spires and towering turrets jutting above the city. Gold gilded every window, every ledge, every roof, sparkling like the brightest crown beneath the afternoon sun. A familiar thrill rushed through me at the sight—the childlike awe that painted the princess' face was the same expression I wore when I first saw Xesta, nearly ten years ago. It was a feeling that never went away, no matter how much time or distance separated us.

I felt it now, a deep tug in my chest that pulled me forward to see everything I could see, to hear everything I could hear, to taste everything I could taste. Xesta felt like a second home. A breath of relief washed through my bones at the familiarity. This place existed outside of everything else. There was no war here. No suffering, no mourning. Only the exuberant, infectious glee of children running from one shop to another, clapping as horses trotted by, squealing with delight when the confectioner offered free treats. Everything was bright and colourful and happy.

And yet, horrors followed me everywhere I went.

We were passing a board tucked into an alcove between two buildings when the princess stopped to stare at it. Brightly coloured posters announced different fairs or circuses or events for the next month.

I paid it no mind, running through the list of things I wanted to ask King Ovono, until the princess spoke up.

"Evhen."

The rest of us turned as one. I immediately saw what the princess was looking at, and my stomach lurched into knots.

An accurate and incredibly detailed portrait of the princess, painted in striking colours, stared at us from the centre of the board. We crowded around the sign, already conspicuous, but there was no denying that it was the princess we were looking at. They even painted her freckles with stunning accuracy.

By order of Chief Mikala Maristela of Marama, and under threat of the royal armada of the Full Moon and Crossbones, anyone with information about the location of Princess Kalei Maristela must report immediately to

The words swam in my vision. Beneath the notice, a reward in gold for information glared at me. My mouth went dry.

"My father's looking for me," the princess in question said, her voice as small as I had ever heard it. She tilted her head back to look up at me, fear standing out in sharp relief in every freckle. Beneath the dirt and grim and lacklustre in her short braid, she hardly looked like the girl in the poster, but there was no denying the fear in her sapphire eyes. "He wants me dead, Evhen."

She truly believed it. Whatever legend or myth or fable she'd read, she believed it. But this time, she wasn't looking at me like I had all the answers. She was looking at me with the fear of someone who had believed one thing her whole life, only to find out it had been a lie, and the very people she trusted the most had been the ones lying to her.

"I'm scared," she whispered, eyes shimmering.

Panic spiked through me when her shoulders trembled. *Shit*. I didn't know how to comfort anyone when they were sad, much less when they were scared, much less when they were terrified about being recognized in a world that wanted them dead. Even Icana, who had helped her through her cycle's pain, seemed to not know what to do.

"Find a cloak to cover her hair," I said to Talen as I grabbed the princess, pulling her into the narrow shadows behind the sign. She hid her eyes, trying to stem the tears, but when I pulled her hands from her face, her palms were wet.

"I'm scared," she repeated.

"I know," I murmured. My fingers caught knots in my hair and snagged on jagged bits of skin on my lips. I sighed through my nose. "I know you're scared. I am too. I've already been attacked twice by people your father sent."

Her face scrunched again, trying to figure out when the second time was.

I forged on quickly. "You were right. I don't like people seeing me as weak or incapable. I thought I would have to prove my capability to lead my people by killing someone, but maybe that's not it. If I had killed you when I had the chance, your father would have decimated Vodaeard. As it is, I hope he hasn't done that yet, but I know I'm no match for him. I'm a kid, Kalei. I'm a fucking scared child. Just like you. Maybe we were never supposed to be in this position, but we can do something about it now."

"How?" she asked, eyes wide, boring straight into my soul.

"Do you love your father?"

"Yes," she said quickly, earnestly, and then frowned.

"Even if he wants to kill you?"

"I don't know," she admitted. "I want to, but—"

"Well, I hate the man. And I'd rather him die than...what was it you said...have him become immortal?" Black seas, thinking about the implications of those two monarchs being immortal—it made me dizzy. "The war doesn't end with your death. It only gets worse."

Understanding dawned in her eyes and cast shadows across her face. This was bigger than either of us had realized, but we were the only two who could do anything about it. Suddenly, it wasn't my duty to decide the fate of the entire world. That heavy weight rested on her shoulders, and she seemed to sag under it. But she had to be strong.

The only thing I was responsible for now was keeping her alive. Because if I died, she would, leaving the world to her parents' cruelty.

We couldn't fail the entire world.

"I don't want to die, Evhen," she said.

My name on her lips was soft and sweet.

Even though I wanted to hear her say it again, I pushed all distracting thoughts from my mind and twined my fingers through hers, squeezing with what I hoped was reassurance. "Me neither."

She nodded, a quick jerk of her chin. "Let's not die together."

Talen had already returned by the time we emerged from behind the sign. He held out a lavender cloak with a drooping hood for the princess.

She flung it over her shoulders, drawing the hood over her white hair. The hem hitched off the ground, leaving her bare feet visible, but it covered the braided thicket down her back.

I was suddenly glad she had let Icana braid it—how tightly coiled it was that it didn't even touch the ground.

"Keep your head down and the hood up," I told her as we made our way up the street towards the castle.

The crowds thinned by the moat surrounding the fortress, but a few families huddled together to have their portraits painted in front of the towering citadel by overcharging amateur artists. A circular courtyard opened up in front of the castle, roads branching off in all directions around the city's massive centrepiece. A white tree stood proudly in the middle of the courtyard, sentry, sentinel, and solitary. I pulled the princess along before she stopped to gawk.

Two guards stood at the edge of the footbridge, helmets glinting in the afternoon sun, spears towering over our heads. More lined the bridge and stood by the castle's grand doors on the other side.

"State your business," one of them said. His gaze burned suspiciously, lingering too long on the princess beside me.

I squared my shoulders. Sweat beaded in my hands and rolled down my back. It was a wonder we had passed through the city gate without anyone recognizing the princess, despite her wanted poster plastered across the city. We wouldn't get nearly far enough if these guards stared hard enough.

What was I so afraid of?

It was the words that lumped in my throat that burned the most. "I am Princess Evhen Lockes of Vodaeard. My parents are friends to King Ovono." My throat tightened as I realized my mistake. "*Were* friends…"

"We heard about the attack in Vodaeard," the other guard said. "They're dead, then?"

My vision tunnelled. The distant, but all too close memory of metal flashing through flesh rang in my ears. "Killed in the war."

The princess tensed beside me, but I hardly heard another word as the guards offered their condolences and bowed.

My nails bit into my palms, hard enough to draw blood.

When they straightened, they said something else that Talen answered. Then the first one led us over the bridge.

A ringing like a swarm of bees trilled in my head as we crossed beneath the gilded lintel. The words had been a lot harder to say than I expected.

A warm breeze wafted out of the castle as we stepped into the grand entrance. Light bounced off the walls. Gold gilded every possible railing and door frame. Even the hanging portrait frames had hammered gold plates.

Strolling through the halls reminded me too much of home.

As children, Alekey and I would play on the staircases at home, sliding down on blankets or sleds, riding down the railings. We even swung from the chandeliers, but only once, always getting underfoot and inconveniencing the servants. We didn't have many to start with, and the handful we did dwindled as we got older and become more independent, but I always remembered the halls being lively and cheerful. Courtesans and nobility were often invited to grand parties before the war got so bad. When the kingdoms around us were pulled into the war first, the halls emptied, the servants left, and the cheer diminished. But home was always a warm place, wide and open, my parents always there to lend a hand to our neighbouring kingdoms.

Eventually, it had gotten them killed.

This castle bustled with activity, people moving to and fro on the stairs and through doors, ducking into hidden passages as they passed. It was as my home should have remained. I missed those days bitterly. I missed my parents bitterly.

The guard told us to wait a moment, but I barely heard him before he disappeared down a hallway straight ahead.

I was still trying to catch my breath, trying to sort through what had happened in the past and what was happening in the present, when Kalei spoke up.

"Are you okay?" she asked.

My consciousness slammed back into me all at once. The room spun around me. I did the only thing I could think to do when my emotions became too much—I shoved a finger between my teeth and chewed the skin until it bled. Tension threatened to unravel me completely. I had a job to do here, and I couldn't do it if I was lost in tears.

"The king will see you, Your Majesty," the guard said upon his return a moment later, bowing again.

"Thank you," I said, wincing at the title. It knocked against my ribs, but it was something I had to get used to. I was a queen.

The guard led us through the back of the castle, past sweeping staircases and grand balconies and vaulted ceilings. Everything glittered in the light of thousands of candles, warm and inviting. Even from outside, the kingdom appeared to be thriving, as though the war had barely touched them here. I knew that wasn't true. The war had touched everyone everywhere. Some just had more resources to fight back.

The guard stopped at the massive double doors to the throne room and my heart lurched into my throat.

The image of Talen whisking me away from the carnage flashed through my mind. It had happened only days ago, but it felt much closer and much further at the same time. I had felt so small in those moments. I looked up at him next to me. Beneath his scruffy beard—seas, how long had we been walking that he was already growing a proper beard?—his face was pale, his chest tight. If my voice of reason was anxious, how would I fare when the doors opened?

The doors ground open, but there was no carnage on the other side. No blood splattered up against the walls or pooled down the aisle or stained the thrones. Only a clean carpet, set between clean pillars, that led to a clean throne. My breath stuttered out of me when my eyes landed on the king at the other end of the hall.

King Ovono rose as I strode forward, Alekey beside me. Talen, Kalei, and Icana trailed a step behind, the princess tucked between the other two as if they were protecting her.

"Queen Evhen," the king said with a booming voice that both rattled and comforted me. "And Prince Alekey! My deepest condolences," he added, sweeping into a bow as he met us at the edge of the carpet. "I am so terribly sorry to hear about your parents' deaths."

My vision blurred again, but I managed a small bow and whispered, "Thank you." A mask of neutrality settled over my features, those jarring memories hidden away once more. I couldn't afford to cry again.

"What brings you to my kingdom amid such turmoil?" he asked. "Of course, I am entirely at your service. You need only ask. Your parents were great friends and even greater allies. I will do anything in my power to assist you in these troubling times."

It was hard to ask for assistance when the cause of these troubling times was standing right next to me, but I forced a gracious smile. "I fear retaliation from Marama. When they attacked, my crew and I fled west in my parents' ship, but now a blockade prevents us from returning home. If you could spare a small fraction of your army to help us cross the border…"

The king turned around with a thoughtful *hmm* and strode back to his throne. He dropped into it with a heavy sigh. "This is troubling news, Your Majesty," he mused. "We have not been wholly unaffected here, despite how happy my people seem. The Marama army is ruthless, no thanks to their hallowed Princess of Death."

A rustle of fabric behind me.

I didn't turn, didn't react, didn't look at the princess.

The king glanced around me, eyes narrowed. "And who's this?"

"Someone we picked up along the way," I said, almost too quickly. I clamped my hands behind my back, nervously picking at the skin out of sight. "She's been affected like the rest of us. Will you help us?" I pressed, bringing his attention back to me. No doubt he had seen the posters in his own kingdom. No doubt he had sanctioned them.

And I wondered, again, why we hadn't been stopped at the gates.

He looked back at me, now disinterested in the tagalong behind me. "More and more refugees have been entering my city. In my opinion, this war has gone on long enough, but it won't end until the girl who can bring the dead back to life is dead herself. No more magic. No more death. No more war."

My mouth ran dry, but all I could do was nod, my heart slamming a painful rhythm against my ribs. Air struggled to fill my lungs. I needed King Ovono on my side. I needed Princess Kalei on my side. And I couldn't have both. "I think," I said slowly, keenly aware of how very still the princess was standing behind me, "the army can be stopped another way."

The king smacked his hand on the arm of his throne. The sound slapped through the room, resounding in my chest. "Bah! Nothing will stop that army. Power like that shouldn't belong to any one person. I'd sooner kill the girl myself than let her parents have more of her wretched magic. There are people looking for her in this city, greedy for gold. Power like that must be snuffed from this world. You of all people should understand that?"

I swallowed and nodded again, unable to form words. Discomfort rolled in my stomach. Is that what I sounded like in the hours after my parents had died? Desperate for revenge and blood? No wonder the princess was scared.

"I'll make a deal with you," the king said, settling back into his throne. "I'll give you a fraction of my army to get past the blockade on the condition you come to me first with any news about the Princess of Death."

Throat dry, I nodded, hoping he couldn't see the terror in my eyes. He grinned at me.

It was a leering smile that sent shivers down my spine. This wasn't the kind man I remembered from my childhood. He had been twisted into something vile, as we all had, by this war.

"Now, Queen Evhen, please do me the honour of allowing me to host a party in your name, as a celebration of your coronation."

FIFTEEN

As soon as the doors to my private quarters closed behind me, I clawed at the cloak as if it was suffocating me, scratching until the fabric tore beneath my nails. I slipped it over my head and tossed it in the corner, gasping for air that wasn't enough to replace the panic in my lungs. The king who wanted me dead was hosting us in his own castle, even after the captain—queen—denied and refused and politely turned down his offer..

My chest heaved as I lurched towards the attached bathing room. The room spun around me and my hip rapped against the stone basin. Hands trembling, I fumbled with the tap, yelping when steaming water spouted out instead of cold.

Suddenly hands were dragging me away from the basin, and I crashed to the tiled floor amid a tangle of limbs, swatting aimlessly

"Get off, get off, get off!" I cried.

Evhen's face swam in front of mine, and I reared back, smacking my hand across her cheek.

She froze.

I froze.

The usual anger didn't come. The anger that I expected, the anger that defined her. It didn't come in a verbal or physical lashing. Red splotched over her pale cheek, but she didn't move to strike back.

"Ow," she said instead, and the most ridiculous thing happened then. I laughed.

A panicked, nervous burst of laughter that sounded more like it came out of my nose and stung as badly. She stared at me incredulously as I wheezed, clutching my stomach when a painful stitch formed between my ribs. Tears rolled down my face and manic giggles bounced off the tile. Each echo sent me into another tizzy.

She disentangled herself from me, watching my panic spiral into something hysterical. "Why are you laughing?" she finally asked, eyes wide, as if I had well and truly lost my mind.

Perhaps I had. Perhaps none of this was real. The last few days and weeks were just one horrible nightmare, and I was going to wake up in my bedchamber to the smell of coconut in my coffee and see my lighthouse in the distance and perform another Resurrection.

Thinking about the Resurrection, and everything I had heard my father say in the infirmary, quickly sobered me. Between gasps, I stared at my trembling hands in my lap, the familiar curve of many scars, the slender joints that held so much power. Nothing about this was funny. Nothing about anything was funny.

"Are you all right?" Evhen asked carefully, peering at me like I was a bowstring pulled too taut, ready to snap.

"No, I am not all right," I said, waving a hand through the air between us. My shoulders shook. "The king wants me dead, you want me dead, my father wants me dead. Is there anyone in this world who doesn't want me dead?"

The king hadn't recognized me even though I stood mere feet from him. Would have said all those things if he had known? Would he have seen me as a child or a monster? Or would he have cut out my heart when Evhen had hesitated? Something in his voice made me think he wasn't the type of person to hesitate.

"That's three people," Evhen said lightly, but she didn't deny she was one of those three. "There are millions of people on this continent alone. Billions more in the world. I'm sure they don't all want you dead."

Was she trying to comfort me? It wasn't working. Maybe I did deserve to die for all the pain I had inadvertently caused. But how was I supposed to know the people I brought back to life aided a war I hadn't known about? A war my father waged in his search for immortality? Another hysterical laugh bubbled up inside of me.

Evhen grabbed my fingers before it unravelled me completely. Warmth jolted through my cold hands at her touch, and she squeezed, rubbing her calloused fingers over the raised scars on my wrists. "Tell me about these," she said.

A distraction. She was trying to distract me.

But Resurrections were the one thing I understood for certain. That was my domain. Even my parents couldn't venture across the realms. No one else could explain or experience the comfort I felt diving into the depths and fulfilling my scared duty.

"Every month on the full moon, I cross into the dark depths, to Death's shores, where I retrieve the souls of the dead and guide them back to their bodies." This was familiar. This was right. As if from outside my body, I noticed my breathing came easier and my heart slowed again to its normal rhythm. "The stone guides me into the depths and guides me out again. The light of the full moon shows the path to me. Its energy gives me the strength I need." A small smile touched my lips as I recounted my journeys. "The souls look like glowing seaweed. I catch them in my net or on my hook. I give life. I do not take it."

A whimper finally broke my voice. "I never knew my gift was being used for violence."

My parents had lied to me about everything, but especially about my power and the reason I dived into the depths every month. I had trusted them—had let myself believe they were doing the right thing.

"I thought I could be brave," I said, dropping my gaze to watch her fingers draw circles on the back of my hands. "I thought I could be brave and fearless like you or just and kind like my father—or cold and distant like my mother. But I'm not any of those things."

She snorted, her hands stilling. "I'm not brave," she said. "I just act like I am. It's gotten me into a lot of trouble. But you don't have to be any of those things. Just be…you."

"I don't know who that is," I whispered.

Her finger caught my chin and lifted my head up. "I think you said it. You give life. You don't take it."

I swallowed. Everywhere her fingers touched, my skin burned. I was used to the cold, but this heat wasn't entirely unpleasant. "What does that make me?"

The warm shade of her eyes softened. "A very good person."

I scoffed and pulled free from her. "You heard the king. Power like mine doesn't belong to any one person. I can't be good if my power hurts more people than it helps." Frustrated, I pushed myself to my feet, smoothing out the crinkles in my dress.

"Then change it." She bounded to her feet in front of me. "You've seen how people treat you before they know you, and all that's based on what your father's done to this continent. Not what you've done to stop it. You can choose to do something about it. Death doesn't have to be the end."

This whole time, as much as I didn't want to acknowledge it, I had thought death waited for me one way or another—by the princess' hand or my father's. But that very princess was offering me another way. A way to survive. To live. To help and heal what I had broken. These people might hate me for the part I played in breaking this world, but I didn't have to let their hatred govern my actions. She was right. I didn't have to let my fear govern my actions. I didn't have to let my parents govern my actions.

I met her gaze. "How?"

She crossed from the bathing room into the bedchamber and picked up my discarded cloak. "We keep your identity hidden. We go to this seas-forsaken party to keep King Ovono on our side. We take his army across the mountains. And then we end this."

"By killing my father." That was the only way this ended.

She didn't say anything, gaze heavy on my shoulders. It was as though she was placing a very heavy crown of responsibility on my head. But she was still giving me the choice to accept it or not.

"I love my father," I told her, trying to find the right words to express how I felt—like I was being torn in two and stitched together in all the wrong places. "More than anything else in this world. The man who attacked your parents is not the father I knew. He was kind and gentle, but I'll never forget the way his voice sounded when he talked about…" I choked on the words, the memory, his detached voice so unlike anything I had ever heard before.

A cloud passed over Evhen's face as she fought the memories rising within her.

I swallowed the burning lump of shame. "He wants this more than anything else in this world. And I can't let him have it. I told you I will do anything to help you if it means he doesn't get it."

The memory of that cold night on the dock flashed in my mind again, rain-splattered and lightning-shattered. I had looked up into the face of the one person who had ever held my life in their hands, and I hadn't seen hatred. I hadn't seen anything except a broken shell of a girl who had lost so much and grieved so long. That was why and when I offered to help her, long before I knew she was the princess, long before I even knew she wasn't going to kill me.

I wanted to be the person who broke down her walls. I wanted to be the person to help her.

"All right," she said. She made a face. "I hate parties."

The next evening, Evhen, Icana, and I were gathered in my room amid a scattered disarray of colours and fabrics across every available surface. Jewels glittered on strings and bands and hooks between the assortment of clothes. Outside the window, the sky was pink and red from the setting sun.

Icana had sat me in the chair by the vanity while Evhen stood in front of us, commanding and commenting and controlling what went in my hair. The poster with my face on it had been painted with the brightest strokes of silver for my hair, the clearest chips of sapphire for my eyes, and the deepest touches of black for my freckles. It was a wonder we hadn't been recognized immediately and an alarm hadn't gone through the city—the lost princess had been found! Someone contact her father!

All that gold and no one made a sound.

Evhen had been the one to suggest a veil to cover my hair. The maids and seamstresses didn't question her strange request, and the queen had met them at the door, grabbing their bundles through the barest crack and refusing to let them enter. Now she held up an opaque purple silk veil hemmed with hundreds of pearls.

"Oh, I like that one," I breathed, reaching for the fabric.

Hissing, Icana yanked me back against the chair with a sharp tug on my hair.

"Careful!" I exclaimed. She resumed her braiding without a sound. "My hair is considered sacred where I'm from."

"And now it's the one thing that will get us killed," Evhen said, folding the veil over her arm. "What about this one?" She held up a gold veil, gauzy lace threaded through with topaz beads. Her nose turned up at it, and she shook her head, not realizing just how closely the colours resembled her eyes.

"Purple," Icana said, fingers deftly moving through my hair and pinning it in a thousand different places. No one had touched my hair in years, not since I was old enough to maintain it myself, but Icana's fingers gently scraping my skull felt like something I hadn't known I missed.

I preferred to keep my hair loose, and people simply moved out of the way. It would dishonour the moon to step on my strands, but it was easier to let it trail behind me than braid it anew every day.

Evhen surveyed the three outfits we had finally settled on. Hers was shimmering gold. The fabric fell in glistening waves from thin straps. She hadn't tried it on yet, but my stomach was already flipping at the thought of so much skin exposed.

Icana's slate-grey outfit was an overcoat with a tail that resembled a gown skirt, open wide at the front to reveal tapered pants. Her shoes had the highest heels I had ever seen, as sharp as daggers.

My dress was midnight black for the new moon. Any other time, I would have requested white to honour the moon, as I did in all things. But the moon was dark tonight—it pained me to think I had already been away for two weeks—so I had chosen a rustling gown of deepest black, tulle over silk, thousands of tiny gems embedded in the folds that sparkled like a clear starry night sky with the smallest movements.

Evhen disappeared into the bathing room with her dress. Through the locked door, she called, "You'll have to wear shoes tonight."

I made a face at the assortment of shoes and slippers. Icana stuck a final pin into my hair and turned me around to face the mirror, and I forgot all about them.

I had never seen my face without wind-caught strands of white surrounding it, but now all the pieces had been drawn back, pinned in an elegant braid that fell only midway down my back. Somehow, Icana had woven strands into something resembling a crown at the top of my head, and even though it was going to be hidden beneath a veil, I admired her handiwork.

I raised a hand to touch the intricate design, but she swatted my fingers away with a stern look. "Do you want to come live in the palace and do my hair every—"

"No," she said without blinking. She tilted her chin towards the shoes. "Wear something tall. It makes your legs look better."

I whirled to face her. "No one is going to see my legs!" I exclaimed, heat searing my cheeks.

"They won't be covered for long once she sees you." Icana winked, and my stomach plummeted at what she was suggesting.

Before I could say anything, my cheeks hotter than ever, the door to the bathing room opened and Evhen stepped out.

The thin gold straps tied at the back of her neck, the strings creating a necklace that wound and wound and wound around her throat, and somehow that was enough to keep the soft material from falling off her body. It clung to her curves like it was meant to fit only her. The back drooped in a waterfall of fabric to her waist, which was cinched with a hidden belt and then cascaded from her hips into the skirt. A slit ran up the side of one leg, revealing much more skin than I ever imagined possible, and it took all the remaining coherent thoughts I had to close my mouth.

Icana whistled, low and long, and the sound startled me out of my head so suddenly I jumped.

Evhen rolled her eyes, padding through a pile of party outfits towards the shoes, rifling through until she found a matching set of gold sandals. With a heel.

I jumped to my feet as she bent over to put them on and snatched up my dress, retreating into the bathing room before Icana could prove me right about the heels. It didn't take long to maneuver the dress over my hair—it was much easier to manage pinned up—and then I stepped into the bedchamber, expecting Icana to occupy the bathing room next.

She had already changed, in front of Evhen, who now sat on the edge of the bed, one leg draped over the other, toes peeking at me from the sandals. I wiggled my bare toes in the carpet, hidden beneath the hem.

Not for long.

The unbidden—but maybe not entirely unwelcome—thought choked me. I turned quickly to Icana, gesturing for the veil as words failed me again.

A knock sounded at the door. The blonde put herself between me and the door, reaching around me to set the veil on my head, careful of the pins, as Evhen answered.

"King Ovono awaits your presence," said the servant on the other side. I peeked around Icana to see him bowing.

I nodded at Evhen. "We'll meet you down there," I said quickly, sticking a foot out by way of explanation. "Shoes."

She nodded at Icana's insistence. As soon as the door shut behind her, and her footsteps faded down the hall, I grabbed Icana's wrists, meeting her keen gaze.

"I want the gold one."

Icana led me towards the ballroom with a crooked arm, earning several curious glances and approving nods. My heart fluttered like a trapped bird in a cage of bones, and I had to forcibly remind myself every few steps that I was not doing this to make an impression on the captain. Princess. Queen. I still didn't know what to call her now, and trying to find the right word sent my mind reeling. I nearly tripped over my own feet, so lost in thought. I had opted for a pair of low-heeled sandals, silver straps wrapped halfway up my legs, but nonetheless stunning.

To every person we passed, Icana flashed her most dazzling, most disarming, and most flirtatious smile. More than one girl swooned, and several boys puffed out their chests. She had already promised a dance to dozens of people by the time we reached the ballroom.

The doors spilled open into the spacious room, a massive chamber with vaulted ceilings decked in gold trim, hundreds of mirrors lining the walls, thousands of crystals glittering in the chandeliers, and more people packed into the space than lived on my island. Floor-to-ceiling shutters at the far end opened to the gardens, full night blanketing the city. Even at a distance, tiny glass orbs with tiny flickering lights were visible, strung between the bushes, over the branches, and around the babbling fountain.

Stars dripped from the ceiling. Real green vines garlanded every banister, every doorframe, every lintel on the way to the ballroom. Gold dusted the floor, caught in gowns and beneath shoes, kicked up into a frenzy amid the stragglers outside the ballroom. Lively chatter filled the air with the intoxicating scent of berry wine and ambrosia. A cool night breeze wafted through the corridors, from the hundreds of flung-open windows, gauzy curtains swaying like many twirling gowns.

We had entered on the second floor, a small balcony draped in pine and jasmine garland, staircases sweeping down to the tiled floor below. The overwhelming scent tickled my nose as I scanned the room. Icana drifted out of my reach to cozy up next to a lithe-bodied girl in blood red. My fingers folded around the banister, watching the sea of bodies sway to the tune of a string quartet in the corner.

Servers darted to and fro between the bodies, nimble on their feet, trays perfectly balanced in their palms, never missing a step. The trays never seemed to empty, though every person present grabbed a goblet or plate.

A flop of dark hair caught my attention at the bottom of the staircase to my right. Alekey turned when he noticed Icana had joined the party. His eyes lit up when he saw me.

Relief washed over me at the sight of someone familiar. Someone who didn't want to kill me. I moved towards the stairs, wishing Icana hadn't left so quickly in case I fell over, gripping the railing so hard my knuckles turned bone white. The comparison seemed appropriate.

I put one foot on the top step, raising my eyes briefly to smile at Alekey, but shimmering gold in the distance behind him snagged my gaze, and suddenly I couldn't breathe.

Evhen stood on a dais at the end of the room—next to the king, a place of honour for the guest of honour. But she was staring at me as though she had never seen me before.

Air fought its way into my lungs. I had never noticed how red her lips were before, slightly parted as she took in the gold veil, the one that matched her eyes, the one that matched her dress. The heat of her gaze burned me to the core. I felt her eyes rake over every inch of me, and suddenly I knew Icana had been right about the shoes.

Movement blurred next to me. Alekey's lanky frame hovered in my periphery, catching my arm as my next step was decidedly more unsteady than the first.

"Kalei?" he asked and then followed my gaze across the ballroom. "Oh," he said in a small voice, his arm already slipping out of mine.

"No," I gasped, seizing his hand and wobbling where I stood. I forced myself to drop my gaze to my feet, to every careful step. Alekey led me down the staircase, and I knew I would never make it back up. As soon as we reached the bottom, he pulled away from me like I'd burned him.

"Alekey..."

He shook his head, dark hair falling out of its coiffed glaze. "She was wrong, to keep all that from me, but I—" Unable to find the proper words to describe his turmoil, he snatched a goblet from a passing server, downed the red liquid in a single gulp, and disappeared into the sea of people.

Talen moved in front of me, scowling down his nose. His arms folded across his chest and wrinkled his crisp black tunic.

"What?" I said, instinctively reaching up to make sure my hair was hidden. Icana had said she'd hidden its length as best she could with the braid and the mesh lace was woven so tightly together not a single strand peeked through. Still, I felt more bare with my hair hidden than with it on display.

He leaned towards me, lowering his voice to growl in my ear so only I would hear his threat. "That is my captain, my queen, and my friend. If you hurt her heart, I will hurt all of you. Do you understand me?"

My tongue knocked against my teeth, and I nodded, gazing past him towards the dais. Some courtier or noble was trying to get Evhen's attention, but her gaze were locked on me, eyes narrowed slightly as Talen straightened. She finally seemed to notice the man in front of her, and the sea of bodies swallowed her up again.

"I need a drink," I muttered, hobbling to the side of the ballroom, where there were fewer bodies.

People milled around the edges, but most occupied the wide open floor, dancing and laughing and forgetting there was a war going on outside these walls. It was hard not to feel like we were in the wrong place, doing the wrong thing.

But the king had thrown this party in Evhen's honour.

157

It would have been rude not to attend. We didn't want to draw any more attention to ourselves, and not showing up to our own party would have thrown too much suspicion on us.

Still, I couldn't shake the feeling of too many eyes on me. I touched the veil again, topaz beads rippling beneath my fingers. What had I been thinking? The gold was a cry for attention. I could have walked in naked without as many people staring at me. But the gold had immediately set me apart, had connected me with the captain and princess—now queen.

My chest tightened with what was becoming a familiar sensation. Before I could scratch at the veil, I plucked up a silver goblet from a server and tossed back the sparkling liquid. It buzzed in my veins and turned everything fuzzy. A silver sheen settled over the ballroom as calmness wrapped around my lungs, easing the panic.

Voices drifted to me through the haze. I spotted a couple nearby, heads bent towards each other.

"A shame what happened to the girl's parents," one said.

I twisted away. That wasn't a memory I wanted to dredge up right now, even if it wasn't mine.

"I heard she ran away like a coward," another voice said. "Pissed her pretty little dress and everything."

"Didn't even stop to mourn them before she took their crowns."

"No one will follow her. I know I wouldn't."

"Look at her. She's distracted. Unfocused. And that dress. Unbecoming for a queen."

I found another drink in a silver goblet and tossed it back before another insult needled its way through the fog in my head. This was despicable. I had never heard people talk so horribly about someone else before, much less a queen. Much less a queen who was standing mere feet away.

"Miss, are you all right?"

A face loomed in front of me, blurry and swimming in my vision. I blinked rapidly.

"Fine," I mumbled. *Was I?* I didn't feel fine. My fingers throbbed, blood pulsing noisily through my veins. I had never heard it pulse like that before. It seemed to push me forward, stumbling through the crowd, a constant buzzing in my ear like angry wasps.

The music became distorted around me. I glanced around the room in jerking sweeps. Something was wrong. Something was wrong, but I didn't know what it was. I didn't see any more silver goblets and… was that the problem?

I shook my head at myself. I'd already had enough to drink. Hadn't I?

I turned around to ask for another silver chalice and locked eyes with my mother. A stunned yelp burst out of my mouth before I realized it wasn't my mother. It was me—my reflection in one of the many mirrors lining the wall. I leaned forward, touching my reflection's eyes. Eyes like my mother. Hair like…hair like…I reached up. Before I could stare longer, a flash of silver sparked in the corner of my eye.

A tray, a silver chalice, and a serving boy with a missing hand darted into a hidden hallway.

I lurched after him, catching the door with my fingertips. With a deep breath, I plunged into darkness.

SIXTEEN

When Kalei walked into the room, I forgot how to breathe. We locked eyes across the empty space, the world falling into muted music and bated breaths as the sea of bodies between us parted. Time halted altogether. The scent of coffee wafted through the room on the ocean breeze she brought with her, tinged with a sweet smell I couldn't place. Maybe the *coconut* she had mentioned? It tickled my nose, warmed my belly, and suddenly I understood all the stories Mama used to tell us as children.

I had dismissed those stories as easily as I had dismissed the princess' legends, but maybe there was some truth in them after all. A thread connected us, and not because she had chosen the gold veil. We were tied together amid this storming sea of happiness, of joy, of celebration, of commiseration, and it was all wrong.

But it felt right looking at her. She was like a breath of fresh air, a cool salt breeze instead of the tang of fish that permeated every port city on this continent. She was a cascading nightfall of silver stars as she descended the staircase with one hand gripping Alekey's arm, the other clutched around the banister.

This was all wrong. Still, I couldn't look away. Not when voices buzzed in my ear. Not when faces surged in front of me. Not when Alekey darted away from the princess as if he had been burned by the heat of my gaze.

Then Talen leaned down to whisper something in her ear, and the spell broke.

I was suddenly aware of my panting breaths and sweating palms, the overlapping conversations and swaying bodies, the too-loud music and too-cheerful melody. An unfamiliar sensation coiled in the pit of my stomach, burning my cheeks. I finally looked away when my father's advisor—now mine—straightened, jerked back to reality by one of King Ovono's many noblemen introducing himself to me at the base of the dais, offering his condolences, muttering things I couldn't hear over the din and rushing of blood in my ears.

I gave him my best impression of a grateful smile, thanked him, and turned to King Ovono beside me. He had kindly requested I join him on the dais for the beginning of the evening as the guest of honour, though I wondered why Alekey hadn't been asked as well.

I had already lost my brother in the crowd, but perhaps it was a good thing he wasn't here. He would have been too miserable to do anything other than pout. In standing here without him, I could at least spare him the constant stream of condolences, though my palms were burning from where I'd clenched my fists so tight blood was beginning to scratch my skin.

"I am amazed your servants had all this prepared under such short notice," I remarked to the king.

This was how court life went, as far as I was concerned. Meaningless conversations under the guise of true interest while everyone else talked about you behind your back. Their judging eyes bored into me from every direction. I could almost hear their whispers, the mocking and downright awful alike.

"A thousand servants with two thousand hands working three thousand jobs," he said proudly, surveying the room with the watchful eye of someone who expected trouble. A chill snaked down my bare spine. "That girl you arrived with. What's her name?"

His hawk-like eyes finally landed on me. A curious glint sparked in their depths, as if he had finally found the trouble he expected.

"Rindi," I said, picking the first Vodaeardean-sounding name that came to mind. "Why?"

161

An innocent shrug of his shoulders. "A king ought to greet his guests by name. I apologize for singling you and Prince Alekey out from your friends. Talen and Icana, correct?"

I nodded slowly, still trying to piece together what he was attempting to glean from me. Talen had been my father's advisor—he had visited Xesta more often than I had in the last few years, so it made sense for King Ovono to know his name. But Icana was only my weapons master, and she wasn't even from Vodaeard. Where had he learned her name?

And why did it matter?

"I was simply so upset at the news of your parents that I forgot decorum completely when you arrived," he explained, returning his attention to the room at large. "Your arrival surprised me, to say the least, Princess Evhen."

A ringing trilled in my ears at the title. He had been so quick to call me "Queen Evhen" earlier. The sudden lack of respect sent warning bells clanging through my head. I scanned the room for the princess, but I had already lost her. Somehow, a glittering gold headpiece was easier to lose than gleaming white hair. The ringing pitched louder.

"If I had known our predicament," I murmured, folding my hands in front of myself, "I would have sent a message sooner."

"Of course," he said. His massive presence beside me sent more shivers down my spine, but I forced myself to remain still. "I can't imagine the stress you're under. It must be difficult, bearing the weight of an entire kingdom at such a young age."

Every eye in the room needled into my chest, though not a single person was watching me. They swayed as gently as ocean waves, mesmerizing, sickening. This was wrong. We weren't supposed to be here. Hot air pressed against me on all sides, stifling the breath in my lungs. And I could feel King Ovono watching my profile, waiting like a viper in a nest to strike me down.

I looked around once more for the princess, and when I didn't find her, the thrumming beat of the drum threatened to pull me into the panic building in my chest. The room narrowed to a tunnel. I fought my way out of my thoughts with careful breaths, recalling how the princess had calmed me down earlier with the simple rock of her leg against mine. I focused on the heads of the dancers, up and down, side to side, and slowly I found myself again.

That calm place of anger within my heart. The only emotion I knew how to handle well.

A slow smile spread across my face. One as wicked as a blade and just as sharp. "Would you like a drink, Your Majesty?"

My eyes slid to his. Satisfaction rippled through me at the blunt annoyance flitting across his face.

"Enjoy the party, Your Majesty," he said instead, returning to the throne behind me.

Talen appeared at the bottom of the dais a moment later, and I nearly cried out at the sight. I scrambled off the platform as quick as possible, pulling him abruptly onto the dance floor. He snapped his mouth shut. At my warning glance, he swallowed his questions.

Without missing a beat, he slid his arms into position, one hand grabbing mine, the other resting on my hip. He moved with the grace of someone who had grown up in court, who had learned all the dances. It was easy enough to let him lead because, for once, I didn't know what I was doing.

"What's wrong?" he murmured, mouth against the shell of my ear. We were the same height now, our conversation hidden with our heads bent against each other.

"I think the king knows," I whispered. His fingers tightened imperceptibly around mine. "Have you seen Kalei?"

"She went to get a drink a few minutes ago," he answered. We turned in time to the music, but I knew he was using the moment to scan the room. "I don't see her. Or Alekey."

He pulled me closer when a weak sob rattled my chest. Warmth radiated off his body in waves, enveloping me in a smoke-scented embrace.

"Icana?" My voice was barely a whisper.

His chest rumbled as he answered, "In the corner, romancing a rather pretty girl in red."

I let myself fall into the sound, let it push past the panic. "If she's not worried, maybe I'm wrong," I said, spying my weapons master in the corner as we spun around again. Her keen eyes would have seen trouble from leagues away.

As it was, she had her head bent into the crook of a raven-haired girl's neck, a blush of scarlet as deep as her dress painting the girl's cheeks. A number of young boys milled about close by, grumbling to each other about her lack of attention for them.

"May—" Talen drew back with a jerk, a surprised expression drawing lines down his face as he looked at someone behind me.

I turned.

"May I?" A young man with golden hair offered a hand, bowing low at the waist.

I raised an eyebrow at Talen—did I really have to entertain this?—but he politely took a step back and retreated to the side of the room. Stifling my annoyance, I let the boy take my hand.

He pulled me towards him, replacing my advisor's hands with his, gentle despite the gleam in his eyes. "You look stunning, Your Majesty," he said, eyes flicking to my face. "My deepest condolences for your loss."

"Losses," I corrected before I could stop myself. The word stung me, and I shifted my gaze away from his.

"Of course," he said. "I hope you don't find this party too dreadful. It is in your honor, after all."

Surprised, I looked back at him, and he winked secretively.

"We have a party like this at least once a week. It's always the same people, the same food, the same boring conversations. Yes, I heard your dog died. Your child is how old? No, I'm no longer in school. Yes, we've met before. No, I don't remember the last time you visited. Your neighbour said *what* about your cabbages?"

Despite myself—despite the panic threatening to spill all over the dance floor, despite the knowledge that there was a war going on be-

yond these walls, despite the fear clawing at my throat at not knowing where the princess was—I laughed. The tension I felt seizing my
muscles snapped, and we fell into an easy rhythm.

"How many of these parties have you been to?" I asked as we spun
around the dance floor. Dresses rustled around me, shoes clacked in
time to the music, and notes swelled up and down. But, for a brief
moment, I didn't feel suffocated under anyone's scrutiny.

"Only about all of them," he answered, rolling his rich brown eyes.
"I live here," he added like he was telling me a secret, mouth close to
my ear.

I tripped, but he expertly covered my misstep.

"Who are you?" I asked, pulling back as far as I could to search
his face.

A frown tugged his lips. "You don't recognize me?" He stepped
back, broke the dance, and swept into a bow. A familiar bow.

My heart slammed back into my throat as a massive presence
shifted behind me, filling the air with commanding authority.

"Mind if I cut in, son?" King Ovono said behind me.

I stared as the prince rose, barely masking my hostility. He flinched
at the look on my face, but disappointment settled over his features
as he nodded.

"Of course, Father," he said, giving one final short bow. "It was an
honour, Your Majesty."

Honour. What a useless thing from these snakes.

Plastering the best attempt at a smile on my face, I turned to the
king. These political mind games were forming an ache behind my
eyes, but I would be gracious. Cautious, but gracious.

"I didn't think kings danced," I said, waiting for him to close the
distance. I should have seen the resemblance sooner—or at least recognized Prince Osno. *Os.* The years had turned him from the young
boy I remembered into a young man, a near-perfect imitation of a
younger version of his father. Without all the grey hair and worry
lines creasing his face.

"A king should be able to dance with all his subjects, at least once," he replied with a mirthful chuckle. He didn't move, arms hovering in position around an invisible body, as if he expected me to fill that void.

"One of us is going to have to make the first move, Your Majesty," I told him. "And frankly, I don't know how to dance."

It was strange, watching the other couples move around us like raindrops in a hurricane and we were in the eye of it. No one dared to end the dance, but every head was cocked towards us, every eye watching us stand at an impasse. If they weren't talking badly about me before, they would now.

"You seemed to be doing just fine with your advisor." He took a single step forward, and like a thread binding us or a mirror reflecting us, I took a single step forward.

"He was leading."

All too quickly, the music shifted, and the king seized me tightly, pulling me into a rapid dance that left my lungs firmly rooted to where I had been standing. My fingers clutched his shoulders, crushing the velvet vest, as he spun me around. When my breath finally caught up to me again, I found my feet, found the rhythm, and found my dignity again.

"Your son tells me these parties are boring," I said, raising my voice slightly to be heard over the clashing music. It was too fast, too loud.

"Are you bored?"

"Decidedly not." Never in my life had a party simultaneously terrified me, annoyed me, and intrigued me. I was curious to see where the night went, if we continued going on in circles like the dance or if one of us would finally reveal the truth. It was another gamble with another uncertain outcome, so I only prayed to the seas that I could hold on just a little longer.

"I'm glad," he said, spinning me at arm's length and pulling me back against his chest, arm locked around my throat. "I would hate for one of my parties to be considered boring."

Before I could gasp for air, he turned me around and grabbed my waist, and then we were off again in a tireless and tiring route around the room.

"Os is doing well," I said, my chest tight. I couldn't get enough air into my lungs, he was moving me too fast, and every limb shook from exertion. If I didn't pause soon, I was going to collapse. "I didn't recognize him."

"You have not yet found a suitor, have you, Evhen?" His question surprised me so much I tripped, crashing into his chest. He caught me, making it appear all a part of the dance, and brought his face close to mine. "Marry my son," he hissed in my ear. The roar of blood drowned out all other sounds except for his horrible voice. "Join our families and our kingdoms. Or I will expose you as the traitor you are."

Political games. That's all this was. But I had never been good at games, and I certainly didn't have the patience for this one. Swallowing the lump in my throat, I lowered my voice. "Are you threatening me, Your Majesty?"

Threats against *Captain* Evhen were one thing. Threats against *Queen* Evhen were another entirely.

He drew back, flashing a white smile. "Is there a reason for you to feel threatened, Your Majesty? Unless, of course, I'm wrong." He blinked, feigning innocence. I scowled to hide the terror rising like bile. "Her father's men came to the city days ago. Did you truly think she wouldn't be recognized at the gate?"

Understanding pummelled me with a sickening lurch in my stomach. I had been foolish to believe we hadn't been spotted. The king had known from the start who she was. This party was all a ploy.

"But I needn't give you over to them," he continued. "Unless you continue this dangerous game. What will your people think when they hear you've been sleeping around with a girl who is not only your enemy but someone who cannot give your kingdom the heirs it so desperately needs? Your monarchy will fall apart. Your people will turn on you. Vodaeard will cease to exist."

As he spun me out at arm's length again, the music slowed, and time seemed to stretch. I saw the entirety of my kingdom's future spanned before me, a once-great city that had survived outside pressure time and time again, only to crumble into the sea because of my foolish heart.

Vodaeard had once been as large as Xesta, but northern invaders had pushed us to the brink. We survived because my ancestors had made the difficult decisions that had kept us alive—cede the north, lest we be toppled into the sea. We had lost our military and two-thirds of our country in the treaty, but we did not lose our monarchy. My family hadn't survived countless attacks just for me to throw it all away to be with one girl.

Time sped up again, and he pulled me back. I gasped as I hit his chest. "I'll abdicate," I blurted. "Alekey can have the heirs." The people wanted my brother, anyway. It had to be the right decision.

"And where is he?" King Ovono stopped dancing abruptly, causing me to trip not for the first time, and scanned the room. "I want to congratulate him on becoming king so soon."

A beat passed as I caught my breath, and then a horrific scream rent the night air from the direction of the gardens, followed by dozens of shouts by panicked party guests. My blood ran cold as I spun towards the gardens. I knew that scream better than I knew my own. It had filled every nightmare since we left Vodaeard, echoing through the chambers of my restless mind, my most horrible vision made reality.

King Ovono's grip tightened on me.

I fought my way out, clawing and scratching like a feral cat. His fingers left stinging red marks on my arms as I yanked myself free. I scooped up the hem of my dress, pushing through the suddenly still bodies of too many guests, and burst onto the glittering porch. Several guests scampered away from a dark section of the garden. Night air bit into my skin. Glass crunched underfoot. Stars speckled the velvet sky like millions of witnesses to my grief.

A string of broken lights led me around a tall hedge to a statue garden. Blood, ink-black in the dark, smeared the stones. A trail of it—oh seas, there was so much of it—spilled over the steps of a white gazebo in the centre of the courtyard. I scrambled up the steps, collapsing into a pool of Alekey's blood next to his seizing body, screaming for someone, *anyone*, to help. My fingers caught his as he gurgled around a mouthful of blood.

"Help!" I screamed again, my throat raw. A crowd formed behind me, murmuring to each other, but no one moved to help. As though this was merely their nightly entertainment.

A figure in black and gold slipped out of the shadows on the other side of the gazebo, dropping to her knees next to me in a puddle of blood. White hair streamed from Kalei's braid. It spread in rippling waves around us, but the dark thoughts swirling in my mind were more like a violent ocean than a gentle stream.

"I can heal him," Kalei said between gasps. Through my tears, I looked at her face, biting down the single question I wanted to ask when I noticed red rimming her eyes and marks marring her arms. Had she been attacked? I didn't have time to ask as Alekey jerked beneath me, blood spurting from his mouth.

"I can heal him," Kalei said again, as Icana and Talen emerged from the crowd, guarding the entrance to the gazebo.

"He's not dead!" I shouted, clamping my hand over the wound in his chest. It was too deep, too wide. The blood kept flowing.

"I don't just bring the dead back to life," she said quickly. "I'm a healer. I can heal him. Let me *heal* him, Evhen!"

My name on her lips shocked through me, and I fell back, nodding.

"I need my necklace," she said, too calmly. She was too calm. This wasn't going to work.

Icana tore the stone from her wrist—the princess didn't question why I had let the weapons master carry it—and tossed it towards us.

She caught it with a sigh of relief, clutching it to her chest as if she had been drowning and the stone had carried her to the surface.

"Knife," she said. When no one moved to hand her one, she turned wild eyes to me. "Evhen, you can do the honours, but I can only heal this wound with my blood. Give me a knife now!"

Icana tossed her shoe, the heel as sharp as any dagger.

Kalei instructed me where to cut her forearm, from elbow to wrist. She barely winced as the needle-like heel broke skin. Blood welled up along the cut in ruby-red dots that swiftly turned into a stream. She shoved me aside and leaned over Alekey, angling her arm over him, whispering words that I had to lean closer to hear: "Open the door, and walk the shore…"

The stone in her other hand began to pulse, short bursts of light that I quickly realized beat in time with her heart. Her blood spilled over Alekey as she trailed her arm up and down, head to toe, the moonstone glowing the entire time.

Its light only began to flicker when she swayed. She squeezed her palm, easing more drops from her veins. Alekey was deathly still beneath her.

I held my breath until I couldn't breathe anymore. This wasn't going to work.

Kalei's arm dropped, and she pitched sideways, smacking her head on the blood-stained boards.

"Kal—!" I reached for her when Alekey suddenly sucked in a shuddering breath. I screamed—in fear, anger, relief, but mostly joy—and flung my arms around his neck, forgetting where we were and who surrounded us.

A low groan escaped him.

I pulled back, the front of my dress covered in his blood.

The wound stitched together beneath the gore and torn fabric. His eyes fluttered open, droplets of blood caught in his eyelashes, spattered over his face, matting his hair to his forehead.

"Key," I murmured, tears streaming through the blood on my own face as I brushed his dark locks from his face. It only smeared the blood more. There was so much of it.

Feet pounded the gazebo stairs. Guards rushed towards the princess' limp body and hauled her up.

"Don't touch her!" I yelled, scrambling towards her, blood slick beneath me.

One of the guards bashed the blunt end of his weapon into my face. Blood burst in my mouth as I hit the ground.

Dazed, I peered through soaked strands of hair as more guards hefted Alekey between them, being significantly more gentle with the prince than they were with the princess. They took him away, back up the path towards the castle, passing through a maze of alarmed guests.

Boots squelched in the blood in front of me. There was so much of it. How could anyone survive that? It reminded me of another grizzly blood-splattered scene, and another king looking at me like I was a pathetic child, and a whimper bubbled out of me before I could stop it.

"Let me help you up, Your Majesty," King Ovono said, grabbing my arm before I could refuse.

I cried out as he hauled me to my feet, the wound in my shoulder splitting open again. His physicians had done the best they could to stitch it only hours earlier. Now it felt as raw and fresh as ever as he pulled me down the gazebo steps.

"I warned you what would happen if you brought that girl here," he growled in my ear.

Guests politely turned away as we passed, as though I was a child being scolded by its parent, not a queen drenched in blood.

My stomach roiled. "Let me go," I begged through gritted teeth, though I had nowhere to go.

Worse still, Talen and Icana had gone missing in the few minutes I had been focused on Alekey.

I didn't want to imagine them locked away in a rotting dungeon beneath this magnificent city, but the picture came unbidden anyway. A sob broke out of me. This was supposed to have been my chance to be a leader everyone looked up to. Someone who made the right choices for the right reasons. Someone who made the hard decisions when everyone expected the easy ones. I needed an army to help me cross the border into my own country, but I wasn't even sure I would make it to see tomorrow.

Seas, I had screwed up.

And now everyone I loved was dead, dying, or missing.

The king dragged me through the gilded halls to a section of the castle cordoned off from the rest, heavy oak doors surrounded by guards with towering spears. The doors opened as we approached—I glimpsed shadows beyond, dark shapes filling the void—and he turned me to face him. My foot twisted on one of the seas-awful heels.

"If you want an army—if you want Vodaeard to thrive again," he said, sealing my fate with the weight of his words, "you will marry my son." He shoved me into the dark room.

I slipped on the hem of my dress, tumbling to the ground in a soft heap of fabric, a bone in my wrist snapping beneath me.

"Don't you want to have a father again?" he mocked, no trace of his earlier—and fake—kindness in his voice.

Screaming, I lurched to my feet and threw myself against the doors as he pulled them shut. A bolt slammed into the lock. The sound ricocheted through my chest, a finality that sent another wave of panic washing over me, but I still bashed my fists bloody against the door, screaming obscenities until my throat was raw.

When I could no longer make a sound, I collapsed against the door, sank to the ground, and let the panic pull me under.

SEVENTEEN

Bile burned my throat when I woke. A searing pain throbbed in my right palm and a burning heat ran the length of my left arm. Agony shot up into my chest when I lurched to the side. Nothing came out of my mouth except a retching sob. The taste of blood lingered on my togue.

"You're all right," a voice whispered somewhere beside me. I couldn't tell the direction. Everything was spinning in my head.

When the sickness passed, I raised my right arm—or tried to. Metal clanged against metal. My eyes flew open, spotting three things in quick succession: first was the manacle clamped over my wrist, second was the captain slumped in a chair, and third was the darkness shrouding everything else in the room. The spinning sensation didn't stop, even when Evhen raised her head from her hands. The dried blood blackening her face and red splotches rimming her eyes only made me dizzier.

My eyes snapped shut. Memories flooded back all at once, filling my head where only moments ago there had been nothing but confusion.

"Alekey," I croaked.

"Alive," Evhen said, voice rough and strained. She sat forward and, without a word, help up a cup of water to my lips. I downed the contents greedily, nausea rolling in my stomach.

Evhen set the cup back down, scrubbing at her eyes. She looked as though she hadn't slept in days, her skin paler than usual, gaunt and sunken. "At least, I think he's alive. He was the last time I saw him..." She trailed off, as if afraid of finishing the thought.

My stomach twisted. I pushed myself up, wincing as the iron shackle bit into my tender skin. "When was that? What happened?"

She raised her head, eyebrow arched. "Don't you want to know about that?" Her chin jutted towards the shackle.

"No," I immediately answered. "Well, yes," I amended, "but I want to know what happened to you first."

"Where do I start?" Her voice pitched high, too close to the type of mania that had unravelled me on the bathing room floor days ago. Tears spilled over, running red through the blood on her cheeks.

Before she could start, I snatched her wrist with my free hand, turning her hand over. Cracked nails and bloody fingertips.

She scoffed. "I tried to get that thing off you."

"Come here," I said, crossing my legs and guiding her to the bed. Someone had replaced my gown with a thin white shift, but Evhen still wore her dress, covered in blood stains. It appeared as though no one had bothered to give us a wash basin. Even her bare leg, visible through the long slit, was covered in dried, brown blood. Scratch marks tracked through the stains where she had presumably tried to claw it off like a scab.

With her sitting opposite me, I felt more exposed than I had in a long time. Recent memories aside from Alekey's gouged body were a blur. When I tried to snag a memory of the party, it slipped like water through fingers, leaving only the unpleasant grit.

I motioned for my necklace. The shackle let me move my hand only so far as the edge of the bed, but I turned my palm over on the drenched sheets. She carefully placed the stone on my burning skin. I didn't fail to notice her gaze froze on the stone-shaped indent in my hand. It was the first time I was noticing it too, but I tried not to think about it as I plucked a strand of hair from my head.

"When were you going to tell me you could do that?" Her eyes traced my movements as I wound the strand over her fingers.

Power kindled in my chest with the familiar words, but when the stone pulsed, it seared my hand. The scent of burning flesh filled the air, and I bit my tongue, groaning.

Alarmed, she jerked back, but her fingers were already healing.

"It's fine," I said through gritted teeth. I tore another strand free and pushed it into her shoulder when she began to protest. She grunted, teeth grinding over each other, face twisted in pain as the wound stitched itself back together. Pieces of broken flesh folded over themselves. The resulting scab, which would heal over in a few days, looked less like a gaping hole and more like a blossoming flower, a sunburst on her shoulder. She blew out a breath, ruffling the messy strands around my face.

The stone tumbled from my grip, bouncing several times across the floor. "I meant to tell you," I said with unsteady breaths, "when I shot you. But then Talen broke my jaw."

She gave me a weak laugh. "I should thank you for saving Alekey's life, though I suppose it doesn't matter." Defeat coloured her voice. "They won't tell me how he's doing. And they won't tell me where Talen and Icana are, either."

Our fingers wove together on the bed. For the first time, I noticed the jagged, crusty cut on my forearm. Her eyes locked on it as well.

"You can't heal yourself, can you?"

"No." Still-drying blood oozed out when I flexed my fingers. A wound like that wouldn't heal overnight. "How long has it been?"

Her voice ground flatly over the words. "Five days."

My stomach lurched as if her words were a physical punch and a wince shuddered through me. Every part of me felt sharp, fragile, as if I was likely to break at any moment. "We've been locked up for *five* days?"

Evhen nodded, twisting away from me. "I've been trying to find a way out, but there's…" She shook her head, hiding her face in her hands as sobs wracked her body.

"Evhen," I said, but that was all I said. I didn't know what to tell her. I didn't know how to make this right. I didn't know how to make any of this right. A pressing weight squeezed my heart. Responsibility. I was responsible for the fate of the world, and I had doomed it.

She dug the heels of her hands into her eyes and angled to face me again. "What happened to you?" she asked. "At the party. You disappeared, and I thought..." She didn't elaborate, but a distinct sheen of hurt glazed over her eyes.

Even though the party was a blur in my mind, I could never forget the way she looked at me.

"Talen said you went to get a drink," she added, as if that would loosen something.

And it did, like a quiet jingle of coins. "I went to get a drink," I said slowly, parsing through the fragments. They flashed like slivers of silver and gold. As if through a fog, I followed the memories, the boy through the servant's door. I pinched my eyes shut to bring the images to the forefront. "I followed a servant into a dark corridor."

And that was when the memories twisted...

I had reached for the chalice and tumbled into the stars.

Silver danced in my veins, turning me into the moon, the thing to be worshipped above all else. An invisible breeze caught my hair, lifting it free from the veil, scattering the pins in all directions. Strands rose to the rafters, banding around the boards, noosing around my neck.

A laugh burst out of me, clear and bright, the sound brushing against the stars. They laughed in turn as the moon rose higher. Darkness retreated from its light. *My* light. I spread my arms to cast the net of light wider even as the twisting shadows began to curl up my arms, press against the silver haze in my head, bleeding like moonblood across my vision.

A dark figure stepped out of the shadows below me, a moonpale face appearing between the coils of darkness. My laughter sputtered out as I stared down at my father. Blood drenched him, head to toe, matting his hair, staining his clothes, dripping from his fingers into a rapidly spreading pool at his feet.

Haunted eyes turned up to me.

An explosion rocked the air, and the moon fell.

I landed on the deck of his ship, choking down smoke-filled breaths. Fire licked the sky and the stars blinked out in the shadows of the frenzy. An undead army surged around me, shouts ripping through the night—no, it wasn't night. This attack happened in the early hours of morning.

Day suddenly shifted in the sky. I pushed myself to my feet as the ship shuddered beneath me. Sunlight danced off many armoured soldiers. They ran to and fro, yanking the sails free, turning the ship around as my father called the retreat from the helm.

I twisted to him. Saw a small ship darting between the armada. Caught a glimpse of fiery red hair on the deck.

I blinked, and the *Grey Bard* disappeared in the crashing waves. An explosion knocked me off my feet at the helm. A scream bloodied my throat. My father crashed to the deck next to me, stomach ripped open with shrapnel. He reached for me, cupped my cheek in his palm, smearing sticky blood across my face.

"*Minnow,*" he moaned.

"I'm here," I tried to say, but my mouth wouldn't move, frozen in horror as blood pulsed and pulsed and pulsed from the wound. I leaned over him, plucking a strand of hair from my head. It crumbled to ash in my hand, blowing away in the death-stenched breeze. Another scream tore my throat as he shuddered.

"Why…did you…let them…hurt me?" he asked between gurgles. Beneath my scrabbling fingers, hundreds of stab wounds opened up on his chest. "Why…did you…let them…kill me?"

"I didn't, I didn't, I won't!" My cries were lost in the gale that caught their sails. A black knife appeared clutched in my hands, and I threw myself away from my father's bloodied body, staring at the bloodied blade. The crew stood in a circle around me, glaring accusations burning right through me. I screamed again, shaking my hand, but the blade was fused into my skin, unmoving.

My father loomed over me, gore spilling out of his chest, his still-beating heart thumping wetly between broken ribs. "Why did you kill me?"

He grabbed my arm, twisting the blade towards my chest.

A scream that wasn't mine ripped through the air. I landed hard on the stone floor of the kitchen pantry. My father was nowhere to be seen.

More shouts. I gathered the folds of my dress and ran from the kitchen, into the garden, towards the gazebo, tears streaking my face and red marks searing my arm…

"Have we learned *nothing* from the attack in the tavern about accepting drinks from strangers?" Evhen said when I had recounted those awful memories.

I laughed wearily, scrubbing tears from my cheeks. "I didn't expect to be attacked at a party in your name."

"Neither did I," she grumbled. A heavy sigh shook her shoulders. "I'm sorry you had to go through that," she added, face pinching as if she wasn't quite sure what to say or how to say it. "It must have been awful."

Shame warmed my face. "Don't…don't apologize," I said, though the words were hard to say. "None of it was real. I don't want to think about it."

Her hand came to rest on my knee in one of the most comforting gestures I had ever experienced from her. I wound my fingers through hers again.

"How do we get out of here?" I asked.

"There's no way out," she said. Her fingers curled into mine, pinching with worry. "I've been looking for five days. There aren't even windows. The only time that door opens is once a day to see if you're awake, to give me a single plate of food, and to change the chamber pot."

"When?"

She shook her head. "No," she said, her tone cold. "It won't work. I tried. And you're tied to the bed."

"Evhen, I can't think of anything else," I told her. "If we can get this off, we have to try something." I rattled the cuff.

"And then what?" A distant look clouded her eyes, heavy with defeat. "There are probably thousands of guards between us and freedom. Even if we can make it through the door, we won't make it down the hallway."

A terrifying thought coalesced in my mind. It eased a shiver across my skin. "Why hasn't he killed me yet?"

"What?"

"He said he would kill me himself. So why is waiting until I wake up?"

Even if I hadn't been unconscious, I was no match for the king. I was no match for my own father. I wasn't a weapon-made-human like Icana or anger personified like Evhen.

A thought formed, distant and hazy, until suddenly it wasn't. No, I wasn't any of those things.

I was much worse.

A cold feeling settled in my stomach. "Do you think there's a crypt beneath us?"

"What?" she blurted, red curls flying around her face as she shook her head. "I'd rather not find out. We're supposed to not die together, remember?"

"I know, I know," I said quickly, running my hand up her arm to calm the shakes—hers or mine, that I didn't know. "I have an idea, but I don't know if it'll work."

Her golden eyes narrowed. "I'll take anything over marrying that viper's son."

"What?"

She wagged her head. "Never mind. What were you thinking?"

Pushing aside my confusion, I sucked in a wobbling breath. "When I told you I can only bring people back to life on the full moon, that wasn't quite true. It's true that their souls can only return to flesh and bone on the full moon. But when there is no flesh for a soul to return to, when there is only bone, I can move those bones at any time. I have to be in control of them the entire time, though. Any distraction will break the connection."

"All right," she said slowly, a look of utter disgust twisting her face. I would take that look of disgust over anything else that flashed through my mind.

"If there's a crypt beneath us, I can raise an army of my own."

Understanding blinked across her face in waves, followed quickly by skepticism. "And how do you plan on getting into the crypt?"

Evhen's frantic screams nearly broke my charade. Her fists pounded against the door, sobs choking her as she called for help, screaming that I was dead. I tried not to think about where she had learned to scream like that, like her world was tearing in half. Footsteps echoed in the hallway outside.

I lay as still as a corpse when the door flew open. My head hung to the side, blood dripping out of my mouth. Somewhere, amid preparing for this, I had broken my wrist in the cuff, but it didn't burn nearly as much as the moonstone against my chest, hidden beneath the collar of my dress.

At my request, Evhen had reopened the gash on my arm to cover me with fresh blood. She had been careful to make sure I wasn't going to bleed out before I even reached the crypt, but there had to be enough to make it look convincing.

And to make sure the guards didn't look too close.

"She just started seizing," Evhen wailed as guards filled the room. "I-I couldn't do anything. She was coughing up blood, and then she... then she..." Her explanation dissolved into sobs.

A pair of heavy footsteps marched into the room a moment later.

Evhen shrieked at, I assumed, the king. "She's dead, you killed her, she's dead!" Fists pounded against something solid, and then Evhen dropped to the ground, whimpering. "You killed her! Are you happy now? You killed her!"

"She killed herself by saving your brother," the king snapped.

I wished I wasn't pretending so I could strangle him for the pained sound Evhen made. Still, I remained motionless, focusing on keeping my breaths slow and even, unnoticeable amid the chaos and blood.

"You could have saved her," the king continued, voice closer to me than it had been a moment ago. "If you had accepted my proposition, I would have had the healers save her."

"No!" Evhen shrieked when the guards lifted me from the bed, limp as a doll. "No, you're lying! You wanted her dead! You killed her!"

A smack, flesh hitting flesh, echoed into the sudden silence, and the doors shut resolutely on Evhen's screams.

We moved through a twisting labyrinth of hallways and corridors, descending deeper and deeper into the castle's bowels. The air grew frigid, and the stones dripped with stale moisture.

"Gods, this hair is even heavier in death," grumbled one of the guards currently holding my tresses.

"Just cut it off," suggested the guard carrying me, his chest rumbling with laughter. "It's not like she's going to miss it."

"Drop her here," said another. "Let the mortician deal with it in the morning."

A door creaked open. Rotting flesh and human waste wafted out, causing more than one person to gag. The guard dropped me like I was nothing more than a corpse, to be disrespected and desecrated, and my nose shattered at the impact. Pain burst across my face, but I held still, breath bated and lungs screaming.

"Hey," said the first guard as they turned away, but the door shut on his next words and their answering laughter.

As soon as their footsteps faded, I lurched sideways and vomited.

Then I looked around the dungeon.

EIGHTEEN

Limbs shaking, I pushed myself up off the floor and lurched for the bed. I didn't make it that far before I pitched sideways and vomited into the chamber pot. A sob—a real, seas-awful, heart-breaking sob—erupted out of me. I pulled my trembling body onto the bed and told myself she was fine. But it didn't feel fine.

It felt like the memories of that morning, so long ago, were crashing down on me all at once. The way I had screamed for help. The way I had begged for my life. The way I had wet myself in fear. The way their blood had splattered the walls, the floor, the thrones. The way another king had stood in front of me and mocked me while he slaughtered the people I loved most. Bile rose up in my throat, and I gagged, clutching my stomach against the pain.

Kalei wasn't dead, though. It had all been an act. A very real, very *convincing* act. And even though I had been thinking about my parents the entire time, I couldn't help but think she could very well die by another king's hand if we didn't get out of this glittering prison in time.

Light slanted through the crack beneath the door, but that was no indicator of time. Exhaustion and fatigue continued to drag at my bones, trying to sink me into oblivion, but there was no way of knowing how much time had passed since the princess had been taken away.

I dropped sideways onto the sheets, ignoring the cloying stench of piss and blood and sweat, and pressed my face into the pillow. Coffee and moonlight and ocean salt. That's what she smelled like, but I couldn't find those scents now.

A whimper broke the silence. There was nothing I could do now but wait. Wait and hope.

Hope and wait.

And pray to the black seas I didn't succumb to terror before it was too late.

The castle rumbled with an earth-shaking shudder.

I lurched upright and immediately regretted moving. Nausea stung my throat and pain stabbed my muscles. Everything ached. My chest felt too tight—lungs squeezed too empty—and needles jabbed at my eyes from a throbbing in my head. It didn't help that I smelled worse than a public latrine. A horrible reek clogged my nose as I staggered to my feet, padding towards the door while the walls shook around me. Whatever the princess was doing, I didn't want to be near it if the quakes were this bad so far from the crypt.

She was very clearly alive. And an army was answering her call.

I tried the door—still locked. Of course. I was still a prisoner. They hadn't even put us in a room with windows. As if we could have survived the fall to the moat below. We were only human. The princess could still bleed.

The image of her covered in blood flashed in my mind again. I pinched my eyes shut, pushing it back down. Thinking about her dying would only send me down a very long, very dark path. King Ovono had been right. She was wrong for me, for my kingdom, but that didn't mean I couldn't fight for her *and* my kingdom at the same time.

The floor shook again. I caught myself against the wall, mind spinning in a thousand directions at once. How was I supposed to get out of here when the only door was locked from the outside?

Before I could move, the door popped open. Open-mouthed, I stared as Prince Osno fell ungracefully into the room, landing on hands and knees. He scampered to his feet and dusted himself off with an air of someone trying to regain their dignity after being caught doing something ridiculous.

"Queen Evhen," he said, nodding his sharp chin at me. I snapped my mouth shut and peered around him into the empty hallway. The only sign of the guards were the indentations of their boots in the carpet. "Um..."

"*Um?*" I echoed incredulously, smacking his arm. He recoiled and delicately set a hand over his mouth and nose. "That's all you have to say?"

"I am sorry," he said forcefully, pinching his eyes shut as if my stench burned. Or maybe he was anticipating another smack. Half of me wanted to give him exactly that. "I had no idea what my father was planning. I never would have agreed to it if I had known."

Huffing, I folded my arms over my chest. "So now what? You free me and I fall in love with you? We run off together and get married up north?"

"I—what—no?" His thin eyebrows drew together. "I mean...yes, I am freeing you. No, we don't have to do any of those other things. Unless you want to..."

"No, I don't want to marry you, Os," I snapped. He flinched like each word was a slap. "Where is my family?"

"Waiting at the city gates," he said, and I believed him. Relief rushed through me like a gust of cold air. "We don't have much time. Or we have a lot of time. I really don't know what's going on." The room tilted. I crashed into him, and we both crashed into the hallway. He grunted, gagging.

Smacking his arm again, I disentangled myself from him. "Stop that. It's not that bad."

"It is much worse, Your Majesty," he murmured behind his hand.

I must have lost my sense of smell, then.

He declined my offer to help him up and bounded to his feet, eyes tearing at what he considered a much worse stench than I thought. Through held breath, he untied a belt from his waist and handed it to me. My cutlass, safe in a new leather sheath. I clutched the sword to my chest and kissed the pommel before hastily tying it around my hips.

Prince Os jutted his chin, and we took off down the empty hall.

"How did you do it?" I asked as we slipped into another corridor. "How did you get them out?" There was no other person it could have been.

Holding up a hand, he paused at another corner and peered around. A crack ran up the wall, growing larger with each rumble beneath us. Plaster and paint rained down. He nodded, and we moved again, the castle quaking all around us.

"Smuggled them out through the crypt," he said. "One by one each day. Icana helped me plan it. Talen went first—supposedly strung himself up in his cell."

I clamped a hand around my neck, fear ripping through me as a portion of the wall gave way behind us. Dust billowed into the air.

"Alekey went next," Prince Os continued, not noticing how visibly shaken I was at his words. "Natural causes."

My eyes fluttered shut. I knew it was all an act, the same charade Kalei and I had planned, but hearing how all my friends supposedly died was somehow worse than imagining them actually dead.

"Natural causes, my ass," I hissed, clinging to the only thing I knew when everything else went sideways—anger.

"All right, he succumbed to his injuries," Prince Os said impatiently, flapping a hand. "Icana, according to the guards, was still alive when they threw her in the crypt. She had strangled one of the guards, and they tossed her in there as punishment. As far as they know, the dead came for her. And now your princess...what is your princess doing?"

"Raising the dead," I said, trying to ignore the way your princess made my toes curl.

Prince Os tripped, spluttering. He glanced over his shoulder at me, then nodded, as if he had very quickly accepted what I said as truth. No questions asked. And thank the seas for that. I didn't need questions at a time like this.

The floor rippled, the carpet rising and falling like waves, causing us both to trip again. The floorboards beneath the carpet creaked and groaned like the deck of a ship in a tossing tide. After a few moments, during which many paintings lining the walls crashed to the ground, the shuddering stopped again.

"I hope you don't mind my saying," he said as we scrambled to our feet once more. "She is incredible."

A small smile graced my lips—not for the first time thinking about the princess. "Yes. She is."

The grand entrance was in chaos when we arrived. Portraits had smashed to the ground, littering the floor with broken shards of gold and glass. Cracks ran along the floor in widening lines. Dust filled the air where parts of the walls had collapsed. And hundreds of guards crammed the space, fighting what look like an army of bones.

It was an *army* of bones, skeletons with mismatched spines and femurs, broken mandibles, several ribs missing, cracked toes and fingers. The guards didn't seem to know what to do when their swords slid in and out, ineffective against a fleshless foe.

It was the most bizarre thing I had ever witnessed, but it seemed to be working. The guards were pushed back from the double doors, leaving a wide path for us. The prince and I ran down the sweeping staircase, just as it cracked, splintered, and collapsed behind us. It was as if the entire castle was coming to life around us to fight back. I hated to think that was exactly what was happening—if the princess was raising *bones*.

The stairs continued to fall as we ran. At the bottom, the prince leapt over a fallen guard and fell into a heap, crying out. I skidded to a stop, grabbing at his arm.

"Go, Ev!" he shouted at me, slapping my hands away. "Fix this whole mess!"

The floor surged. A guard screamed as a chasm ripped through the foyer and more bony hands clambered out. Fingers curled around ankles, pulling more bodies to meet the bones below.

"This place is going to collapse!" I shouted back. Overhead, a soft tinkling sound jingled through the din. I craned my neck back. The massive chandelier swayed, crystals raining down. Cracks in the wall raced towards the hook that was holding it in place. "Give me your hand, now!"

He slipped his hand into mine. I yanked him towards the door as the chandelier broke. Crystals shattered with a beautiful melody.

In the span of a breath, Prince Os shoved me towards the doors. Stomach dropping, I tripped over the threshold, twisting. Too slow. The chandelier crashed on top of him, and my shout was lost amid the screams.

Without anyone left to help me, I scrambled to my feet and raced over the bridge. The entire city was in an upheaval—smoke and dust billowing in massive clouds into the air, raining ash down on the rumbling streets. Terrified shouts echoed off the stone, coming from everywhere at once. The cobblestones broke apart under my feet as I sprinted for the city gates. Buildings around me tumbled into the spreading chasm. And all the while, more and more bones poured out of the underside of the city, crawling and clawing towards the light.

Lungs screaming in pain, I finally turned around. The castle was a twisted jumble of turrets and spires, the tallest towers collapsing inwards as the bottom levels heaved and quaked.

And there stood Kalei on the bridge, in her blood-spattered white shift, moonlight glowing in her unravelled hair. The stone around her neck pulsed in time to the beat of bone feet marching through the city.

The ground shook. Knees scraping stone, I watched the princess rain destruction down on this city in the form of millions of bones buried beneath the streets. Xesta was a graveyard, beauty built on battered bones and buried bodies. Gagging at the thought, I scrambled away from the heaving stones, the city breathing and dying at the same time. Strong hands pulled me up, and I grabbed onto Talen's shoulders.

Kalei continued to march towards us. Rows and rows of bones surrounded her like guards, marching in time, surging out of the cracks and hollows of the city. This power required her undivided attention. She had said as much earlier. But I feared she was so far gone, entranced by her own magic, that she wouldn't be able to wake herself from it.

Behind her, the castle—Xesta's crown jewel—collapsed in a burst of dust and glass. The shock knocked us backward.

"Kal!" I shouted over the screams and wails. The bones and gaping skulls turned to me all at once. Talen dragged me backwards, towards the gate.

We were not her enemy, but the skulls looked at us—even without eyes—like we were. I yanked my arm out of Talen's and rushed towards her. "Kalei!"

A shudder ran through the city. Attention divided. One by one, the bones closest to us fell, breaking apart to ash where they landed. Then more fell, like a wave, and the moonlight faded from Kalei's hair. Her unfocused eyes found me across the haze of dust and death.

Then she dropped just like her army.

NINETEEN

My eyes flew open a moment later. I knew it was only a short lapse because Evhen hadn't reached me yet. She was running with all haste through the dust, crunching through—

I screamed.

A graveyard of bones surrounded me. Skulls, sternums, ribs, femurs, various pieces of hands, feet, shins, and arms were scattered amid the dust. Empty. Hollow. Dry and cracked and as dead as ever. Nothing moved in the street where only moments ago *everything* had moved. They had been everywhere. Now they were all dead. My hand brushed against a spine. My elbow cracked through a skull. I couldn't get away from them—they were everywhere—gaping mouths, sunken cheeks, and hollow eyes stared at me everywhere I turned.

I screamed again, scrambling away from the lifeless bones.

Evhen slid through the dust, scattering chips of bone. She brushed the dirty powder off my dress—by the moon, pulverized bone was in my hair!—and told me over and over I was all right.

Everyone was all right.

Everything was all right.

But nothing was right because, for the first time in my life, the dead didn't move. The bones didn't sing their waking melody. They didn't strain in the crypt to tell me their stories. Because I had witnessed their stories firsthand. And now, they were as still as the crypts. No more stories to tell.

With growing horror as Evhen pulled me to my feet, I realized why I was never supposed to wake them. Why the bones of the dead were never meant to see the light. They moved and danced for me in the crypt, but their stories had already been told and lost. Such things were never meant to be heard. Such horrors were never meant to be released.

And I had woken them all. All their anger and fear and sorrow and pain—I had felt every aching second of it, every moment from their lives that had been pushed so far down only their bones remembered. The worst parts of their lives—the most painful, the most agonizing. The way thousands of them had died by sword or fever or hunger. My skin crawled with the memories of the countless people lost to time.

Evhen yanked on me, yelling at me, careless of where she stepped.

The crack of bones erupted all around me, popping like explosions in my head. I wailed for it to stop, wailed for the children and babies that had died by their parents' hands, wailed for the elderly that had curled up in corners to fade away, wailed for all the people who sought better lives in this glittering jewel only to have those dreams shattered in the gutters.

Evhen suddenly veered to the side, slipping through bone dust and ground marrow, cursing quietly. She pulled me into a narrow alley. We burst into a side street a moment later and then ducked into a cramped space between two half-collapsed buildings that was hardly wide enough for us to stand shoulder-to-shoulder.

I slipped from her grip, sinking to the ground as what remained of my energy seeped from my muscles.

She crouched in front of me, hands on my knees, talking, mouth moving, but I didn't hear the words.

A slap shattered my thoughts.

Cheek stinging, I turned wide eyes to the captain, hovering over me like a vengeful spirit. Through the din in my head, her words found a place.

"They've blocked the gates. We have to keep moving."

Panic laced every word, every shallow breath, as she pulled me to my feet again. My cheek didn't hurt as much as my pride, but I knew we were in trouble. *I* was in trouble. Somewhere in the back of my mind, I knew I had hurt many people. And more people were going to be angry about that.

"Where are the others?" I asked as we emerged onto an empty street. Dust continued to rubble down, but nobody remained on the roads. Nobody alive, at least. There were bodies and bones and blood. I tried not to look at them as we passed.

"They got out," Evhen said, voice tight. It sounded like she didn't believe it, but really, really wanted to.

Hoofbeats echoed through the eerie silence. She cursed again. There was so much dust and death shrouding the city that even the sun couldn't shine through. Everything had taken on a dull brown tint. Or maybe that was just the blood running in rivers down the road.

We ducked into an empty store, the door dangling by a single hinge. Part of the ceiling caved inwards. A hole in the floor gaped into murky blackness. We crouched under the window, hearts in throats, holding our breath as a battalion marched through the street on horseback. Someone paused and approached the store. My eyes fluttered shut.

Warmth radiated from the centre of my chest. A familiar thread tugged inside my bones. I reached for it and pulled it towards me, clinging to the one thing I understood more than anything else in this world.

A sharp snap bit into the back of my neck, and the thread unravelled through my fingers, taking with it all the power and energy.

My eyes flew open to see Evhen gripping my stone in her palms, gaze not on me, but on the window. Tension wound in her jaw.

The guards passed with a cursory glance inside. Deeming the wrecked building an unlikely hiding spot, they moved on, hooves on cobblestones, armour chinking a steady beat.

When the sound faded, only then did Evhen look at me. Incredulity sharpened her glare to a knife's edge. "What exactly were you thinking to do?"

I pressed my lips into a fine line. If there was anyone in this moon-damned world who could rebuke me for using my powers, it was not her. The only one who could tell me what to do with my powers was *me*. And the only one who could guide me was the moon. No one else could make those decisions for me. No one else could tell me what was right and what was wrong. I had already learned that the hard way, and I wasn't going to let anyone else tell me what to do now.

Still, there were more bones that hadn't woken, but my heart felt ready to burst out of my chest at the thought of waking them—knowing them, *being* them. I wanted to feel that power again, that strength, but not at the cost of knowing those untold stories.

With a huff, Evhen straightened. Dust turned her hair the colour of dying embers—the red hidden beneath a touch of grey and black. She ran her hands through the curls and made a face at the ash coating her fingertips.

"There's a small gate," she said, plan forming as she spoke, "where the city's waste runs into the ocean. We might be able to get out through there."

"No," I said, drawing out the word.

She cocked an eyebrow at me, a cutting retort already forming on her tongue.

But I kept talking. "There are tunnels running beneath the city. Whole catacombs. I sensed them when I woke the bones." It was a simple thing, to wake oneself from slumber. It was another thing entirely to wake bones from endless slumber. One never meant to be broken. But there was no other way to describe the action. They slept, they woke, and they raged.

Evhen peered into the street. A shaft of light speared through the cloud of death, casting shadows across her ashen face. "Where do these catacombs let out?"

192

"The bones could guide us," I said, reaching for the stone. It was dangerous, this power. But despite the pain and agony, I *wanted* it. I couldn't explain the desire in my soul to reclaim that power. Perhaps it was because my whole life I had only touched the surface of the moon's gift. Had only done what my parents asked and nothing more. And now I was free of that. Free of their pressure to blindly trust.

With a shake of her head, she wrapped the cord around her wrist once more. "Only if we get lost," she said, holding my gaze, a challenge in her sun-bright eyes.

Because even she knew taking a hidden route beneath the city was better than trying to hide up here. We were the only people aside from the guards roaming the streets. Everyone else was either trapped or dead.

"How do we get in?"

I pointed to the hole in the middle of the floor. "They all came from somewhere."

Gulping, she leaned over the hole. Nothing moved within the dark depths. No lights shone, either.

"It's going to be pitch black down there," she said. Her eyes, when they found mine, were wary. Uncertain.

"It's just like diving into the depths," I said with forced lightness.

She flashed me a dark look as I dangled my legs over the precipice. "*I've* never dived into the depths," she reminded me.

"Then I hope you're not scared of the dark."

As it turned out, I shouldn't have worried the captain would be scared of the dark. Because the depth of her fear was so much worse. She was completely *terrified* of it.

We had landed in a pitch-black chamber, and the first thing she had done was grab my arm tight enough to draw blood. She pressed herself closer as we walked forward.

The air was tinged with the cloying scent of long-forgotten bodies. The smell of ocean salt hid beneath the scent of sweat and blood, stinging my nose.

I steadied my breaths. The darkness of the depths was as familiar to me as the brightness of the moon. But this was a different kind of darkness. This was pressing, suffocating, deathly still. I put my hand out towards the wall, edging forward until it hit something solid. And bumpy. And—I recoiled.

Evhen yelped in surprise at my sudden movement, then apologized under her breath. "What is it?" she asked, a whisper of air tickling my neck.

I closed my eyes, though it made no difference in the dark. "More bones," I said, breath shaking. "The walls are bones."

"Great—that's great, that's *fantastic*," she babbled, pressing her forehead into my shoulder.

Her breath warmed my skin, the only thing I had to fight off the chill.

The cold was familiar. It seeped into my bones. My teeth chattered as I put my hand out again, brushing along the gentle curves of craniums. The only place to go now was forward. There would be no trail of blood and moonlight to guide me back to the surface.

"K-Kalei," the captain said, teeth clattering, as we made slow progress through the tunnels. She seemed to realize her fingers were latched onto my arm only when they dented my bone. She loosened her grip slightly. "T-tell me a story."

I pried her fingers from my arm and twined them through my own. We both winced at the sting as her palm brushed the stone-shaped indent in my skin. Her hands were as cold as mine.

There was only one story I could think of.

"In another time, in another place... When the world was young, and water covered its surface, a piece of the moon fell from the sky..." I recounted the tale of the first chief and his quest for immortality, the girl who had touched the moonstone first—and her bloody death.

Evhen listened to my words weaving the tale around us. The bones lining the walls rattled as if they knew the story firsthand. She jumped at every small noise—stones clattering high above us, rubble tumbling into the darkness, chips of bones peeling away as we passed.

My skin felt icy by the time I finished the story, tears frozen on my cheeks. The ground sloped upwards, but the tunnel seemed to stretch on forever. Cold darkness gripped my heart with icy claws. Death waited before us.

Her hands had stopped trembling. A sigh gusted out of her, warm against my neck. "You really believe your father knows of this power."

"Yes." I sniffled, an ugly, undignified sound that echoed through the tunnel. "He said he would have it by the Blood Moon next month, but I've never heard that term before."

"The Blood Moon?" she echoed, a frosty familiarity coating her voice.

I shivered, glancing over my shoulder to where I assumed she was. All I could hear was her feet. All I could feel was her hand. "Do you know it?" A hollow feeling sank into the pit of my stomach. It was the one part of my father's maniacal ramblings that I hadn't un-ravelled yet.

"It's a rare event," she answered. "It only occurs once every fifty years or so. The moon turns red as blood…like in the story…"

The moon turned red as blood that hour…

"It's just a story though," she argued—as if she was trying to con-vince herself it wasn't real. Immortality wasn't real. "I mean…the first chief wasn't immortal, was he?"

I shook my head before remembering she couldn't see me any-more than I could see her. "It seems unlikely. The world would have known about immortality long before my parents. But the moon turn-ing red as blood… a Blood Moon. That must be the only time the ritual can occur."

She grunted as her toe hit something. The hollow sound it made smashing into the wall caused me to wince. Another skull broken. Another story silenced.

"Two weeks," she said on an exhale. Only now realizing how dire our situation was.

Two weeks until my father planned to kill me.

The reality of my impending death caused the tunnel to pitch around me. I pinched my eyes shut as a wave of shadows surged ahead of me. Fear crashed over me, easing a gasp from my lips.

The ground rushed up to meet me. A cage of ribs shattered beneath my knees. Shards of bone pierced through my flesh as I reached out to catch myself. The bones swirled around me in the darkness—stories I could never tell and memories I could never live. Precious bones that had been destroyed and hated by this world. All mine to hold. All mine to know. I felt more connected to them in this gloom than ever before, even more than when I pulled souls from the depths. These were the stories I had to protect.

"Kalei!" Evhen exclaimed. Her hands landed on my head, my hair, my shoulders.

I sensed her crouch next to me, carelessly brushing bones away.

"Don't touch them," I snapped, smacking her hands away. I pulled the bones towards me, forming a shield around them, dragging them into my lap. "Don't you dare touch them!"

If I'd ever had a purpose in this world, it was for these bones. The ones untouched by war, but in agony all the same. The bones of the forgotten, people pushed to the edges, turned to ash in memories.

"Kal...what's wrong?" Her voice was farther away now. She must have stood up.

My stomach clenched as a sob broke free. "You don't think about all the bones you've trampled, all the people you've hurt, all the lives you've lost. You don't think about any of that, but they all have stories, too. They all had lives, and they were all taken! Don't touch them if you can't respect them when they're gone."

I was the Princess of Death. I gave life, and here I was surrounded by stories silenced much too soon. It wasn't fair to accuse Evhen of ignoring them—she didn't know any better. She didn't understand. But I had a responsibility to share them. I had a responsibility to make sure no one else suffered the same way.

My fingers ran over a length of bone. A crack in the middle of it tore into the skin on my cheek, opening a long cut from mouth to ear. Warm blood dripped down my neck, settling into the hollows of my hips and trickling down onto the bones beneath my feet.

At the spill of blood, new power surged in my veins, even so far from the light of the moon. It thrummed with urgency.

The bones lurched, and I bit back a scream as the shards collected in my arms shot into my skin like many thorns, needles, daggers. They continued to writhe, rattling as something much more powerful than the stone woke them.

Blood.

Evhen suddenly crashed to the ground next to me, scrabbling at the floor as *something* pulled her in the opposite direction. Her fingers latched onto mine. Screams echoed off the bony walls, sharp as nails.

The bone in my other hand jerked. I dropped it and grabbed Evhen with both hands, straining.

Jolting pain burst along my side. Whatever held her let go when I cried out in pain. The rib I had cradled stabbed through my own ribs. It found a place within the cage around my heart. Agony ripped me apart as it shoved my own ribs aside to settle.

Evhen's hands clamped around my arms.

The movement sent a fresh wave of pain rippling through my body. I cried out for her to release me, but she hauled me to my feet, ignoring the tears, blood, and pain.

As she lumbered forward under my weight, part of the ceiling above us crumbled inwards. Writhing bones poured down on us, falling from the tunnel's ceiling. Evhen threw her arms over my head, but a tiny shard of bone landed on my collar and shot into my jaw. Beneath my bare feet, a broken femur pierced through my heel, driving up past my shin and tearing the skin open. I hit the ground hard, clawing at my skin. Bile filled my mouth. Pain lanced across my jaw.

Weak daylight filtered through the broken ceiling. Shadows twisted to blot out the light. They pulled and tugged at my bones, at the bones that weren't mine, dancing just out of reach—waiting. As long as I kept my eyes open, they would remain at bay.

Evhen pulled me through the gaping hole, using the fallen bones as a ladder, and we landed in a heap in dew-wet grass. I coughed into the dirt, blood dripping from my mouth, my nose, and my eyes. The shadows lurked at the side, animalistic beings with bones for eyes and claws for fingers that dug into the grass. Each scrape felt like it was happening inside my head.

Maybe it was. I couldn't tell what was real and what wasn't anymore.

As Evhen turned to me, her concerned voice floating through the early morning air, the shadows lunged.

TWENTY

Xesta's city walls faded into a tangle of trees behind us as I dragged Kalei through the forest. Early morning sunlight chased away the shadows and gloom of the catacombs, but the memories lingered, heavy in the maple-scented air. Nothing followed us.

Nothing except death.

Where the light touched the ground, it fell on gold and auburn and ruby leaves crunching underfoot. Autumn had come unseasonably early to the south. Decay sprouted through the underbrush, moss and lichen clung to tree bark, and the leaves continued to spiral downwards, breaking from their branches to join the bramble below. Somehow, we had lost a full day and night in the catacombs. Or—I was loathe to think—more.

If what Kalei had told me was true, we had less than a fortnight to reach Vodaeard and stop her father. But that would be impossible if we didn't reach the mountains soon.

A feat made further impossible if the princess didn't wake up. She was limp in my arms, ice cold and painfully still, as I pulled her between the twisting roots of a tall oak. Sweat beaded her forehead and drenched the front of her dress, but it was the blood that concerned me. It was everywhere where those seas-damned pieces of bones had struck her—her cheek, her jaw, her hands, and the most horrific gash along her leg where a bone had crawled up into her thigh. Her dress was torn at the waist, ripped to shreds where something had pierced at her side. Blood stained the white fabric—some of it fresh, some of it old—all of it hers. It slicked her arms, neck, and hair.

I crouched next to her, craning my neck back to peer through the thick canopy. Sunlight filtered in thin strokes through the fluttering leaves.

"Kalei," I whispered, brushing her hair back from her face. Even my hands were slick with her blood. There was so much of it.

The image of Alekey drowning in his own blood flashed before my eyes. With a strangled gasp, I pushed it away. Worrying wouldn't save the princess.

Fighting through the exhaustion in my limbs, I hefted the princess onto my shoulders, dragging her unceremoniously through the underbrush. Her hair dragged through leaves and snagged on roots. Sweat quickly drenched my back. Cloying panic rose from the dirt like bones and threatened to drag me into that cold, desolate place of unfeeling. I chewed my lip to shreds—the pain keeping me present and focused.

A trickle of water babbled gently through the trees nearby. I followed the sound to a stream winding through the moss. It was hardly more than a stride across, but it ran steady and cold. I set the princess down against a log—apologizing when I banged her head—and dipped my hands in. The ice-cold shock lanced up my arms, causing me to hiss in relief. My knees sank into the springy earth, and I dropped to my elbows, splashing water over my face.

After I had scrubbed the blood and dirt and sweat and piss from my body, stripped bare to let the dress dry, I sat back on my blistered heels and stared at the princess. She hadn't moved, a pale sheen to her sun-darkened face, now ashen. Dust and dirt clung to her like a second skin, pieces of bone still embedded in her hands and feet.

I didn't know what horrors she was facing in her own mind, trapped somewhere between the living and the dead, drowning in a darkness I couldn't see. I didn't know how to help her fight this, and that thought alone made me think I wasn't capable of helping her fight anything.

Gritting my teeth, I pulled her towards the stream. Maybe I didn't have to help her fight. I just had to help her survive.

The dress peeled off her body like a bandage, catching on the broken bits of skin and clinging to the sticky splatters of blood. She smelled worse than I did, if that was possible—like rotting flesh and putrid waste. The wounds oozed gore. Bits of blackened and bleached bone poked through her skin, buried beneath her flesh, but at least they weren't moving like maggots anymore.

As I tossed water over her, landing like icicles on her skin and hissing like coals on her wounds, I wondered if a septic infection would be the thing to kill her first. I did my best to scrub her down, careful of where my fingers lingered, the stream running red and black. While I washed her skin, I noticed the gashes weren't as deep as I first thought, but no less ugly.

The cuts sizzled with the motion of wiping away broken flesh, clumps of moss acting as rags and salves. I could name a hundred uses for saltwater and seaweed, but not enough for a moss that grew along the faintest trickle of water in the heart of a forest. Hoping against hope that it would be enough until we—I—found proper medicine, I started washing the blood and bone out of her hair.

Sunlight shifted through the trees, slanting towards afternoon, when the princess finally made a sound. My back was to her. A small portion of her hair dunked in the thin stream in front of me, so I didn't notice her move until she spoke.

"Cap—"

I started violently, scrambling away from her hair only to twist around and land bare-ass-first in the stream. She jumped at my reaction, snatching up the dress to cover herself as I yanked mine towards me, the gold silk falling over my lap. Clutching the fabric to my bare chest, heart rabbiting, I stared at her across the water. Red crept up her neck in pulses. My own cheeks flushed with searing heat.

"I...haven't finished washing that," I said, jutting my chin towards the dress she'd pulled up to her neck.

"Did you...were you...was I...what happened?" she spluttered, finally landing on the question I felt I could answer without embarrassing myself, or her.

I pulled myself out of the water and plopped on the other side. "I think you got possessed by bones."

It was the only thing that made any sort of sense, even though nothing about any of this made sense. Sense hadn't existed in weeks. But there was no other way to explain what I had seen.

"That's not possible," she murmured. Her eyes dropped from my face—a cold breeze shivered down my spine in their absence—and landed on the thicket of tangled hair in the water. Most of the blood was gone, but the bones remained—latched onto her hair as well as her flesh.

"Tell that to the extra bone in your leg."

The moment the words landed, confusion rippled across her face, chased with the horror of widening eyes as she looked down and shoved aside the scratchy white fabric of her shift. A wince hissed between her teeth when she touched the torn flesh, running from heel to thigh.

"I'll let you...um..."

"Thank you," she whispered, understanding what I couldn't say.

I backed away from the stream, slipping behind a tree where I tugged the hideous gold dress over my head. It was still wet, squeaking over my air-dried skin, and the colour had dulled from gold to russet with bloodstains that refused to come out, but at least the stench was gone. Small mercies for all my troubles.

The forest was not the place I wanted to make camp, but hunger gnawed at my stomach, so I searched the underbrush for edible berries and mushrooms. Again, a hundred uses for something other than moss nagged at me, but I was not at sea. I was in a forest, and I needed food.

I circled back to the water after several long minutes—long enough for the princess to wash her dress and put it on—arms laden with a pitiful pile of dark berries and pale mushrooms. She sat on the edge of the stream, running her fingers through her damp strands. The gown hung in tatters around her hips.

"I'm not sure I like these," she said upon my approach, picking at the bones threaded like beads in her hair. She tugged on one, letting it fall back with a huff when it didn't budge.

I touched a shard as I passed. "Hmm. Better than those, I suppose." I nodded to the pricks embedded in her hands. She winced as she flexed her fingers between the needle-sharp points. "At least they're not moving anymore."

With a thoughtful nod, she twisted around to face me, abandoning the fruitless attempt to cleanse her hair of the dead.

I emptied my bundle into the crook of a tree.

"Poison berries!" she exclaimed.

"What?" I gasped, jumping away from the pile.

She giggled, that bright sound finding a place within my heart that hadn't known joy in a long time. "They're not actually poisonous," she explained. "Not for humans, at least. Wild hares use them to hide their warrens because predators won't go near them. They're delicious in tarts." She picked up one and popped it in her mouth, grinning at me.

"Yes, all right, poison berries that are not actually poisonous by nature," I said slowly, watching her carefully for any sign of sickness. "Totally makes sense."

"Only by name," she said. "Some of those mushrooms, though, I would not recommend eating."

I made a face at the deceptive pile, suddenly no longer hungry. "How do you know so much about wild food? Do you grow poison berries on your island?" I raised a skeptical eyebrow as I settled against the tree, folding an arm over my crooked knee. The slit in the dress spilled over my leg.

"I had a lot of hobbies," she said, a hint of sadness colouring her voice. "My parents said power like mine was supposed to be protected at all costs. That meant I was never allowed to leave or have friends or wander the island. Even the servants weren't allowed to be alone with me."

"That sounds…really lonely," I said, idly picking at the berries in the pile next to me, rolling a plump piece between my fingers. Even after the war touched our nation, Alekey and I still had friends. We were still free.

She sat against the log at an angle from me, our feet close enough to touch if she wanted to close the distance. She shrugged. "Like I said, I had a lot of hobbies. Guitar. Knitting. Painting. Reading—mostly reading. Our library had a great selection of exotic flora and fauna encyclopedias." Her eyes sparkled the way they did only when she talked fondly about her home. Something that was becoming increasingly rare.

"And stories about how to gain immortality?" I added.

She laughed, the sound less mirthful and more bone-weary. "And stories about how to gain immortality," she echoed. A memory pulled her eyebrows together. "Those stories sank with your ship."

The sharp reminder cut through me with a painful twist in my ribs. "It was my parents' ship," I told her. "Was one of the only things I had of theirs."

What would they have said, if they were alive, knowing I had let it sink in a storm? What kind of captain could be so careless with something so precious?

"That's not true, Evhen," she said. "You have a whole kingdom that was theirs."

I raised my gaze, biting back tears. My first instinct was to snap at her for being so naive and foolish. But as my tongue hit my teeth, I realized she was right. Vodaeard had been their greatest gift to me, even if I didn't want it at first. But I wouldn't have it for long if her father eradicated it in his homicidal quest to find the other piece of moonstone.

Even worse was King Ovono's threat—something told me I hadn't seen the last of him.

"Let's hope it's still there when we cross the mountains," I said, grimacing at the uncertainty in my voice. I couldn't let my fear get the best of me now. Vodaeard was strong. Even without a Lockes heir on the throne, they wouldn't succumb so easily to Chief Mikala's tyranny.

The princess nodded, popping another berry into her mouth. "Evhen," she asked around the juices, "what happens if we don't reach Vodaeard by the Blood Moon? If that's the only time my parents can do the ritual, why don't we wait? Let it pass without incident."

It seemed like such an easy solution. But the simplest solutions had never been the ones that worked, in my limited experience. There was always a price for its uncomplicated nature.

And then it struck me, like a hammer to the chest. "That's why he didn't kill you," I breathed.

"What?"

"King Ovono," I said, spitting the name like a curse. "Despite our small size, Vodaeard is the second largest port city on the southern oceanic trade route. If we do nothing, if we hide and wait, I fear your father will take all his anger at missing his chance for immortality out on my kingdom. Vodaeard would be scratched off every map. King Ovono would seize control of every single trade route in these waters. He'd have more power over the seas than your father's armada. He didn't kill you because he wanted that to happen."

"Why Vodaeard?" she asked, voice breaking beneath the weight of realization. "Why you?"

It was the same question I had been asking myself since it happened, but that single, small kernel of concern dug deep into my heart and didn't let go.

"Because," I said with a tone of defeat, "I told your father where the moonstone was."

TWENTY-ONE

We spent the night huddled together in the hollows of a twisted oak tree. Barely visible through the branches and roots and clouds, the moon shifted towards the quarter, growing larger and brighter behind the hazy cover of wispy grey clouds. Just over a week to the full moon. Just over a week to the day when my father planned to sacrifice me—his daughter—for a *chance* at a fable.

Evhen shifted next to me, a night terror wracking her limbs.

I hadn't missed the way she chewed her lips or picked her fingers until they bled. It was something she did when she was nervous or agitated or bored. Any moment she wasn't moving was spent picking flakes of dead skin from various parts of her body. She didn't seem aware she was doing it most of the time, but when she did catch herself, she would stop and focus her attention on something else.

But watching her shake herself awake from a nightmare made me think the worry went much deeper than what she could control on the surface. She sat up with a gasp, panting. She heaved a sigh and shoved her hands through her hair before her fingers caught the peeling skin on her lips.

"Why do you do that?" I asked.

"I don't know," she said with a small shrug. She looked sideways at me, resting her head on her knees. The painful reality of the truth in her words shone in her dim eyes, even with the copper hair falling in the way. The strands were darkened by the shadows of night slinking through the trees. "I've always done it," she continued. "Drove my maids mad—but there's no real reason for it."

"Are you scared?" I pressed. It didn't make sense to harm her body in that way—at least my scars had a purpose.

She scoffed. "No." Her nose wrinkled at the pointed look I gave her. A frown found its way back to her lips. "I'm scared of ghosts. That's it."

"Ghosts?" I echoed, surprised that such a ridiculous concept could rattle someone like her. "Ghosts aren't real."

"You don't know that," she said, almost too quickly.

I fought a laugh. Death's domain was my second home—I would know if ghosts existed in any realm. But I remembered how she reacted in the catacombs, surrounded by death, and I thought maybe the concept wasn't so ridiculous after all. The ghosts of all those bones didn't exist in this realm, but they did live on in my mind in memories. Maybe we just called ghosts different things. Who was I to laugh at that?

"I'm sorry I dragged you into the catacombs," I said instead.

She shivered, wrapping her arms around herself, sticking a finger between her teeth to gnaw at the skin. "We didn't have a choice," she reminded me. Her gaze travelled upwards, to the hazy sky. "We should keep walking. We might be able to reach the southern pass in a few days."

I craned my neck back, counting the specks visible between strips of clouds. The sky was so different here. Stars I had never seen before dusted the void. The moon was in a slightly different position, following a path closer to the horizon. Only by a fraction, but it had pulled me off course as soon as we landed in the west. It had been strange, following its energy as if I were constantly listing sideways. Hopefully, that pull would balance when I returned home.

If I returned home.

The idea that I might not settled like ice in my stomach. Evhen had spared my life over and over again, even before I knew she was the princess I sought, but Death still waited at the end of this dark tunnel. This time, in the form of my beloved father. I hadn't truly realized that I might never see my island again, my lighthouse. There had always been the possibility. Now it was fainter than the faintest stars.

She pushed herself to her feet and offered her hand to me. We left the hollow and followed the stream through the trees, letting it guide us until the sun dusted the sky with rose and peach.

"I don't remember this forest," Evhen said as afternoon leaned towards night.

A stifling wind shifted through the trees, smelling of ocean brine and clogged earth. My hair stuck to my neck, weighed down with the heavy air. In the distance, a low rumble shook the sky.

"We're too far north," she noted as the first drops splattered on the canopy.

"What does that mean?" A drop landed on my forehead and rolled down my cheek. I brushed it aside, but another replaced it, and another.

Soon the leaves above us were sagging with rain. Thunder grew closer, rumbling in quakes that shook the forest floor. Pewter clouds hung low over the trees. Night fell, suddenly and all at once, with a sheet of stinging raindrops.

"It means we're too close to the mountains," she called over the driving wind. "We don't have time to—"

A crack of thunder split the air between us.

Lightning forked overhead.

"We won't make it to the southern pass in time," she continued. "We'll have to cross the mountains."

The dirt turned to mud beneath our feet, squelching with each step. Rain streamed in my eyes, turning the whole forest into a murky river of green and gold shadows. Lightning dazzled my eyes, close enough to taste the shock on my tongue as it split a tree in half not too far from us.

I yelped as the bark crackled and crashed, branches cracking as it collapsed.

"We have to find shelter!" I called to her.

"Where?" she shouted, all her frustration tainting that single word. The sound of it scraped my nerves.

If she was going to yell at me for offering a plan, I was going to—I took in a deep breath through my nose, let it out slowly. Shouting wasn't going to solve anything. We had done enough of it already.

"There has to be a cave or—town!" I blurted, pointing through the pouring rain.

"What?" She shook her hair out of her eyes.

"Town!" Lights floated in the river of my vision, bright yellow beckons through the gloom. We hadn't been facing that direction when the storm hit. We might never have noticed it amid the snapping thunder and falling trees.

Evhen gave a cry of relief that turned into a cry of alarm as lightning slammed into a tree next to us. She ducked as a massive branch broke from high above us, smashing through more branches on its way down, tossing splinters and twigs. She threw herself out of the way before it shattered against the forest floor like a broken spear, teetering on its end. It tilted in her direction, cracked bark smattering against the ground. A cry broke on her lips.

I whipped a strand of hair towards the branch, wincing at the many bone shards digging into my palms, and yanked it sideways. The branch fell with a ground-shaking thump. I pulled my hair back before it rolled to a halt and rubbed my scalp.

Evhen scrambled to her feet, her dress torn in more places than the alluring slit, and glanced from me to the branch and back again. "Let's not do this again," she said, and somehow I knew she didn't mean this storm. It was another storm we were both remembering—and the promises made in anger and desperation.

I nodded, grabbing her hand. We followed the steady lights to a quiet, rain-battered town nestled between two foothills, a single road running through the centre. Snowcapped mountains speared the stormy sky directly ahead of us.

The road wound through the crags and disappeared into the peaks, barely visible between flashes of lightning. The forest fell away behind us. Scraggly trees fought to grow along the side of the mountains, pressing up in the cracks running through the town, bent in the gale that whipped snow from the mountain caps.

Lightning crashed into the side of the mountains every few breaths. The peaks rumbled with answering thunder. Evhen caught my gaze, my own concern reflected in the gold of her eyes. Crossing the mountains in the still season seemed unlikely, given their height. Crossing after a storm like this would be near impossible without a guide to lead us through the twisting paths, especially if we wanted to avoid the sudden sharp falls and wrong turns that would be hidden beneath the snow and ice loosened by the gale. But that was a worry for tomorrow. Tonight, we had to find shelter.

We found it in a tavern at the heart of the small village. A handwritten sign outside misspelled vacancy.

Evhen shoved the door open.

The smell of ale hit my nose, hanging in the air as thick as the smoke curling from the fireplace in the corner, turning my stomach at the memory of silver-laced poison and blood-splattered visions. Sticky liquid covered the floorboards, more painful than the brambles of the underbrush on my bone-studded bare feet. Several patrons glanced up, turning up their noses.

"Look what the storm dragged in," one said in a mocking tone.

A girl, no more than eight or nine years old, jumped off the counter, face pinched into a scowl. "Hey! What do you want?" she barked, as commanding as any barmaid, though I had very little experience with the profession. "You can't be in here without shoes."

"We were robbed," Evhen said. "We need a room and a guide to lead us through the mountains."

"Ha!" one of the patrons bellowed, spitting into a bucket near the fireplace. "Mountain's luck finding anyone who'll take you this late into the season."

"I'll take my chances," Evhen told him with narrowed eyes until he ducked his red face into his drink again. "A room," she repeated to the girl.

"How's you gon' pay for a room if you've got robbed?" she shot back.

"The Vodaeardean coffers should cover the cost."

Discomfort twisted in my stomach. The patrons ogled us, leering and sneering. From what I remember—the last few days were a blur—the queen wanted to keep us hidden from prying eyes. And there were more than enough of those here.

The bar girl laughed, a scraping sound like nails on stone. "The *What*-ean coffers? What are you, some princess?"

"Ev," I warned.

She tilted her head at the girl, hand resting on the hilt of her cutlass. "Yes, I am *some* princess. More, even. I'm *Queen* Evhen Lockes of Vodaeard. The kingdom on the other side of those mountains."

The girl ran her tongue over her teeth. "Hmm," she pondered, her stare raking up and down Evhen's body as though she wasn't the least bit frightened of the drenched golden girl in front of her. "I've never heard of ya."

Boisterous laughter rippled through the room. Fists pounded on the tables. Feet stomped under benches. This was probably the most entertaining thing these people had experienced in decades, and it was at Evhen's expense.

A strange emotion roiled through me, clawing up my throat with burning fingers. I had been angry before, but not like this. Not like the captain. This was her rage finding a place in my bones and making it mine.

I stepped around Evhen and looked down my nose at the girl.

She tilted her head back to smirk up at me.

"Perhaps you've heard of me," I said in a low voice. "The Princess of Death who raises lost souls and protects the dead."

Blood spilled in an oozing stream into my palm. With gritted teeth, I flung the drops onto my hair, holding her gaze as the shards of bone in my palm trembled.

A scream built up in her throat as, answering the call of spilled blood, the shards in my hair lashed out in tendrils of white, shattering cups and mugs out of the hands of several astonished patrons.

"Will the Waterean coffers pay for those as well?" the girl asked in a timid voice, eyes wide.

Evhen nodded while the room spun around me, pain shooting through my hand and hair.

I fought the nausea rolling in my belly when the bones settled again.

The girl directed us to a room upstairs, eyeing me warily. Attempting to summon some of Evhen's chilling rage, I gave her a toothy grin.

The stairs creaked as we climbed to the second floor. A draft blew down the hallway from the cracked window at the end, but it held up against the torrent outside. The floorboards tilted sideways as if the whole building was listing to the side, likely to blow over in the next gust. Wind and rain shook the wall, the sound like needles driving into my head.

The door to our room scraped against the floor and leaned crookedly against the wall. There was a single bed in the middle of the room and one small window covered with black curtains. I pitched towards the bed, catching myself against the frame as Evhen crossed to the window, peering through a slit in the curtains.

"That certainly got their attention," she muttered, twisting around to face me, the curtains settling back into place with a rustle. Concern formed lines between her eyes. "Are you okay?"

"Not particularly," I said, groaning. "Can you—" My head spun, the room fading to black for a brief moment. "Help me wipe off the blood? It makes it worse."

"Let's avoid doing that in the future," she suggested.

I nodded, ducking my head and sucking in short, sharp lungfuls of air.

Evhen rifled through drawers and closets until she found a cloth and sat next to me, taking my hand gently in her lap. Her fingers flitted over mine, softly brushing the blood away from the bone shards.

My hands looked like grotesque beds of thorns without all the pretty roses to hide their ugliness. As she worked, I counted the shards—six in each hand, embedded in random parts of my palms and fingers. One shard shot all the way through my knuckle. When all the blood had been wiped away, I breathed easier. The bones ceased their painful tugging on my hair and flesh, settling once again into something akin to discomfort and just as horrific to look at. A semi-relieved exhale shuddered through my ribs.

"Was it a good idea to announce our presence here?"

Evhen sighed, pacing to the window again. "Get some sleep, Kalei," she said. "We're going to need all our strength to get through the mountains."

I heard what she didn't say. *To get through the border*. Because the mountains would be the least of our concerns if my father's armada was waiting for us on the other side. We were two girls against an undead army. The odds were not in our favour.

"What about you?" I asked as I settled against the pillow. My ribs hurt too much to rest on my side, so I tilted my head towards her, shifting so pieces of hair bone didn't jut into my back.

Tension crowded along the stiff set of her shoulders. "I'm going to find a guide and new clothes."

Exhaustion yanked me under as quick as a downpour before she even turned to leave.

TWENTY-TWO

When I returned to the tavern a few hours later—wearing thick pants and a warm cloak with a bundle of clothes for Kalei in my arms that the merchants had happily accepted my tattered gold dress as payment for, and no mountain's luck finding a guide to lead us this late into the season—the place was in an uproar. Rowdy laughter could be heard halfway down the street. I shouldered the door open, shaking raindrops out of my eyes—and stopped short, mouth falling open, clothes tumbling out of my arms.

Kalei sat on the counter running along the far wall, leather-clad legs swinging back and forth as she regaled a crowd of people. She currently entranced them with a grand story involving a lot of hand gestures.

Someone in the group laughed. Music swelled from a hidden source. Lively chatter filled the air. Mugs of ale clanked together, and the fire sparked in the grate, hotter than before. Smoke and cheer wafted through the room. Alarms careened through my head as her eyes landed on me.

"Ev!" she called, grinning. *Black seas*, she was drunk. Announcing our presence so boldly was one thing—getting drunk in a group of strangers was another thing entirely. Rage turned my vision red as she listed off the counter—someone caught her and straightened her—and strolled towards me, throwing an arm around my shoulders.

"This is my friend Captain Evhen," she announced to the group of inebriated men and women. They cheered, toasted me, and drank.

I roughly threw Kalei's arm off me, sending her stumbling back towards the counter.

Someone lifted her onto the bar, and she took a long drink of something dark and foul.

Through narrowed eyes, I scanned the room, looking for I didn't know what. Someone to blame.

"We haven't been the best of friends," she continued, words slurring. "She tried to kill me the first time we met. And a few times after that. Several times, actually. I really don't think she likes me all that much, but *I* didn't do anything wrong. It's my father she hates. He killed her parents, but really, that doesn't have anything to do with me. But here we are!"

"Here we are!" The cry rose throughout the room. My heart firmly lodged in my throat at her words, each one worse than the last, a knife of memory twisting in my ribs over and over again.

"To Ev-Evhen!" she shouted, raising her bottle. She winked at me, tipped the bottle to her lips, and then frowned into it. "It's empty," she whined.

Another bottle was passed over.

I pushed through the rancid crowd and snatched it from Kalei's fingers. Someone protested my actions, as if I was spoiling all their fun, and shoved me away before I could pull the princess off the counter. The edge of the bar dug into my back as the group formed a circle around Kalei, blocking her from view except for the frustratingly long strands curling like a moonlit river along the floor.

A laugh bit into my neck behind me.

Scowling, I turned to glare at the young bar girl, seated primly on a stool to watch all the events unfold in her tavern behind the safety of a counter. I leaned forward, grabbed her collar, and yanked her face towards me. "Who gave her the first drink?" I growled.

Her small face turned red as she struggled, a wicked glint in her eyes. "I ain't saying," she said.

I shook her.

She grunted. "I don't know! But threatening the one person who can get you 'cross the mountains ain't the way to find out, *Princess*."

I let her go with enough force to make her realize I was not in the mood for games.

She matched my scowl with equal ferocity. "I ain't seen nobody give her no drink. She walked in like that twenty minutes ago, spewing nonsense, and started telling all these grand tales. Really fascinating stuff. Least she hadn't dropped her hair trick yet."

"Right," I grumbled, eyeing the crowd around Kalei. Someone had not only given her the first drink, but they had given her new clothes as well. A billowing blue shirt tucked into tight black pants that tied at her waist. They fit her perfectly. *Too* perfectly. Someone had eyed her for far too long to get her measurements exact.

My stomach soured at the thought. I was going to have words with her after she sobered about accepting drinks from strangers. That twice-made mistake was supposed to stay firmly in the past.

"Has anyone been—" I glanced back at the bar girl, surprised to find her face a hair's breadth from mine, brown eyes boring into me with icy intensity.

"It's an act," she whispered, leaning back to casually examine a cracked fingernail.

"What?"

"What?" she echoed—as if she hadn't spoken the first time, eyes wide with innocence.

I rubbed the ache forming behind my eyes. This whole situation was giving me a headache. Was *I* the drunk one?

Kalei caught my stare over the group surrounding her, eyes glinting brightly in the light of the crackling fire. Smoke hazed between us, masking the distinct glow of fear shining in her gaze. With a crooked smile, she turned her attention back to the group, laughing along as she dove into another story.

Nails dug into the peeling skin on my bottom lip, scratching at a broken scab. My fingertips came away bloody, but still, I worried.

There wasn't anything else to do in this situation. I felt as helpless as when I cowered in the throne room, watching my parents die, and I hated that feeling. But if this was all just an act, I had to trust the princess—had to trust she knew what she was doing.

"This tavern is a tinderbox," the bar girl whispered to me over the counter. "I'd really rather you not make it explode, so whatever you're thinking, *don't*."

I didn't really care if this tavern and everyone in it exploded.

Kalei's voice drifted to me through the smoke and din. "She's not a very nice person at all," she was saying, pitching her voice too loud.

My teeth ground against each other.

"In fact, she's downright loathsome! Pretty to look at, but if she would only keep her awful mouth shut. We wouldn't be in this mess at all."

Her words lodged in my chest like a rusty spike. Even if she was acting, she was acting very well. The inability to react grated on my nerves. There was a reason I had announced our presence earlier, but she was making it so difficult to play along.

"She could never be a real queen, running her mouth like that."

A breath gusted out of me, rattling loose the frustrated sob that had been building up in my chest. All my life people had told me I wasn't fit to be queen—too brash, too bold, too brazen. Too irresponsible. And when my parents died, too weak. Too cowardly. No one here knew who I was, but they had whispered the same things in Xesta, even as they danced at a party in my honour. They said I had run at the first sign of trouble. That a true queen would have stood her ground and faced her enemy.

Hearing the same accusations out of Kalei's mouth stung worse than if they had come from anyone else. The words lodged beneath my skin like the pieces of bones under her flesh, melded to my own, writhing as painfully as a thousand pins in my veins.

A sheen of red glazed over the room, aided by the sparking fire in the grate. I fell back into the comfort of anger and rage, letting it fill the void my parents left in my heart.

"Don—" the bar girl tried to warn me.

I bent, gathering up the princess' long hair. Then I yanked.

The group around her parted between the stream of white hair. Kalei tilted her head at me, seemingly unaffected. She mouthed, *Don't*.

Clenching my jaw, I pulled again. She yelped, tumbling off the counter. The other patrons weren't sure what to do, glancing from the princess to me, eventually deciding that this was not a fight they wanted to break up. The mood in the room sobered, but Kalei's wrath was as hot as mine.

"Ev," she warned again, fingers curling around her moon-blessed hair.

Eyes blazing, I pulled her towards me.

"Evhen!"

Chest heaving, she stared at me across the small space. Hurt shone brightly behind the veil of tears in her eyes.

My hair is considered sacred where I'm from.

I dropped her hair as a jolt of memory shocked my fingertips.

"Is something wrong here?" a masculine voice asked.

"No," Kalei said, forcing a smile to her lips, but I recognized the sense of unforgivable betrayal that darkened her eyes when they shifted to me again. "I'm fine."

We weren't fine, though, not in any sense of the word. A shiver cramped my spine as the man stepped into view beside me. Decay wafted from his body. I didn't have to look to know he was one of the men who had threatened Alekey on the road to Xesta.

The one who had burned my hand with poison.

The hand that now twitched towards my cutlass.

"Another round!" Kalei called, trying to maintain her act that had fallen apart the moment I had moved. The other patrons grumbled. The tension in the room was thick enough to cut with a knife.

"No, thank you, Princess," the man said.

My hand jumped to the hilt at my waist, but the trill of his sword filled the air as he swung it around and laid it across my neck. I winced at the kiss of cold steel against my skin.

"Everyone out," he growled.

The patrons wasted no time scrambling for the door, leaping over tables and knocking over benches in their haste, abandoning drinks and food. Out of the corner of my eye, the bar girl slipped out of sight behind the counter.

Kalei settled back onto a stool, running her fingers through her sacred hair. As if this were a mere court meeting and not one of the many dangerous situations we had found ourselves in lately. "Noa."

"Princess," he said, bowing his head respectfully. I scoffed, earning a shallow nick across my throat. "Show her the respect she deserves," he hissed at me. He angled towards me, drawing his arm back so the tip rested in the hollow of my neck. "Or I will cut your throat open."

"Noa," Kalei said again, voice low. She sat up straighter, but her face was a stony mask.

"Bow," the man growled. His sword dug deeper. A trickle of blood welled up beneath the blade, dripping down my chest. I had no doubt he would do what he said. My options were limited. Non-existent.

Holding Kalei's gaze, I lowered myself to my knees.

The hurt in her eyes shifted to pity and then slammed straight to horror as the man snagged a hand in my hair, yanking my head back to bare my throat to his sword.

Panic quickened my breaths, the sharp edge of his blade scraping along the tendons in my neck as I swallowed.

"Let her go," Kalei said, struggling to keep her voice even. She rose from the stool and took a step forward before the man's grip tightened, easing a sharp gasp from me. She froze where she stood, a debate raging in her beautiful blue eyes.

"You trusted me once, Princess," the man said.

The familiarity and reverence in his voice grated against my ears. My blood roared in response.

"I trusted my parents," she replied. "They betrayed me."

"They protected you," he argued. His voice was gentle when he spoke to her, small even.

I knew that tactic. Talen used the same one on me many times. He was making himself appear weak and small, so that she would feel in power, large. Another viper in another nest but deadly all the same, his words poison.

"We have only ever honoured you, Princess. All of us would gladly die a thousand more deaths for you. You are the only thing that matters in this world, and we will do what we can to protect you from people like her who only want to use you for themselves."

Kalei looked down at me, uncertainty creasing her forehead, but there was nothing I could say or do to convince her otherwise. This man would twist whatever I had to say to fit his argument. She had to figure this one out on her own. She had to follow her heart. And if her heart was where I thought it was, she would come with me across the mountains. She would end this war by my side.

And if I was wrong, I would be dead in a few minutes, and Kalei soon after.

"All of us?" the princess echoed. Her eyes darted to the door behind us and she shrank back. My heart thumped loudly in my chest.

"We came to bring you home," the man said.

The hairs on the back of my neck stood on end. We were trapped.

"Please, Kalei. Come home. Your parents miss you. They only want to know you're safe where you belong."

But she wouldn't be safe with them. She had been the one to first realize her parents' plan. She had been adamant in believing the legend. So why did she hesitate now?

"I am safe." She took a step back. "I am where I belong."

"On the run with these criminals?" He shook his fist in my hair. My lip curled at the stinging kiss of his blade. "They'll be hanged for their crimes. You belong with us. You belong with your parents, safe in the palace, not the gallows."

Kalei shook her head. Tears rimmed her eyes, but didn't fall.

His words were finding spaces through the cracks in her resolve. This was a man she trusted.

I couldn't let him rattle her any more than she already was.

Steel rang outside.

Kalei's gaze flew to the door.

As the man hauled me to my feet, hairs snapping from the top of my head, movement shuffled behind us. A chair cracked down on the man's spine. He stumbled forward with a grunt, the attack not quite as effective as a sword to the gut.

But it was enough of a distraction for me to unsheathe my cutlass and arc it through his wrist.

With a howl, he clutched his arm to his chest, the severed appendage tumbling to the ground, sword clattering across the floor.

Blood spurted from the wound as he turned to me, eyes blazing. He took a step towards me, but Kalei scurried forward, knocking his knees out from under him with carefully aimed whips of her hair. He hit the ground with a thud, glaring up at me as I tucked my bloodied blade beneath his chin.

"I've already died, bitch," he snarled. "I'm not afraid to die again."

"You won't come back a second time, Noa," Kalei told him in a low voice. "No one does."

"Oh good," I said, voice like ice, lifting his chin with the flat edge of my cutlass. "It'll be my honour to send you back where you belong."

"Wait," Kalei said, placing a hand on my arm. It was hard to ignore the thrilling shock it sent through my skin. "I need him to send a message to my father."

"And what makes you think he'll send it?"

"He will." Her eyes sparkled with deadly promise. The man paled as she leaned close. "Noa, please listen carefully and make sure my father hears all this. Tell him he was wrong about me and he was wrong about the world. Tell him I won't let him continue to destroy it. Tell him I'm coming to meet him in Vodaeard and I will not let him have what he's searching for. Tell him this will end. This war will end. His quest will end. Or I will end him." Her voice cracked on the last word, but steely resolve shone in her eyes.

"You can't win this," he replied as a window pane shattered inwards. Something smoking rolled across the floor and exploded in a blinding flash of light and a deafening pop.

I slapped my hands over my ears.

The man jumped to his feet, smacking my sword away and shoving me backwards.

I crashed into the bar, unable to see the princess through the afterimage of white light painted over my vision. Beyond the ringing in my ears, I heard the distant sound of the door slamming open and people filling the tavern.

A hand clamped around my wrist and tugged me backwards. Stumbling as I struggled to get my feet under me, I vaguely realized someone was pulling me from the room, and then my boots crunched on gravel. I blinked rapidly, shaking my head to dislodge the ringing and flashing, trying to figure out where I was.

When my vision cleared, the back of the tavern loomed in front of me. Fields to the rear. Mountains ahead.

I was alone.

I spun around to jump back into the fray, but the bar girl appeared in the doorway, shoving Kalei into the mud. Then she slammed the door shut in our faces.

The princess grabbed my hand, and we ran.

Blood streamed from her ears, and even though she was on her feet, she stumbled, face pale beneath the fear. She looked to be on the verge of passing out.

We skirted along the low stone wall running behind the tavern until the smoke from its chimney was a pale smudge in the distance behind us. The storm had rolled over, turning the fields into mud and rivers. Lightning continued to crackle, charging the air, but the rain had passed for now. Night had well and truly fallen over the small village, each house a hulking shadow, dotted with candlelight. We followed the wall until the village was also a speck. Tumbling green hills rolled ahead, disappearing between the mountain slopes.

Howling wind cut through the mountain pass ahead, tugging at our clothes, the high whistling sound layering on top of the shrill ring clanging in my ears. I winced, pressing my palms to my ears as we forged ahead, delving between the slopes. A dirt path curved ahead, twisting over the rocks, and we followed it for some time as night pressed around us. Even the moon didn't shine down here. Hardly a star sparkled through the piercing peaks high above. Gusts slammed into the side of the mountain, raining down loose rubble and snow. My teeth chattered. A shiver curled my toes. We were still much too close to the village, but no one would be foolish enough to follow us into the mountains at night. After a storm. No, no one would be foolish enough to brave these peaks.

When the high of near-death passed and we were shivering too hard to move forward, we found refuge in a small overhang, where the wind wasn't as fierce.

Kalei dropped to the ground, curling her knees to her chest, fright glittering in her eyes as frost nipped at her skin. Her jaw was clenched so tightly I was sure she'd break it again with a strong enough shiver.

I crouched in front of her. My fingers were already frozen from the cold as I gripped her chin and gently tilted her head to the side. The blood had stopped flowing from her ears, but it stained her neck in streaks of rusty brown. I pushed her hands away as she reached up, reminding her of the blood-greedy bones in her palms.

"Can you hear?" I asked.

"N-not well," she said, rubbing her ear against her shoulder. "What was that?"

I shook my head, rubbing my ear as if that could dislodge the pressure. "I've never seen anything like that before," I answered. The little explosives had been designed to stun us, but they could have done so much more damage. Mountain's luck we hadn't been more seriously injured. Or worse.

"How did that girl get us out?"

I had wondered the same thing. "She knew your act was just an

223

act," I said, trying to find the right words to say around the shame. I should have trusted her. "You knew that man."

Kalei nodded, squirming. "My father's advisor," she said, face pinched in misery. "He's a good person. He's just doing bad things because my parents made him. He found me when I went down to get a cup of coffee. I trusted him, but I knew it was a bad idea to accept anything from him. I played along, let him think I was drunk and had my guard down. The bar girl was the only one who gave me drinks, dyed water—nothing more. I was just waiting until you came back." Icy tears pressed against her eyes.

I pushed myself to my feet, secretly relieved. "You made the right choice," I assured her.

"Did I?" she snapped, surprising me with the force in her tone. It was as sharp and biting as the cold whipping through the alcove. "You heard what he said. I'll be hanged. You'll be hanged. There's no forgiveness for traitors and criminals."

"We can't be hanged if we don't get caught," I told her.

Kalei snorted derisively. "It's hopeless," she said darkly. "We won't survive these mountains. There's an army waiting for us on the other side. And my parents still hold all the power."

I ground my teeth together. She spoke as if we had already been defeated, but it was hard to argue to the contrary. We didn't have a guide. We didn't have proper clothes. The mountains would kill us before the army even had a chance.

A thought formed in my mind like a slow-moving glacier, crystallizing like ice. "Maybe not," I said.

She looked up at me between strands of hair and bone.

"The lights came from this mountain," I explained.

She perked up. "What lights?" She looked around, making her hair slip over her shoulders. The bones rattled in a disturbing symphony as they clanked together.

"Every month, the sky would light up over the mountain. Every month on the full moon."

Her brows pinched as she pieced it together. "The other half of the stone," she breathed. "It responds to mine, too."

Grimly, I nodded. Even if we got to the stone before her parents did, we'd be chancing a deadly mountain without a guide. It was dangerous—I hoped it would be worth it.

"I told your father where the lights were," I admitted in a whisper. "He could already be searching for them."

Her gaze dropped to the stone sitting around her neck. "It glows when I heal, as well," she said thoughtfully. She pushed herself to her feet and approached me like a timid animal. Her eyes held mine, steady, unwavering.

Breathing unevenly, I nodded. It was our only chance.

She scraped a fingernail across the gash on her arm and lifted her hand to my neck, to the shallow cut on my throat, chest rising and falling in a steady rhythm. Her breath fanned my face as she pressed her finger against my neck, whispering the words I had heard her say when she healed Alekey, an almost song-like quality to her voice. "Open the door, and walk th—"

Light blasted from the stone around her neck, filling the small shelter, and rayed out into the night with blinding intensity. Reeling back, I screwed my eyes shut, twisting away from the light, but it was everywhere. It burned through my eyelids, hot and cold at the same time. Where it landed on my skin, it prickled. My body tingled at the sensation. And then, slowly, the wind picked up again, cutting through the overhang, howling in the pass, and the light faded. Shaking, I opened my eyes.

The princess was on the ground, her arm flung out, holding the necklace she'd ripped from her throat. The black stone quivered in her palm. Burn marks exploded like the sun's rays across her chest, her hand blackened where the stone rested.

I tried to kick the necklace out of her grip, but it wouldn't budge. It was fused into the indent in her palm. I bent, grabbing at it, but the burned stone scorched my fingers. I drew back sharply, gasping. Thin rays of light still emanated from the stone, piercing through the night like star trails.

"Kalei?" My voice cracked. My throat burned, as though the light had cut through every part of my body and left me raw and open. I glanced down. Blood seeped through hundreds of needle-thin cuts on my chest. I swore as the pain caught up to me, lancing like icicles up and down my body. "Kalei," I said, shaking the princess' shoulder. "Wake up."

Panic rippled through my body when she didn't move. The cave tilted around me. Terror squeezed the air from my lungs. I shoved my hands through my hair, twisting around helplessly. My chest hurt, my lungs hurt, my head hurt. Even looking at the faint light strobing off the stone felt like a knife stabbing through my eyes. Breathing became too difficult, too stifled, too hot in the cramped cave.

And the princess still didn't move.

"I can't do this," I gasped, staggering towards the mouth of the cave, staring out into the vicious night. What good was this shelter if the danger was inside? Snow whipping off the mountain slopes drove towards us on the violent wind. Even nature itself didn't want whatever was in this cave. I squeezed my eyes shut, chest rising and falling without getting any air into my lungs. I couldn't do this on my own. White spots danced behind my eyelids. I scrubbed at my eyes, trying to rid the spots from my sight, but it only made them worse. They swirled around, faster and faster, like the snow blowing off the peaks. "I can't do this," I said again, fingers tingling in numb, abject horror.

We had failed.

I had failed.

As shadows swirled before me, two frail arms twined around me.

For a moment, I stiffened, before exhaling and collapsing against Kalei's chest. She smelled of moonlight and stale coffee. Bone-studded hair scratched my face.

Her arms, much too thin and weaker than ever, squeezed around me tighter, as tight as they could go.

My own were pinned against my sides and I couldn't move them to return the embrace, even if I wanted to. My breaths shuddered against her, shoulders wracking, but slowly the panic and fear bled out of me. In the span of a few brief moments, our hearts were beating as once. A slow, private dance.

Kalei shivered and tilted backwards. I caught her, and together we sank to the ground. Her eyes rolled back, only the whites visible for a horrifying moment, as if she had slipped entirely from this realm into another. Then she blinked and jerked upright, clawing at the air.

"Please stop doing that," I whispered. I had seen her faint enough times, and one of these days, I dreaded she wouldn't wake up again. My fingers, blue and frozen and trembling, stroked her cheek, pushing wet strands of white hair out of her face.

She reached up, hesitantly touching my face—as if seeing it for the first time—and caught the icy tears that stuck to my eyelashes. "Only if you promise," she said between uneven breaths, "not to do that again."

I nodded, unable to get enough air into my lungs. The overwhelming anxiety was a dull knock against my skull, no longer a hammer driving me into despair, but every part of me still felt hollow. "What did *you* do?"

"I healed you." Shivers coursed through her body. Her lips were blue behind the healing bruises, eyes like chips of ice in a snowstorm. "Took away some of your fear."

"I didn't know you could do that," I whispered, winding my fingers through hers. Her right hand was still closed over the stone.

"Neither did I," she admitted, teeth chattering. She followed my gaze and turned her hand over, wincing as she unfurled her fingers. The stone glared up at us, blacker than night, surrounded by a black stain of jagged skin. "That's new."

Her eyes trailed up again, to the blood dripping down my chest, pinprick holes in my shirt. If I could guess—and that was a pretty big if—I suspected the moonstone had been calling out to its other half, rays of light directing itself towards its location, and I had simply gotten in the way, as though I had been standing in the way of hundreds of needles.

The princess had suffered worse. The centre of her chest was black and raw under the burns, and the stone was still embedded in her palm, an ugly brand. She had probably tried to throw the stone away when it exploded in light. It was now bound to her in ways neither of us could understand.

"I can heal those," she said, gesturing to my wounds, realizing with silent understanding that she had caused them as well.

I shook my head as she raised her palm to stare at the seas-damned black stone again.

"It feels weird."

"Does it hurt?"

The princess wasn't bleeding. It was as though the stone had burned straight through her skin, fusing into the bones, the heat immediately curing the broken skin and stemming the blood. Even the scorch marks on her chest weren't bleeding. They didn't look fresh either. They looked more like something bad had happened a long time ago, permanently stained on her skin, a horrific reminder of some long past event.

Kalei shook her head, puzzled. "Not really. It hurts less than the bones. It's more…uncomfortable…than anything. Maybe this is a good thing," she added, closing her fingers over the stone. Light still sparked through the gaps. "We can't join the two pieces if it's stuck in my skin."

"We should still try to follow the light before it goes out," I suggested. The light was streaming in one direction, multiple thin rays like threads spearing into the night. No matter which way the princess twisted her hand, the light continued to shine in one steady direction. Deeper into the mountain pass. "Are you all right to walk?"

She nodded, pushing herself to her feet. "Is it a good idea to go out there?" She peered into the gloom beyond the mouth of the cave.

As I saw it, we didn't have much of a choice. The light could fade completely by morning, and then we would be stuck again. Now at least we had something to follow. Even if we didn't survive the mountain, at least we would have tried.

Movement shifted outside our cave.

The princess tensed and jumped up to cower against the far wall.

My hand dropped to my waist and found it empty. Renewed fear spiked through me as a flickering orange light appeared on the path outside, growing bright and brighter until a torch preceded a hand and then a body.

The bar girl peered into the cave with wide eyes, donned in furs too big for her small frame. She grinned at the miserable sight of us.

Kalei breathed a sigh of relief behind me.

"How?" I blurted, the only word I could use amid the tangle of similar questions storming in my mind.

"The lights," she said, mimicking explosions with her hands. She dipped her chin towards the stone firmly stuck in Kalei's hand. "Does it do that often?"

"No, it doesn't do that *often*," I snapped.

Kalei scurried forward, opening her palm.

The girl poked at the stone, then yelped when it burned and stuck her finger in her mouth.

"You've also seen the lights," Kalei said, voice bright with excitement.

The girl nodded, holding her torch out to me. I stared at it for a moment, until she shook it impatiently, and I finally took it from her. She slipped a heavy bag off her shoulders and started pulling out fur coats and mittens, and boots for Kalei. "Deep in the mountains, once a month, as bright as the sun." She mimicked the rays of lights again. "Just everywhere, light! It usually goes away after a few minutes, but I've tracked it."

"You've *tracked* it," I echoed in disbelief as she shoved a coat into my arms.

"What do you think I am, a coward?" she snapped at me.

I raised an eyebrow at the bite in her tone.

Kalei's face gleamed as she wiggled her fingers into a pair of mittens.

"Look," the girl said, blowing ratty hair out of her face. "I don't know who you are or why you're here, of all places. This town is a dump. I've wanted to get out my whole life, which—by the way—hasn't been long at all! I'm not very old. But where would I go, a simple bar girl who all the drunkards think they can toy with? Nowhere. That's where. Now I'm going somewhere! That light's gotta mean something. I know it. I've always known it. So shut up and I'll help you get out of these mountains."

Kalei laughed at the bewildered look colouring my face. "She's braver than I was when I first met you," she said, eyes glittering.

A forceful memory slammed into my head—Kalei, fury in her eyes, courage at her back, slapping me across the cheek as a maelstrom raged around us on the dock. And before that, in her lighthouse, quick and nimble, and lightning-fast. She had been anything but scared in those moments, but perhaps I had only mistaken her fear for bravery.

The princess was grinning at me now. How could she be smiling so much? I had nearly spiralled into a deep panic, a dark void pressing in on me from all sides. And now Kalei looked as though she expected me to blindly follow this child into the ruthless mountains based on nothing more than what she said she saw.

But I was already blindly following one girl across the world. A girl who had seized every part of me—mind, body, and soul. I thought I had been the one holding the princess captive, but it was becoming clear that it was the other way around. She had captured my heart and held on as fiercely as the stone embedded in her skin. And I would follow her anywhere. To the Endless Seas and beyond.

I sighed. "Lead the way," I said, sweeping a hand towards the imposing mountains on every side.

TWENTY-THREE

I'd been lying when I said it didn't hurt.

For two days, my chest burned as we trudged on the dirt and stone path that twisted between massive slopes on either side.

It wound upwards through the hills, leading us precariously close to the edge of steep drops, and then angled downwards again to almost flat terrain. Snow and hail whipped down the sides, tugging at our clothes and our hair, freezing us down to the bone. I shivered deep in the fur coat, shoulders hunched to my ears, eyes trained on the ground in front of my feet.

The girl had brought shoes. It was an oddly thoughtful gesture from someone who had no business being near us, but I could hardly feel my toes within the leather, anyway.

Every part of me was chilled, bone scraping like ice picks under my skin. The only thing that was hot was the stone lodged in my right hand. Even beneath the mittens it burned, hot and heavy, the light pricking through the wool. My chest hurt as much as my hand, more so because my lungs were struggling to get enough air. I tried to block out the pain, but the wind cutting through the pass only intensified it. Shoved into the deep pockets of the coat, my hands trembled, shoulders tense as I continued shivering, unable to stop my teeth from chattering in my still-healing jaw.

The instant the necklace exploded, I thought I had died. It was all fiery pain and white light and then nothing. The explosion had burst across my chest first, spreading like fire through my veins, and I vaguely recalled ripping the cord from my neck, but that was when I fainted. Sometime after that, I had seen Evhen at the mouth of the cave, frantic thoughts running wild, black mist swirling around her mind like dark worries. I hadn't thought—simply wrapped my arms around my captain and let the darkness consume me instead.

I hadn't understood the black mist or the twining shadows at the time, but now I did. I felt them crawling under my skin, pricking at my ribs, wiggling into my heart like the pieces of bone embedded in various parts of my body. The shadows had latched around the stone in my hand, trying to dislodge it.

And now I couldn't stop shivering. I had been cold before—every time I healed someone, I left a little bit of my warmth in them, and cold chased me away from the depths as viciously as Death himself during every Resurrection. But this was a bone-deep cold, a soul-crushing cold. Aside from the burning sensation in my palm and chest, every other part of me was formed from ice. The kind that burns and numbs. Frosty fingers had circled my heart, my lungs, my stomach. Every breath dragged in more cold air, cutting up my throat like shards of glass. My teeth chattered so hard I thought they would shatter in my mouth. It angered the bruises covering my jaw.

Not even the fires of the damned depths could warm me. If I died out here, if there was anything waiting for me on the other side of the Dunes of Forever, it wouldn't be enough to warm me. Nothing could stop the chill from snaking through my veins, coursing like blood through my heart, settling over me until I was sure I'd become an ice carving. The great Princess of Death, dead at last. Frozen to death in a barren wasteland with nothing but criminals surrounding me and a hole in my chest where my heart should be.

The rock in my palm gave a great jolt, and I cried out, tumbling to my knees, drawing my arm to my chest as if that could stop the pain lancing through my veins. It raced into my chest, radiating through the burn marks over my heart.

Evhen was at my side an instant later, holding me as my body quaked uncontrollably.

My necklace pulsed and throbbed, stealing all of my strength. My hand fell limp to my side, the light spinning in a circle until it pulled in one direction, many threads drawn taut.

The bar girl leaped out of the way at the last second—barely saving herself—as the light sprayed past her.

A cough wracked my body. Something cracked at the force of it, and I whimpered, blood bubbling up. It dripped over my mouth, down my cheeks and neck, warm and oozing, the only thing I felt other than Evhen's frantic fingers trying to wipe it all up.

"You said it didn't hurt," she accused.

It was all I could do to focus on her voice and not the shadows swirling around the edges of my vision. I recognized the creature taking form in the writhing darkness. The same creature that chased me through the depths on Resurrection Day. The one that screeched and clawed and stole. Death's messenger, come to claim me at last.

But I was the Princess of Death. It was *I* who stole from Death. I saved souls and thrived on the chaos in Death's dark shores. I was not scared to dive into the depths to bring back what was lost—to steal back what had been stolen. And I had always known I would stray too close to Death's door one day. I just didn't think I'd be trying to cross a mountain and stop a war when I did. A weak laugh scratched my throat at the mere thought of nature taking me before anything else.

But I was still the Princess of Death.

Death dare not take me now. Death dare not come close to me.

I commanded death. I overcame death. And so, I put what little strength remained in my withering soul to push Death back once more.

The shadows surrounding me stuttered. The stone in my palm scattered light and shattered darkness.

Then I slipped into a very dark, very lonely place.

(B)lack water lapped at my ankles, neither cold nor hot. I recognized the beach at once. Souls glowing like seaweed littered
the shore. People I knew in life. People I had yet to meet. And people
I will never meet. All fluttered in this windless place, twitching as I
neared and falling still again as I passed. My fingers yearned to reach
out, scoop them up, and bring them home—wherever home is, whatever home is—but something prevented my arms from moving.

I looked down at my hands. Black veins crawled over my skin,
twining around my fingers like thread, circling over the pale half-
moon scars on my wrists. No fresh cuts. So how was I here, where
the souls of the deceased call to me and Death skulked like a shadow,
waiting to devour, if I stayed too long and strayed too close? I paused.
The beach continued on forever in either direction and the souls glow
along its indefinite length. So many souls. So many dead.

A dreadful moan rose out of the sand behind me. My spine tingled, but I didn't turn around. The sound lifted, carried over the souls,
growing louder and louder until every soul wailed around me. My
knees hit the sand as I clamped my hands over my ears. Water sloshed
around me. The wails endured.

An unfamiliar form strode out of the watery grave towards me.
Skin glinting like scales covered an ambiguous body. Eyes too big for
a face stared down at me.

I craned my neck back, slowly lowering my hands. "What are
you?" I asked, voice raspy. There was no air here—I shouldn't have
been able to talk. This place was wrong, yet strangely familiar. Comforting. But I was already part of this place. I accepted that long ago.
It was in my bones, in my soul, went where I did—was what I am.

I was Death, and this was my realm. And so I could speak—could
command. Behind me, the wailing souls fell silent at my will, but they
did not leave. They would never leave. There were no Dunes of Forever for them to husk away on. No one to bring them back to the living.

"We are the same," replied the creature in front of me. Its tongue
clicked against sharp teeth. "We are both blessed and cursed by the

Moon, protectors of magic. We are healers, killers, traitors, survivors. We are the first, and you are not the last."

More pale faces appeared in the water, slimy hair hanging in streaks. Silvery tails flicked through the black waters.

"You're sirens," I whispered.

The siren nodded. "And we give gifts and we take gifts and we bear all. You bear all as well. Protect, heal, kill. Survive, little moon. That is what the stone calls to. Survival, life, chance, and more."

My brow furrowed. "How can I survive if I am already dead?"

The creature laughed. It was a sharp, biting, and cold sound. "You are not dead. Not yet. We cannot cross the realms of life and death. Only you can grant life and grant the impossible. We cannot. We cannot cross the realms, so you cannot be dead."

It sank back into the water, a tail forming where the legs were. Scales climbed over skin, over face, over mouth. "Survive, little moon."

"How?" I called as it dipped beneath the waves.

It reappeared a moment later with the others. Glittering black eyes watched me. "Survive," was its only answer before it slipped below the surface once more and was gone.

The howls of the dead renewed behind me. But I was not dead, so this could not be Death's dark shores. They were not *souls*. Not yet. Everyone the war hurt was here, but not everyone the war hurt was dead. Many lived.

And I would live. I would make it right.

A gust whistled through the windless place and Death's messenger screeched, finally jolting me from the soul-scattered shores.

Smoke prickled my nose. Char and soot swirled close to me, brushing ashes along my face. Light flickered just beyond my closed eyes, warm and red against the darkness behind my eyelids. Nearby, the pop and crackle of firewood. And, even closer, the scratch of rough-woven blankets pinning my arms to my sides.

As wakefulness dragged me out of slumber, I twitched a finger on my left hand. Good. Then I tried my right. Nothing moved. Even when I shoved all my will into my fingers. My eyes flew open, sleep and nightmares forgotten in an instant, and I clawed at the blankets suffocating me.

A figure loomed at my side, shadowed against the fire behind her.

Then Evhen's face hovered close to mine, blurring in my vision as I fought my way out of the blankets.

"You're all right, you're all right," she murmured, over and over, trying to push me back down.

But I wasn't all right.

I wiggled my arms free, ignoring Evhen's protests to take it slow, and raised my right hand. The dull moonstone caught the light of the fire, embers sparking in its blackness, still firmly lodged in my palm. But it was worse. Black lines swirled around my hand, twining around my fingers, circling my wrists, just as they did in my dream. My nails were black, cracked, and stunted.

I pushed my sleeve up, breath sticking in my throat as the threads curled over my arm, up my elbow. I clawed at my shirt, tugging it down. The inky lines ran towards the centre of the burn on my chest, falling inwards as if the mark was a black hole sucking everything in.

"What is happening to me?" I croaked.

Evhen winced, sitting back on her heels. She rubbed the back of her neck, glancing across the space at the bar girl.

I was about to snap again, but my eyes snagged on the curved stone above me, the rough-cut walls, the crackling fire pit. I twisted around. "Where are we?"

"The mountains," Evhen answered. Reaching behind her, she grabbed a waterskin and held it out.

I snatched it from her. The ice water soothed the burn in my throat, the fire in my stomach. Everything was hot and searing, not the reprieve from the icy cold I had hoped for. "What happened?" I asked.

"First, you lied," Evhen said, a frown tugging at her face. "Then you fainted." She got up from her crouch and returned to the fire, sitting with a huff that rocketed through me like a knife. Her expression twisted into something akin to a glare, not entirely hostile but unpleasant all the same.

How could she be angry at me for fainting? I didn't exactly have a choice in the matter. Besides, it was all the stone's doing. I had no say in what the stone did, where it wanted me to go, what it wanted me to do. I grappled for control over my breathing. "How long?" I asked.

"Three days," she answered in a clipped tone. She rubbed her hands together and held them out to the fire. Her heavy gaze fell on me across the flickering flames.

Oh. It wasn't the fainting after all.

I rubbed my palm against the blanket, the jagged stone catching loose threads. It itched something terrible and burned even worse.

"Ev," I murmured.

Her spine straightened, a jolt rattling through her from head to toe, but she didn't say anything. She wasn't angry at me for something I couldn't control—the pain in her gaze said as much. But there was an accusation there, anger at something I could control, and chose not to. If this was the last time I would face her wrath, I'd gladly take it over what else came next.

"Can we have a moment?" I asked the bar girl. I didn't take my eyes away from Evhen. She was my captain now. And she deserved my respect. My honesty. My trust.

Talen's warning rang in my ears as the bar girl shuffled out of the cave, his dark threat weaving through the memories of a glittering gala and deadly drinks. *If you hurt her heart, I will hurt all of you.* The warning continued to ring, louder than the pounding of my heart, as I shoved aside the blankets and crawled over to Evhen, kneeling by her feet. This was the second time I had knelt before her, but I knew it wouldn't be the last.

Evhen kept her gaze locked on the fire, tossing up walls to keep the pain out, but when I brushed my fingers over her knees, her shoulders slumped.

"I thought we were past lying," she said, turning to look at me finally. Her ruined hand came to rest on my cheek, setting my skin on fire in the most pleasant way. "Kal, when will you be able to trust me?"

"I do," I said, throat tight, voice straining. The words didn't feel like a lie, but they didn't feel like the truth either. I shifted, curling the fingers of my good hand around the fingers of her good hand. "I *do* trust you, Ev, but I thought this was something I had to endure alone."

My palm twinged, but it was Evhen's thumb idly brushing over my cheekbone that made it hard to concentrate on what I was saying.

I swallowed and forged on. "I can't help you truly understand what I'm feeling. This—" I gestured to the black lines crawling over my arm, my chest. "All of this terrifies me and no one can tell me what it means. When I fainted, I dreamt about a place—I call it Death's dark shores, the same place I go to on Resurrection Day to retrieve the souls of the dead. During the Resurrections, I can't speak or breathe and if I stay too long, Death sends a messenger to chase me out. But this time was different. I spoke with the sirens. Ev, their power is..." I took a deep breath. "It's as strong as the moon. They're like me. Moon-blessed."

She was silent, but bumps rippled over her skin despite the fire crackling before us.

I continued. "In my dream, I became Death. That place became *my* kingdom. And it wasn't just the souls of the dead there. It was every person my parents hurt in their war. Thousands, millions of people—everyone hurt by this war. It's my duty to protect them, to stop their deaths from happening. Depths below, I do not know how to do that, but I know I can do it with your help." I turned slightly and stared unflinchingly into her gaze. "And I trust that you'll be there to help me. I trust you with everything I have and everything I am. But can you trust me still? Even with all this pain and suffering?"

Her hand had gone still on my cheek. Slowly, she dropped it onto my right hand.

Ashamed and frightened by the black veins scrawled over my skin, I tried to pull back. I was Death incarnate, and these marks branded me as such. Not the half-moon scars around my wrists or the moonlight caught in my hair.

But Evhen grasped my fingers firmly, lightly touching the stone embedded in my skin. She didn't pull back when it burned—it seemed to cool at the captain's touch. For the first time, I didn't feel it singeing my palm.

Evhen's eyes flicked up. Firelight sparked in their depths, like crystals on a sun-touched sea.

"All of you," she whispered. Her fingers tucked a stray strand of hair behind my ear, and her gaze dropped to my mouth for an instant, but an instant was enough to undo weeks of anger, rage, and frustration. I rose on my knees to meet her halfway.

"Uh, princesses?" the bar girl shouted from outside, shattering our quiet moment before anything came of it.

Evhen jerked upright, hand jumping to her empty waist again. She scrambled to her feet and edged past me towards the mouth of the cave.

I blew out a ragged breath, clamping a hand over my chest as if I could ease the rabbit-quick thudding of my heart. My eyes fluttered closed. We were bad for each other—opposite ends of day and night—leading each other to the other's death. But still.

Voices drifted to me from outside, familiar and urgent. I twisted around and pushed myself up, trying to tamp down the thrill that crept over my neck.

Outside, Alekey was squirming out of Evhen's tight embrace. He caught my gaze over her shoulder and winked at me. The sun was just falling between the mountain peaks behind us, a thin trail of light spearing down the path and lengthening our shadows. His golden eyes caught the light as he finally broke free.

My mouth quirked, my heart soaring at the sight of his floppy, dark hair. "Your Highness," I said, dipping into a bow.

A laugh cracked his lips wide. "Princess." His eyes snagged on the burns raying from the middle of my chest. "I've missed something, haven't I?"

I shrugged, slipping my right hand behind my back, even though the light hadn't faded from the stone yet. It was still calling out to its other half, tugging at a thread in my heart. "Nothing too exciting. How did you find us? Where are Talen and Icana?"

Alekey shoved a hand through the mop of dark hair on his head. "We got separated outside of Xesta, and the only thing I could think to do was go home. I was nearly at the mountain's southern pass when I saw this…weird occurrence in the sky. I figured you had something to do about it."

"The lights," the bar girl said, nodding to herself.

"Who are you?" the prince asked.

"Inconsequential," she said, waving a hand.

Frowning, he turned back to me. "Am I right, then?"

I nodded, pulling my hand out from behind my back and unfurling my fingers.

He lunged forward, grabbing my palm and twisting it around, staring at the way the light continued to shine in one direction. "Whoa," he breathed. "That's…that's certainly weird."

"It also hurts," I said, smacking his hand away.

He grinned sheepishly.

"We're trying to find the other half," I explained.

"We're a little bit behind schedule," Evhen added, giving me a sidelong glance.

"What happened?" the prince asked, worry edging his voice.

"Inconsequential," the bar girl said again. "We're all up—I think those two kissed—so let's go! I've spent too long trying to get out of that town to die in these mountains now."

"Wait, what?" Alekey spluttered, glancing between me and Evhen, blinking rapidly. "They kis—what?"

"No," Evhen said sharply, and I pressed my lips together, fighting the grin that spread across my face. She wouldn't look at me. "Besides, it's too late to go anywhere now. We'll leave in the morning."

The bar girl groaned, stomping her feet petulantly. She stormed back into the cave, curses flying from her mouth.

"I like her," Evhen said as we watched her leave.

Alekey glanced over his shoulder, wringing his hand together. "We should leave her," he said. "She's just a child."

"A child who could die out here alone," Evhen argued, frowning. "Key, what's wrong? You weren't followed, were you? How did you lose Talen and Icana?"

A stab of fear cut through me, something I had simply brushed off when Alekey said they'd gotten separated. But they wouldn't let themselves get separated from the prince—not after what happened in Xesta. They would have travelled with him to the ends of the earth, to the depths and back, just as they would have followed their queen. So why was he alone?

"Yeah, yeah," he said absently. "I wasn't followed."

The moonstone thrummed in my palm, light spearing out of it. I winced, closing my fingers over the stone, but the light still seeped through, growing brighter and brighter. A low hum sounded in my ears, vibrating up my arm.

The royal Vodaerdean siblings shielded their eyes.

"Stop!" I cried at the stone, willing it to cease as I had willed the souls into silence. It pulsed a steady beat, the hum a continuous sound in my ears, but the light faded back to thin slivers.

That was when I heard the footsteps over the dull hum.

Dozens of pairs of feet crunching over snow and dirt. The metallic shift of armour plates, the shrill ring of swords. My vision tunnelled, spots dancing in front of my eyes.

"No," I moaned, understanding hitting me.

Alekey stepped away from his sister. "I'm sorry, Ev," he said, jaw tight.

"No," I whispered again. The final rays of sunlight landed on the army rising over the hill in front of us, my mother's severe black dress whipping in the wind, my father's glinting armour catching what remained of the light.

"You led them here," Evhen said in a small voice. Her fists clenched at her sides, tears rimming her eyes.

Alekey winced. "I had to," he said, voice wobbling. "They took Talen and Icana. They said they'd let them go."

"How could you?" Evhen whispered. She faced the approaching army of dead soldiers, chin high, tears dotting her cheeks like diamonds. There was a fine line between bravery and foolishness, and Evhen straddled it perfectly. "Kalei, go," she said between gasps. "I'll hold them off."

Hearing her wasn't easy over the hum and footsteps, but breathing was even worse. I sucked in sharp gasps, eyes locked on my mother and father. The stone ached in my palm as the decision to abandon her raced through my mind. I couldn't, not after everything we'd been through.

"Kal, go!" Evhen said again.

My gaze slid to her, her honey eyes sad, hurt, betrayed. Her fists clenched and unclenched. Fists and knuckles would do nothing against steel and sword.

We were supposed to not die. *Together*.

"No," I said, shaking my head, swallowing the pain of betrayal and fear. "They'll only kill you. Both of you," I snapped at Alekey, hoping he understood the severity of his actions—the consequences he had wrought upon himself and his sister. He flinched back.

"I'd rather die than let them kill you," Evhen said through her teeth.

"How noble!" My mother's voice cut through the mountain pass, louder than I had ever heard. It broke through the stony wall around my heart and crumbled it with one stroke. I could never master my emotions in front of my mother, and she cut me down with a single stare. "Kalei, come here."

My feet stumbled forward.

Evhen caught my wrist and shook her head, golden tears caught in her eyelashes.

"I have to do this," I whispered, raising a hand to brush the tears away. More fell into their place. "I won't let you die for me, Ev. I'm sorry it's taken me this long to realize it," I said quickly as two soldiers approached us. Their armour clanked together like a death knell. "I'm glad you took me away from my lighthouse that day. Please don't fight them," I begged as the soldiers seized her arms and yanked her back, knocking her to the ground on her knees.

Evhen snarled, thrashing, her rage as fiery as her hair.

A hand clamped around my wrist, dragging me backwards. My mother's sharp gaze drilled into me. I had always known it would end like this, but seeing her standing here, at the end of all things, only made the truth more painful to witness. There had never been love in her eyes, and now there was only pure loathing.

"Please don't hurt her!" I pleaded with her as she pulled me away. "Please! You can't kill her, Mother!" I strained to look back.

Evhen fought against the two men holding her down, tears streaking down her face as the moon rose over the mountain peaks beside us. It was nearly full.

My mother continued to drag me forward, away from the only person who had ever shown me real love.

"Don't kill her, please!" I cried, my voice carried on the wind whistling through the mountain pass, knocking against the steel of armour and sword. "Please! She can help me find the stone!"

My mother dropped me on the ground, glaring down at me. Her nostrils flared. She jutted her chin towards the soldiers. "Bring them."

I glanced back, clutching my blackened hand to my chest, as the soldiers cracked their swords over Evhen's and Alekey's heads, and they both slumped to the ground. Hot tears blurred my vision. My father's boots appeared in front of me, and I tilted my neck back.

He was fully healed, but I had never seen such anger in his eyes before. "Oh, Minnow," he said, hauling me to my feet.

My arms were so thin from what happened in Xesta that his entire hand circled above my elbow, fingers touching on either side.

"We truly hoped it wouldn't come to this."

My arm went numb in his grip, the black swirls stark in the moonlight. It was nearly the full moon, and my power clawed beneath my skin, burning through the moonstone in my palm. I whimpered as the pain intensified around the bones protruding from my palm.

His other hand caught my wrist, twisting it upwards. The light pulsed beyond us, coursing through the mountain pass, twisting and winding. Somewhere in the back of my mind, I knew what that meant—we were close to the second half—but my thoughts were preoccupied with Evhen and the two soldiers dragging her between them, following as the rest of the army turned around.

"Interesting," my father murmured, gazing in the direction the light arced. "Minnow, dear, how much do you know about the Blood Moon?"

A chill coursed through me.

"Enough," I growled. All my life, they had been the monsters I feared, and I had been too blind to see it. It was clear now, as he hauled me forward without another word, following the rays of light. "Stop!" I cried, shaking my arm in his grip. "I can walk on my own."

"And what will stop you from running away?" my mother said quietly beside me. She looked so out of place on this mountain, but somehow fit the perfect picture I always had of the thing that would eventually kill me.

"Why would I?" I muttered. "All the people I love are right here."

My mother snorted. It was a delicate sound that was as out of place as her presence was. "The girl will be hanged for her crimes."

"No," I gasped as the world around me tilted.

"Now, now," my mother cooed. "She's a criminal. It's where she belongs. And now you're where you belong as well."

"Don't fight this, Minnow," my father added. His voice was soft and kind again, but all I could hear were his murderous words, over and over again.

"No," I said again, dislodging his grip. My chest heaved. "I won't stop fighting. I will never stop fighting you."

"How quaint." My mother laughed, a trilling sound that brushed along the snow-capped path. "Do you really think she loves you? Look at you. You're a mess."

My lip curled, but the fight was bleeding out of me with every breath. My heart stuttered in my chest. There was nothing I could do about this. They held the power. They always had. And with the rock embedded in my palm, the lights guiding the way to its other half, they would find the moonstone. They would have everything they wanted. They would have immortality. They would have the world.

Evhen would die. I would die. Would we both disappear into the depths with all the souls I couldn't save? Or would the queen's beliefs take her far away from me—to a shore I couldn't reach even in death? I didn't have an answer. I didn't have a future in order to even know the answer. There was nothing I could do about the inevitability building up in front of me. The light at the end of the dark tunnel had grown dim.

It wasn't a light I should strive towards at all. It was Death's door, waiting for me to come knocking one last time.

That was my fate, so I stumbled towards it.

I was Death, and I was going home.

My parents had a camp set up in the valley at the bottom of the hill, beyond which I could see the ocean in the distance, black against the night sky, and a small city dotted with lights.

Vodaeard.

I heard Evhen suck in a sharp breath behind me and twisted around, but Noa loomed in front of me as she was hauled off to a nearby tent. I turned away from my guard and former friend, eyes locked on the kingdom ahead of me. Some small part of me had wanted to see Evhen's home, but not like this. Not at the brink of failure. We had come so far. Had been through so much. I didn't want to go any farther because it meant I had failed. It meant my parents had won. I dug my heels in, stubborn, heart slamming into my ribs hard enough to bruise.

"This is it," I muttered to Noa. I chanced a glance at him—his jaw clenched, his eyes forward. I wrapped my arms around my waist. "I always liked you. I admired your loyalty. I knew you would keep my father safe wherever he went. So thank you, for bringing him safely this far."

His eyes shut. I twisted away from him, looking towards my parents' tent. It flapped in the breeze, blue and silver linings. Their crest waved above it, the waves and stars I had always loved. Maristela. The star of the sea. For the first time in my life, the sight sickened me. Coupled with the full moon and crossbones snapping from every other tent, I felt downright ill. Far below us, I knew that same flag flew above Vodaeard. I didn't even know what crest it had replaced. Vodaeard belonged to my parents now. This was only a small fraction of the army that had invaded Evhen's home.

I turned away again, but everywhere I turned, another awful flag waved, another awful soldier walked by, another awful reminder of my failure drove nails under my skin, as painful as the bone shards, as sharp as the black veins. My arm stung. The moonstone pulsed impatiently, pointing me in the direction it wanted me to go. It had betrayed me. This thing I had admired for so long, this power I had controlled, had betrayed me. My face tilted up to the moon, nearly full, hanging above us like a guardian. Its power tugged through my soul, calling out to me.

I couldn't control the moon any more than I could control my fate. It had been working against me this whole time.

The moonstone seared my skin. I winced, closing my fingers over the rock to douse its light, narrowing my eyes at the face of the moon. Burning flesh pricked at my nose. I squeezed my fist tighter, and the rock cut deeper into my skin, blood dripping between my fingers, angering the bones embedded in my flesh. It sizzled against the stone, seeping into the black rock that consumed everything else, and then light shot forth from my palm, as bright as day, racing in an arcing path through the mountains. Crying out as the pain intensified with each pulse of light, I dropped to my knees, ducking my head from the moon's glow, hand trembling in the dirt.

Survive, little moon.

The words the siren said to me in my dream crept through my mind like fog, a slow, slithering veil that blanketed all other thoughts. I had to survive. Somehow, in this dark, never-ending night, I had to find a way to survive.

The power the moon granted me wasn't just about bringing back life to the lifeless—it was about survival. Surviving everything the world tossed at us. Surviving death. Overcoming that permanent end again and again. The moon darkened, and the moon brightened. It survived. The dips and valleys that marred its face were a testament to all that it had survived. And it continued to glow and give strength.

It was no accident I had been blessed with its power. It saw something in me, just like Evhen saw something in me. A chance to survive. To overcome. To find the light in the night. But if my moon had wanted me to survive all this time, it wouldn't have given me this power in the first place. Not if this power would only ever lead me to my death. There was more to it—I had learned that in the catacombs beneath Xesta—but I was beginning to think the moon had never cared about me.

With a sinking feeling, I realized what I had to do to survive. I had to find the other half of this stone pulsing in my hand—the other half of the one thing that gave me purpose in my whole life—and I had to destroy it. Evhen had been right. This power shouldn't belong to any one person. And the power it could grant certainly shouldn't belong to people like my parents.

I lurched to my feet, grabbed my hair in a bundle, and ran.

Noa shouted behind me, and I heard my parents call for a pursuit.

I stumbled into the snowbanks curving up the side of the mountains and dropped the bundle of hair. It whipped behind me like a cape, fluttering on the wind, reflecting the impassive glow of the moon above. The light streaming from my palm pulsed and danced through the air, twining around the mountain like a river. White threads, like my hair, pulled me up the mountain. The bones beaded in my hair clattered, but the sensation of them was becoming a comfort. Familiar. Even the extra bones seared under my skin didn't hurt anymore.

I scrambled over a short rise and stopped abruptly. The light swirled around a small crater, its edges blackened by the force of the thing that had fallen so long ago, filled with loose rubble and snow. If it wasn't for the light arcing into the middle of the pile, I might never have seen it. The stone in my palm strained, pulling me towards the hole, towards the thing that rested within.

Dots burst across my vision and pain lanced up my arm as I scratched at the crater, but before my fingers reached the bottom, someone clamped a hand on my shoulder and pushed me away. Dizzy, I collapsed to the ground, gasping for air, each breath sharper than the last. My hands quaked.

My mother reached into the pile with a hand clad in black leather and withdrew a midnight stone, its sharp edges piercing the light of the moon. It vibrated in her hand, swallowing the rays of light that cascaded into its depths.

My fingers twitched over the stone in my palm, the hot pain drawing me downwards. I didn't hear what she had to say as I closed my eyes, the creatures in the dark shadows writhing around me once more.

TWENTY-FOUR

The dungeons beneath my castle smelled of rotting flesh and something putrid.

I rammed my shoulder into the cell bars again, long since numb to the cold iron bruising my arms. Shackles weighed my hands down, rattling against the bones in my wrists, but I didn't feel their cool kiss against my skin anymore. I didn't feel much of anything except the fear that had snared around my heart like arrow bolts digging under my skin with every breath. Everything else was cold, empty—numb.

"Ev," Talen said wearily in the corner, not bothering to raise his head as he spoke. He hadn't moved much in the three days since I had been thrown in here. He had already been here for a few days before that, and he looked weak, skin drawn taut over his bones, muscles lost from lack of nutrition. His scraggly ginger locks now brushed his jawline. He needed a shave and a haircut.

Maybe he had accepted defeat, but I hadn't. This was my home. This was my kingdom. I wouldn't be trapped beneath my own castle while my princess suffered above. I hit the bars again and sank to the ground, the chains around my wrists and ankles clanging noisily.

Three days. Three days I had been locked down here with my crew, my friends, my family. I had no idea what was going on above our heads, no idea where Alekey was—if he was even alive. All I knew was that the moon grew fuller and fuller each night. It was all I could see through the slitted window near the ceiling.

What were they waiting for? They didn't need any of us alive, so why were we stuck down here? Why was I still alive, guilt and fear and shame eating away at my bones? Was this to be my punishment? Fade away until no one remembered me—Captain Evhen Lockes, princess of the seas, war orphan, unwanted queen? I had failed. I had brought death and destruction into my home, and there was nothing I could do about it. Even my crew had broken apart under my rule. Alekey had betrayed me, Talen could hardly move, and Icana had appeared late yesterday, beaten, bruised, bloodied, battered. I didn't know what kind of information they had tried to torture out of her. She hadn't stirred in her cell across from us since.

I drew my knees to my chest and rested my forehead against them. I had failed. The moon was going to be full tomorrow night, and I couldn't save the princess from down here.

For so long, I had wanted to be a hero, first to my people—to prove I could lead them when they doubted me. Then to the princess—to protect her from the rest of the world when it tried to hurt her. But I couldn't save her from this fate. It was embedded in her very skin. It had led them right to the other half. And it would lead her right to her death.

She would die up there in the light of the full moon and I would die down here in the darkness.

"Ev," Talen said again, voice hoarse. I raised my head to see him looking at me, his gaze clearer than it had been in three days. "You did what you could do," he continued. "Stop hurting yourself over it. She's not worth it."

Anger flared in my chest, bright and sudden, and was gone a second later. Heat crept over my cheeks. My nails scratched at the loose skin on my fingertips. "You're wrong," I said, voice faltering. A sob threatened to break within. "Everyone's always wrong about her. She *is* worth it."

Saving the only person who had shown me a glimmer of light in dark days would always be worth it. But it was hard to see past the iron bars in front of me. My vision only went so far as the gallows. Already I felt the noose around my neck, tightening with every breath.

It was worth it. If only for a short time. And if I could, I'd do it all over again. I'd do it right.

I'd save the world.

Talen sighed. Even he couldn't argue with me anymore. My voice of reason had gone mute. And that silence was so loud—spoke so much.

"Talen," I said quietly, shifting to face him. "She saved my life."

"So did I." His voice was flat, emotionless. He sighed, hiding his face. "I only ever cared about you, Ev. I didn't want to see you get hurt. And…you're hurt. Because of her."

I shook my head. It was true I was trapped, my future dark, my neck about to be broken, but none of that was Kalei's fault. Talen had saved me the moment he pulled me from the throne room, but the princess had saved me in more ways than I could explain—body, mind, and soul. I had been lost, in a very dark place, before she showed me the light.

"You really do love her," he said, bleak resignation in his tone.

"I do," I whispered. I hadn't said the words out loud before, because I knew they couldn't last, and now they hung in the stale air between us. It was a truth neither Kalei or I had been brave enough to look in the face. I didn't think of myself as very brave at all, and now the dank and the dark were forcing me to face this truth, to look at it, to acknowledge it with everything that I was and had.

Once, I thought I had been brave. I thought killing the princess was the single bravest thing I could do. It meant ending the war. It meant avenging my parents. It meant proving to my people that I was capable of leading them, even if they didn't believe it. Even if I didn't believe it. That was the brave thing I fought for, but I'd hesitated. And in hesitating, lost my courage. Lost my false bravery and wasted it on a dream, a fantasy. A horrific need to prove myself that had blinded me to the truth.

I was a queen without a crown, and I didn't need to prove my worth to anyone. But I wasn't brave enough to see that. I wasn't brave enough to acknowledge the truth of my feelings. And I certainly wasn't brave enough to fight my way out of this cell and die on the other side.

Kalei had been willing to die to save me, even when she knew the truth about her father's war. And, like the coward I was, I didn't have enough courage to do the same for her.

Down the corridor, a door opened against the stone floor. Heavy footsteps stormed towards our cell, the sound piercing through the panic clenched around my heart. I jumped to my feet, weighed down by the shackles, as two men appeared in front of the bars. I recognized the one with the missing nose. He tapped his hip as his companion fumbled with a key to open the cell door. My cutlass glinted beside his sword at his waist.

"That's mine," I hissed, lip curling.

"Funny," he said, filling the cell with his rotting stench as they moved towards Talen in the corner. "I didn't see your name on it."

Fear jolted through me, rattling the chains. "Look harder," I said. My father had had it engraved with my name when he gave it to me last year.

He didn't respond, hauling Talen to his feet. My first mate didn't even fight back, too weak to hold himself up.

"No," I said, putting myself between them and the door. "You'll take me."

"Cap—" Talen murmured.

"You'll take me!" I said again, voice rising to a shriek. I wouldn't see Talen tortured.

The man with the missing nose shoved me aside, cracking a hand across my face.

I dropped to the ground, chains digging into my wrists. "No!" I cried, grabbing at his feet as they shuffled past me. He twisted, kicked his foot up. Blood burst in my mouth as I fell backwards. I coughed, spitting a wad of blood and saliva on the ground. Hair fell into my face as I looked up at them with hate in my eyes.

"You know who I am," I said through my teeth, remembering their threats on the road to Xesta. We know who you are, Your Majesty. "You'll take me instead."

"Ev—" Talen warned.

I couldn't bring myself to look at him, to see the fear in his eyes. I knew he would rather die than let me face them alone, but I couldn't let him do that. Not for me. Not when I still had one chance to make this right.

The two men looked at each other and then tossed Talen back into the cell. He landed in a heap with a groan, struggling to push himself up as the man with the missing nose grabbed my arm and dragged me into the hall. The door clanged shut behind me.

The courtyard above the dungeons was empty. Night fell like a shroud around us, brilliantly lit by the moon above. It cast a perfect glow on the gallows, the rope that would soon be around my neck. As I was led across the space towards the castle proper, I imagined I could hear my neck breaking, snapping in the stillness. My people wouldn't be there to watch, to mourn. I'd die alone.

The man took me on the direct route to the throne room, and the noose tightened with every step until I couldn't breathe. I wasn't brave enough to face that room again, not so soon after I watched my parents die. I wasn't brave. I wasn't strong. I was only a girl who missed my parents terribly and hadn't slept since for fear I would see their dead faces if I closed my eyes.

The doors were already open when we arrived. I remembered them being shut when that monster arrived with his army. Remembered my parents telling me it would be okay, that we were safe.

I knew they had been lying, but the memory still stung. I blinked hot tears from my eyes as the man led me down the long carpeted aisle to the dais at the end. There were no guards. I hadn't even seen any in the dungeons, as though the two usurpers in the throne room had scrubbed my kingdom clean of anyone who would oppose their invasion. It made me wonder what happened to whoever had stepped in during my absence. Shame warmed my face.

The chief and chieftess of Marama sat on my parents' thrones, black stains against the stone, all sharp edges over the soft cushions. The man with the missing nose shoved me to my knees in front of them, his hand tight where the soft place where my neck met my shoulders, I thought he would snap my neck. Better here than at the gallows.

"So you are the pirate who kidnapped my daughter," the chieftess said thoughtfully, leaning forward ever so slightly. A sharp nail tapped against her sharp chin as if she was a living statue, all stone. Looking at them now, on thrones that didn't belong to them, it was easier to separate them from the princess—they looked nothing alike. These people were the monsters. "Tell me, pirate. Who else was involved in my daughter's kidnapping, so that I might have enough rope?"

My throat constricted. It had been my plan to kill the princess. My crew had only gotten me to safety before I was also killed in this very room. "No one," I said tightly. "I alone kidnapped the princess. I alone sought to kill her."

"Do not lie to me," the chieftess said slowly, settling back in her seat.

"What reason do I have to lie?" I said through my teeth. "You've taken everything else from me. You've taken my family, my crew. Be done with this already." I tried to emulate some of the princess' stormy courage, but fell short. "You don't belong on those thrones, so finish this and take your army and leave." I only wanted my people safe. It didn't matter what happened to me now.

"I don't know who you think you are, child."

I bristled. It was one thing for my people to think I wasn't fit to lead, but it was another thing entirely to be dismissed by a complete stranger. A stranger who sat on my mother's throne.

"I am Queen Evhen Lockes of Vodaeard," I said before the usurper had a chance to continue. "You murdered my parents and now sit upon their thrones. This is my home. These are my people are you tormenting, and I will not stand for it."

"I remember you," the chief said suddenly, studying me. His dark eyes rested heavily on my shoulders. "The little whelp who begged as I cut out their hearts."

My ears rang with the memory, too close. It had been exactly a month. The last time I had seen this room, it was bathed in blood— the thrones splattered, the walls covered. No, a month wasn't nearly long enough to forget such a horrific day. My vision swam.

"I should have killed you," he murmured, sitting back. "Soon enough." He waved a hand, and I felt as though that single gesture sealed my fate. With such a bleak future, what point was there in being brave when I was going to die, anyway? Bravery and foolishness were so close together, I couldn't draw the line between them. I might as well say what I needed to. So I sank back into the only thing I had ever known. My anger. My rage.

"Yes, you should have," I said in a low voice. "But I'll thank you for failing to do so then. It only means I have a chance to spill your blood as you spilled theirs."

The hand on my neck squeezed, but it didn't matter.

"Watch your tongue, girl," the chief growled. "You are still a prisoner."

"And your daughter is still *my* prisoner."

The chief lurched forward, but the chieftess' hand came to rest on his, placating. Her chilling gaze cut through me. "Why her?" she asked. Her eyes sparkled in the light of the chandelier, the same shade as Kalei's but significantly icier. She wasn't so easily angered.

"She's an abomination," I said. It was the truth I had held to for so long. "Power like that should not belong to any one person. Her death was the key to stopping this war."

The chieftess dipped her chin, a grin cutting across her face. "You must have known your plan would have ended with your demise."

As all my plans did. I grinned, a little bit wild. "I was willing to die if it meant taking her with me."

"What changed?" the chief demanded.

The same question Talen had asked that fateful night when my ship sank.

"Nothing changed," I said, though it was hard to lie when the man with his hand around my neck could feel the rapid flutter of my heart.

"You had every chance to kill her," he said. "Why didn't you?"

The queen tilted her chin. "You think she loves you," she mused.

My stomach dropped at her phrasing. No, no, I was almost positive. There were still some barriers we had to overcome, but we trusted each other. More than trusted. *Everything I have and everything I am.* There was no doubt in my mind what the princess had truly meant when she said those words. But there was that seed planted so easily.

This woman was a liar—I couldn't believe a word she said. Yet, the thought nagged at the back of my mind, an uncomfortable, churning wave. One that threatened to steal me out into a stormy sea.

My breathing hitched as the chieftess leaned back, a cruel grin spreading across her thin lips. They hadn't so much picked my walls down stone by stone as demolished them utterly and completely with one stroke. My heart was bleeding my truth across the stones where my parents had bled.

"I want to see her," I said before I could clamp my mouth shut.

"No," the chieftess said, blinking impassively as that single word tore down the rest of my resolve. "You trifled with something you don't understand, and now you must face the consequences."

"Something I don't understand?" My voice rose, echoing around the tomb-like chamber. This wasn't my home anymore. "I think I understand killing your daughter well enough. How are you going to do it, anyway? I know the legend. There was only one chief. One person who gained immortality. How is she supposed to give it to both of you?" It was a desperate attempt to create discord between the usurpers, but I didn't understand magic at all. Certainly not when it came to life and death.

The woman's eyes glittered, and suddenly my only regret was not saving Kalei from these monsters sooner. "Who is to say she can't? You couldn't possibly understand that which doesn't concern you. This is a family matter. But you wouldn't know about that, would you?"

Her words slammed into me like a punch to my stomach. Angry tears pressed against my eyes as I drilled into her with a venomous glare. "Get off my mother's throne, you usurping bitch."

She rose with feline grace, her heels clicking on the stone as she descended the steps. The carpet muffled her approach.

I squirmed, snarling, lip curling.

The woman gestured, and the man hauled me to my feet. I barely had time to get my feet under me before the chieftess' hand cracked across my face, a stinging burn welting against my skin.

"I have never known such a disrespectful brat," she said, voice low.

"Respect is earned," I snapped, spitting at her. "You haven't even earned it from your own *daughter*."

I thought she was going to slap me again, but then her fingers, nails like claws, dug into my arm and bodily dragged me from the throne room. I writhed, feet stumbling, but the chieftess was surprisingly strong for her stature. She hardly seemed burdened by my flailing as she pulled me through the empty hallways, towards the grand entrance, into the courtyard.

I thought she was only dragging me back to the dungeons, to my dank cell beneath my home, but then she cut a sharp turn and angled through the untended gardens towards the cliffs that overlooked the ocean. Nothing much grew in the gardens, the salt air too hostile for most plant life, but what did grow was tough and resilient. Like me.

I lost all of that toughness and resilience, foolishness giving way to outright fear, as the woman pulled me along the rocky path. The sound of crashing waves drowned out the thud of my heart.

"No!" I screamed, trying to plant my feet, but the chieftess continued to jerk me forward. "No! Please! She'll never help you!" My fingers grabbed at her arm, only catching bits of swaying cloth.

We stopped at the edge of the cliff, the world spreading out below our feet. Waves crashed against the rocky slope, inky black capped with white, shining silver in the moon's glow. I had stood here so often, watching the gulls circle above the fishing boats, listening to their cries, the creak of old boats, and gentle lapping of the ocean. The waters had always called to me, a tug in my soul like the ebb and flow of the waves.

I was destined for the water, destined to sail forever. That was why I masqueraded as a pirate, because the ocean was as much a part of me as breathing. My father taught me how to sail before I could run. We were seafarers, through and through.

I had never been scared of the ocean before. I only thought I feared the ghosts sunk in its depths.

My feet brushed the edge of the cliff, rubble tumbling to the waves below. The chains linking my wrists to my ankles rattled.

"Beg," the chieftess said, pushing me to my knees in the dirt.

"I am!" I gasped. My fingers curled into the hard-packed dirt. Wind blasted into my back, easing a sharp cry from my lips. My hair, dirty and greasy from days below ground, blew into my face. "Please. You can't kill her."

"More."

I gasped, squeezing my eyes shut. The wind slicing off the cliff brought cold tears to my eyes. Or was it the fear? "Please, I am begging you. I don't care for my life but don't kill her. She's innocent." I tilted my head back, tears frozen on my cheeks. "Please don't hurt her. I love her. I love her, I love her, I love her!"

The chieftess' hand curled around my arm again, dragging me to my feet.

I swayed, gasping for breath. The world tilted around me, and the stars tumbled in the skies.

The woman gripped my chin. Nails dug into my jaw, pricking my skin hard enough to draw blood. I winced, caught in the whirlpool of her icy gaze. The same colour as Kalei's eyes, and yet so different.

"You want to see my daughter so badly?" Her lip curled. "She'll meet you in the depths."

Then she shoved me backwards off the cliff.

The wind snatched my scream—and the rest of my breath—from my lungs. And then, mere moments later, I slammed into the frigid waves, cracking something in my torso with the force of my landing. I gasped down a mouthful of water. The chains tangled around my wrists and ankles, working to sink me. A wave crashed overhead, pushing me back and forth with the undertow as I fell below the surface. Pain lanced up and down my side, sparking small explosions in my head.

Gritting my teeth through the pain, and what little breath left in my lungs bubbling through my nose, I kicked my legs uselessly as the undertow tugged me down. Light sprayed across my vision. The ocean blurred around me, the surface too far away for me to see. The icy water numbed the pain in my side and froze everything else. My arms fought to untangle the chain, to claw for the surface, but nothing moved when I thought they did. My chest jumped as my lungs screamed for air. Fresh pain burst across my chest.

Then nothing.

TWENTY-FIVE

I woke from a torturous nightmare, screaming and thrashing under the covers that weighed me down like the ocean waters in my dream. Beneath the fabric, the stone in my palm burned, hissing as it melted skin and bone. I screamed and screamed and screamed until my throat was raw and torn.

The door to my room slammed open as I lurched out of the bed, collapsed to the ground, and vomited blood onto the floorboards. I raised my head at whoever entered—traitors, all of them—and screamed my rage. Blood dripped from my mouth, nose, and eyes, falling like tears down my cheeks.

Someone grabbed my arm, the spiralling black veins spread like ink spills over my translucent skin, and jabbed a needle into the underside of my elbow. I thrashed, yanking my arm away, spraying black-tinged blood, and collapsed against the bed. My arm burned as I kicked my feet at whoever was trying to approach me. I couldn't see anything except images of Death pressing cold, dead lips to my mouth, stealing my breath, stealing my life, stealing my soul. Choking me. Drowning me.

I curled up against the side of the bed, moaning, rocking back and forth as if the ocean still tossed me. The moonstone scorched my palm, fire racing up and down the swirling black veins, burning my flesh from underneath. It seared my chest. I clutched my hand to my heart to ease the pain, but it only made it worse, the heat leaping off the stone and into the mark on my chest. A whimper broke from broken lips.

Whatever they injected into me coursed through my blackened blood. It prickled, then numbed. My heart raced and my breathing slowed. My eyelids fluttered as the pain dulled. Not gone, it would never be gone, but this was almost bearable.

"What happened?" a severe voice snapped from the doorway. I raised my head to see my mother, dressed in her usual black-on-black, standing in the middle of the room, an intense look in her icy gaze.

Concern flitted across my mother's features. But that wasn't possible. She had never been concerned about me before.

My head fell forward again as exhaustion dragged at my bones.

"She woke up screaming," someone answered. A voice I knew but couldn't place.

My mother crouched in front of me, picking up my burning hand from the floor. She examined the jagged flesh, roughly twisting it this way and that. I barely even felt the stabs of pain jolting through my arm.

"Hmm," she murmured and stood again, letting my hand slap to the floor. Useless. Dead. "Get up. It's time."

Warning tickled my ears. I lifted my head, my vision blurring. "Time?" My tongue felt too heavy, too dry. "Where's Evhen?"

"Don't worry yourself," my mother said sweetly. "You need all your strength for tonight."

My head spun. "Tell me," I croaked. The pain was coming back, jabbing needles through my head.

"I told you not to concern yourself." My mother narrowed her sharp eyes.

"Where is Evhen?"

"The pirate is dead, Kalei," she snapped. "Stop being ridiculous. She never loved you. You wasted too much on her."

261

I rocked back against the bed, breath rushing out of me. "No," I whispered, tears burning my eyes. A sob burst in my chest, the fragile place where it felt like a blade was tearing my heart in two. Over and over, the knife came down with every unsteady breath. My fingers curled around the burning rock in my palm. I pinched my eyes shut. Tears sizzled, hot and fast, where they landed against the black marks crawling all over my skin.

"Now, now," my mother said, clicking her tongue. "Don't spill tears for her. She's not worth it."

"You don't know her!" I screamed, opening my eyes to glare up at her. "She saved me!"

"Saved you?" she echoed with a curt laugh. "Dear, she kidnapped you. She tried to kill you. We saved you from her. The little prince saved you from her. He saw the truth before it was too late."

I slammed my fist into the ground, the stone unmoving in my palm but biting all the same. How dare she try to use Alekey's betrayal against me? If I ever saw him again, I'd commit my first murder.

Agony tore through my chest, cutting me up from the inside. I curled inwards, sobs shaking my shoulders, each one more painful than the last. My wails filled the room and the castle, chased away to the ocean depths by the moon's steady, impassive glow. Between the pain in my hand and the pain in my head and the pain in my heart, I barely noticed my mother snapping at the servants to make me ready for the Blood Moon.

The moon was full tonight. My power coursed like fire through my veins, adding to the pain. As the servants undressed me and slipped a black gown over my head, I wailed. This was no ordinary Resurrection Day. There would be no ceremony. There would be no honouring the moon.

My bare feet dragged against the floor as they pulled me through the hallways, my head lolling forward. I didn't even have the strength to look up, to see where I was going, to gaze upon the moon one last time.

The three days since we had arrived in Vodaeard had been comprised of forced complacency—salves and teas and injections to keep me unconscious in a state of unbeing. To keep me bound to their will. I was weak, ill, thin. It was hard enough to keep the nausea down, much less fight back.

This was what they had always wanted. A perfect daughter to do their will. To do as she was told.

And they were telling me to die.

The full moon lit a path for us past the courtyard, past the gallows, past the garden. Somewhere, distantly, someone cried out to me, but I couldn't raise my head to search for the voice.

The soldiers led me to an open square near the docks. A pale beach stretched towards the cliffs on one side and disappeared around a bend on the other. Soldiers crowded the space, the beach, and the docks, silent as the crypt and just as dead. No one stood out to me, though I had brought them all back to life. No one stood up for me, though I had given them all a second chance.

A platform—two wooden posts atop it less than a body's length apart—sat in the middle of the square.

My parents watched from a distance as the two men hefted me onto the stage and dropped me between the stakes. The soldiers grabbed my wrists and drove me to my knees, spreading my arms wide and securing them with rough rope to the posts.

Pain flowered across my chest. I struggled to inhale.

I faced the moon, as I always did on Resurrection Day. It hung low on the horizon above the ocean, barely skimming the surface, its white glow reflected in the gentle waves. Threads of power tugged beneath my skin, straining against the ropes that held me still, easing a cry of pain from my dry lips. The light of the moon drew me up, pulling at the burn marks on my chest. Where it rested in my palm, the moonstone roused, answering the call of magic. I bit my lip hard enough to draw blood. A trickle slipped down my chin and throat, raying out from the burn marks. It seared my skin.

And as I watched in horror, the moon—my beloved moon—turned blood red, the colour seeping across its pale face like fog.

My back arched as a scream clawed at my throat but made no sound. Someone in front of me fainted. One by one, the previously dead people crowded on the beach dropped. Their souls crammed under my skin, writhing against the black veins and additional bones that kept them prisoners. The people who had never died, soldiers in an army I had never known about, shifted uneasily, staring at me like I was the monster everyone else believed me to be.

My mother crossed the stage towards me, a glittering black knife in one hand, the other piece of moonstone in the other.

The rock in my palm lurched as its other half drew near.

Bile rose in the back of my throat.

My mother knelt in front of me, her blue eyes a mirror to mine as she searched my face.

I had always known her to be cold and distant like the stars, so I was surprised at the flicker of fear in her gaze.

"Please," I whispered through bloody lips.

She caressed my cheek, heedless of the knife biting into my skin. "Where did I go wrong with you?" Disappointment replaced the fear in her eyes, and she reached for my ruined hand.

The stone wiggled and trembled as it fought to be released. When it finally came loose, tumbling into my mother's waiting palm, it felt less like removing a thorn and more like losing a limb.

My throat was too ravaged to allow a scream. My eyes fluttered as my mother slipped a cord over my neck, the whole moonstone rock coming to rest against my chest. It bumped against the burn marks over my heart, so heavy the cord dug into the back of my neck. I slumped forward again, the souls of the dead clamouring through my veins to reach the moonstone. Where it waited. Pulsed.

My mother pressed the knife to the inside of my arm. Steel cut my skin open with a cold kiss, a gentle whisper in the still night. Blood welled up and dripped down. The souls writhed along the black threads twining up my arm and settled into the black rock over my heart, caught in the swirl of impossible magic.

My heart stuttered. I didn't even know how I was supposed to grant this power, but that seemed like a distant worry. My mind was struggling to catch up to the present, where my blood was staining the stage, spilling in a steady flow that left me dizzy, weak, faint. I was back in my nightmare with Death tugging me to the depths— stealing my breath, my life, and soul, with a cold kiss.

The tunnel into the depths washed over me, the blacks of night and the reds of blood and the greys of stars swirling around and around like coloured water falling over itself. I plodded towards the piercing light at the end, unable to turn around, unable to fight. Blood sprinkled the ground behind me, normally a ruby path to guide me home. But there was no going home after this. This was the last time I would dive into the depths.

And I was meant to stay there.

My hands reached for the usual tools I used during Resurrections—the net and hook. But before my fingers could brush them, the door ahead slammed open and yanked me onto a black beach. A slate sky above. No clouds, no light. Black waters burbled around my ankles. Souls littered the length of the beach like glowing seaweed.

The closer to the water they were, the brighter they glowed. Towards the barren landscape beyond the Dunes of Forever, they were fainter. I had never ventured that far, but that was where my destiny lay. Where I would husk away after I had given my life and the life of hundreds of previously dead souls to my parents.

My fingers itched to save the souls. To guide them back to the moon's light. But my energy was draining faster than ever. Ice coated my fingertips. I was already becoming part of this place. Still, I continued on towards the dunes. The souls husked away, blown to ash on an invisible wind. Beyond this dead place, this place of undying, I sensed my life force bleeding out of me, rushing into someone who cradled me as I died, called me Minnow, and brushed bone-studded hair out of my face.

Frost crept up my palms, crackling over the black flesh in the middle of my right hand. It wound over the black veins and half-moon scars on my wrists.

I was going to die here.

A screech rent the abysmal sky. Death's messenger, come at last.

I whirled around—and saw a soul apart from the others, black waters lapping around bare ankles, sunset-tousled hair fluttering around a pale face.

As I stared at the soul, too bright in this bleak place, a creature with wings of leather and shadow soared out of the sky, careening towards me.

No, not towards me. Towards the soul. That beautiful, bright, bold soul. It looked at me with golden eyes, too sad for such a place of unfeeling. Distantly, I realized I knew this soul. And it didn't belong here.

The creature howled, sweeping low, wings skimming the surface of the water.

As memories waded through the water as beings with fishtails, the creature swooped low. I knew this soul. This soul did not belong here.

I lunged.

Black ice crackled against the soul's chest as I shoved it out of the creature's path. It tumbled into the churning black waters, its light winked out as it sank. The creature raged, teeth snapping, and its wing nicked me as it arced back into the sky.

I fell backwards, hitting the blood-drenched boards with enough force to rattle my teeth, my hands unbound from the posts.

My father scrambled away from me, eyes wide in horror, white light shining in his veins. As he stared, my mother reached for me, her wicked blade dripping black blood.

Heart slamming in my throat, I snapped the cord from my neck and slammed the stone onto the stage. It shattered, and pieces of black rock scattered in all directions.

TWENTY-SIX

I gasped, coughing, spluttering blood and water onto the rocks. My ears rang with a piercing shriek that sounded like my head was being split open. As water lapped around me, frigid and icy, the ringing faded to a dull screech, a constant sound like the rush of blood.

A pale face loomed over me, and I yelped, scurrying back. My hand slipped on the sharp rocks, slicing my palm open. Blood trickled into the water.

"Oh," the siren said, snatching my hand and pressing wet lips to the blood.

I yanked my hand back, making my head spin with the movement. "What happened?" I croaked, voice hoarse, throat raw. I tasted blood and bile.

"It is Resurrection Day," the siren said, glancing to the side. I followed its gaze, but my eyes snagged on the horrific moon rising against the black night. It was blood red, the dark colour marring its face, bleeding into the ocean. I sat up, wincing at the pain in my side. I put a hand against my ribs.

"The Blood Moon," I said, and the siren nodded, turning back to me.

The creature studied me, eyes glowing faintly, two eyelids sliding shut in a blink. "You are blessed—captain, princess, queen. You have survived death, survived life, survived chance. Because you live, you must take a life."

Something clattered onto the rocks next to me. The siren reached down and withdrew a blade of bone from the stone.

"Bring me their hearts," it said, grinning viciously, teeth sharp.

I shivered as it slipped back into the waves. When nothing moved in the wine-dark ocean, I glanced around, trying to orient myself. I was on the far side of the city, away from the docks, on the other side of the cliffs that jutted out behind my castle.

A path climbed up the rocky incline towards the grazing pastures in the north.

Pushing myself to my feet, I craned my neck back to stare up at the looming cliffs. Something tugged at my mind, a memory, something close and fearful, but I couldn't place it. The cliffs stood impassive, witness to something horrific, but they wouldn't tell me what. I imagined I saw a figure cut in black with severe lines and sharp edges, standing on the cliff and watching while something fell, dark against the black night.

When I blinked, the image was gone.

What had happened here?

A different memory pressed close as I raced up the twisting path towards the hills. The sensation of falling was something I couldn't remember clearly, but landing—I had felt the landing. I had felt the waves crash over my head. Felt the ice fill my lungs. Felt the Endless Seas beckon.

At the top of the hill, lungs aching with the strain, I paused a moment to stare at the moon. Its blood-red face rose higher. Witness to all. I had run out of time, but somehow I had also been granted more time than I ever should have been afforded.

What had happened on this cliff?

Somewhere on the other side of the castle, near the beach, a scream rent the night. I tripped, raising my head at the sound. I was too late. They were killing my princess.

I ran faster.

The courtyard in front of the castle was empty. The gallows had been cleared away. A single guard stood at the gate to the dungeons. Like a ghost, I lunged from the shadows and buried the bone knife into his chest. He gurgled as he fell. Blood stained my hands as I searched his pockets for the key.

No one stood guard at the bottom of the stairs. The door creaked open under my hand, and I sped down the hallway to Talen's cell. The key squealed in the lock, rusty from years of disuse. Hunched in the corner, Talen raised his head, streaks of long hair matted in his face.

"Ev?" he croaked. He rubbed his eyes, the skin around them puffy and red, and pushed his hair back. He desperately needed a shave. "Ev..."

He burst into tears.

I dropped to my knees in front of him, surprised when he latched a hand around my arm and pulled me into an embrace so tight my ribs pinched together.

"Tal." I wiggled in his hold. "Come on. We have to save Kalei. The ritual's started."

He only gripped me tighter.

"*Tal,*" I repeated, urgent.

"They said you died," he choked against my hair. He pulled back, cupping my face, fingers trembling over my cheeks. Tears glimmered in his eyes. He drew back suddenly and sharply. "You told me your ghost would haunt me. This isn't real."

I sat back on my heels, my heart thumping wildly in my chest. My throat burned with every breath, sharp stabs like knives jabbing at my lungs. The memory of falling crashed over my head, and my fingers dug into Talen's arm, a gasp scratching out of my throat. "I fell." My brows came together. The figure I had seen—the chieftess. My eyes narrowed. "I was pushed."

And I was alive.

I shook my head, pressing the heel of my palm into my temple. Black ice shattering. A creature screeching. A breath in my lungs as the siren's face appeared above me on the beach.

"Talen, I'm real," I said, voice breaking as I folded my hands over his. His eyes scanned my face, searching my gaze as if he couldn't believe I was really here.

But he was holding me. I was real. I was alive.

"What happened?" he asked, fingers gripped in mine. The strength was returning.

My chest tightened. "I don't remember everything. Just falling, cold, and darkness. I woke up on the rocks at the base of the cliffs and a siren told me to kill the chief and chieftess."

"A siren?" he echoed, raising an eyebrow in a very Talen-like manner.

I brushed off his concern. "I owe them a debt for sparing me. Besides, they gave me a gift and I intend to use it." I showed him the bone hilt.

His mouth quirked down. "I don't like it," he whispered, his voice-of-reason tone brushing my spine.

I pushed myself up and helped him to his feet, grunting. "I'm not making any more plans that are doomed to fail," I told him. "First, we get out of these cells, and then we put one foot in front of the next, and see what happens from there."

This whole time, my weapons master hadn't stirred in her cell. I rushed over to unlock it, bending next to her and brushing limp strands of hair from her face. "Icana, please fight. I need you."

"I'll get her out," a voice slipped down the corridor. I spun towards my brother, hovering in the shadows by the door, face darkened with shame. Relief at seeing him alive cut through me with all the intensity of a blunt knife, quickly replaced by the explosion of anger at his audacity to show himself here after his betrayal. Talen put a hand on my arm, barely calming the rage that thrummed in my veins.

Talen put a hand on my arm, barely calming the rage that thrummed in my veins."Leave him to rot down here when this is all over," my advisor said. He ushered me down the corridor, putting himself between me and Alekey when I lunged for my brother's throat.

Alekey flinched but didn't move to defend himself.

Talen and I hurried through the darkness.

At the top of the stairs, the empty courtyard spread out before us.

I gasped in a lungful of cool night air, tainted with the distant spill of blood and the ever-present scent of salt. Tears pressed against my eyes. If I let them fall now, they would never stop, but seeing my brother had loosened something inside of me, and I wasn't sure I knew how to rebuild what had broken. Trust that went deeper than trust. Alekey was family, and he had betrayed all of us. Some things were too painful to forgive.

A frigid wind whistled through the courtyard, whisking my tears away. "Let's go save Kalei," I said, focusing on the struggles that lay ahead, not behind.

The light of the red moon above us turned everything a dull shade of ruby, like a rose-coloured veil had dropped over Vodaeard. It made the sight on the beach even more gruesome. The hundreds of soldiers gathered on the shore, lining the docks, filling the space where a stage faced the open ocean. Most of them lay on the ground, motionless.

And on the stage, the princess sagged forward, blood dripping from gashes on her arms. It spilled bright red over the stage, as if the moon's light seeped into every drop and amplified it tenfold. Moon-light shot down the length of her bone-studded hair. Even at a distance, I saw the moonstone pulsing around her neck.

The chief held Kalei in his arms, smoothing back her hair as light poured out of her veins and into his. The black threads beneath her skin turned white when they seeped into him.

There were very few shadowy places to hide among the rocky dunes. In a crouch, Talen and I scurried downwards. Even with the red glow of the moon obscuring everything, we had to be careful as we weaved through the stone.

But I knew these rocks better than anyone. We crept along, the bone knife a feather in my grip until I spotted the stage again between the crags. Now I could see Kalei's face, twisted in pain, blood dripping from her nose and mouth. Her chest heaved as something swirled inside the moonstone necklace against her chest.

As I stared, the air around us shifted.

Her eyes flew open, the brilliant white fading to sapphire. She threw herself out of her father's arms and shuddered against the bloody boards.

The chieftess stalked towards her, as if to claim her prize. Blood blacker than night dripped from the wicked blade in her hand. I raised from my crouch, drew my arm back, and aimed my own blade at the wicked woman's heart.

Before I could throw it, Kalei circled her fingers around the moonstone, ripped it from her neck, and shattered it against the stage.

TWENTY-SEVEN

My power spluttered as the moonstone shards skittered off the stage. The twining threads beneath my skin stilled. The white light hazed around me, fading from my hair but still there when I blinked.

Beyond the stage, the beach was littered with souls—no, not souls. Dead soldiers. All of them silent. *Still.* Some of them turned to dust in an instant, blown away by the wind whisking off the ocean, long dead.

"What have you done?" my mother screeched, lurching to pick up the broken pendant. She clutched it to her chest, the silver shards of the clasp stabbing through her hands. Her iron fingers dug into my arm, pulling me upright.

"No!" I screamed, thrashing.

But nothing stirred under my skin. No magic, no dark power I didn't understand, nothing more I could give her. The black threads circling my arms were as still as the bodies scattered on the beach around me. Even the moon had gone dark.

She shoved me back against one of the blood-stained posts and slammed the shattered silver pendant into the centre of my chest.

I screamed, back arching, head thrown back as agony ripped through my body once more.

The fragment of moonstone that stuck to the bit of silver dug into my skin, past the burn marks, settling somewhere deep within my chest. It writhed and wiggled like the extra bones under my skin, sharp edges coming to rest against my heart.

My eyes fluttered, and then everything went stark white. Black figured dotted my visions, hundreds of bodies against the whiteness—no beach, no ocean, no moon, only a barren white landscape and black bodies. My hands gripped the black figure in front of me and life poured off me like smoke, like blood, coursing down the lines twined over my arms.

This was all wrong. In the legend, the chief had killed the girl to gain immortality. My father hadn't been the one to cut me, yet he was glowing white next to us. Now my mother demanded the same gift, determined to snuff out my life to extend hers.

Black veins turned white, seeping into her skin.

She tilted her head back to laugh, letting the life consume her, welcoming the power. But her elation was cut short by a gasp.

I blinked, and the white faded from my vision, replaced with a blood-red moon and a wine-dark sea.

We looked down at the tip of a bone knife protruded from her chest.

Over her shoulder, Evhen snarled and twisted her wrist.

My mother gasped again, stepping back from me. Blood bubbled out of her mouth. She pitched backwards off the stage. The fall was short, but she was dead before she hit the ground.

I stared in horror at her twisted body, the bone blade sticking out of her chest, the threads of life that now blackened her skin and made her appear older in her final moments. She looked nothing like my beautiful, alarming, terrifying-as-the-sea mother.

I sank to my knees at the edge of the stage.

All around me, there was movement as soldiers struggling to comprehend what had just happened to their chieftess. They surged forward to kill someone—anyone.

But time slowed for me. It stretched out to eternity. Death whispered in my ear. Death, with her pretty face and sweet lips and fingers around my neck like claws, pulled me down to the watery depths.

There would be no escape this time.

TWENTY-EIGHT

I caught Kalei as she pitched forward in a dead faint. I carefully lowered her to the stage and brushed pieces of bone out of her face. Her skin burned beneath my fingers where they grazed her cheek, a sheen of sweat on her brow, breaths shuddering in her chest.

"You should have stayed dead!" a voice shouted from behind her.

I stood to face the chief, lifting my gaze from Kalei's frail frame to her father, whose veins continued to glow. "My parents taught me to survive," I spat.

"They didn't do a very good job of it themselves," he said.

Anger pulled at my stomach. "We are not our parents."

Rage flashed in his eyes, and his sword arced down.

I ducked, my foot slipping off the edge of the stage, and I tumbled next to the chieftess' body. Coughing sand and blood out of my mouth, I looked up as he leapt down, blade angled towards my chest.

A flash of metal slipped under his, raining sparks down on my face. The heat of the clash singed my skin.

Talen grunted, my cutlass quivering in his hands. With gritted teeth, he pushed the chief back.

The enemy ducked under the stage, scurrying away from the din surrounding us as half an army rose to demand blood for their chieftess' death. The sound of swords and shouts filled the air, a chaotic battle unfurling around me.

More people were coming out of the shadows. *My* people, forcing their way to the beach to fight this war. I stood on trembling legs, heart soaring, watching as they pushed our enemy back. Reclaiming our home. *My* home.

And there it was, that thing I loved so much about Vodaeard. The courage and bravery and resilience.

Talen pushed my sword into my hand.

The hilt of my cutlass molded to my fingers with familiarity.

"Go," he said, jutting his chin. "We'll take care of her."

"We?"

A dark arrow whizzed over our heads, slamming into a soldier surging towards us. I looked towards the cliffs.

Sliding down the incline, fitting another arrow to her crossbow, my weapons master shone in the moonlight, blonde hair flying. It was longer now than I had ever seen it. She skidded to a stop by the stage and wobbled, catching herself, face pale.

"I'm fine," she said, waving away the concerned remark readying on my lips. "Go."

I ducked under the stage and followed the chief's retreating form around the dunes, through tough trees and battered bushes.

The red glow of the moon was starting to fade, but the amount of blood the princess had already spilled remained splashed across my vision as I followed his glinting armour. The sandy beach soon gave way to rough stone. Rocky dunes rose around us, sharp as knives, forming a small alcove near the crags. I shifted my cutlass in my good hand as the chief turned to face me.

Alekey squirmed in his grip, a black knife pressed into the hollow of his neck.

A gasp snared in my mouth at the terror flashing across my brother's face.

"Key…" I breathed. He wasn't supposed to be here. He was never supposed to be here. As angry as I was at him, he was still my little brother and I still had to protect him. My lip curled. "Let him go."

"Didn't my men warn you what would happen?" The chief eyed me down the length of my cutlass. "Put that down before you hurt yourself."

I took a step forward.

He drew back, the tip of his knife digging a small hole in Alekey's neck. Blood welled up in ruby drops.

"You took something important from me," I said through my teeth. "I won't let you take him as well."

"Then put your weapon down," he enunciated, his grip tightening on his dagger.

Key winced as the colour drained from his face. "Ev, please."

"I'm the one you want," I growled. My cutlass quivered in my grip, but I refused to lower it. Lowering it meant defeat. I wasn't beaten yet. "Take me instead of him."

There was a shuffling behind me, and I was vaguely aware of soldiers filling the small space, steel ringing through the air. My blood pounded in my ears. I couldn't lose Alekey. Not like this, not after everything that had happened. I wanted him to suffer more than anything for betraying us, but not like this.

"No," the chief said, a smile spreading across his face.

How did such a monster as him raise such a daughter as Kalei? There was no resemblance between the two.

"See," he continued, as if he were discussing a business proposition and not my brother's life, "if I take you now, then it's over. But if I take your brother, I keep you in line for as long as I need."

My legs wobbled. Someone broke away from the group of soldiers behind me and clamped a hand on my shoulder, driving me with little effort to my knees. The cutlass clattered out of my grip.

"There's a good girl," the chief said, dragging Alekey out of the alcove and towards the water. "I'm sure we'll be seeing each other again soon, *Your Majesty*."

Tears splattered onto my hands, turning the stones black.

The man shoved me as the soldiers turned to follow their chief.

Biting down a ferocious scream, I snatched up my cutlass and lurched to my feet, twisting around.

Before I could move to retaliate, the soldiers turned in unison, swords arcing towards my heart.

My breath slammed into my chest as I froze. I couldn't fight through all of them.

Unable to move, unable to fight, all I could do was watch as the chief dragged my brother through the crags and disappear around the bend. His soldiers followed and left me alone in the hollows.

A tremble began in my lower lip.

Key was gone. My parents were gone. The princess was…

No. Kalei wasn't gone yet. The ritual hadn't been completed. She was still alive.

Rocky resolution fitted the pieces of my heart back together.

I couldn't save Alekey.

But I could save her.

I turned and fled back to the stage, guilt nipping at my heels. They would call me a coward for leaving Alekey, as they called me one for leaving my parents. But I didn't care what they thought anymore.

Icana sat against one of the bloodied posts on the stage, breathing raggedly, crossbow propped in her leg. An assortment of dwindling arrows scattered the stage next to her. She raised her head at my approach, chest rising and falling in a way that concerned me.

"The chief?" she asked, a wet cough rattling her body.

I hopped up onto the stage, squatting in front of her. It was hard to tell what was her blood and what wasn't, but something oozed from her side every time she breathed. "Icana…" I said on an exhale.

"The chief," she said again, more forcefully, eyes like two daggers. She would never say she was scared, but it was there in the flutter of her hands and uneven breaths.

I shook my head. "He…he took Key."

A breath wracked her chest. Gritting her teeth, she pushed herself to her knees. A groan whistled between her lips.

"Icana, sit down." I tried to make my voice firm, like I was giving her an order, but I couldn't stop the way it wobbled.

"We have…to go after him…" She coughed, blood splattering.

"He's gone," I said, the finality in my tone hitting me in a place I had forgotten existed. I inhaled sharply. "I have to save the princess now."

Her gaze flitted past me.

She raised her crossbow and loosed a bolt.

I heard it hit armour and someone fell with a thud. Then she collapsed backwards, her weapon skittering from her fingers. Her whole body trembled.

"Icana!" I cried, catching her hand. Not Icana, too. Tears blurred my vision as I raised my head towards the moon. "Don't let her die," I ground out, glaring at its marred face.

Before all of this, it had just been the light to rule the night. But I had seen enough of its magic to know it had more power over this world than simply pulling the tides. If it cared about the world it lit, if it cared about the princess it had blessed, it wouldn't let either of them die.

"I'll take care of her," Talen shouted from the other side of the stage. "Go save your princess!"

The pale moon watched me as I dragged Kalei away.

She burned in my arms, skin clammy and covered in sweat and blood. Kalei was so frail, all jutting bone and ashen skin, black veins crawling over her arms. Her hair stuck to her temples, the bones threaded through its strands snagging across the sand.

A whisper like a cold kiss followed us down the beach, a shadow in the corner of my eyes, a ghost peering over my shoulder, a shiver tingling down my spine.

Soldiers clamoured around us, heedless of my struggle with the princess's limp body.

As I passed her dead mother, I remembered what the sirens had asked of me. I hefted the wretched woman onto her side and yanked the bone knife from her back. With heavy breaths, I carved open her chest and reached in, closing my eyes as another memory swelled in my mind. The organ squelched in my fist as I drew it out, severing it from her chest with a few vicious strokes of the bone knife.

My stomach roiled as I shoved it into my pocket.

I pulled Kalei to the rocks by the water, away from the noise, away from the destruction, away from the pain. But pain seemed to go wherever we went, embedded so deeply in our lives. We could never be free of the torment that had brought us together or the suffering that had brought us this far.

I felt threads pull taut in my heart, stretching, stretching, *stretching* as the princess grew weaker. Somehow I knew it would snap if I couldn't bring her back, and that was a pain I wouldn't survive.

I knew it was bad seas to trifle with siren magic, but I swore to myself that this was the last time. Their magic, bound in some similar way to the moon as the princess, was the only thing that could save her. The moon above had grown distant, cold, and pale. Its power didn't flow through Kalei's veins anymore. Something dark remained, ugly and even more dangerous. Something that was eating her soul.

I carefully set the princess against the rock and turned towards the sea. It was calm, unmoving, an unbroken dark mirror. I clambered forward until the water lapped at my ankles, biting and cold.

Another memory surged forward. Black water. Black sand. Black sky. I hadn't meant to be in that place of undying. That was Kalei's realm, her afterlife. Mine was the Endless Seas.

But what if they weren't so different after all?

I pushed the memory down. If the princess survived this night, I would ask her about it later.

"Help me!" I screamed into the night. My voice drifted across the water like a skiff, but nothing answered. "Please! I need your help!"

Still, nothing moved under the glassy surface of the sea. Nothing rose to my call.

I sank to my knees in the grit. "Please. I need her. I need her to live."

Silence drowned out the thudding of my heart. I threw my head back and screamed at the sky. I didn't have the power to command life or death, and I certainly didn't have the power to command the sirens.

They only came when they wanted.

A breath caught in my torn throat. My fingers dug into my pocket and withdrew the slippery heart. Blood coated my fingers, oozing down my arms, as I raised it to the sky.

A dark face bobbed out of the water.

I stared at the approaching siren, a hateful expression in its dark gaze. Scales gave way to skin as it scrambled over the rocks to face me. I shrank back, holding out the heart with bated breath.

"A life for a life," the siren reminded me, teeth snapping. "Equal exchange. You live—someone dies. She lives—another dies."

"No," I said through chattering teeth. A cold wind blew off the ocean, gusting through the crags. "She brought me back to life. This heart…is for her life. I don't care about mine, just save hers."

The siren narrowed slitted eyes at me. "She is dying."

"But she isn't dead!" I cried. My voice broke against the surface of the water. "She can be saved. I just don't know how to do it."

"You have been touched by the moon," the creature said. A forked tongue flicked between sharp teeth. "By her. We will take the heart, but you must give up something of yours in exchange."

"Anything," I blurted. A driving rain hit me all at once. It churned the waves and slanted off the ocean, pelting my face like ice.

"It will not be easy." The siren hovered over Kalei, tapping a black nail against black lips. Its eyes cut to me. "Her father lives. Immortal. But the ritual was not completed. So she is only partly dead. She will always be dying. It will not be easy."

"I will give anything to save her." Everything I had. Everything I *was*. It all belonged to her.

"Memory."

"What?"

"Something essential must be given to preserve what she is losing." Its eyes drifted to my cutlass. "That."

I unsheathed my blade, but hesitated. What memories did it hold?

The engravings on the blade caught the moonlight. *My dear Evhen. Follow the seas.*

My eyes fluttered closed as I realized what I had to give up. My father had given me this sword and told me to follow my heart where it led. To scour the seas and find adventure.

And my heart had led me to Kalei.

Memories of my parents were the only thing I had left. But if they could save Kalei—if they could save my brother…

Fighting tears, I dropped the cutlass to the stone.

The siren snatched it up and chucked it into the waves.

A thread snapped inside my chest, memories unravelling like a fishing reel, sinking alongside my blade with a resounding crack that shook the foundation. Blinking furiously, I palmed tears from my cheeks and offered the heart.

With a wicked grin, the siren picked it up like it was a precious jewel and bit into it. Gore spread across its sharp teeth, dripping down its chin. Bile stung the back of my throat as it leaned over the princess, spreading the blood across her forehead, chest, arms, legs. It finally set the mangled heart above Kalei's and flipped backwards into the sea, a cackle filling the rumbling air.

I blew out a breath and twisted to face jer. Her body shook with tremors, her hands trembling against the rocks. Black marks covered her entire right arm, nearly indistinguishable from the gash in her palm where the stone had been embedded in her flesh. The same marks rayed out from her chest under her mother's heart. I knelt next to her, grabbing her hand and bringing it to my cheek. Her skin burned.

"Please come back to me," I whispered. A tear splattered from my cheek onto Kalei's chest. When I left these shores only a month ago, I never imagined I'd be back here, where it all started, at the end of all things, weeping as the very person I had wanted to kill was dying in front of me.

I had already lost everything else. Why did I have to lose this bit of brightness as well?

A distant conversation, one that seemed so long ago, drifted through my mind like fog over the sea. *Respect is a mutual transaction.* But it wasn't respect we had been clamouring for from each other. It was trust. Trust that I wouldn't kill her before we reached Vodaeard. Trust that she would remain true to her word to help me. And when everything had gone wrong and trust should have been shattered, it had already started to grow roots, a seedling spreading through our lives.

She had trusted her parents, and they betrayed her.

I had trusted my brother, and he betrayed me.

What we had, what she had given me, went beyond mere trust. She had given me so much more than that, and I had been too blind to see it.

No, not blind. *Scared.* I had closed off my heart to anyone and everyone the moment my parents died. I had been too scared to let anyone in because everyone I loved had been taken from me.

But Kalei was here, and she wasn't dead yet.

I bent my forehead to hers so the storm couldn't snatch my words from me, not when our breaths mingled. "I love you," I whispered.

Her eyelids fluttered.

I drew back as she gasped and lurched upright.

The heart tumbled from her chest, but she didn't notice it as her hand scrabbled at her throat, clawing at the mark burned into her skin. Her nails frantically dug into her flesh, drawing blood, scratching herself open.

A piece of bloody moonstone fell into her palm. It seemed to cling to her, a string of blood hanging between the stone and her chest, its sharp edges cutting into her fingers as if it strained to replant itself in her soul.

She yelped and hurled the stone away. It splashed, a massive crack sounding through the world as it exploded, and then sank, far from the light of the full moon.

Her wild gaze found mine. "Ev?" Her voice cracked.

"All of you," I blurted, searching her face for any understanding of what had just happened or what had passed between us and finding only pale moonlight caught in her sapphire eyes. "Everything you have and everything you are—I love all of you, Kalei."

TWENTY-NINE

lood dripped from my fingers. Some of it was mine, some of it not, all of it slick and browning. The moon was cold and distant behind us, rising steadily over the glassy black waters, its song silent in my heart and its power purged from my veins.

"Kal?" Evhen panted behind me as we scrambled up the banks.

I glanced back at her, shivering when my eyes caught the moon's face. Talk to me. My moon was quiet for the first time in my life. A stab of pain, of grief, jabbed through my ribs.

"What do you remember?" Evhen asked, turning her face up to the sky. Pain twisted her features, and blood matted her hair. She was covered in as much blood as I was, but I had no way of knowing if any of it was hers.

Over the ridge, the sound of battle broke the night air. The clang of swords and cries of pain nailed against my head. I winced. "Nothing," I lied.

Evhen grabbed my wrist as I turned towards the fray. "Kal, please don't lie to me," she said, her voice cracking.

I stared down at Evhen's fingers—they trembled over the black marks inked into my skin, weak and crusted with blood, nails cracked and chewed to the quick. I pulled my wrist back.

She let go with a jerk, eyes wide, pleading. Scared.

"They need our help," I said, heart stuck behind my teeth. The truth lodged in my throat. I remembered everything. But if I stopped to talk now, I might never climb up the banks to stop this war.

The tang of blood and moans of pain filled the air as we climbed over the rocks. Dead moonlight shone on a dead beach, the sand red with the spilled blood of Marama soldiers and Vodaeard citizens. I choked on the stench of death, the bodies of my people outnumbering the Vodaeard dead. I would never be able to bring them all back.

I would never be able to bring *anyone* back. Never again. My power had gone as still as the crypts, a dead thing in my bones.

But the gaping hole in my chest, where the moonstone had burned through flesh and bone, screamed in agony as I weaved through the bodies. The soldiers were still fighting, weapons ringing through the air, sparking in the torchlight, running with blood.

"Stop!" I screamed at them, my throat ripping with the force. "Stop this!"

Wind howled down the beach, so powerful it knocked me to my knees amid a puddle of blood. My hair whipped around me, the shards of bone caught in the gale and strands fanning out before me, sweeping over piles of bodies and trails of blood, the dull white turning red. The vicious wind screeched past my ears, the same sound Death's messenger made in the depths, and when it settled, the moans of the dying faded to silence as they were whisked away.

I raised my head as the silence stretched. My hair landed amid the tangle of bodies, soaked with the blood of my people, soaked with the blood of people I helped kill. No one moved on the beach, staring at me as I pushed herself to my feet. The soldiers in the Marama army hesitated, the cresting wave and stars emblem stained red on their armour.

"Stop this violence," I said, voice shaking as it rose over the beach, the bodies, and those still breathing. "Your chieftess is dead. This war is over. The dead here will stay dead and you will finally know what it's like to mourn. Put down your swords. There is nothing left for you to gain from this. Put your weapons down now."

A figure moved in my periphery, a shadow in the corner of my eye, and one of my mother's guards appeared, a snarl twisting his features, sword arcing towards my head. I scrambled back, tripping over a heavy dead body. As I shook my hair out of my face, an arrow burst through the man's chest, splattering my face with blood.

"No," I whimpered, watching the shock and pain and fear flash across his face. He coughed, congealed blood spraying into my eyes as he pitched forward. He landed with a thump beside me, his face turned to me, frozen in death with an expression of pure loathing. Another body added to the pile.

Palming tears and blood from my face, I turned away and rose to my feet. As anger surged through me, I turned back to the startled soldiers, cheeks hot, chest heaving. My voice trembled, but not from the cold or the fear. "Every life I brought back, I gave a second chance! And you used it to murder!" I yelled, pointing a shaking finger at the man whose name I didn't even know. I stepped over his body before the urge to kick him consumed me.

I scrambled towards the stage, still slick with my blood. "I am trying to give you a second chance now! Your army is broken. You're outmatched and you continue to fight. Why? I can't bring you back anymore. No one can grant you immortality. No one can give you a second chance at life if you're dead. But if you put your swords down now, you don't have to die. This is your second chance. Surrender, and you'll live. The choice is yours."

Talen stood guard in front of Icana whose pale hair dusted her bloodied face. He held her crossbow.

"Shoot anyone who resists." I whispered the sharp words, knowing I was condemning more of my people to the Dunes of Forever.

"With pleasure," he said, nocking another arrow.

I grimaced at the cruelty in his voice, the grim glee with which he aimed the crossbow.As I rounded the stage, two arrows flew in quick succession. The sounds of them hitting their marks knocked me to my knees in the dirt, a sob bursting out of my chest.

Evhen appeared through the haze of blood and death and wrapped her surprisingly strong arms around my frail frame. I leaned into her, muffling my cries against her shoulder.

The bitterness of death didn't hang around her as heavily. She smelled like salt water and something else that tickled my nose, a scent not unpleasant but peculiar—magic, the edges of the depths curling against her hair. She had been touched by something I couldn't understand, but she still smelled like Evhen—felt like Evhen. Only now she was *more*. Different. Special.

Another arrow sang through the night, and I screamed against Evhen's shoulder. I'd lost everything, and I was still losing. A great emptiness settled in my soul as she clutched me closer.

"Everything's gone," I whimpered against her chest. "I lost my parents, I lost the moon, I lost you, I lost...I lost my power." What was I without my power? What was I if I couldn't heal, couldn't cross the boundary between life and death, couldn't brave the depths to retrieve lost souls?

"You didn't lose me," Evhen said, fingers tangled in my hair, at the nape of my neck. "I'm right here, Kal. You didn't lose me."

"You died!" I fought to free my arms, but she only held me tighter. "I saw you in the depths! You died and don't say it's fine because I can't lose you again and I can't...I can't let you die again." I wouldn't be able to save her again.

"I'm still here," Evhen murmured into my hair. "Feel that heartbeat? I'm still here, Kalei. I'm not going anywhere."

I felt more than just her heartbeat—I felt her fear trembling through her body, felt her truth in the words she spoke, felt her love in her tight embrace. My shoulders shook as I gasped in Evhen's arms, fighting for a proper breath. I had lost so much, but this moment was real. I wanted to stay in it forever.

But good things couldn't last indefinitely. Death still lurked behind me, breathing down my neck, sending a shiver down my spine. I wasn't supposed to be alive, and Death was angry.

"It's over now," Evhen whispered. "Let's go home."

I didn't have a home anymore. The Marama army I hadn't even known existed covered this beach with my home's blood. Even if there were still people on my island, I couldn't go back to them. I couldn't face those memories, of a glittering prison I once felt safe in, reminders that I had done more harm to this world than help. But I had to remember what happened here today. I had to remember what I had caused, what I had lost.

I shoved myself out of Evhen's arms. "I need to see their faces."

"Don't do that to yourself," she said under her breath.

"I need to see who I killed," I insisted, searching the ground and bodies as if they would give me the answers I was looking for. But I didn't even know the questions I was asking.

Evhen grabbed my arm. "You didn't kill anyone," she said, eyes bright. "You didn't do this, Kalei."

"I might as well have."

I pulled my arm free with little effort and drifted towards the bodies near the stage. The undead who had been the first to fall when my power surged. Their souls had crammed beneath my skin, stolen from them again to give life to someone else, someone even more undeserving. I remembered watching them fall, feeling them writhe in the veins crawling over my skin, hearing their wails in my mind as they flowed into the moonstone. My eyes fluttered shut at the memory.

I wasn't supposed to be alive. The ritual was supposed to kill me, and though it felt like it had, I was still alive. Impossibly, painfully alive. My power had been lost the moment it had been used beneath the Blood Moon, and yet I was still alive.

My gaze landed on a small form huddled against the leg of the platform. As I approached, it became clearer with every step that the girl was dead, blood shining down her front. Crouching, I pushed thick strands of messy hair from her face. She was just a child. Throat slashed. Shutting my eyes again, my hand rose to my own, finding only the black stain that still burned.

Behind me, Talen and Evhen spoke in hushed whispers.

"The chief?" he asked, his husky voice carrying on the sea-salt wind.

My fingers tightened against my neck. I opened my eyes, moving along the front of the stage.

"Escaped," Evhen answered flatly. "With Alekey."

My heart jumped into my throat. My father was still alive. He had taken everything from me, and yet he was still alive. It didn't seem fair, that after everything, he had gotten exactly what he wanted.

Minnow, he had always called me. A small fish our people used as bait. A weak thing. Was I weak now? I had done the impossible. I had granted immortality and survived. My body might be weak, but I wasn't. And I was going to prove that to the world.

Stony resolution settled around my heart as I wound through the bodies in front of the stage. This world that had hated me and feared me. This world that hadn't known me.

I was going to prove I was stronger than my enemies. That I was stronger than the moon's dead energy. Now that dead light shining in the night only pulled the tides. It didn't pull me anymore.

I hadn't been blessed by the moon. I had been cursed by it.

A dagger glinted amid the dead bodies. I snatched it up. The pommel was carved with the full moon and crossbones insignia of the Marama navy. It hadn't always been that banner. My parents had changed it from the volcano peak when they realized my power. A testament, not to me, but to the moon that would give them unimaginable power.

I twisted to face it where it hovered over the still ocean. Its energy didn't flow in my veins anymore. I wasn't bound to it anymore. Its light didn't shine in my hair anymore. Hair that I once thought was sacred—hair that I had never cut.

I swept its heavy length away from my neck and placed the blade against the bone-studded strands.

Evhen turned. "Kal—"

With a quick jerk, the dagger's deadly edge cut cleanly through my once-sacred hair. It fell to the ground with a smack, its weight no longer a familiar comfort but a dead thing. The still-embedded bones twitched in pleasure. The strands—once a shining white, now a dull grey like ash—fluttered in the breeze. They wafted away down the beach, lost threads that had once connected me to the moon. But no more. That connection had severed the moment I lost my power.

I was no longer captive to the moon I had worshipped my whole life. No longer captive to my father or my mother or my island. Something more powerful than the moon's energy rose within me.

Rage, boiling my blood.

The silence of the crypt settled around me as the bones embedded in my skin sang a waking song to answer the swell of blood magic in my veins.

THIRTY

The Princess of Death was dead, after all.

All that remained was Kalei Maristela, my star of the sea, screaming her rage into the night.

And she terrified me.

ALEKEY

EXCLUSIVE HARDCOVER

CHAPTER

ead bodies spilled out of the streets. Cobblestones cracked and roads ruptured as bones clambered out of the catacombs beneath the city. In the hazy distance, shrouded by smoke as the palace collapsed, Kalei stood on the bridge we had crossed in good faith days ago. It was impossible to see her features from here, through the dusty veil of destruction, but there was no doubt she was responsible for *this*.

Icana tugged me impatiently towards the gates, but all I could do was stare at the princess, awe and horror combining into an uncomfortable churning sensation in my wounded stomach.

"Alekey, we can't—" she panted, cutting herself off when Evhen's shrill voice cut through the horrific sounds of marching bones. It was a dull, hollow sound, like a loose pebble rolling around in a stone dish, but knowing that it was the rattle of bones knocking against each other, held up only by magic, made me shudder.

Ahead of us, Talen was trying to pull my sister back, away from the collapsing streets and walking dead. A sound like thunder echoed through the city as thousands of skulls turned to look at Evhen all at once, and she stumbled back. In fear, I realized, an emotion I rarely saw from my sister. She was the bravest person I knew, but even she had her limits.

This display of power was pushing those limits, but Evhen still shoved Talen away and called out to Kalei again.

The ground beneath us shuddered. I winced, hand pressed against my stomach. I'd learned that Kalei had healed me, but it seemed some of the wounds went too deep to be healed but whatever magic she possessed, and I worried they would reopen before we got out of this city alive.

I didn't know which was worse—dying here, buried in the rubble of a destroyed kingdom caused by an army of bones, or dying in Vodaeard, in our own home at the hands of a man who killed my parents?

The ground lurched like a wave, throwing us backwards, and Icana pulled me towards the gates while ignoring my protests to wait, to wait for Talen, to wait for Evhen and Kalei, to wait and see what was going to happen.

A shudder ran through the stones beneath our feet, followed by a shock wave that sent us stumbling through the broken gates. I gritted my teeth against the pain in my side, nodding to Icana when she paused to look at me with a question in her eyes. We couldn't stop now. We could only hope that Evhen and Kalei got free too.

Parts of the outer wall had crumbled in the surge. The many roads leading into Xesta's capital were littered with chunks of white stone, making it hard to navigate the paths that were swarmed with people fleeing the city. We passed more people with blood on their faces than not, and no one turned their attention on us, figuring we were just travellers who got caught in the unfortunate demise of the greatest city in the world.

Not the people who had brought the demise.

The farther southeast we went, the less crowded the roads became. Far ahead, several days by my guess, the mountain range that bordered Vodaeard broke the bright blue sky with a jagged white line, but my sights were set behind us, to the plume of smoke rising from the ruins of Xesta. It wafted towards us, blackening the sky.

"Talen has gone ahead of us," Icana said, surprising me by reading my mind.

I twisted, spotting my friend emerging from the last of the rubble on the road ahead. He shielded his eyes as he waited for us to catch up.

"And Ev?" I asked. Dust coated my throat. I blamed it for causing me to cough, and not the fear spreading like ice through my chest.

Icana pressed her mouth into a thin line and didn't answer. There were certain things she would lie about—namely anything that got Evhen out of trouble—but she wouldn't lie about this. I only wished she could reassure me that my sister was going to be all right, but I supposed that would also be a lie. There was no way any of us could know.

We scrambled up the small rise to meet Talen, who immediately started examining me for any injuries. Dust fell from my shoulders as he dragged his hands over me.

I finally squirmed away, cheeks warming. "I'm fine," I muttered.

He frowned down at me, less friend and more father, a resemblance that made me uncomfortable. Talen had been my father's advisor for a few years, but he wasn't old enough to have a child my age. It always made me feel helpless when he looked at me like that.

"You are the prince," he said. Not like I needed the reminder. I already knew that I was the preferable heir to the throne, which—I suspected—was why I'd been attacked at the party, but I didn't have any interest in taking the throne from Evhen unless she explicitly abdicated. For now, I was acting on the assumption that she was still alive.

"I need to make sure you're all right." Talen's gruff voice softened.

"You were supposed to make sure my sister was all right," I snapped, pushing past him to continue on the road. If we reached the southern pass in a few days, we'd be in Vodaeard before the next full moon. With Xesta in ruins, we couldn't waste time. Even if the idea of leaving Evhen behind filled me with guilt.

"She's resourceful," Talen said. I glanced up at him and caught him staring into the distance behind us. "She's with the princess. They'll both be fine."

I rubbed the bandages crisscrossing over my stomach. They were dirty and sweaty and itchy. "You sound like you're trying to convince yourself."

Talen sighed as he twisted away from the ruins to follow me. "I am." He rested a hand on my shoulder, careful of my wounds, but it still felt like he was placing a heavy weight on me. The kind my sister had been carrying forever. Responsibility. "I'm sorry I didn't stay with her. It all happened so fast. But I know she would have wanted me to be with you."

"Icana's capable," I grumbled, gesturing to her where she lopped ahead of us. Somehow, none of the city's dust had landed on her—or if it had, she had already brushed it off.

"We should get off the road," she called back. "Her father's men were clearly there. They might already be watching the roads, especially after that display."

A small town sprouted up in the distance ahead of us, and we agreed to spend the night there and gather any supplies we would need to make the week-long journey through the pass into Vodaeard. We'd lost all our money when King Ovono imprisoned us, and all we had were the clothes we'd been imprisoned in. Icana's and Talen's suits were made with fine enough materials that they could potentially sell them, but mine was ripped to shreds, barely hanging on my shoulders. No one would buy, or even trade, for it.

Until we reached the town, there was nothing but rolling fields and farmland, so we were forced to walk along the main road with some stragglers from the city. Icana walked in front, her keen eyes able to spot danger in the distance, and Talen walked behind me, his bulk of muscles able to stop danger before it reached me. It was an unspoken rule among us, how they guarded me and Evhen, and my sister's absence was a hole in our formation. Guilt gnawed at my bones. If only I hadn't been attacked…if I hadn't been so jealous of my sister, I wouldn't have gotten drunk so quickly…

I rubbed at my eyes, annoyed to find them wet. I had almost died. There was no reason I should feel guilty when I had been the one holding my guts inside my body. Evhen hadn't been right to keep those secrets from me. Even though her absence made it painfully clear how seas-damned we were, I was still upset with her. And, as bitter as it felt in my heart, as much as I had hoped she'd gotten out of the city, I also hoped she was feeling just as guilty as I was.

We found a tavern at the edge of the town, and while Talen ordered some non-alcoholic drinks, Icana slipped back out to procure some money for food and board. She didn't specify *how* she would find the money, and I didn't care enough to ask. I slouched in the corner of a booth against the wall, eyeing the door suspiciously. It felt as though every time we tried to enjoyed a drink, we'd been drugged or attacked. I was immediately wary, even when Talen slid into the booth next to me and pushed a mug in front of me.

My lips puckered at the first sip. "Seas, I need something stronger."

"No," Talen grumbled, watching the door for Icana's return. "You got drunk at the party and wandered off and someone tried to kill you. I'm not letting you have alcohol ever again."

I shoved the drink away. "Alcohol is a part of court life. You can't fault me for enjoying it."

"Wine is," he emphasized. "And you don't enjoy it. You abuse it."

He was right, but I wasn't going to give him the satisfaction of hearing me admit it. When the war had finally reached us in Vodaeard, I had found the only way to cope with the fear was to drink it away. And it worked, for the most part. Until my parents died. Then I drank to forget. To stop seeing their ghosts in my periphery. To stop hearing what I imagined their screams sounded like. To stop feeling so helpless while Evhen threw herself into danger, and I hid from it. That was the difference between us—she wanted to fight, and I wanted to flee. How could anyone think that would make me a better leader than her?

I was a coward when it really mattered.

I muttered something unpleasant beneath my breath and took another sip. It wasn't a horrible drink, but I wanted the buzz. I wanted the effect of alcohol, because I was starting to get a headache without it.

Talen ordered food and more drinks—he changed mine to water when he realized I wasn't going to drink this seashit stuff—and eventually the uncomfortable sense of dread that had been building ever since we sat down finally crashed over us when the door opened, and we noticed it was dark out, and Icana still hadn't returned.

"Fuck," Talen said, hand drifting to his empty hip. Habit. My own fingers trembled on the handle of my mug, trying to hold it steady as I took another sip, but the dread was quickly blossoming into fear, and seas, I wanted a drink so badly.

He shoved up from the table. "Let's go."

"What if she comes back?" I whispered. Our food remained untouched and unpaid for, and despite everything, I felt bad for leaving without paying. My sister wouldn't think twice, but these people had livelihoods that depended on monetary exchange for goods. It wasn't right to leave, even if there were other patrons who could pay.

Talen gestured for me to get out of the booth. "She won't. We need to keep moving."

We didn't get very far. Night blanketed the town, and we kept to the alleys where the buildings leaned dangerously close together, roofs touching, blocking out even the light of the moon and stars. Which was why neither of us realized we were being herded into a dead-end alley until the brick wall rose up in front of us, and the rotten stench of death wafted through the narrow space on the stale wind.

Talen shoved me behind him as we turned to face the mouth of the alley. Men in black and grey armour barred the exit, each of them looking, for lack of a better word, dead. Some of them had missing limbs, others marred features on their faces. Bile churned in my stomach at the varying stages and putrid stench of decomposition clogging my nostrils.

Talen shifted into a fighting stance, hands fisted in front of his face. I admired his courage, because we both knew he wouldn't be able to fight through all of them, and even though he had only been my father's advisor, he had vowed to give his life for ours.

We both knew this situation did not call for it.

Still, he would fight.

The line of men parted, and someone stepped into the alley that I knew at once, even though I'd never seen him before. I had already been hiding on the *Grey Bard* when he killed my parents.

But he looked so much like Kalei—there was no mistaking the chief of Marama.

Two days later, we were in Vodaeard. Talen had tried to fight, predictably, and had gotten a broken nose for it before I ordered him to surrender. His face was still black and blue when we stepped out of the chief's carriage into the courtyard outside the castle. *My* castle. My home, which looked so dreary without our crest waving from the flagpoles. Instead, they had been replaced with black banners depicting a full moon and crossbones, a symbol that would brand itself behind my eyelids and taunt me whenever I closed my eyes.

Some undead soldiers led a cuffed Talen away from the castle proper while the chief gestured grandly for me to follow him through the main doors. Each step aggravated my wounds, my body reminding me what I'd gone through just to be back here, in chains, walking the same halls I'd fled almost a month ago while the man in front of me slaughtered my parents. Nausea rolled through me in waves as we descended into the cold bowels of the castle, steps carved right out of the black cliff, until we stopped at a nondescript door in the cellars. A dank smell permeated the air down here, cold and cloying. Icy fingers clawed down my throat with every breath.

"Before we begin," the chief said, "I want to remind you."

"Of what?" I asked, trepidation making my voice shake.

"Of what happens when people don't cooperate with me." He pushed the door open, and a horrible stench blew out. I gagged, looking at him questioningly until he gestured for me to step inside.

The room was icy, a cold so deep I felt it through my shoes, breath puffing in the air as I approached the stone slab in the centre of the chamber. Light bobbed along the floor from the lantern in the chief's hand, landing on a white sheet when he stopped on the other side of the slab.

And the distinct hills and valleys of two bodies beneath the sheet.

I recoiled, straight into one of the dead's arms, who gripped me tight as I squirmed. The chief ripped the sheet aside, and I bit down on my tongue, shutting my eyes and twisting my head away. Vomit stung the back of my throat. I swallowed it, tears burning my eyes.

"Look at them," the chief urged. "This is the fate of your entire country if you don't help me find my daughter. *Look* at them!"

The dead soldier wrapped his fingers around my throat, pinching tight until my eyes flew open in panic.

A strange sensation settled over me when my gaze froze on my parents—a numbing chill spread through my veins, and the roaring noise inside my head went silent. They were so...still. There was no expression on their slack faces—eyes closed, deaths accepted, lives ended. My vision went blurry when the chief pulled the sheet back further, revealing gaping holes in their chests, flesh bloated and torn and red, jagged bones sticking out at odd angles, broken cages as if their hearts had leapt free.

But no—they'd been ripped out. The man who stood across from me had carved them open, reached in, crushed their hearts in his fist. While Evhen watched. While I ran.

I vomitted.

They dragged me back up through the cold castle corridors, and I didn't realize where they were taking me until we were at the doors to the throne room, and my body seized. This was where it happened. *This* man did *that* to my parents beyond *these* doors.

I kicked at the dead man's ankles—he either had absolutely no feeling in his feet or he simply didn't care—but when the chief opened the doors, there was nothing to indicate something horrible had happened here. The room beyond was not painted with blood. It wasn't the portrait of regicide I had imagined.

It was, aside from the chief's undead army lining the walls, the same throne room where my parents held court every week. The same throne room Evhen and I had once turned into an ice rink. The same room where Evhen had sat in our father's throne and declared she didn't want it.

The chief of Marama sat there now, next to Kalei's mother on my mother's throne. I almost believed she was a statue for how still she sat, but her ocean blue eyes cut through me.

The dead man pushed me to my knees on the carpet, and I looked around for any sign of my parents. Blood, a bit of clothing, jewellery—something to remind me that they had been alive a month ago. But they had been wiped clean. Erased.

Replaced.

Anger rising like bile in my throat, I lifted my head to glare at the two people sitting on my parents' thrones. I tried to summon some of my sister's bravery, but it suddenly tasted like ash in my mouth when I noticed the hunched figure next on the ground next to the chief.

Icana, blood still dripping from her mouth. She dragged her head up, saw me, and tried to stand, to put herself between me and the chief, to protect me as she had always protected my sister.

The dead man next to her, half of his nose missing, slammed a fist into her stomach, and she hit the ground hard, coughing.

"No!" I cried, straining. A claw-like hand in my shoulder kept me in place. "Stop, please. I'll help you. Just don't hurt her. Don't hurt them."

Icana tried to shake her head at me—she would never give up so easily—but the man backhanded her with a smack that echoed through the stony chamber. She spat a glob of blood on the ground at his feet.

When he fisted a hand in her collar, and drew back to punch her again, I jumped to my feet. "Stop! I said I'll help you. Don't hurt her!"

The chief smiled and waved a hand. The gesture was dismissive, but it felt like a sentence. I watched as Icana was dragged out of the room, hissing like a cat, and then I looked back at the chief.

Guilt, shame, and rage rattled through my head.

"Promise me you won't hurt them," I begged. This was my home. These were my people. Without my parents, without my sister, it was my responsibility to keep them safe. From where I stood, I could only do that on my knees.

The man rested a hand over his heart. "You have my word."

Words didn't mean anything when his actions told me exactly what kind of man he was. A monster and a murderer.

"Now," he said, leaning forward, too comfortable on my father's throne. "Tell me everything."

I opened my mouth, but the woman next to him spoke up.

"Careful, boy," she said in a voice as soft as silk, but a tone as sharp as a knife. "I am very good at picking apart lies."

In the end, I told them everything.

ACKNOWLEDGEMENTS

I never would have guessed that when I first starting writing this book—four years ago when the world shut down, in a frenzied, blurry forty days—that I would be able to hold it in my hands now, instead of only in my head. My mind is like a sieve, so trying to think about what the last four years have entailed would be an arduous task, and trying to remember who has been there throughout this process is near impossible. There's a lot to say about what goes into creating a debut like this, and not nearly enough space on a page to write it. So instead I'll say, broadly, thank you to everyone who made this possible.

Specifically Zara, editor, publisher, friend. Without Inimitable Books, I wouldn't have found the courage to send this book into the wild. We started small, but these unforgettable stories are mighty. Thank you, from the deepest trenches and farthest reaches, for taking a chance on Kalei and Evhen and their messy crew of noble pirates.

To Sam, who was there when all I knew was "Rapunzel with necromancers." Thank you for every encouraging word and your unwavering faith in these characters.

To the OG writing crew—Bri, Brian, and Michael. I'm forever grateful I found you that day on Reddit. Your support helped me grow.

Jessi and the Wander Writers. I'm still upset the pandemic cancelled our plans for Florida but I'm glad I could meet everyone in my home city.

To VE Schwab, who doesn't know me, but whose words and wit inspire me every day. If my prose can be as sharp as hers one day, I'll know I made it. The *Grey Bard* is for you, V.

To my parents, who may never actually read this book because I've hidden such a large part of my life from them. Maybe one day I can be my true self. At least they didn't force me to become a doctor or someone who was good at math.

And lastly to you, the reader, the dreamer, the star-gazer. Without readers, a book is just a stale, dead thing. It's the readers who being it out of obscurity, out of the confines of an author's mind, making it a living, breathing reality. I'm so excited to share this experience with you. Kalei and Evhen are yours now. Take care of them until the next book.

ABOUT THE AUTHOR

Kay Adams is a fantasy author living in big-city Ontario surrounded by a massive TBR pile and an equally massive teapot collection. A graduate of the University of Toronto's Celtic Studies program, Kay began weaving worlds and creating characters using a mix of folkloric fascination and celestial curiosity.

When she isn't writing, she can be found scrolling TikTok until her time limit runs out, existing in the same vicinity as her two cats Goose and Ducky, or staring at her rainbow library until a book she wants to read magically materializes—except the books she really wants to read are the ones she's writing. *Heirs of Bone & Sea* is her first published book.

LAFORI

COSTUN

AZRIA

OXIMEEN

SIREN LAGOON

MARAMA